HAMMER TO FALL

Also by John Lawton

JOHN LAWTON
HAMMER to FALL

Grove Press UK

First published in the United States of America and Canada in 2020
by Atlantic Monthly Press, an imprint of Grove Atlantic
This paperback edition first published in Great Britain in 2021
by Grove Press UK, an imprint of Grove Atlantic

1 3 5 7 9 8 6 4 2

A CIP record for this book is available from the British Library.

Paperback ISBN 978 1 61185 472 5
E-book ISBN 978 1 61185 905 8

Printed in Great Britain

Grove Press UK
Ormond House
26–27 Boswell Street
London
WC1N 3JZ

www.groveatlantic.com

per

Marcia

You cannot fold a flood
And put it in a drawer,
Because the winds would find it out,
And tell your cedar floor.

—Emily Dickinson

I

Peanut Butter

§1

East Berlin: July or August 1948

Das Eishaus: The Egg-Cooling House, Osthafen

"So, Sadie says to Doris—"

"Doris? Что такое дорис?"

"Doris is just a name, Yuri. A woman's name. Doris, Debbie, Diana . . . doesn't matter. Just a fuckin' name."

"Da. Da. Еврейское имя?"

"What?"

Frank turned to Wilderness, the exasperation beginning to show in his face. Wilderness translated.

"He's asking if it's a Jewish name."

"Oh. Right. Yeah. If you like. It's a Jewish name. Anyway . . . Doris says to Sadie—"

"No," said Wilderness. "Sadie was talking to Doris."

"Oh for fuck's sake. Who's telling this gag? You or me? So . . . Sadie says to Doris, 'My Hymie's such a gentleman. Every week he brings me flowers.' And Doris says, 'Oh yeah, my Jake is such a putz, if he brings me flowers it can mean only one thing. I'll be spending the night with my legs in the air!' And Sadie says, 'Oh, you don't got a vase?'"

Frank laughed at his own joke. All but slapped his thighs. Wilderness managed a smile. He had heard it before. Three or four times, in fact, but Frank was never one to preface a gag with, "Stop me if I told you this one already."

Yuri looked nonplussed.

The kid next to him, one of those string-bean youths they had nicknamed "Yuri's Silents," was smirking. He looked to be about the same age as Wilderness himself, but Wilderness was twenty going on thirty, and this kid was twenty going on twelve. He always looked nervous—scared shitless, as Frank would have it—and perhaps he, a mere corporal, thought it only prudent not to laugh at a dirty joke his boss, a gilded NKVD major with shoulder boards as wide as landing strips, couldn't get.

Yuri got swiftly back to business.

"Sunday? One hundred pounds?"

Frank glanced quickly at Wilderness. Wilderness nodded.

"Sure. One hundred pounds of finest PX Java."

Yuri stuck out his hand. He liked to shake on every deal. Even though they'd been trading coffee, butter and anything else the Russians had on their shopping list for months now, he shook every time as though resealing a bond between them. Wilderness did not think Yuri trusted Frank Spoleto, but then he wasn't at all sure he trusted Frank either.

They were about halfway back to the jeep. Wilderness could see Swift Eddie at the wheel, deep in a Penguin paperback, oblivious to all around him. And he could hear footsteps running behind them.

He turned.

It was the "Silent." His great flat feet slapping down on the pock-marked tarmac.

"I am sorry. I mean not to surprise you."

He was a Kolya or a Kostya . . . one of those abundant Russian diminutives foisted onto children and rarely abandoned as adults. He had the look of an adolescent, features scarcely formed, his face dominated by bright blue eyes that seemed far too trusting to work for an NKVD rogue like Yuri. His Adam's apple bobbed above his collar. His long fingers disappeared into a pocket to produce . . . an empty jam jar.

Frank said, "What's on your mind, kid?"

"Can you get me this?"

Wilderness said, nipping in ahead of Frank, "Our deal is with Major Myshkin. We don't undercut him and we don't deal without him."

Frank rolled the jar in his hand, showed Wilderness the label.

"I don't think Yuri will give a damn about this, Joe."

The label read,

COUSIN KITTY'S GEORGIA PEANUT BUTTER

And then, egregiously,

YUM, YUMMY YUM YUMS

"Is true," said Kolya/Kostya. "The major will let me buy."

Wilderness shrugged. Who was he to stand in the way of a deal, however petty?

"Can you get it?" he said to Frank.

"Sure. If not this brand, then something like. If there's one kind of peanut butter coming out of Georgia, there must be fifty. If this is what he wants. I'll find something. God knows why he wants it. The stuff sticks to your teeth like Plasticine."

"Is . . . личное дело . . . personal, yes?"

"Whatever. Fifty cents a jar, OK. And greenbacks. Capisce? None of those Ostmarks you guys print like toilet paper. US dollars, right?"

"Of course," the kid grinned. "Grrrrinbaksy."

"How many jars?"

"Hundred."

"A hundred?"

"A hundred . . . to begin with."

"OK, kid, you got yourself a deal. Now shake on it, just like your Uncle Yuri, and me and my partner here will head back to civilisation."

They shook, and Kolya/Kostya said, "Major Myshkin not my uncle. I am Kostya—Konstantin Ilyich Zolotukhin."

As they climbed into the jeep, Frank had his moan.

"Do any of them have a sense of humour? 'Uncle' was just a tease. And Yuri . . . what in hell happened to him? It was as though I'd asked to fuck his grandmother."

"Maybe he doesn't like Jewish jokes."

"Never thought of that. Do you reckon he's Jewish? I mean, what kind of a name is Myshkin?"

"A Russian name," Wilderness replied. "And you can bet your last dollar it's not his real name. By the bye . . . how much does a jar of peanut butter cost back home?"

Frank's hand sliced the air, tipping an imaginary fried egg onto an imaginary plate.

"Around twelve cents."

"That's quite a markup."

"Markup from what? We steal the stuff. And how would the kid ever know the right price? He's going to hop on a plane to Shitcreek, New Jersey, and hit the local grocery store?"

"I meant. Fair play. That's all."

"Fair play. Jeezus. Joe, this is no time to grow a conscience. If he'll pay fifty cents then we collect fifty cents."

§2

The problem had always been their own people. The military police of the French, British and American occupying forces. The Reds left them alone. Wilderness assumed that they'd all been told by Yuri not to mess with his "*Schiebers*" . . . his smugglers. Since the airlift began, the MPs did not cross the line to East Berlin, but on occasion they were not past demanding the odd, random search—and on occasion producing papers showing they were in Intelligence cut no mustard and a half-hearted, odd, random search took place. None of them had ever thought to open the jerry cans mounted on the jeep—all packed with contraband.

There was no room in the cans for the peanut butter, so it sat in a sack in the footwell. So what if it got confiscated? The goods that mattered were the ones that passed for currency . . . cigarettes and coffee. And who among the English MPs would know what this stuff was? If needs be, Wilderness was prepared to swear it was bunion ointment or pile cream.

Come Sunday, they delivered the coffee.

Yuri paid up, in the usual manner, as though each dollar was flayed from his own back, and disappeared.

They were left alone with Kostya, who beamed with delight at his purchase, and paid without pain.

"I even got you the same brand," Frank threw in.

"Da. Most happy. Cousin Kitty. Most happy."

"To begin with, you said. A hundred jars to begin with."

Wilderness would not have offered to extend this deal. It could not be long before crossing West to East became a logistical impossibility. They had far bigger concerns than piddling amounts of peanut butter.

"I will . . . let you know."

"Kid, you sound just like a New York theatrical agent talking to a Forty-Second Street hoofer. 'Don't call us, we'll call you.'"

"At the club. I call at the club. At *Paradies Verlassen*."

"OK. But time and tide wait for no man, as Shakespeare says."

"Chaucer, you dimwit," Wilderness said as they left.

"Chaucer, schmaucer. I should care."

§3

Later that week, the *Schiebers* gathered at the *Paradies Verlassen* club, as they did three or four nights of seven. Wilderness thought they must look odd—odd to any onlooker. A bit like the enlisted version of the Three Stooges, none remotely resembling the other: Frank in his US Army olive green, Eddie in his Artillery khaki and Wilderness in RAF pale blue. One captain, one lance bombardier and one corporal who knew in his bones he'd never make officer. If they only had a French-man handy they'd be a representative cross-section of the occupying powers of West Berlin, but Frank had a thing against the French, and Wilderness knew from experience that the French would be the last to forgive and forget and hence would never make good *Schiebers*. Neither forgiving nor forgetting was essential to smuggling, which entailed trading with the likely next enemy and the certain last enemy, but a self-serving indifference to old wounds was. Occasionally they would add a splash of dirty-brown and a little brighter blue to the mix—the NKVD uniform of Yuri, Major Myshkin . . . all jackboots, epaulettes and red stars—but Yuri rationed his visits.

Tonight, the dirty-brown and blue was worn by a woman—her uniform far better tailored than the baggy sacks that Yuri wore. Wilderness caught sight of her across the room just she yanked on the cord of the *Rohrpoststation* and sent a note hurtling through the pneumatic tubes that crisscrossed the ceiling to land, half a minute later, in the net above his head. She waved, blew him a kiss that meant nothing.

Wilderness unfolded the note.

"That damn Tosca bitch?" said Frank, part statement part question, squirming in his chair to look across the room.

But Tosca had picked up her book and resumed reading, and Frank seemed to look right past her.

"Yes," Wilderness replied. "Seems she wants a bit of a chat."

"You kill me with phrases like that. The English art of understatement. When she rips off your balls with a bayonet, try understating that."

Wilderness, as with so many of Frank's moans, ignored this. He crossed the floor, past the man tinkling idly at the piano, to her table.

"Major Tosca."

"Corporal Holderness."

Whilst she was always "Major Tosca" to him, usually he was just "Wilderness" to her. Once in a while, he was Joe. If Tosca addressed him by his real name, let alone by his RAF rank, he was probably in trouble.

She beckoned to a waiter. Ordered two vodka martinis, and Wilderness (real name Holderness) sat, waiting to hear what was on her mind.

"You guys don't give up easy, do you?"

Wilderness loved her voice. New York. Raspy. Like grating nutmeg. There was much to love about Tosca. Everything Frank would fail to appreciate. Thirty, maybe thirty-five at the most, with eyes like conkers and tits like Jane Russell.

"Do we need to give up? The blockade isn't working. We both know that."

"Plenty of you *Schiebers* have given up."

"The ones who have given up are the ones your people have shot. And so far they've all been civilians. You don't shoot at uniforms."

"You got a good shield in Yuri."

"I know."

"It might not be as wide a shield as you imagine."

"Meaning?"

"You been going East more often than usual. You have a new deal, a new customer."

Wilderness said nothing.

"In short, you got Kostya."

"And he works for Yuri."

A brief silence as the waiter set glasses in front of them, and Tosca took a first sip of her martini.

"I'll miss these if they ever drag me back to Moscow. New York, London, Moscow. I have to ask myself. Am I on a losing streak?"

"Kostya," Wilderness prompted.

Tosca pushed a note across the table to him:

Can you meet me Tuesday 7pm at the Café Orpheus in Warschauer Straße opposite the station? K.

"I don't mind playing the messenger for you. But make this the last time."

"I'm not happy about these deals to begin with, so . . . yes. We complete on this one and we're out."

"Good. I do not want Kostya hurt, so do not hurt Kostya. Do not *get* Kostya hurt. He's the son of my oldest friend. Besides, he's just a kid."

"I'm just a kid."

"No, Joe, you're not just a kid. You were born old. Make this the last time you sell anything to Kostya. The shit will hit the fan one day soon. I want Kostya kept clean. If he works for Yuri, OK. Yuri can bullshit his way out of anything. He's a survivor. And Spoleto? Do we any of us give a fuck what happens to Frank?"

"He's my partner. I care."

"Admirable. Don't let caring get you killed. Above all, don't let your caring get my Kostya killed. Capisce?"

"*Capisco.*"

§4

The Warschauer Straße U-Bahn station was just within the Soviet sector, a boundary defined at this point by the River Spree. It was the easternmost stop on a line that began out at Uhlandstraße and crossed the river on the upper deck of the Oberbaumbrücke, a Victorian monstrosity, not unlike Tower Bridge in London, that had taken a pasting at the very end of the war—not from the Allies, but from the Wehrmacht, who had blown the central spans to slow down the Russian entry into Berlin. The lower deck was for vehicles and pedestrians, and had been the scene of a couple of shootings in the last few weeks.

They crossed without incident. They were less than two hundred yards from the Egg Palace and most, if not all the guards would be on Yuri's payroll.

There was no Café Orpheus.

They parked the jeep in front of the Café Unterwelt. A cultural slip of tongue or memory that made sense to Wilderness and Eddie but was wasted on Frank.

"I hope the kid doesn't turn out to be total fuck-up. Orpheus . . . Unterthing . . . who knows?"

The café was aptly named. A pit of a place lacking only brimstone and sulphur, presided over by man wearing a grubby vest and several layers of grease. He said nothing, just jerked his thumb in the direction of the back room.

Kostya was not alone. He stood up as they entered, gestured to the woman seated next to him, and said, "This is Major—"

Frank cut him short.

"Are we dealing with you or with some major we never met? What is this? Does your army have more majors than grunts? Everyone's a fucking major!"

"Со мной будете говорить."

"What did she say?"

Wilderness said, "Calm down. She says to deal with her."

The woman looked up. Dark-skinned, thick black hair falling in ringlets to her blue epaulettes, nut-brown eyes like Tosca, but sadder eyes, far, far sadder. She looked to be roughly the same age as Tosca but perhaps she had not worn so well. God alone knew what life she might have led—women like this had driven tanks from the Urals to Berlin only a couple of years ago. Women like this had taken Berlin and crushed the Nazis.

She had a jar of jam and a jar of Cousin Kitty in front of her, and was spreading what looked to be grape jelly and peanut butter onto a slice of black bread.

"Oh, God. That's just disgusting," Frank said.

"В один прекрасный день будет возможно купить такую смесь в одной и той же банке."

Kostya translated. "The major says one day you will be able to buy grape jelly and peanut butter in one jar. Progress."

"Yeah, well it's disgusting. Like eating ice cream and meatballs off of the same plate."

Wilderness said, "Frank, shuttup and let them get to the point."

"The major asks this of you. We are wish to buy one thousand jars."

"Not possible," Wilderness said.

He felt Frank touch his arm, watched the major bite into her gooey feast.

"No so fast, kid. Could be doable, could be."

"Even if you can get hold of a thousand jars, we don't have enough hiding places in the jeep for a thousand jars of anything."

"Excuse us," said Frank, with an uncharacteristic show of good manners, and hustled Wilderness to a corner by the door.

"It's a cool five hundred, an easy five hundred. Are we going to turn down money like that? Who cares if we have to carry it out in the open? Our guys are lazy, the Reds don't give a shit and if we're caught, we throw 'em a few jars and carry on. It's not as if it's coffee. It's not the brown gold. It's sticky kids' stuff in a fucking jar. You think anyone's gonna start World War III over peanut butter?"

Wilderness said nothing for a few moments, looked back across the room, catching the major with a look of pure gastronomic delight on her face.

"OK. But that's it. No more irregular runs after this."

"Irregular?"

"We stick with coffee and butter. We stick with what we know pays and we deal only with Yuri."

"OK, OK."

Frank approached the table.

"One thousand it is. Fifty cents a jar. Five hundred dollars."

The major wiped her mouth on the back of one hand.

"Двадцать центов за банку."

Wilderness said, "She's offering twenty."

"No way. I might go to forty-five."

"Скидка для навала."

"She wants a discount for bulk."

"Are you kidding? This is bullshit."

The major got to her feet.

"Twenty-five," she said, suddenly no longer in need of an interpreter.

"Forty."

"Thirty-five."

"Done," said Frank.

She spoke rapidly to Kostya, so rapidly Wilderness could not follow, but Kostya said simply, "Noon, Friday?"

Then she bustled past them before either Frank or Wilderness had answered.

"Well, I'll be dipped in dogshit."

"That would be justice," said Wilderness.

"Kid, your buddy drives a hard bargain."

"Buddy? What is *buddy*?"

"You know. Pal, chum . . . mate . . . fukkit . . . *tovarich*."

"No, not my pal. Это моя мама."

"What?"

"He said she's not his buddy, she's his mother."

"I don't fucking believe this."

"Yes. Yes. My mother, Volga Vasilievna Zolotukhina."

As Tosca had called her, "my oldest friend."

"Volga?" Frank said.

"Da. Like the river."

Frank rolled his eyes, a burlesque of incredulity.

"Would you believe I have an Aunt Mississippi?"

Kostya looked to Wilderness for help, baffled by Frank.

"Ignore him, Kostya. We'll be here at noon on Friday."

§5

At noon on Friday, they pulled up by the Café Unterwelt. Eddie drove. Wilderness and Frank sat awkwardly with knees almost to their chins and their feet atop small mountains of jam jars. It felt ridiculous. It looked ridiculous. Wilderness was amazed they hadn't been stopped for the sheer fun of it.

They parked behind a Red Army half-track, purring diesel fumes into the summer sunshine. Two Silents stood by the rear doors. But these were not Yuri's Silents—young men with scarcely flesh on their bones, chosen for their brains, not their brawn—these were hulking bruisers, as tall as Wilderness or Frank and twice as wide. True to type, neither spoke, and the *Schiebers* made their way to the back room.

Major Zolotukhina was at the table, playing patience with a frayed deck of cards. Red Queen on black King. Black seven on red eight.

There was no sign of Kostya.

"Тысяча, да?"

"She wants to know if we got her the thousand jars."

"I got nine hundred and thirty-six."

"Не важно."

Even Frank understood that—an easy carefreeness close to universal *de nada . . . di niente.*

Suddenly she shot to her feet, as rigidly to attention as a short, stout woman could be. She saluted. Fingertips touching the peak of her cap.

The *Schiebers* turned. A tall, slender figure had appeared silently in the doorway.

Wilderness could hear Frank revving up to say something and got in first.

"Just salute, you idiot. And hold until she returns it."

Frank raised his hand, whispered, "What the fuck is this?"

"It . . . is a full-blown NKVD general."

"Are we busted?"

The general was looking them up and down, assessing, deciding . . . hands clasped behind her back like a member of the British royal family. Then she quickly returned the salute for all three of them, stepped past the men and spoke softly to Zolotukhina.

" Ты здесь пряталась, а?"

(So, this is where you've been hiding?)

Then they both grinned like schoolgirls and hugged as though they had not seen one another in months.

As she left, almost over her shoulder the general said, "Не опаздывай."

(Don't be late.)

Momentarily Wilderness wondered, "Late for what?" but it didn't matter. None of this mattered, they'd collect their money and go. And never come back.

Outside, Eddie stood with his hands in his pockets, conspicuously not helping the Silents load nine hundred and thirty-six jars of Cousin Kitty (smooth and crunchy) into the back of the half-track.

"I make that $327.60," said Frank. "Call it $325 for easy."

Wilderness translated and then translated Zolotukhina's reply.

"She says Kostya holds the money. He'll pay us this evening."

"What? Does she think we're fuckin' dumb?"

"She says he's having a tooth out right now, but he'll be here at eight with our money."

"And you believe her?"

Making a virtue out of necessity, Wilderness said, "Frank, you need to know who to trust."

Frank let it go. Let Volga Zolotukhina go. Not that either of them could have stopped her. He was seething a little, but too many thoughts dogged his brain.

"So we come back one more time?"

"Yep."

"And who was the top skirt?"

"You know, you're wasted in Intelligence. That was Krasnaya. I'd bet money on it. Only female general in the NKVD."

"Kras what?"

"Krasnaya. Short for Krasnaya Vdova—the Red Widow. Hero of the revolution. They all took noms de guerre. I think she began as Red Hammer . . . a name she is supposed to have adopted in exile in Switzerland over thirty years ago. She came back to Russia on the sealed train with Lenin and Krupskaya—"

"Krup who?"

"—But then her husband was killed in the civil war . . . so she's been the Red Widow ever since. Krasnaya for short. There were posters she's said to have posed for. That cartoon style of severity they call Socialist Realism . . . Delacroix made bold and simple . . . heroic, beautiful young woman . . . you know the sort of thing, billowing peasant skirt, red headscarf, unwavering steely gaze . . . machine gun on one arm . . . a baby on the other. They say the baby was really hers, too."

"So did I just meet a piece of history in this pistol-packing momma?"

"Something like that."

§6

All over England on a summer's evening as warm and light as this one, men would be at their allotments lifting potatoes, brushing the caterpillars off brassicas, binding over the green tops of onions—many of them in an old battledress from the all-too-recent war. Khaki or blue. Retained, worn, not out of any prolonged sense of pride but out of a pragmatic sense of waste-not-want-not.

To see Germans still in threadbare Wehrmacht jackets was commonplace and never less than thought-provoking. Who could possibly wear it with any sense of pride? Who could possibly wear it without some sense of shame? Who in the country that was all "want" because it had been all "waste" would dream of throwing it away?

Three old soldiers sat in front of Café Unterwelt, sipping distastefully at acorn coffee and smoking God-knows-what in needle-thin roll-ups. One lacked an eye, one an arm and the third a leg. They were the lucky ones. The unlucky ones were still in Russia.

Wilderness always kept what he called his "bribe pack" of Woodbines in his pocket—two or three cigarettes passed around seemed to ease any negotiation and cost him nothing.

He put the packet on the battered tin table in front of the men. A hand reached out for them. No one spoke. No one looked at him.

But Frank spoke.

"You're wasting time and money on these bums, Joe. They don't know the meaning of gratitude. Fukkit, we should have shot the lot."

He pushed open the door of the café. Mercifully without another word.

The one-eyed man spoke.

"He's right, you know. We'd be better off dead. Tell him to come back and shoot me. But first let me smoke one of your English cigarettes. Most kind."

Wilderness wasn't sure if the man had smiled or smirked sarcastically. He followed Frank, drawn to the sudden outburst within.

Frank had Kostya up against the wall, body-slamming him into the plaster.

"Whaddya mean? Whaddya mean?"

Wilderness shouldered him aside.

"Frank, for crying out loud!"

Kostya slumped to the floor.

A trail of blood crept across his chin, but then Wilderness remembered he'd had a tooth out and Frank probably hadn't hit him—yet.

"He's trying to scam us. Says he hasn't got the money!"

Wilderness pulled Kostya to his feet.

"Is this true? Your mother says you hold the purse strings."

"*Shto?*"

"That you keep the money for both of you."

"Тогда моя мать не сказала правды."

Frank erupted.

"In English, you sonovabitch!"

"He says his mother lied to us."

"All dollars I ever have I am give to you for first hundred jars. My mother keep other monies."

"OK. So where's your fuckin' mother now?"

Wilderness echoed Frank, used a softer tone, but still one of concern.

"Kostya, where is Volga now? Does she have our money?"

"My mother since three o'clock on road to Moscow. Her . . . подразделение . . ."

"Her unit," Wilderness prompted.

"Отозвано."

"He says her unit's been recalled to Moscow."

Frank kicked over the table. "Shit, shit, shit."

And Wilderness recalled Krasnaya's last word to Volga Zolotukhina—"Don't be late"—and in the mind's eye he could see a mile-long column of tanks and half-tracks crawling across the dull plain that was Prussia.

"This comes out of your hide, kid."

"No," said Wilderness. "Take it out of my hide, or if you really feel you need to hurt someone there's a bloke outside who's already asked you to shoot him."

"Three hundred bucks, Joe!"

"Peanuts, Frank. If you're really that upset about it . . . take it out of the stash. Take it all out of my share and forget about it. Kostya hasn't scammed you. His mother has."

"What was it you said? I need to know who to trust? *I* need to know who to trust? It's you who needs to know who to trust!"

Wilderness sincerely hoped that was Frank's last word on the matter. His impulse was to walk out, take the jeep and leave Frank to find his way back west on the U-Bahn. But that would mean leaving him alone with Kostya.

Frank's cap had fallen to the floor in the scuffle. Wilderness picked it up, knocked off the dust and handed it back to Frank. "Here. Take the jeep. I'll find my own way back."

Frank put his cap on, with a couple of overly demonstrative, fastidious adjustments. Then he feigned a lunge at Kostya, growling as he did so. Kostya fell back against the wall. Frank laughed and left.

Wilderness held out a hand to help Kostya up and, as he did so, heard Frank encounter the Wehrmacht veterans once more.

"Losers!"

§7

Wilderness went home to Grünetümmlerstraße, to his lover, Nell. He was "Franked" out—a common enough condition—quite possibly Eddie's permanent one—and while Nell could never be a guarantee of a relaxing time, an easy time (he was not at all sure she understood the idea of "easy" in any language) she did at least provide balance, being almost the moral opposite of Frank, who after all was all but devoid of morals.

Yet again, as every evening since the blockade of Berlin began, the canned food—the solid stuff, as Frank would have it, the stuff they stole from the PX and the NAAFI on a daily basis—sat unopened on the dresser as Nell and Wilderness ate an "austerity" meal of whatever was available for honest Deutschmarks at the local honest market. Tonight it was cabbage-and-bread soup with a hint of fresh parsley grown in their window box—a poor man's *ribollita*. On the dresser were prawns in aspic, two foot-long salamis and a dozen cans of Green Giant yellow sweet corn. And Wilderness's threatening to pawn the can opener if she didn't use it did not dent her resolve for a second.

"*Wir sind Berliner*. We are Berliners, Joe. The common fate of our people is our fate. We live like Berliners, we eat like Berliners."

Substitute "Londoner" for "Berliner" and still the idea meant nothing to Wilderness. On Forces Radio, Flanagan and Allen's "Maybe It's Because I'm a Londoner" had been the hit song of 1947. Wilderness thought it pure schmaltz. He'd no more "love" London than he'd do "The Lambeth Walk." It was all nonsense. Fate? Fate was never common. Fate was what you made of it.

Nell's one concession to the black market was eggs from Yuri's *Eishaus*. But that was sentimentality, not vice. Since 1945, when Yuri had become her mother's lover and protector, protecting her from an army of Russian rapists, Yuri had brought eggs. She would never reject his eggs, it would be like rejecting the memory of her mother. Wilderness merely wished that Yuri brought them more often or that today he had bought some himself and passed them off as a gift from Yuri. Lies and more lies.

Wilderness had no problem with lies. You lied and you were lied to. A good *Schieber* survived by being able to know when he was being lied to whilst lying himself. Not that he liked lying, not that he disliked lying. What was there to have any feeling about? Lying was life—the air you breathed. But . . . but he had told Nell so many lies, and in his heart—that hysterical, unreliable organ—perhaps he wished he hadn't or perhaps he wished that the necessity to lie wasn't there?

He'd lied to her between the sheets tonight.

He was relishing the silence that was not quite silence. The sensual rhythm of Nell's breathing. The perfect mechanical rhythm of the piston engines in the airlift planes overhead—all those Lancasters and Yorks, all those Douglas C-54s—into Tegel, into Gatow . . . all the food to keep a city, well . . . half a city, alive. And the imperfect arrhythmia of takeoff and landing. What was it? A plane every thirty seconds? Every sixty seconds? The Cold War's metronome. It might become music. It had long ago ceased to be simply noise.

She spoke first.

"You went East today?"

"Yep." *True.*

"You'll have to stop soon. If the airlift goes on, smuggling will become so much more dangerous."

"Yep." *True.*

"So," a fingertip traced the edge of his left ear, and her lips breathed warmly on his neck. "You will stop, won't you?"

"Yep." *Lie.*

If she knew what he was planning now, knew what tangled thoughts had woven their way into a mental web, knew what he and Frank had cooked up next . . . she'd leave him. Of course there'd be no more runs to the East with a jeep full of black market goodies. He'd found a tunnel. If the Russians controlled the surface, he and Frank would control the underground, deep beneath the Tiergarten, all the way to the ruins of Monbijou on the far bank of the Spree. And if Nell ever found out . . . she'd leave him.

Nell Burkhardt was probably the most moral creature he'd ever met. Raised by thieves and whores back in London's East End, he had come to regard honesty as aberrant. Nell had never stolen anything, had lied, if at all, only in omission and, her association with Wilderness notwithstanding, led a blameless life, and steered a course through it by the unwavering compass of her selfless altruism.

Oh yes, Nell would definitely leave him.

§8

All the same, it came as a surprise when, a few months later, she did. Even more of a surprise was that he would not set eyes on her again for fifteen years, that the 1950s would roll into the 1960s without a glimpse of her.

From time to time he'd hear of Nell—Nell became, after all, little short of famous—from time to time a woman using *L'aimant* by Coty would pass him in the street, in London or Paris, Rome or Helsinki . . . and his head would turn involuntarily or his feet would follow, helpless. On one stupid, stupid occasion he'd caught up with a woman, touched her arm, seen the look of fear and commingled scorn in her eyes as he said Nell's name, then apologised and retraced his steps. He'd learn to mask whatever he might have felt, that little frisson, that tingle in the spine, the goose-pimples up and down his arms, beneath the desirable, inescapable necessities of being first a husband and latterly a father.

He still told lies, but now he lied for England.

And of course he lied *to* England.

Vienna

§

Vienna, The Imperial Hotel: September 1955

I am not drunk, he told himself with the drunk's acute sense of euphemism, I am tipsy.

Perhaps it was the booze. Perhaps it was the innate connection between being off duty and off guard. The first blow, to the belly, doubled him up, and the second, to the face, sent him to the floor scarcely conscious. He'd just about taken in the fact of the attack when he found himself dragged by his shirt collar to the bathroom. His eyes returned to focussing in time to see the bath full of water before his head was plunged in.

When he thought he was dying, hands yanked him back up, he sucked in air, and as his head went down again a voice uttered one of the few words that was common to most European languages: "Idiot."

After the third dunking, the hands let him go, and he fell against the side of the bath, wheezing.

He looked up. The little Russian was sitting on the painted wicker chair by the bathroom door—a semiautomatic in his right hand.

"Идиот," he said again. "You treat me like an idiot."

Wilderness got to his feet. Stripped off his sodden jacket. He felt blood on his face and in his mouth. He leaned over the basin, spitting. The gun stayed on him.

"At the Gare du Nord, you are out in the open as though you think you are invisible. On the Orient Express you linger over your meals and gaze out of the window as though you have nothing better to do."

Wilderness stuck two fingers in his mouth and wiggled a loose tooth. Then he cupped water in his palm and rinsed a pink trail into the basin. He looked in the mirror. This bloke wasn't wearing gloves, and there were no prints on the mirror. He'd been very careful in his search and wiped it down—or he hadn't looked.

"In Venice you . . . you English have a bird word for it . . . you *swan* around like a tourist . . ."

"Bamdid," Wilderness said.

"Что?"

"Band-aid."

The Russian just waved the gun.

Wilderness opened the cupboard. His Browning .25 was still taped to the back of the mirror. The Russian could have found it. He could have emptied the magazine. He could have stuck the gun back up. But, then, the point of taping it up had been that any movement of the tape would probably show. It looked to be as he had left it, but there was really only one way to find out. He'd know by the weight as soon as he had it in his hand.

He took out the roll of Elastoplast and closed the door.

The Russian set down his gun in his lap and lit up a cigarette. Cocky, casual, but he could grab the gun in a split second.

"And in the Nordbahnhof this morning, you practically waved a camera in my face. And still you think I do not notice you. English, you treat me like an idiot."

Wilderness tore off a strip, slapped it on the cut on his right cheek.

The discourse rattled on. "Idiot, amateur, dilettante, бабочка." Accomplished bore finds captive audience. Indeed, it occurred to Wilderness that the bugger might have gone to the trouble of sandbagging him simply to be able to give him a piece of his mind.

He opened the cupboard door, put the roll of Elastoplast back, pulled the Browning free and aimed.

The Russian just grinned—cigarette in his left hand, fingertips of his right resting on his gun. He took another long drag on his cigarette, exhaled a plume of utterly contemptuous smoke.

"You're doing it again. Treating me like an idiot. I know you English. You're all just amateurs. Play the game, chaps, play the game. Sticky wicket, googly, maiden over. You think of Agincourt and cannot begin to imagine Stalingrad. What an absurd nation you English are. I know all about you. Gentlemen and players. Professionalism is vulgar, practice is cheating. Gentlemen and players? Ha! You won't shoot. Your kind never does."

Wrong, wrong, wrong.

II

Tea and Stollen

§9

West Berlin: Late September 1965

Willy Brandt was a nice guy, one of the good guys. Everybody said so. There might be Germans who would never forgive him for fighting against Germany in the war or for accepting Norwegian citizenship, but foreign politicians adored him. He'd got on well with JFK, reasonably well with LBJ and De Gaulle and very well with England's new prime minister, Harold Wilson—he could almost hear the phrase "Good German" on his lips, but hoped he never would.

Brandt hated losing.

He'd spent what seemed an age in Bonn, just lost the election for chancellor of the Bundesrepublik, otherwise known as West Germany. Now he was back in Berlin—his old job, his old office—suffering from . . . what was Churchill's term for it? . . . "Black Dog Days."

His chief of staff found him lying on the floor, his head propped up with a thick book—*Goethes Sämtliche Werke Band VI*. The Grundig radiogram, which sat in the corner squat as a harmonium, softly playing Schubert's Swan Song.

"Miserable stuff," Nell said. "Is this the mood you're in?"

"Yes. And no."

She put a cup of coffee within arm's reach. Pulled up a chair and looked down at him. "The staff—your staff—would like to see something of you. They'd like a word from the mayor of West Berlin, not the hermit of the *Rathaus*."

"Instead they've got the return of the prodigal loser."

"Never cared for self-pity and dare I say it's out of character."

Brandt eased himself up, wrapped his hands round the mug of coffee.

"I said I'll never run again."

"Yes. We all heard that. It was the last thing you said before you fell down the well."

"Before the dog bit me . . . much more appropriate. But . . . I was lying."

"To the staff? To us?"

"To myself."

Nell shrugged.

"Well. Plenty of time to change your mind a dozen times if you want. No election for four years."

"This government won't last four years. I need to keep . . . to keep a finger on the pulse in Bonn."

"Why are you telling me this?"

"Did you enjoy our time in Bonn, Nell?"

"I say again, why are you telling me any of this?"

"I want you to go back. I want you to be my eyes and ears in Bonn."

This required no thought, so Nell gave it none.

"No."

"Is that your last word?"

"Until you start your charm offensive and wear me down."

"What can I do to make the prospect appealing to you?"

"Nothing. I hated Bonn. It's a hole. It's a company town and the product is politics. I'd sooner be in KdF Stadt making Volkswagens. At least the product is tangible. Bonn is what I imagine Washington to be . . . the cave dwellers . . . everything is politics, every other person is a diplomat . . . the man you sit next to on the tram is a Swedish delegate, the woman ahead of you in the market queue is the British ambassador's secretary. None of it, none of them is real."

"You wouldn't have to live there. Just . . . regular visits."

"The answer's still no. Fire me if you like, but I'm staying in Berlin."

"I know . . . I know . . . you are the Berliner and I'm not. There are times I feel like a stranger in my own land. Let me finish the coffee you so kindly brought me and then I might be fired up enough for the charm offensive."

"Fine. I'll be in my office—in Berlin."

§10

At six o'clock Nell did not go straight home. Instead she went to Grünetümmlerstraße, to the house she had lived in, all those years ago just after the war, with Joe Wilderness. Two years in that flat above Erno Schreiber. Another lifetime. Joe had moved on—or rather she had thrown him out—she had moved on. Erno had not. Erno had stayed. Erno had grown old in a three-room flat he had occupied since he walked home, slouching not marching, from Amiens on the Western Front in 1918, and decided the best use for his *Pickelhaube* was as a coal scuttle.

A young woman was poking the fire in the iron stove, shovelling in a few lumps of coal from the steel helmet, as Erno fussed about his tea and teapot. She was blonde, pretty—about the age Nell had been when she had finally moved out—the bloom of youth upon her, worn with a carelessness Nell had never managed.

"You know Trudie," Erno said, not asking a question.

But Nell did not know Trudie.

"Ach . . . she has your old room."

Trudie closed the stove door and stood up.

"I'm Nell," said Nell. "Nell Burkhardt."

"Of course," Trudie replied. "Erno often talks of you and of Joe."

Nell glared at Erno. It was an unwritten rule. They did not talk about Joe Wilderness.

But Erno merely smiled and set three cups on three saucers, and tore at the wrapper of a stollen cake.

"Not for me, Erno," said Trudie. "I will leave you to talk."

A scant exchange of the pleasantries of departing and Nell and Erno were alone.

He put a knitted tea cosy on the pot, eased his backside into a sagging armchair. "So, you think out of sight is out of mind?"

"I don't want to talk about Joe. I didn't come here to talk about Joe."

"You don't have to come here to talk about anyone. You are welcome even in silence."

She sat opposite, perched herself on the hard edge of the chaise longue. "But I did come here to talk about someone—Brandt."

"So—pour tea, cut cake and tell me."

When Nell had finished, Erno said, "You've never lacked ambition."

"Meaning what?"

"You have been trying to set the world to rights since you were nine years old. Your mother always said to beware your stamping foot and your po-face."

"I was, I know, a rather serious little girl. Mea culpa."

"And now you are a very serious woman. Why else did you ever take up with a rogue like Joe or an old rogue like me—because we made you laugh?"

"Let's not talk about Joe."

"Ask yourself, Nell—what will serve you best? Following Brandt or not following Brandt? He has the same ambition, the same messianic urge, the same preposterous belief in himself."

"Preposterous?"

"If Brandt ruled the world, every day might not be the first day of spring, but East would talk to West, North would talk to South and no one would go hungry."

"As you said, preposterous."

"You have hitched your wagon to his star."

"But . . ."

"But?"

"But Bonn. Erno, it's the dullest place on Earth."

III

Omelettes

§11

The Palace of Westminster, London:
May 19, 1966, about 4 p.m.

Cloudy with Sunny Intervals

"Where is Bernard Alleyn?"

Fifteen minutes earlier it had been "Where is Leonid L'vovich Liubiumov?" One man, two names, but he did wish they'd make their collective mind up.

It was the third time Reg Thwaite had asked him that. This time, noticeably, pointedly without rank or status. Not Flight Sergeant Holderness, not even Mister.

Wilderness returned the compliment.

"I think I answered that question several minutes ago. I don't know," he lied.

"If you had answered me, I'd not be asking, would I? A Soviet agent, a Soviet agent in your charge, vanishes without trace—I'll ask you a hundred times if I have to. Where is Bernard Alleyn?"

The chairman intervened.

"I think, Flight Sergeant, that Sir Reginald would like your 'I don't know' placed in some sort of context."

"Context?"

Wilderness felt Burne-Jones edging nearer, straining for proximity, everything short of scraping his chair across the parquet.

It was unusual for a parliamentary committee to question a serving MI6 officer, almost without prior protocol. Burne-Jones had been insistent . . . it would all take place behind closed doors, there'd be no stenographer, and as Wilderness's immediate superior he'd be there too, half a pace behind.

"Run through the details of the handover."

"Again?"

Wilderness felt Burne-Jones at his ear.

"Just answer the question, Joe."

"All right. Once more. It hasn't changed in the last half-hour. It won't be any different. Alleyn and I walked out to the middle of the Glienicke Bridge—"

"Ah . . ." A rustling of papers on Thwaite's part, the pretence of consulting notes. "Why was that? Why just the two of you?"

Wilderness could find it easy to hate Reg Thwaite. A working-class Yorkshire Tory MP, a privy councillor, who had taken it upon himself to be the voice of the patriotic working man, a barrack-room lawyer who had no truck with socialism and had made himself the scourge of what he saw as a secret service dominated by the English upper classes. He hated the old boy network, and even Wilderness's East End accent carried no reassurance that he might be the antithesis of anything that could be termed "old boy."

"More people, more guns, more possibilities of someone getting shot," Wilderness replied.

"And you didn't have Alleyn handcuffed?"

"No."

"And you say no shots were fired?"

"No one even drew a gun," Wilderness lied.

In reality, he and Yuri had stood in a face-off, pointing guns at each other's heads. He'd no idea if he could ever have shot Yuri or Yuri him. He'd known Yuri since 1947, as plain Major Myshkin. At some point in the murk of Soviet history he had become General Bogusnik—another case of one man, two names.

"Alleyn crossed to the East German side as Geoffrey Masefield crossed to the West. They stopped for a moment. Got a good look at each other. Too long a moment. I watched General Bogusnik fold up in pain. Alleyn went to grab him, Masefield followed. Between them they got him back to his own people at the far end of the bridge. That was the last I ever saw of Alleyn."

He hoped he'd placed the right emphasis on the final sentence.

"And what did you do?"

"I stayed on the American side of the line and I waited. I stood there with my hands in my pockets in a freezing wind and I waited. I thought

Masefield would return, but when I heard engines start, I knew he wouldn't. I knew the deal was off. I walked back into the American sector and drove into West Berlin."

The Americans had backed him in this pack of lies. If they hadn't, he'd be in the shit. He assumed it had been in both their interests to bury the truth—that Alleyn had crossed back with him. Frank Spoleto had been there—the CIA man posing as an Ad-man posing as a CIA man. As long as the grunts jumped when Frank barked, Wilderness didn't care. Frank owed him no favours. He'd no idea why, but it must have suited Frank and the CIA to agree to his story. But—somebody had said something. There was a careless whisper in the air or pricks like Thwaite wouldn't have their teeth into him.

"The last you saw of him?"

"Yes."

"And where do you think he went after that?"

"I've no idea. Bogusnik died. That was common knowledge within ten days. They gave him a state funeral. Someone else will be looking after Alleyn. He could be on a pension with a row of medals on his chest, he could have a desk job, he could be propping up a bar with Kim Philby, he could be in a gulag."

Thwaite looked pained. Mentioning Philby might have been showing the red rag to the bull, a one-person incarnation of everything Thwaite hated about the toffs. But he looked to his left, to the Liberal Party's sole representative on the committee—J. Fraser Campbell, MP for islands in the North Atlantic where the sheep outnumbered the voters two hundred fifty to one—and passed the baton.

"Thank you, Sir Reginald. Could we come to the incident that took place a few hours later? At the Invalidenstraße checkpoint?"

"I got Masefield out," Wilderness said bluntly, and sensing what was coming next threw in, "I did my job. Or did you expect me to leave him there?"

"Is it part of your job to create diplomatic incidents?"

"Mr. Campbell, I'm an SIS field agent. In the field everything is a potential diplomatic incident. If it weren't, we'd be known as the Obvious Service, not the Secret Service."

"So you don't deny this was a diplomatic incident?"

"I don't deny it. I don't care. I did what I had to do. I did my job."

Campbell shoved a sheaf of papers to one side, spread out a newspaper, spun it around to show Wilderness the headline and photographs: *Der Tagesspiegel*, six months old, dated the day after the *incident*. He'd seen it before. The West Berlin press must have been nifty to get there so soon. Night shots, the stark unreality that flashbulbs create . . . the wreck of a car, the prat of a British officer he'd confronted, the bent barrier . . . it all looked as though he'd just walked out of shot seconds before.

"The barrier crashed," Campbell was saying. "Our side confronting their side, shots fired, men injured. Do you have any idea how hard it was to placate the East Germans?"

Wilderness had no recollection of any shots fired, but at the moment he crashed through the barrier in that borrowed Austin Healey he would not have noticed a bomb going off.

He flicked up a lock of hair, not so casually that they could fail to notice the scar on his forehead.

"No shots were fired. The only people injured were me and Masefield. And I don't care about placating the enemy. This was a skirmish at a Berlin crossing point, not the Cuban Missile Crisis."

The British border patrol weren't telling any lies on his behalf, but then they didn't have Frank breathing down their necks. What they had were photographs. The camera never lies. And Wilderness wondered whether this meeting would be taking place at all if there'd been no photographs.

"But weapons were drawn?"

"You don't draw a rifle, you just point the bloody thing."

Wilderness heard another whisper from Burne-Jones: "For God's sake. Remember your manners."

Too loud a whisper. They'd all heard.

Thwaite again, "I find your attitude very hard to credit, Flight Sergeant Holderness. There's no room here for your resentment."

"And I find your questioning very hard to stomach. You shouldn't be sitting here in judgment on me like the three wise monkeys."

"Then what should we be doing? If not our duty?"

"I did *my* duty. I got Geoffrey Masefield out. A hapless bugger who should never have been there in the first place. Instead of whining about diplomatic incidents you should be giving me a fucking medal."

Burne-Jones was on his feet at once.

"Sorry, gentlemen, but I'm afraid this meeting is suspended until further notice. You will understand if I say that I need to talk to Flight Sergeant Holderness alone."

Thwaite had to have the parting shot.

"I'd understand if you said you had to smack his bottom."

§12

It being a Thursday when Burne-Jones and Wilderness emerged into New Palace Yard, Wilderness had no expectations of an early resumption. On Fridays members of Parliament dashed back to their constituencies in the pretence of consulting the electorate, while shooting grouse or shagging mistresses. The earliest he'd be summoned again would be Tuesday.

Burne-Jones held up his furled brolly and hailed a cab. Turning in the open door he said, "Go home, Joe."

"Shouldn't that be 'go home and look to your sins'?"

"No. Go home and look to your wife and children. If you can't be a good spy, at least be a halfway decent son-in-law."

A bit of a stinger. Nothing like the bollocking he might have expected. All the same he thought he was a very decent son-in-law to Burne-Jones and had no opinion at all on his own merits as a spy.

He watched the cab head west, glanced up at Big Ben and, realising it would soon be rush hour, turned into Westminster Bridge Road and headed for the Underground.

It was Saturday afternoon before he heard from Burne-Jones again. He was watching wrestling on ITV—the antics of Jackie Pallo and whichever lumpkin knew part B of the same routine and had been selected as fall guy. Judy had taken the twins to Hampstead Heath in the custom-made double pushchair the Burne-Joneses had given the Holdernesses for Christmas.

Wilderness turned the volume down and picked up the phone.

"Joe."

The upper-class drawl of his father-in-law, a single syllable drawn out to sound almost horizontal.

"Dinner this evening?"

"I think we can manage that. Judy's out at—"

"No. Just you and me. Madge will be going to the theatre. The Whitehall. You know how fond she is of farce."

He did know. Madge had dragged both of them to some awful tosh over the last few years. The current Whitehall farce was an attempt to make a comedy out of a Soviet defection.

"Isn't it still *Chase me, Comrade*? She must have seen it by now?"

"Twice, as I recall, but it's the last night, and she's taking a very special guest, Nureyev. Upshot, I have the place to myself. Shall we say seven thirty?"

So, a bollocking at the dinner table. Alec being one of nature's gents, they'd at least get through the soup course before he laid into Wilderness.

§13

There was no soup course. After a stiff martini, during which Wilderness had answered half a dozen questions about the character/behaviour/ university place/career prospects of his two year-old children, Alec had invited him to rip up a French stick while he deftly tossed omelettes over a naked flame at the dining table.

"An omelette should never feel remotely leathery to the tongue," he pronounced as the first turned a somersault.

He sounded so knowledgeable. All the same Wilderness knew he couldn't so much as peel a potato if left to cook a proper meal. If he mentioned Elizabeth David, his father-in-law would raise an eyebrow and say "who?" It was not so much his party trick as just another toff thing. A leftover from his days in the Officers' Mess. A gentleman should always be prepared to toss his own.

"Eat it while it's at its best, Joe, don't wait for me."

A couple of minutes passed in silence. Burne-Jones flipped his own omelette onto his plate, took a mouthful and sighed at his own artistry.

"It's good," Wilderness said. "It's very good."

"Don't blame yourself."

"I'm not. You cooked it."

"I meant Alleyn, Masefield . . . that pompous ass Thwaite."

"Fuss about nothing," Wilderness replied.

"Quite . . . but . . ."

Inevitable, thought Wilderness; he was here to rebutt the buts.

"But what?"

"Something set them off. Someone or something poked a sleeping pig with a stick."

"So?"

"I'm tending towards the notion that it's the Invalidenstraße incident that rang all the bells. After all, the Glienicke Bridge is American turf and they have little choice but to accept the Americans' version of events. But Jock Campbell is not exaggerating. Invalidenstraße took some sorting. The Germans are utterly schizoid about things. They admire the guts and the dash for freedom whilst deploring the damage to their efforts at an Eastern Bloc *Politik*. But for Invalidenstraße I'm not at all sure Alleyn would be an issue. Our lords and masters might not have noticed him. But it remains, they have noticed. Pity you wrote off the car. Made too good a photo. Bigger pity our blokes couldn't get it all straight before the press arrived, but there you are."

Or, thought Wilderness, there I wasn't.

"I got Masefield out. Surely no one thinks I should have left our Geoffrey behind?"

"No . . . no one does. I think it may well be your methods . . ."

"Tell me another way. I got him out without a shot fired."

"And therein lies the saving grace. Not a shot fired. If there had been—well it doesn't bear thinking about."

"What do they want? What do they expect?"

"Dunno what they expect. Perhaps some evidence that Alleyn had reached Moscow?"

Wilderness shook his head.

"That's . . . that's naïve. To name one example. It took the Russians five years to admit Burgess and Maclean were there. Why would they trumpet Alleyn's return? There's no pattern."

"It's just that our people in Moscow have picked up nothing. Absolutely nothing."

"But the Russians aren't complaining they didn't get him back. So it's meaningless. The Russians will do what they will do. And right now they're using Alleyn's presence or absence to create dissent here."

"Do you really believe that?"

"Probably not."

"Do you have any idea at all where Alleyn might be if not in Moscow?"

"I'd only be guessing."

"Then guess."

Wilderness had last seen Alleyn in Charlottenburg six months ago. He had given him an Irish passport. A fake, but a good fake. One of Erno Schreiber's small masterpieces. Alleyn would only hit trouble when or if he came to renew it. He'd also given him the address of his ex-wife in Dublin. He'd made no arrangement to get Alleyn out of Berlin, he'd left him to it, but it would be a man of very little imagination, let alone one who had lived a double life for fifteen years—English civil servant and Soviet secret agent—who could not navigate his way back to England using the hundred quid in fivers that Wilderness had also given him.

It would be a fairly safe guess to say that Alleyn was in Dublin.

"He could be anywhere," Wilderness replied.

"Anywhere except Moscow?"

"That's right."

"Joe, I think we are only a matter of days away from some arse like Reg Thwaite coming straight out and accusing you of turning Alleyn loose. An action Reg may well consider to be treason."

"I shall deny it."

"No you won't."

"Eh?"

"I got called upstairs yesterday."

Ah.

Upstairs.

The office of C, Sir Dick White, head of MI6.

"You won't get the chance to answer the question. Dick wants you out."

"Out of the Service? Alec, for fuck's sake!"

"No no no. Out of the country. Joe, Dick White doesn't want you answering that question. In fact, he doesn't want the question asked in the first place. The only reason we can give, the only acceptable reason, that is, for you not answering a parliamentary summons is if affairs of state intervene."

"I say again, eh?"

"We can post you abroad, tell 'em it's a top secret mission that only you can do. We pretend you're 007 or some such tosh. They'll all have seen a Bond film. Reg Thwaite surely has? He's a dead ringer for that Goldfinger chap. If not, then they're all of a generation to have grown up on Richard Hannay. They probably think that's what you do."

"I carry a gun. I wear a well-tailored suit. I don't have a homing device in the heel of my shoe."

"Quite. Nor do you have a pen with invisible ink. We invent a mission, then we just let their imaginations settle into a rut of Buchan's or Fleming's devising. Within a few months they'll have forgotten about you."

Wilderness found there was always a certain pleasure in being told he was "on a mission."

"So. Back to Berlin," he said, heightening the pleasure for himself.

"Er . . . 'fraid not. You and Berlin are a poisonous combination right now. I think it might well be the only place we couldn't send you."

"Ah. The criminal always returns to the scene of the crime?"

"Quite. No, we have something else in mind. Persereiikkä."

"Spell it."

"Er . . . P . . . something something lots of *i*'s . . . lots of *k*'s. And an umlaut thingie on the end. It's in—"

"I know where it is. I just wanted to be sure you'd got it right. You're sending me back to fucking Finland?"

"Yeees."

"It's bollock-freezing."

"It's summer. They have hours and hours of daylight."

"Persereiikkä is inside the bloody arctic circle!"

"Which is why they get all that daylight."

"And in winter they get none."

"Really?"

"Alec . . . it's stuck where the sun don't shine. Tell me you'll get me out before winter."

"I can't make any promises."

It was not, he knew, a take it or leave it. It was a take it. A stark choice between the midnight sun and the abominable Reg Thwaite.

"So, what's the mission?"

"Well . . . simple really. Allied nation . . ."

"Alec, Finland isn't in NATO."

"Not all our allies are in NATO."

"Norway is. Iceland is."

"And Sweden isn't, so what does that prove? As I was saying . . . allied nation . . . a thousand miles of border with the Russians, quite possibly the most heavily defended border this side of Korea . . . and . . ."

"And?"

"And that's about it, really."

"A watching brief?"

"If you like."

"Watching what?"

"Watching a thousand miles of sensitive Russian border."

"Do I get wellies, a walking stick and a packed lunch with it?"

"Joe. I'll say one word to you, and if you persist in this line I will go on saying it—Thwaite!"

"Nothing ever happens on that border and certainly not as far north as Lapland."

"Thwaite!"

"There's only one border crossing."

"Thwaite!"

"The cordon sanitaire is about a hundred kilometres deep."

"Thwaite!"

"On their side it's considered a punishment posting!"

"That's as may be. If I wanted to punish you there are far worse postings than Finland. Nevertheless—Thwaite!"

Not wishing a further "Thwaite," Wilderness acquiesced.

"OK. Finland? What don't we know about Finland already?"

"Wrong approach, Joe. Most of what we knew about Russia's intentions towards Finland went belly-up eighteen months ago when Khrushchev got the boot. For a very unpredictable man Khrushchev was pretty consistent about Finland. If he made one statement on the matter of Northern Balance and Finnish neutrality, he made a dozen. I hate to say it, but with hindsight you knew where you stood with Khrushchev. The new chaps . . . completely unknown quantities. Probably itching for another scrap after Cuba."

"If we knew where we stood with Khrushchev, why were we all surprised by the Berlin Wall?"

"Don't try to muddy the waters. You know what I'm talking about. New men in the Kremlin. We can take nothing for granted, and hence we need to look again at things Finnish . . ."

"You mean *I* need to look again?"

"At last, on the same page, are we?"

Wilderness had met Khrushchev—and had made an impression. In '61 as the wall was going up. By pure luck—as Wilderness saw it, good luck—he'd been standing in Bernauerstraße when the man made a clandestine visit to see his handiwork. Emerging from an unmarked car, barely disguised by cap and muffler, he had recognised Wilderness at once as one of the myriad Western spies present at his meeting with JFK in Vienna—but, then, it was said he had a memory like an elephant. He had spoken civilly to Wilderness and Wilderness to him. He'd even landed an invitation to visit the Soviet Union . . . as if. He'd never put it in a report. He'd never told Alec. It might not be his ace in the hole, but it was a card to be played at the right moment, and this was not that moment."

"Take Sunday to pack. Have a quick word with Eddie on Monday and then . . ."

"Bugger off to Finland."

"Quite. Coffee?"

§14

Part of him dreaded getting home. Judy Jones was the sort of wife who necessitated regular trips to Petticoat Lane for the cheapest crockery the stalls had to offer, as she threw so many plates and cups when angry. The scar on Wilderness's forehead was as likely to have been caused by one of Judy's spinning Bosanquet googlies as by anything that had happened in the field.

But—she was on the sofa, red dress, a bottle of decent claret breathing, two glasses on the coffee table, one of his Brubeck LPs on the turntable, the lingering melancholy of "Blue Shadows in the Street."

"Alec told you?"

"Yep. Said not to blame you."

He slipped off his jacket and sat next to her. She slumped almost at once, head in his lap looking up at him, a glass of wine resting on her sternum.

"There's more."

"Tell me."

"He said if this war were a hot war not a poached-egg war, you'd have got your medal. Parliament may think you're a menace, MI6 quietly thinks you're a hero."

"Quietly? More like silently. And I don't want a medal. I never wanted a medal. I only said that to annoy the hell out of Reg Thwaite."

She held up the glass.

He knocked half of it back.

"Sweetest, dearest, husband mine . . . why did you let Bernard Alleyn go?"

He set the glass back on her chest, took pleasure in the rise and fall of her bosom, watched her fingers twine around the stem, inhaled the familiar, provocative waft of Judy's scent—*L'aimant* by Coty. The same scent he had given to Nell Burkhardt all those years ago in Berlin. He'd met Judy's scent long before he'd met her—her room in her parents' house being designated the guest room while she was at Cambridge, and Wilderness so often the designated guest. He'd fought his own memory to forget/remember and once acknowledged had installed barriers to compartmentalise his mind, the little Berlin Walls of the skull. Not always successfully. If needs be, he would remember and recite the list of books on her shelves . . . Jane Austen, L. M. Montgomery, Noel Streatfield . . . and see the red ballet pumps in the bottom of the wardrobe . . . the pile of Frank Sinatra 78s . . . the paraphernalia of an

English schoolgirl in the 1950s . . . nothing to remind him of Nell. But all bound by the spell of *L'aimant*.

"Joe?"

"Sorry. What?"

"You were daydreaming."

"Was I?"

"Why did you let Bernard Alleyn go?"

"You think I did?"

"I know bloody well you did."

"I suppose . . . I suppose I liked him. Certainly more than I liked Geoffrey Masefield. Bernard was a family man. He cared about his wife and kids and just wanted to be left alone to be an Englishman. I gave him the next best thing. A place on John Bull's other island. With any luck, if it all went in accordance with my lack of a plan, he's living as an Irishman. Masefield? Masefield was a fantasist."

"A fantasist you couldn't abandon to his fate?"

"No. He didn't deserve that."

A pause. He could hear Judy thinking.

"Mum thinks the MPs are using what you did as a way of getting at Dad. She reckons someone in Six is ratting the two of you out to the greenarses."

Greenarse—Burne-Jones slang, handed down to the current generation. Slang for MPs who "do bugger all but polish green leather benches with their arses."

"It's a pointless attack if that's what it is. Your dad has less than eighteen months to retirement. But she may be right. The sins of the son-in-law. However, it will all blow over."

"You're sure?"

"Their case—their nosiness—rests on two things. The supposed diplomatic incident at Invalidenstraße and the suspicion that I turned Bernard loose. That I took the law, their law, into my own hands. Neither amounts to anything. They admit the *incident* fell a tad short of the diplomatic—it would have taken a few bullets and a body to make it that—and Bernard . . . well, *they* set him free, not me. Wondering where he might be now is a pointless speculation. They'd already agreed to swap him for Masefield. That the swap didn't take place is neither here nor there. Only the Russians have a right to whinge, but they're not. It's not as if I'd busted him out of the Scrubs. The English had already agreed to give Bernard his freedom. They turned the key and he walked out. That should have been an end of it, and it will be an end of it."

"In a month or two."

"Or three or four."

"Oh God. As long as that?"

"Possibly. You could work on the old man."

"I'll try, but there are times when I think he's daughter-immune. I could always come and visit. I've never been to Lapland. The girls could get to see a real reindeer . . . on Dancer, on Prancer, et cetera."

"Well, it might be brilliant cover. A British agent with wife and kids in tow. Who would ever suspect me?"

"OK, maybe not such a good idea."

"But . . ."

"Yeeees?"

"If you really wanted to go. The battle for Finland is a war of words. Neither East nor West is allowed a base there . . . more acutely I think neither East nor West would dare put a base there . . . so we swamp the poor buggers in propaganda thinly disguised as culture.

"If you want a grant to stage *Twelfth Night* in your local village hall in South Bumstead, Hampshire, the Arts Council will likely as not tell you to fuck off . . . but say you want to put it on in a snowbound wooden hut in Saariselkä, then the British Council, that is to say the Foreign Office propaganda arm, will throw money at you. So if you want to visit Lapland, I reckon your best bet is to suggest putting on a nude ballet featuring the over-seventies, atonal score by Schoenberg, sets by Mark Rothko . . . Ken Russell can direct . . . all the easy, accessible stuff . . . and you'll probably pick up a whopping great grant and an OBE as well."

Judy feigned thought. He heard no cogs.

"Over-seventies? Nude? What would you suggest? *Swan Lake*?"

"No. Far too Russian."

"You know what? I don't think I'll bother. But since I won't be seeing you for three or four months, I don't think we should waste another minute."

She handed him her glass.

Stood.
Fumbled a moment with the hook at the back of her neck.
Stepped out of the red dress.
And walked away.
All he had to do was follow the trail of underwear.

§15

She slept. As so often, he didn't. He stared at the red knickers hanging from the lampshade, a trick at which she never missed. The enduring lesson of years of netball and lacrosse.

Overhead a plane descending into Heathrow . . . not *a* plane but *planes* . . . and for a moment he could hear the purring propellers of RAF Yorks and Lancasters . . . not the whine of jet engines . . . not London, not London . . . but Berlin.

Odd thing, memory.

§16

Wilderness, being a field agent, had no desk at 54 Broadway.

Eddie Clark had his office and was welcome to it. Eddie also had Wilderness's former assistant, Alice Pettifer, and was welcome to her too. And as her well-honed sarcasm bounced off Eddie like chip fat off formica, the scope for tension was greatly reduced. She liked working for Eddie, and let Wilderness know it.

"I need a bit of space, Alice."

"Well you're not getting your office back. It's Eddie's. Try the library. Lots of space there."

"OK."

"Besides, I hear you're off to the frozen north later today."

"Tomorrow, Alice."

"Boss says today."

"Have you booked a flight?"

"No. Top of my morning list, though."

"Make it tomorrow. I need a bit of prep time. As you say, the library would be a good choice. And route me via Berlin, would you?"

Telling Alice to do something was not always easy. Not a natural subordinate—one day, Wilderness thought, she might end up running MI6—she worked better if given reasons.

"I want to read whatever is latest from Finland and there are a few loose ends in Berlin."

"Joe, don't give the buggers in Parliament an opportunity to recall you. They'll be in session tomorrow morning. Old King Thwaite will be calling for you louder than he calls for his fiddlers three. You really need to be unavailable to them."

"I will be. Tell everyone I'm flying out this evening, and I'll spend the night at Eddie's. Get me to Berlin by lunchtime and I can fly into Helsinki tomorrow night. Just don't let Alec know."

She smiled. She could melt him with that smile. She loved a conspiracy—another reason she might end up running the place.

The "latest" from Finland was thin. A file he could read in a couple of hours. His assertions to his father-in-law—"Nothing happens there"—and to his wife—"It's a war of words"—had been precise.

It hadn't always been that way. When he'd last been to Finland in the late 1950s, if you threw a stone in the street you hit an Allied agent. It was . . . no better word . . . *crawling* with spooks.

Under the terms of an international agreement between the USSR and Finland—the Finnish-Soviet Treaty of Friendship, Co-Operation and Mutual Assistance 1948, a diplomatic mouthful usually abbreviated as FCMA—Finland was tied into a deal that necessitated neutrality, yet somehow defied neutrality. If Germany and its allies ever threatened either country, each would come to the aid of the other. A NATO in miniature. Two nations rather than fifteen. But therein lay the problem of neutrality. NATO, since the admission not of Germany but of a big bit of it called West Germany, a country unacknowledged by the USSR, might now be deemed to be the ally of Germany, a country that had only a theoretical existence but which in the minds of both Finns and Russians was still a potential invader. If in doubt one need only look at recent history.

It was nonsense. Germany, at least the Western bit, was no threat—but if the heart has its reasons, so does paranoia.

Hence, Finland's neutrality was an uneasy one. It had fought the USSR to a standstill in 1940 but knew it could never do so again. It could only live within the shadow of the beast. Hence, again, the other beast, NATO, the West, the American sphere of influence . . . needed careful handling. The trick to remaining an independent, neutral country was not to provoke either side.

Like Burne-Jones, Wilderness had a quiet admiration for Khrushchev. "As good as his word" might be overstatement, but in 1956 he withdrew Soviet troops from their base at Porkkala, just south of Helsinki—a base on which they still had a two-year lease—leaving Finland entirely free of foreign military bases. Norway and Sweden had none, Iceland just one at Keflavik—a US base Icelanders were willing to see closed until the Russian invasion of Hungary four months later gave them cause to change their mind.

And so began the great Finnish foxtrot. One foot forward, one foot back.

Finland, it was blithely assumed by all Western analysts, would like to be part of the West, it was "natural," this in a political world where nothing was natural—yet it found itself obliged to decline Marshall Plan aid, to decline membership in the Common Market . . . all to foster what everyone knew to be an illusion—neutrality. Neutrality was a line drawn in water.

Rather than neutral, Finland was the next great battleground-in-waiting. The next battle would not be a Stalingrad or an Iwo Jima . . . it would be swift annihilation. Wilderness had found it chilling when an old CIA chum, with too much Scotch inside him, had blurted out the real, if deniable, US policy: "We'll nuke Finland rather than let the Commies have it."

To the north, Lapland, home of reindeer—on Dancer, on Prancer, on Donner and Blitzen—and Father Christmas. Wilderness had never been that far north. He knew it had been left as "scorched earth" when the Finns drove out the Germans towards the end of the war—wooden towns reduced to ashes, bridges blown and roads mined. Twenty years later mines were still being unearthed. Even without such man-made devastation it was a scarcely habitable region, extending up into the arctic circle, that had the misfortune to be where NATO (in the shape, the peculiar shape, of Norway) and the USSR met. A land rich in resources, but a land of few people, that might well be the most photographed and mapped spot on Earth. Until 1944 Lapland had had a spur leading to the Arctic Ocean at the port of Petsamo, a thin strip of land, no more than fifteen kilometres wide in places, a Finnish thread dividing Norway from Russia. Now, the two countries wrapped around Finland like fingers making a fist.

In the fifties there had been mad missions: Finnish veterans of World War II recruited to operate across the border in Murmansk and Soviet Karelia. Wilderness thought there must be a room at MI6 he didn't know about—the Department of Silly Schemes, whose sole purpose was to think up suicidal spy missions. What idiot decided to have men fly over Karelia in a hot-air balloon? They might just as well send Noddy and Big Ears in their red and yellow car toot-tooting all the way. It was a looking-glass war from which few returned. And men being spent, technology took over.

The USA and England photographed the entire border with the USSR in the late fifties, and then every inch of coastline. Sweden and Norway sent Intelligence officers into Lapland to photograph all they could—it was said they bought up all the glossy tourist postcards—and then mined east-west roads. Only a couple of years back the CIA had attempted much the same thing, and for once, Finland had retaliated and expelled them.

Since then things had gone quiet. The spook numbers fell to tick-over levels. Finland quietly censored itself—Pasternak's *Doctor Zhivago* was not welcomed in any language—and just as quietly supplied the British and Americans with what they asked for. Ostentatiously they staged war games, imagining not a Soviet invasion but a NATO one. Just as ostentatiously they welcomed not Wilderness's over-seventies nude ballet, but things not much better or not much different: lecture tours by prominent English writers; the exquisite romantic, Dame Thora Ashby; the prince of the kitchen sink, Arnold Beeston; a tour by the Sheffield and Rotherham Sinfonia . . . and thousands of subtitled film shows devoted to the delights of the English stately home, life in the Shires, the British Commonwealth, Princess Margaret's wedding . . . endless endlessness.

The greatest propaganda coup, Wilderness thought, hadn't happened. The Beatles had played Sweden, they hadn't yet played Finland. Perhaps they never would. But he'd bet money someone at the British Council had asked our four cultural ambassadors in Cardin jackets to earn their MBEs.

Now—it was undeniably quiet now. As he had said to Burne-Jones, "What is there we don't already know?" It was quiet because Intelligence had reached saturation point. The latest file was not only thin, it was six months old. Burne-Jones might be right. Lapland was due for another look. Nothing undermined Intelligence like complacency.

Wilderness read everything back to 1962, then read pickily from each year until 1948.

By six o'clock he was feeling print-blind, when a blob appeared between him and the window.

An Eddie-shaped blob.

It was a curious phenomenon, a bit like baldness—once attained it never seemed to change much. Premature aging passed off as eternal youth. Eddie wasn't bald, but he'd been tubby since the day they met at the Cambridge spooks' language course in 1946. But he got no tubbier. He liked his grub, and his favourite word in the English language was probably *cake*. At the best of times food was never far from his thoughts, and six in the evening wasn't the best of times so much as the hungriest of times. He was Caesar's man—"fat, sleek-headed, such as sleep a-nights."

"I hear you're staying with me tonight?"

"Yes. Not a good night to be at home. Not a good night to answer the phone either."

"Then maybe we should eat out. There's a crackin' chippie on Borough High Street."

Chippie—perhaps Eddie's second-favourite word.

"It's Monday. Chippies don't open on Mondays."

"You've been abroad too long and too often. This is Swinging London. It never closes."

"Really?"

§17

The cod was Friday's cod. And the batter was soggy. However, Wilderness would not be the one to fault the mushy peas, and if this was to be his last taste of England for the indefinite future, he wasn't displeased with Eddie's choice. He'd have preferred claret to Tizer, but you can't have everything, even in the city that never closes.

A polite burp into a clenched fist indicated that Eddie was getting to the point of speech and might not be plying his right elbow for a minute or two.

"Boss reckons Reg Thwaite is trying to nail your balls to the floor."

"He's right. Hence the suddenness of this posting to Finland. This . . . fiction."

"And it's all about Bernard."

"Yep."

"Have they asked about me?"

"No. I don't think they will. I left you out of my report on the Glienicke Bridge. You were never there. You were back at the hotel. The last you saw of Bernard was when Frank and I left for the bridge. If asked that's all you need to say. But, hate to spell it out Ed, you are small fry. They're not after you."

"I love hearing it spelt out. There's safety in being small fry, always has been. I couldn't work for dodgy buggers like you and Troy if there weren't."

"How is Mr. Troy?"

"Bored. Trying to bury himself in growing leeks and raising pigs, but bored all the same. His brother's delighted to have him off the streets. Freddie's capacity to fuck up life for Rod quadrupled when Rod became Home Secretary."

A pause while Eddie ordered jam roly-poly with custard.

Then, "Berlin?"

"Loose ends, Ed. I'd rather see them tied up before Alec drops me down in nowhereland."

§18

Memory was a flood he could not fold. So he accepted it. Every time he went back to Grünetümmlerstraße he knew he would be drenched by wave after wave of memories, mostly of Nell Burkhardt. So he stood awhile on the landing outside Erno Schreiber's door and looked up the staircase to the one-room flat he had shared with Nell all those years ago. On one visit it had been empty, an unlikely gap between tenants in a city where every room could be let twice over. He had looked around. Furnished a stripped room with the bits and bobs that had littered his mind for years.

Temptation had him set one foot on the step up when the door to his old flat was yanked open and someone danced lightly down the stairs to the landing. A young woman. Much the age Nell had been when she left him—but nothing like her. Tall and blonde, a lightness to her smile that Nell would never manage. A child of the postwar era—history had not yet inscribed its frown.

He must have struck her as hesitant or lost.

"Guten Tag. Sie suchen Herrn Schreiber?"

(Good day. Are you looking for Herr Schreiber?)

Without waiting for an answer she banged on Erno's door.

"Erno, du hast Besuch!"

Then to Wilderness.

"Er wird ein bisschen taub, weißt du."

(He's getting a bit deaf, you know.)

She skipped lightly down the stairs and out into the street. Wilderness had not spoken a word, but it was as though she had seen the spell cast around him and had broken it simply by not being Nell.

Erno's door opened slowly.

He was stooping a little. He pulled off the eyeshade he wore for close work—in the middle of forging some document, no doubt—and peered out.

"Joe? My, my . . . *so eine Überraschung!*"

"Sorry, Erno. I didn't have time to warn you."

"No matter, no matter."

He ushered Wilderness in. Summer or winter, his rooms were always crepuscular—deep, dark corners and contrasting pools of bright light from the reading lamps he had dotted around. Wilderness had scarcely known him to open a window, even in June, and the fire was never permitted to go out.

"So, you met Trudie?"

"Yes. Quite a looker."

"At my age I wouldn't know or care—but she keeps an eye on me. At my age perhaps somebody should."

Wilderness had no idea how old Erno was, but he'd seemed old when they met almost twenty years ago.

"Let me put the kettle on, and over tea you can tell me what brings you back to Berlin so soon."

Wilderness told him.

Perhaps everyone needs someone from whom they have no secrets. A role no wife or husband can play.

"Hmm," Erno said at last. "Lapland? I don't even think I want to think about Lapland. The very word makes me shiver. How can I help? Some paperwork you need? I may be getting deaf, as Trudie said, all too loudly, but my eyes are still fine."

"No. No papers. I have a new identity. Or I will as soon as I can be bothered to open the envelope. I'm here for the loose ends. Westminster is out to get me, and I'd rather not give them the chance."

"What loose ends, Joe? The biggest has to be Frank. The last time we were all together in this room you knocked him to the floor."

That had been a decisive, perhaps fateful day. All of them in that room. The last supper of the *Schiebers*. Within a matter of hours he had turned Bernard Alleyn loose, decked Frank with a right hook, had Yuri die on him and seen Nell for the last time.

"No. Frank is backing me. The CIA is backing me. I don't know why but I conclude there is some advantage for Frank in not ratting me out. Frank has put it on record that Bernard crossed into the East. Perhaps his better nature has emerged."

"I doubt that, unless his better nature is coloured green and has a picture of a dead president on the front. So, what loose ends did you have in mind?"

"Do you hear from Bernard?"

"Surprisingly, yes. A card in the New Year. All the usual good wishes, and another about two weeks ago. He seems to have discovered the joys of cricket. Apparently they play a lot of cricket in—"

"Don't tell me. If I don't know, it's one less lie to tell."

"And . . . ?"

"And Nell. She was here that night. I met her at the street door. As she was leaving."

"I cannot hear your question, my boy."

"Did Nell and Bernard ever meet?"

"Yes."

"Did she know who he was?"

"Of course. Eddie was here that night. You think Eddie can keep a secret?"

No, in that respect Eddie was badly prepared to be any kind of spy.

"Your masters will not come looking for Nell, surely?"

"No, I don't think they will. But Nell has a fatal flaw. She's honest. If asked . . ."

Erno pooh-poohed this with a simple wave of the hand.

"They won't ask, you know that. She is . . . out of reach. And I don't just mean geography. She is . . . how to put it . . . risen."

"Not with you here, Erno."

"Brandt lost the election for chancellor of the Bundesrepublik last year. But this is Germany. We can change governments as rapidly as most men change their socks. Everyone knows Erhard won't last, and when he goes Brandt gets another chance. He is but a step away from the Chancellery. So, he has Nell shuffling back and forth between Berlin and Bonn as his . . . hmmm . . . representative on Earth, his apostle of the gospel of coexistence, his . . . Nell the Baptist. She's there right now, as it so happens."

Wilderness found this close to incredible. As long as he had known her, Nell had sung the song of Berlin. She was a Berliner. She'd lived nowhere else, been nowhere else since the day she rode her bike back into the ruins of the city in 1945. And Bonn . . . what was Bonn? It would be a one-horse town if somebody happened to ride in. The rest of the time it was a cultural desert. He'd never spent more than forty-eight hours in Bonn at any one time, and each time it had seemed forty-seven hours too long. It was just a small town in Germany. Nell would be bored silly—*keine Berliner Luft*.

§19

USSR Murmansk
Oblast Rayakoski or Thereabouts:
May 1966

When icicles hung by the wall, Marinin's arse was red and raw.

Child of a peasant family, he held the institution of an indoor lavatory to be a triumph of Soviet planning, to say nothing of Soviet plumbing. A man utterly loyal to the state, a Komsomol member since the age of fourteen, willing to suffer hardship for Marxism-Leninism, could grow decadent in a warm cubicle with a bolt on the door. It was a level of privacy previously unexperienced. With a hint of guilt nestling in a corner of his mind, he would slide the bolt back and forth, delighted at the sound it made and the idea it represented. Peace, privacy, the individualism of a good shit. But for one thing . . . the waxy, shiny Red Army–issue bog roll, every sheet stamped with a hammer and sickle, lacked absorbency and seemed to glide across Marinin's arse ineffectually. It came in boxes, one hundred forty-four rolls to a box, twelve boxes a month, delivered to this far-flung outpost of the Republics. Until the bright May day delivery stopped, and it came home to him that shiny bog roll was far better than no bog roll.

In his official capacity as Clerical Corporal in Charge of Stores, he put in a telephone call to Murmansk HQ.

"No bog roll? . . . Ha ha ha," said the bloke on the other end.

"If an army," Marinin replied, "marches on its stomach, it does so a lot better with a clean arse!"

"OK, OK. Keep your underpants on. I'll ask Moscow."

Three hours later a reply came through on the teleprinter.

```
              TOP SECRET
                 FYEO.
      National shortage of paper.
It is the duty of every Soviet Citizen to
               improvise.
      Waste will not be tolerated.
```

Followed by a name of which he'd never heard, bearing the rank of lieutenant colonel.

Later the same day Marinin posted a notice in every room in the camp instructing clerical staff to save all printed paper, including tele-printer printouts and envelopes, regardless of classification.

He thought he'd get an argument from the resident KGB-nik, Konstantin Ilyich Zolotukhin, but Zolotukhin merely said, "So now we shove our secrets up our backsides? Where could be safer?"

By the end of the day Marinin had two eighteen-year-old privates quartering classified documents and nailing them in sheaves of fifty to the back of lavatory doors.

It was close to a return to reality, but not quite. The pleasure of privacy, the audible reassurance of a sliding bolt was somehow diminished as the harshness of the new paper registered with his arse. It wasn't shiny, it was in all probability marginally more absorbent, but the damn stuff just wouldn't flush. It was at least three times the thickness of bog roll. It would never flush.

Marinin issued a chit for twelve galvanised buckets, one for each lavatory, and in the morning instructed a hapless private that he was to empty them each evening onto rough ground behind Hut 3, and when he had enough for a bonfire he was to burn the contents.

After breakfast Marinin sat on the loo, slid the bolt a few times to enhance his defecatory pleasure, and gazed at the quarter-sheet of paper in his hand.

```
          Troop Movem—
          Armored Cav—
          Fourteenth D—
          Commencing Sept—
```

Fragmentary.

Less than interesting.

He crouched and wiped and tossed the details of a 150,000-man Red Army exercise on the Finnish border into the bucket—a pot for some other greasy bastard to keel.

IV

Fig Biscuits

§20

Wilderness was on the plane, ten minutes out of Tempelhof, before he thought to open the envelope Alice had thrust at him on Monday evening.

Her notes began, "Joe, all you need to know," ran for six pages . . . and ended, "Please remember to burn after reading or at the very least don't leave it lying around."

In between he had been assigned a new identity, an embassy pass and a new passport in the name of Michael Young. Mr. Young was to be a Second Secretary/cultural attaché (that old lie) at the British Embassy in Helsinki.

He flipped through the passport. Diplomatic status. A fake history in the inky triangles and ovoids made by the rubber stamps of half a dozen countries Mr. Young had visited in the last three years . . . Belgium, Luxembourg, Holland . . . my, but this man was a real adventurer, always kicking the dust off his shoes . . . all the world's trouble spots . . . television's Danger Man in the flesh . . . and Wilderness began to worry that he might not be able to make his version of Michael Young sufficiently boring. He had the rank of Second Secretary—not a bad place to begin if boredom and anonymity were your goals.

"You report to Head of Station: Burton, J."

Burton? Which Burton. He'd known a few Burtons in the service. There'd been Jimmy Burton back in Vienna . . . but Wilderness was pretty sure he still was in Vienna—and there'd been Jerry Burton in Beirut, but Jerry had gone into Kurdistan or perhaps it had been Kazakhstan . . . one of the Stans . . . and never come back. He wasn't nicknamed Reckless Sir Richard for nothing.

No . . . he hadn't a clue which Burton, J this was.

A plain postcard was paper-clipped to the last page of Alice's instructions. Handwritten and unsigned was ". . . and leave the fucking gun behind!"

Even if he'd read that before leaving London he would not have done it. He could hear Alice's argument in the mind's ear: "A cultural attaché doesn't need a gun, Joe. Ballet dancers don't shoot back!" He'd got his Smith & Wesson .44 in his briefcase, and everything he carried bore the status of "diplomatic bag." No one would search it.

§21

The British Embassy in Helsinki was beautiful. A rose-pink house, the "Villa Damsen," on the Baltic seashore at Kaivopuisto. The British had owned it almost since the Grand Duchy of Finland had been formally recognised as an independent state at the end of the Great War. Wilderness had never seen it. He wondered if he'd ever get to see it. All the mundane stuff of "chancery"—communications, archiving, missing passports, stranded tourists . . . spying—was conducted out of more mundane offices at 34 Korkeavuorenkatu in the centre of the city. Receptions were held at the Villa Damsen—those sorts of evenings when women wore long frocks and men wore medals, if they had them, or sashes, if they came from the sort of country that thought men in sashes didn't look like buffoons.

Wilderness probably never would get to see the Villa Damsen. He had no medals—he'd never understood the logic of medals . . . did you get them for getting shot at or merely for surviving, whether shot at or not? His dad had medals, but then his dad had been a homicidal maniac. And Wilderness certainly didn't own a buffoon sash. The poshest garment in his wardrobe was his dinner jacket, one of Alec's cast-offs. What Ambassador would invite a Second Secretary in a secondhand dinner jacket to socialise? What ambassador would invite an MI6 officer to socialise? What ambassador in his right mind would invite an MI6 officer under a cloud of suspicion to socialise, with or without his own dinner jacket, sash or medals?

It was a short walk in summer sunshine from Helsinki central station to Korkeavuorenkatu. He sat a while in a park he'd never learned the name of, looked around, pondered, remembered his previous visits to Finland.

Helsinki probably wasn't the most boring city in the world, but it might be a contender. He'd never found much to like or dislike about the place. Hardly a recommendation. The newer bits were on a grid system. Hardly a recommendation—yet, as a tram whizzed by on the Esplanade (a word more readily associated with a rare childhood trip to the seaside at Southend) he thought of trams . . . and cobblestones . . . and trams *and* cobblestones and realised any city that still had both would never feel wholly alien. London had no trams now and only a handful of cobblestones, but the sight of a rattling iron galleon gliding on rails set in cobblestones was another glimpse of a vanished childhood. Perhaps he'd get to like Helsinki. If this was a punishment posting, there were surely worse places he could have been sent?

Burne-Jones had sent him here in '59. The last of a series of visits, which had mostly consisted of waiting, of cooling his heels in any number of the city's plethora of bars, watching Frank Spoleto get drunk. Waiting for some kind of border incident to manifest itself or utterly fail to manifest itself.

In '59 Wilderness and Frank had been the reception for a Soviet defector . . . or was it '58? No matter. It was . . . what? Ancient history. He hadn't seen Frank for at least six months and with any luck he'd never see him again.

He looked at the Finns, silent on park benches, heads tilted to the sun, eyes closed, oblivious to the screeching trams. Doing nothing, saying nothing. Simply happy to be in summer sunshine. Happy as pigs in shit. They did that a lot, he recalled. And in autumn a sea mist could wrap itself around the city, and that too reminded him of London, of the "yellow fog that rubbed its back upon the windowpanes." Sea mist smelled a lot better and didn't stick to the back of your throat like chewing gum.

So far, so good.

§22

The chancery was about as unprepossessing as architecture can get. A gigantic, filthy slab of a building, six or seven storeys high, occupying half a block.

He dropped his bags in Burton's outer office. A girl—that is, a woman in her late forties—was standing behind the desk flicking quickly through papers and muttering to herself.

Wilderness said, "I'm here to see Mr. Burton."

The secretary looked up, a pale, heart-shaped face, framed by a mop of greying curls.

"Mr. Burton?"

"Yes. You know . . . the boss?"

A face already grumpy turned sour on him. A look that mixed impatience with disdain.

"And you are . . . ?"

"Young. Michael Young. I'm the new Second Secretary."

She let the sheaf of papers fall back into the in-tray.

"One moment. I'll see if Mr. Burton is free."

As close to "bugger off" as one could get without uttering the actual words. She disappeared into the inner office, closing the door behind her.

Wilderness waited. Several minutes passed.

Then the door opened, and she said, "Mr. Burton will see you now."

She held the door as Wilderness passed, and, still inside, shut it quietly behind him. The room was empty. Just a big desk with three phones and the usual in- and out-trays and a couple of hard-on-the-arse chairs facing it for visitors. There was no one else there but Wilderness and the secretary.

She looked through Wilderness as if he were invisible, walked straight past him and sat behind the desk.

"Do sit down, Flight Sergeant Holderness. You're only Michael Young when I'm through with you."

Burton . . . Burton . . . Burton, J. Oh fuck. Jenny Burton from the Bonn Station a couple of years back. The one they called the Brocken Witch.

"I'm surprised we haven't met before, but Bonn was never your stamping ground, was it?"

Wilderness sat.

"Berlin," he said simply.

"And your reputation in Berlin precedes you. In fact, I'm amazed the things you got up to in Berlin last year didn't sink you. But . . . that's why you're here, isn't it? Alec wants you out of the way."

Wilderness said nothing. If she was going to prattle on about his reputation, he'd neither defend nor agree.

"Let's get one thing straight from the start, shall we? You won't be playing Cowboys and Indians on my turf. You won't be pulling any stunts like the one you staged at Invalidenstraße. You're a cultural attaché."

She held up a hand, palm facing him, before he could interrupt.

"Now I know you'll say that's only a cover but to be an effective cover it has to be real. Whatever Burne-Jones has set you by way of a mission, you will operate as a cultural attaché. You will do the job. I gather you've a brief to look at Lapland. That's fine. There's plenty of culture you can spread around in Lapland."

Wilderness felt his heart sink. The over-seventies nude ballet was rapidly evolving from joke to reality. She made culture sound like a brand of margarine.

"My instructions from London," she went on, "are that you observe, that you gather information and you report your findings, if any, to London . . . through me. You are not an agent, you are an observer. There'll be no shoot-outs. Do you understand me, Holderness?"

"Of course."

He put on his best fake smile. He doubted Alec had asked for any findings to be routed through her. As Station Head, she'd every right to expect it, but he'd be the one to judge.

"When my secretary, Janis, returns from lunch, she'll assign you a car and a flat. You're free to find your own flat if you wish, but you'll have to pay for it yourself out of your salary. The car will have diplomatic plates. Do not tamper with them, do not remove them . . . everything you do here is as a diplomat. But don't let that delude you into think-ing you're immune from tickets for parking or speeding. You're not. We play by the rules. Any questions? If so . . . save them till Janis gets back. You can go now."

An American quasi-obscenity occurred to Wilderness—wham, bam, thank you, ma'am.

§23

The outer office was still empty.

He found a coffee bar two streets away and sat nursing his wounds and counting his blessings.

Wounds = too numerous to mention.

Blessings = zero.

He counted again. Nope . . . still zero.

§24

He gave it half an hour. Drank a second cup. Hoped that by the time Janis got back the Brocken Witch would have gone out.

She had. Her office door was wide open, and a woman about half the Witch's age was bashing away at an electric typewriter—one of those newfangled IBM golf balls that tinged technology with magic.

"Hello," she said, sweeping a lock of thick, black hair out of her eyes. A northern accent, Yorkshire or Derbyshire, a far cry from the arch Roedean or Cheltenham tones of Jenny Burton.

"You must be Mr. Young. Been expecting you. In fact, I was expecting you yesterday. Ne'er mind, you're here now."

Mannishly, she stood up, not much shorter than Wilderness himself, a good five feet ten inches of her, and stuck out a hand for him to shake. Just when he thought the whole world was agin him.

"Janis Bell. 'Ave you met the boss? Sorry. Mustn't call her that. Mrs. Burton. You've met Mrs. Burton?"

"Yes. I was called into the headmaster's study about an hour ago."

Janis laughed.

"Don't. You'll get us both shot. Mrs. B's a stickler for most things. Starting with respect."

"Then I won't tell you what they call her in Bonn."

"Please don't. What I don't know I can't blab, now, can I?"

She sat down and riffled through the papers on her desk till she came up with a brown envelope identical to the one Alice had given him.

"Flat address and car keys in here. Take a look at the flat and let me know if you can stick it. It's just up the hill, on the left. A sort of jaundice-yellow building."

"Stick it?"

"They're all a bit, y'know, crummy. If I were on a bigger salary, I'd move meself, but . . . anyway, best not complain, eh, Mr. Young?"

"Actually my real name's Holderness."

"I'm expected to observe your cover. You're either Mr. Young or Michael."

"Let's give him a nickname. Call me Joe."

She tapped her front teeth with the rubber end of her pencil.

"The thing is . . . the thing about Mrs. Burton is she likes order . . . everything in its place . . . a bit like that motto my gran used to have over the cupboard under the stairs . . . 'A place for everything and everything in its place.' That hangs over Mrs. Burton's desk, it's just that it's invisible. She'll expect you to be Michael Young."

"Pigeonholed?"

"Yep. Loves her taxonomy. I'm pigeonholed as her 'Chirpy Yorkshire Terrier.' Judging by your file you'll be her 'Man with the Six-Shooter.' You don't have a six-shooter, do you?"

"No," he lied.

"Cos if you did . . . and if you got caught with it . . ."

"I understand."

"Doesn't pay to shatter her expectations . . . you don't have a gun . . . and I don't use words like taxonomy."

§25

The exterior of the block of flats was promising. Art deco, a yellow he knew must have a specific name, but he could not recall it. Patent-yellow? Or was patent a shade of green?

The interior broke the promise. Crummy was precise. Any hint of Art Deco had vanished long ago in a postwar refit. The official embassy flat was a classic example of the East German style of design and décor. Not designed to make you feel at home, but to make you feel there was no such place as home. Trendy Scandinavia—all that Swedish component shelving and chairs like dog baskets—hadn't got a look in. Every chair sat you bolt upright as though to slouch were a sin. In contrast, the mattress was soft enough to give you lumbar agony. And every possible surface was finished in a deckled-cream, wipe-down plastic. The dining table looked less likely to be the scene of a convivial meal than an autopsy.

The block of flats bore the inept name of Paradise Apartments—insult added to injury. He'd keep it. What did it matter? He'd be long gone before winter.

All his life he'd resisted sentimentality. He'd had no love for either parent—a drunken mum and a psychopathic dad—and the only reason his dad had got as far as committing suicide was that Wilderness had not got around to killing him. All his affection as a teenager had centred on his maternal grandfather, Abner, and the old man's mistress, Merle. With them gone there'd been no discernible affection in him until Nell, and with Nell gone—walked out never to return—there'd been none till Judy. But Judy had wooed him. Never one to be passive, Judy had taken all the initiative and unleashed the flattery of a slow seduction on him. She'd taken a couple of years to do this . . . Wilderness resisting only inwardly, wondering what her father would think . . . until the day he'd gone round to the house in Holland Park and asked for her hand in marriage.

Now, alone in this sterile outpost of Stalinallee, he found he missed Judy and the girls more than ever before. The switch that so readily changed him from husband and father to field agent didn't seem to be clicking in. Sitting for a few minutes on the rock-hard couch, looking out across the street, through a dirty, blackened window, at a towering, redbrick, faux-gothic monstrosity—something that had failed the audition to be St. Pancras Station in London and been plonked down here instead—he felt a seeping sentimentality . . . and what good is a sentimental agent? All the same, he counted his blessings once more and came up with a total of three.

He shook himself. The dog who came in from the rain. Muttered a quick "fukkit" and went in search of his car.

§26

The car was not a car. It was a beast. A Mercedes Benz Unimog 404. He'd driven one during his time in Lebanon. It looked like a cross between a Land Rover and a tank and was about the size of an English dustbin lorry. This one had been set up for Finnish winters—a hard top, and a set of snow chains in a box bolted to the chassis. For some reason there was a metal tube about twelve feet long welded to the roof. The Mog looked great—a child's toy writ large—but it would not have been his first choice—accelerated like a dopy tortoise, and struggled to reach even sixty miles per hour.

That was probably why they'd chosen it.

§27

In the morning Janis Bell introduced him to more embassy staff. To the cypher clerk, to the other second secretaries, among whom was one Eric Farr: Requisitions and Materiel. Not all second secretaries were spies, except in Soviet embassies.

"Does Farr know who I am?" Wilderness asked as she led him down the corridor.

"Oh yes. Not your real name of course—but he knows why you're here. He's used to it. Used to people like you, I mean. He'll brief you on the culture thing, and he'll do it with a straight face. Does everything with a straight face. Do try and take him seriously."

"Why do you say that?"

"In our very brief acquaintance, Mr. Young, I might just have leapt to the conclusion that you don't take things particularly seriously. Well, things that take place in offices, anyway."

"Leap away," Wilderness said.

"We also serve who only type and wait."

She tapped on the door they had come to and as a voice said "Enter," she shushed Wilderness with a finger to her lips and whispered, "Now, best po-face!"

A small man, a round, pleasing face, about the same age as Wilderness, running prematurely to fat—well-dressed, a better suit than Wilderness owned, although he would not have been caught dead in a waistcoat, matching or not.

After handshakes, ritual enquiries about life back home—Surrey, Virginia Water and Waterloo station all cropped up in the first few sentences—and platitudes about England, Australia and the ashes, Farr said, "I bet you're wondering about the Mog?"

"I was rather."

"It serves its purpose very well."

"What purpose?"

"British Council Travelling Cinema."

Wilderness reached for his best po-face.

"Very few small towns in Finland have a cinema, but as long as they have something like a village hall, we can show them an English-language film. We've a marvellous selection. I've done the run-up as far as Puolanka myself a couple of times. Always a good reception. But the screen is almost twelve feet across, so the Mog is really the only vehicle big enough. Plus, it will get you there in anything short of a blizzard, and I gather from Mrs. Burton that your brief is to get up into Lapland and . . . er . . . do whatever it is you chaps do. And if you can do it whilst spreading the gospel of English culture then everyone's happy. Perfect cover, I'd say. Not that I know anything about . . . er . . . whatever it is you chaps do."

Such innocence. Such a mockery of innocence.

"It's OK, Mr. Farr. I'll try not to shoot anyone between reels."

§28

In the afternoon Wilderness turned out the contents of the Mog. It wasn't hard to figure out what went where with a 16mm projector and mono sound system, which was just as well since no one was offering to tell him.

But the film library . . . Farr's marvellous selection.

Ye gods, he thought, what are they thinking of?

He doubted there was a film less than ten years old. Some of them were twenty years old. He'd seen at least a dozen of them with Eddie when they were training in Cambridge and as many more in the days of courtship before he and Judy married.

The Titfield Thunderbolt—made in 1953. Rustics fight to stop closure of their railway branch line.

The Battle of the River Platte—made in 1956. The Royal Navy blockades Montevideo and the Graf Spee scuttles itself.

Passport to Pimlico—made in 1949. A London borough declares its independence and puts an end to rationing.

Kind Hearts and Coronets—also 1949. Alec Guinness plays umpteen members of an aristocratic family while an utter cad murders his way to a dukedom.

All marvellous . . . in their way . . . in their time . . . but this wasn't their time . . . this was 1966. London was swinging. Eddie had assured him it was. Monday was no longer just washing day, chippies open and all. What possible impression of England was the FO trying to convey? Would Finland resist the temptations of communism on an ideological diet of unchanging rural life and wartime British pluck?

He moved to the shorts, the fillers put on between what were commonly known as the big and little pictures, in between the tubs of ice cream (vanilla only) and fruit lollipops—fifty episodes of *Look at Life* . . . "The Coffee Bars of Soho" . . . "Driving a Tube Train" . . . "A Day in the Life of a London Cabbie" . . . somewhat more up to date . . . but a yard and a half wide of the mark. Cultural cliché if not cultural white-wash . . . a world in which the British could still point to all "the red bits on the map."

The Americans and the Russians put men into space—the British looked after their branch lines and looked back nostalgically to the days when they sank Nazi warships. It was all so . . . resistible.

He mentioned this to Janis Bell over coffee the next morning.

"Draw up a list and give it to Eric. He'll get you anything you want. I know what you mean. It looks like an outdated vision of England, but the truth is, it isn't anyone's vision. It's a lack of vision. Eric's realm is paper clips and mimeograph machines. If you ever have need of a 'Top Secret' stamp and red ink pad, he probably has a cupboard full. And the last time he went to an English cinema it was probably showing *The Titfield soddin' Thunderbolt*. If he's driven the Mog up north it's only because there was no one else to do it."

Wilderness drew up his list:

This Sporting Life
The Entertainer
Live Now, Pay Later
A Hard Day's Night
Darling
The Ipcress File

A different cinema, a different England. A harder, more cynical England. Self-reflecting, not self-regarding.

He thought about *The Spy Who Came in from the Cold*, which had been released just the year before. He and Judy had seen it in Leicester Square. Richard Burton, for once not overacting, for once not seeming too big for the screen he was in—but then he had pause to think . . . what impression of England did *that* create?

He wrote it down. Then he crossed it out. Then he wrote it down again. Then he asked himself, *Is this too close to home? . . . Isn't anyone who does what I do potentially an Alec Leamas? . . . Is that how I'll end up? Caught between East and West Berlin with a bullet in me?*

So he crossed it out again.

§29

It took Farr four days to get the films Wilderness had asked for. Less than anticipated. Wilderness had hoped it might take him a fortnight. No such luck. Farr, if he had an opinion on Wilderness's restatement of the Foreign Office's vision of England in 1966, refrained from expressing it beyond "All good stuff . . . I suppose."

In the interim he memorised Alice's notes, drank a thousand cups of coffee with Janis Bell and avoided the Brocken Witch—not that he needed to. Once the chain of command had been established, she seemed to have no further interest in him. On the one occasion they passed each other in Janis's office she spoke not a word while her eyes said, "Still here, are you?"

In the evenings, he coordinated Alice's notes with road maps of Finland. He was to fit in two or three "shows" on the journey north ("Flying the flag, Joe") in one-horse, one-reindeer towns . . . Yksikoirankaupunki . . . Kolme-kuolleen rotan kylää . . . Napatakiinni . . . wonder at Finnish's preponderance of double consonants, double vowels and umlauts . . . and arrive in Persereiikkä, Lapland, a convincing representative of the British Council, "spreading" (that bloody word again) Anglo-Saxon culture and somehow managing not to think of it as flogging glass beads to the natives.

And as evening fell to night, he'd open a bottle of Estonian "Burgundy," stare at the faux-gothic eyesore on the opposite side of the street and count his blessings.

Nada . . . niente . . . they'd gone again.

§30

Finland being, as he thought of it, unchanging, likeable, yet somehow avoiding invoking the word "dull," nothing in the journey north surprised him. He'd seen the endless rows of silver birch before and the spindly plantations of pine, so regular as to make one think that everything in Finland strived for a near-perfect verticality. But—he'd never relaxed *into* Finland; every other visit had been *the job*, every aspect of it wrapped in the fabrications of urgency. This wasn't even half a job. This was the slain shadow of a job. So he took time off. Each morning, and each afternoon ahead of his cinema shows, he'd pull the Mog over to the side of a lake—there always was a lake, and he had concluded that nowhere in Finland was more than half a mile from a lake—and watch the water ripple.

Just before he pulled into Napatakiinni, he sat on a rock by a lake unknown and watched an old geezer fishing.

The fisherman seemed to sense his presence and turned to see who compromised his idyll.

"*Englannista?*"

"*Mistä tiesit?*" (How can you tell?)

"*Näytät englantilaiselta.*" (You look English.)

"*Todellako?*" (Really?)

"*Vihaan saksalaisia.*" (I hate Germans.)

Hardly surprising.

"*Vihaan venäläisiä.*" (I hate Russians.)

That too.

"I . . . I . . . I lika English."

"*Hauska kuulla.*" (Glad to hear it.)

"Winstoon Churrrchill."

Wilderness wondered where this might be leading.

"Duke off Edinburger."

None the wiser.

"Mick Jagger."

OK, so it was leading nowhere.

Just like his job.

§31

Persereiikkä was five or six times the size of the villages he stopped off in. Perhaps three thousand people. Big enough to have its own cinema, and big enough to have its own office of tourism—*Matkailutoimisto Suomesta*—run by one Niilo Pastorius, a man charged with enticing hopeless romantics to visit Lapland and watch the northern lights dance in the winter sky—and also charged by the *Suojelupoliisi*, the Finnish Secret Service, usually simply the *Supo*, with the watch on the border. Wilderness had been to Persereiikkä once some six or seven years before on nothing more than a "familiarising" mission. He'd never met Pastorius—couldn't even remember the name of the bloke who'd enacted the fiction of tourism officer at that time.

The Office of Tourism was on the far side of Persereiikkä, next to the river. He drove the Mog across town—it was just about familiar, entirely made of wood, like some frontier town in Wyoming or Nevada. And it was deathly quiet, spreading itself in pristine silence, mostly just a single storey high, under the clearest blue sky he'd ever seen—not a single plume of smoke, not a whiff of pollution. A hint of something, something old, something half-remembered, something burnt.

The exception to wooden buildings was the Office of Tourism. It looked like a prefab off a London council estate. It might have been plonked down off the back of a lorry only hours ago. It differed only in the makeshift addition of a pitched steel roof and a front wall of triple-thickness plate glass, plastered with posters presenting the joys of life in Lapland.

A man about his own age stood in the doorway—about five foot nine, blond, with watery blue eyes and, when he spoke, the hint of a lisp.

"Pastorius. Call me Niilo."

"Fine. You can call me Joe. It'll keep things simple."

"I thought I had to call you Michael?"

"Joe will do fine."

"I can lock up now you're here. I've booked you into the White Nights Hotel. Check in and we'll have drink. And I can . . . brief you. If that really is the word?"

"You're not sure?"

"Oh I'm sure. It's just that brief might be almost too literal. You've just landed in the town where nothing ever happens."

§32

Wilderness wasn't sure what the tourist season was in Lapland. It seemed to him that it marketed itself as a winter wonderland, and made as much as it could of the constant crepuscular winters when most daylight was reflected light. The White Nights seemed neither full nor empty. People drifting in and out. They were only a couple of weeks away from the longest day—the phenomenon of days to come with no sunrise or sunset—and a midnight sun. He had no idea which was the more attractive to the visitor, as, much to his wife's annoyance, he had hardly ever been anywhere as a mere visitor and found it hard to think like one. There'd always been *the job*—a job that smothered a multitude of marital evasions. More than ten years on Judy would drop hints that she was still waiting for a honeymoon. He was sure she'd like the midnight sun, she just wasn't going to get to see this midnight sun. There was a song. He was sure there was a song. Hampton? Ellington? Ella? He couldn't remember.

The bar at the White Nights was too full to talk.

"It's not even half full, Joe. Wait two weeks, then you'll have to fight your way to the bar," Pastorius said.

"I'd be happier outside."

"It's not as if anyone would be listening."

"Let's not take that risk."

They walked along the river, westward—into what in another latitude might have been a sunset.

"'The town where nothing ever happens' can't be wholly true," Wilderness said.

"Why's that?"

"If it were true you wouldn't be here. So backtrack a little, tell me what happened to bring you here . . . better still, to keep you here."

Pastorius breathed deeply.

"Do stop me if you've heard all this before. I'll go back just a few years—we don't need 1917 or World War II. Khrushchev."

"Abracadabra."

"I'm sorry?"

"You just said the magic word."

Pastorius smiled.

"Point taken. Two years after his downfall and he's still the most evocative name in whatever game we're playing. The ghost in the machine. Khrushchev . . . Khrushchev hit all our panic buttons when he invoked the treaty my parents' generation signed in 1948 and demanded joint military exercises back in '61. You can blame Eisenhower for that. U2, Gary Powers, a general increase in the level of Soviet paranoia. I'd have difficulty telling you which is cart and which is horse, but around the same time it became obvious that Russia was upgrading the surveillance system on the border. I got here only a year ago, and we were still uncertain as to what they were up to. How good was their radar, how many more troops were just out of sight? The Americans have their satellites, the Emperor Ming has his death rays . . . all of it a bit impractical, not close enough to the ground.

"So, I tried an old-fashioned approach. There are a lot of charter pilots here . . . I say a lot . . . a dozen perhaps . . . mostly foreigners, Canadians and Australians, stragglers from the last war . . . who make a passable living simply because our railways are nonexistent and our roads bloody awful. They pick up a lot of cargo work. But if you've flown a Spitfire . . . well, I imagine it's dull work . . . and when I offered them double the money to skim the border and test out the Russian radar, they jumped at it. A piece of the action. It's known as 'ferreting.' It went well until about three months ago . . . three went out . . . two came back. Since then the survivors won't make any more runs across the border. They have . . . how would you say? . . . other fish to roast."

"Fry," said Wilderness, somewhat awed by Niilo's command of English. "Could I meet them anyway?"

"The pilots? Sure. They work out of Joeerämaa. It's about an hour and a half north of here. It's tiny. We can go up together in the morning and show another film tomorrow night. Perfect cover."

"Is it? I feel as though I have 'spy' stamped on my forehead."

"The diplomatic plates?"

"They scream 'spy.'"

"No, no I don't think so. It's too obvious. And as such it's good cover. Hiding in plain sight. Everyone knows the British are trying to nurture cultural resistance to communism, so your presence here is completely expected . . . you'd be much more suspicious here as an Englishman without a purpose."

"But I'm sitting here talking to the chief of the tourist bureau. Michael Young might be a tourist. Why couldn't I be a tourist? Why couldn't that be my purpose?"

"Curiosity born of innocence shows. Yours is born of knowledge. That shows too."

§33

They drove up together in the Mog. Pastorius shut up shop and casually hung a sign on the door. Wilderness's Finnish didn't extend quite as far as "Mennyt Kalaan," but the squiggly drawing above it left no room to misunderstand: "Gone Fishin'."

He let Pastorius drive.

§34

Joeerämaa was as small as any of the villages Wilderness had set up cinema in. It stood on the shores of a large lake, on the very edge of the Finnish Border Zone—a forty-five-kilometre strip, forbidden to visitors without a permit and to overflying by aircraft.

So, the flyers had set up right next the lake. They'd carved out a landing strip for their wheeled planes—two of which sat at the water's edge. For all that he had served twenty years, nominally, in the RAF, Wilderness knew next to nothing about planes. The bigger one was a Cessna Bobcat . . . a light freighter with a sizable capacity—he didn't think they'd made them after the war, so it had to be at least twenty years old. The other was much smaller. A two-seater. He'd no idea what model. And out on the lake, a floater, an amphibious de Havilland Beaver, painted blue below and a mottled greeny-brown above. Basic camouflage. A few years ago it had been a regular on TV and cinema newsreels, as the supply plane for the Commonwealth Trans-Antarctic Expedition. British pluck's last fling. Every English schoolboy could recognise a Beaver. It was a workhorse of a plane. It was said you just roll a barrel of beer straight off the quay into the belly of the aircraft.

Wilderness and Pastorius arrived just after noon. The Aussies lounged in deck chairs at the lakeside. Each with a bottle of beer. Each in grubby vests and Y-fronts. One of them smoked, the other lobbed alluvial stones into the water—to skim would have meant standing up and, clearly, that was too much effort.

They'd pitched tents, literally. Like a couple of infantry soldiers told the advance had stopped for a while. It looked more like the Desert Campaign than Lapland. Striped awnings on birch poles, an oil drum barbecue, a washing line of boiler suits and check shirts strung between the trees, a windup gramophone and a pile of 78s—an even bigger pile of empty beer bottles. A rusting mountain of engine parts. And a capacity for relaxation that Wilderness thought very Australian and very un-English.

A record spun down to nothing, the last refrain:

> *And every one was an 'Enery*
> *She wouldn't have a Willie nor a Sam*
> *I'm her eighth old man named 'Enery*
> *'Enery the Eighth, I am!*

And then nothing but the splash of stones in water and the gentle rustling of birch leaves in the breeze.

Pastorius broke into this slackers' paradise.

"Momo Brubeck, Bruce Kennedy," he said. "This is Michael Young, from London."

Wilderness had come almost instantly to hate this part of the fiction.

"Call me Joe," he said.

"Just as well," said Bruce. "Momo's really a Mick and two Micks is two too many, eh Momo?"

"Fuck you, you old dag," Momo replied.

They hauled themselves to their feet. Big men, running rapidly to seed—beer bellies hanging over the wide elastic of their underpants—hair bleached perpetually blond. Wilderness had heard Aussies washed it in lemon juice to keep it that way.

"Who's for a beer?"

Alcohol was prohibited in most of Lapland. Pastorius had explained this to Wilderness on the way north.

"You might buy a beer or a glass of wine in a tourist hotel, but there's no such thing as an off-licence—no shelves in the village grocer's stacked with cans and bottles. Doesn't stop anyone, of course."

It didn't stop these two for a moment. Before Wilderness could even answer, Bruce had stuck a bottle in his hand.

"What brings a young Pom like you to the land of the midnight sun? As if I couldn't guess."

"By all means, guess."

"You're one of Niilo's spook pals. Got to be."

Wilderness turned to Pastorius.

"Is there anyone who doesn't know? Has it been on the national news?"

"Relax, Joe. These two are forever playing the joker. But they're the men who'll tell you what you need to know now. They work for us."

"And what is it you need to know?"

"The last few flights?" Pastorius said. "Gavin?"

"Gavin?" Wilderness echoed.

"Our partner. The Canadian. We lost him in March. Sit yourself down. It'll all make more sense with a map in front of us."

Bruce spread out a map. It covered about one hundred kilometres of the Finnish border with the Murmansk Oblast, past Rayakoski, without reaching Murmansk itself.

"We made a couple of dozen runs. Low over the Finnish side. It's illegal, but Niilo here tells his pals at the radar stations to ignore us. Mind . . . if the Russians had nabbed us, you'd have denied us in a flash, wouldn't you?"

"Of course," Pastorius replied.

"Keep low over the border, gain height over Russia, see what we can see, see how long it takes them to spot us."

"You mean how long it takes them to launch a fighter?"

"Nah. They get to launch a fighter, we're fucked. Can't outrun it and nothing to shoot back with unless you point a shotgun out the fuckin' window. Nah. A simple pulse detector. I made my own. Dead simple. Like Meccano. Not always reliable, but simple. If I weren't such a lazy bastard, and if the valves in it weren't Russian-made, I'd patent it. But . . . what it tells us is how low the Russkis can sweep, and where they have no cover. They've extended their border zone to a hundred K, and while they've been building their radar network for several years now, it's patchy. I reckon they're still building it. It'll take them a couple more years. But they're getting better. Last time, I reckon, we underestimated them. Went in too high. Went in here, as matter o' fact."

Bruce stabbed at the map with a nicotined forefinger.

"They've set their radar steadily lower as they put in more masts. We've got a good picture of everything between here and here . . ."

His hands framed a good sixty kilometres of the border.

"Since last winter their coverage has pretty much doubled. Still not complete, though. Meanwhile, you can still fly in and out if you're careful—but I can't think of a reason why anyone would ever want to do that. There's bugger all happening down there after all."

"Smuggling?" Wilderness said.

"Easier overland . . . the ground patrols are scant . . . the border leaks . . . it's porous."

"So a man could get through one of these leaks?"

"You're not thinking of paying them a visit, are you?"

"No . . . I was thinking more, do they pay us visits?"

"Possible," Bruce said. "But I doubt it. They'd stick out like a sore thumb. I reckon Finns can smell a Russian. What do you reckon, Niilo?"

"There are no Russian agents that I know of."

This struck Wilderness as complacent, but he made no comment.

"Most of what leaks," Bruce continued, "are refugees, and these buggers just send 'em straight back."

"We have no choice." Pastorius said. "We sup with the devil."

"Yeah? Well you need a longer spoon."

Wilderness tacked them away from the subject.

"How did you lose Gavin?"

"Pranged his crate," said Momo.

"No he fuckin' didn't. Gavin was the best pilot of all of us. He was a bit older than us. He flew Spits in the Battle of Britain. Momo and I backed up D-Day. Not exactly a cushy number but nothing like it was in 1940. Gavin was a bloody good pilot. He didn't prang his plane. They shot him down. They got a MiG up. Bang."

"You're romanticizing it, mate. He went up pissed, flew into a tree and came down dead. It's as simple as that."

"All the same," said Wilderness, "they do have antiaircraft guns."

"MiGs are ten times more dangerous. Antiaircraft . . . odds favour the plane. A MiG? They're like my uncle Monty's dog. Once they get their teeth into you . . ."

"And Niilo tells me you won't be making any more border runs."

The two Aussies exchanged glances. For once in agreement.

"Yeah . . . well . . ."

He'd learnt next to nothing. It had been a pleasant day out. Nothing more than that.

"We're still making a living," said Bruce. "There's enough freight business to keep us going. And while Niilo's extra cash was pretty handy . . . well . . . no offence mate, but we none of us really liked spook stuff . . ."

"That's OK. I understand," Pastorius said.

"The border's quiet as a grave. It doesn't need us."

"Yeah, quiet as Gavin's grave," said Momo.

"We're happy as just a couple of dodgy bastards."

"Amen to that."

And Wilderness was happy to let Momo have the last word.

§35

They set up the mobile cinema in a prefabricated hut that seated about a hundred people.

Wilderness chose *Darling*, an Oscar winner written by Frederick Raphael, directed by John Schlesinger, starring the rapidly rising Julie Christie.

The two Aussies came, all but welded to their bottles of beer, but so was everyone else. The film went down like a lead balloon. When it was over, Wilderness swept up a couple of hundred metal bottle caps and listened to Momo put in his requests for future screenings, uncertain whether to file or ignore.

"Ya know what I like. A good, smutty comedy. Women with big tits. The odd knob joke. How about a *Carry On*? Saw a cracker the last time I was in London. *Carry on Cabby*. Sid James. Do they come any better than Sid James? Bring us that one next time, mate. Forget the arty farty stuff."

Perhaps Farr was right. Perhaps the Foreign Office was right. Perhaps the game was pearls and swine. If so, there was no other game—nothing was happening on the Soviet border. He could summarise his first week in Finland on the back of a matchbox.

§36

Back at chancery, Wilderness reacquainted himself with the cypher clerk. One Charles Chaplin, a man with the phrase "no relation" permanently on his lips, who wrote like a schoolboy in an exam—left arm crooked around the paper to prevent cheating.

Long ago, somewhere between the Berlin Airlift and whatever folly followed as night to day, Wilderness had worked out a nonstandard code to use with Burne-Jones when one or other of them felt privacy (secrecy might be more accurate) to be paramount. The only flaw in this was that Burne-Jones wasn't very good at it and on occasion would reply with "Gorgonzola? What are you on about?" or "What's got only three legs?" neither of which bore any relation to the message Wilderness had sent.

He placed his new message in front of Chaplin.

"What's this? I'm supposed to do the encoding. It's what cypher clerks do."

"Just send it as is."

"Mrs. Burton likes to see everything that comes in or out."

"It's personal. A quick note to my father-in-law . . . we have . . ." Wilderness improvised.

"We have a family wedding coming up."

"She won't like it."

"Then don't tell her. It's nothing worth bothering Mrs. Burton with."

"OK. On your own head and all that."

Holderness to Burne-Jones:
—Why did you send me here?

The replies:
—Why do you ask?
—It's beginning to feel like a punishment posting.
—Well, it's not. You're there to keep a watch on the border.
—Nothing ever happens on the fucking border. I went there this week and came back empty-handed. It's moribund.
—No, it's dormant. Not the same thing. Think of it as Mt Etna.
—Think of it as a punishment posting.
—Honestly, it's not. I had to get you out of the limelight. So it made sense to send you somewhere where there was none.
—Eh?
—There's no point in removing you from the scrutiny of the shiny-trousered buggers in parliament because of one scandal, crisis—call it what you like—if you are then in a position to create another. The beauty of Finland, O son-in-law mine, is precisely that nothing is happening—ergo, you can't fuck it up. Joe,

```
just play it safe and keep your nose clean. Do
NOT go poking around. If there's bugger all to
report then report bugger all. Fig biscuits.
Over and bloody well out.
```

Well, Wilderness thought, I've been told. For a second or so he wondered what "Fig biscuits" might have been before Burne-Jones mangled his encoding, but it didn't matter. He'd been told. He'd been sentenced . . . to boredom.

§37

It was more than a week before he loaded up the Mog again.

A consignment of *Carry On* films from London had elicited a gleeful "marvellous" from Farr, and when Wilderness joked that they'd missed out *Carry On Khrushchev*, Farr said he hadn't heard of that one but it would go on next week's list. Abracadabra.

Meanwhile, Sir Mackenzie Herron, emeritus professor of classics, Wadham, Oxford, was in town to deliver his party piece—a series of talks (illustrated with what Farr called "magic lantern" slides) on the Etruscan tombs of Volterra and Tarquinia.

Wilderness was driver and "magic lantern" projectionist. Possibly the only "magic lantern" projectionist with his own Smith & Wesson .44. It almost hurt Wilderness to admit to himself that the talks were actually interesting. He found that driving the old man from one small town to the next . . . Turku . . . Tampere . . . was far from boring. Once the professor was off his own subject, his views on the England from which Wilderness was exiled were quite unpredictable.

"Voted for Wilson. After all, his moment had come and the Tories were in total disarray, but he's a ruthless bastard. You won't recognise England when he's finished with it. Brown's a nicer man, but a piss-artist. It was tempting to vote Liberal, but I stuck to my guns. Been Labour since the general strike in '26. No point in backtracking now."

Wilderness listened intently to this radical in sheep's clothing and the only sticky moment came when the old man asked how Wilderness had come to be in the Foreign Office—by which he clearly meant Intelligence.

"After all, you're not the sort of chap they usually recruit, are you? In my day . . . and I was at Caius just before the first war . . . you got a tap on the shoulder from the college chaplain, an invitation to take tea, and if you didn't get your backside groped the next thing you knew you were in MI5."

"And if you did get your backside groped?"

"Then he'd singled you out for his own purpose, not the state's. If he groped you, you'd never get recruited. He felt he was queer enough for the secret services. He wasn't recruiting anymore."

"And?"

"I punched the old pederast on the jaw and did my bit for Britain in the Argyll and Sutherland Highlanders instead. Gassed at Loos. Being buggered by the chaplain was probably preferable to being gassed. But *you* . . . how did they find you?"

"You're assuming I'm a spy?"

"Of course you're a bloody spy. Or did you think I'd lived my life in an ivory tower?"

Wilderness was not certain what to say next. Was "spy" really written on his forehead?

"Mind you," Sir Mackenzie went on, "you don't have to tell me. We could go back to talking about tombs."

V

Vodka

§38

He arrived in Persereiikkä around three o'clock the following Thursday. He'd done two film shows along the way and approached Persereiikkä from the east.

The screening would not be until seven thirty. He called on Pastorius at the tourist office.

"Let's grab a bite to eat beforehand."

Then he checked into the White Nights Hotel.

It was crowded, it always was, but that was predictable if only he had given a moment's thought to the matter of the midnight sun. It wasn't just the title of a Lionel Hampton record from his teenage years, it was one of nature's wonders, and drew crowds by the thousand. Wilderness had wondered about the formalities . . . so many men in suits . . . but was more concerned by the blackout curtains, without which sleep might be impossible for some, but which for Wilderness were far too reminiscent of a childhood in the London Blitz. He'd leave them open. Sun or no sun. Blitz or no Blitz.

§39

"I have to go up to Joeerämaa in the morning. The Australians. Care to come?"

"Might as well. I got Momo the piece of tosh he wanted."

"Tosh?"

"The film he asked for."

"Oh. Alright. I was just thinking perhaps we should talk to them again."

"Niilo, what would be the point? They haven't flown the border in months and they won't fly it again. The fact is . . . my cover has become the reality . . . 'you are what you pretend to be' . . . that's a quotation. I forget from whom. All the same, it's all getting rather transparent. The Aussies saw right through me, and much to my surprise so did the old English professor I took on the road this week. People look through *cultural attaché* and see *spy* . . . and they're all wrong. The illusion *is* the reality."

"Very philosophical. I'd no idea you could be such a miserable bastard, Joe. Now what delightful piece of propaganda do you have for Persereiikkä this evening?"

"*Saturday Night and Sunday Morning.* It's about a bloke who works in a bike factory."

Pastorius pulled a face. "Bike factory? Really?"

"It's a comedy. It's actually very funny."

§40

The Finns laughed but once—when Albert Finney, as the antihero, Arthur Seaton, pinged a fat old gossip on the backside with his air rifle. The rest . . . the satire . . . the all-but-relentless digs at England in the sixties . . . fell flat. Humour was not, whatever Wilderness might have thought, a universal language.

§41

As they approached the lakeside a dot in the sky took form. Then took wings. By the time they'd parked the Mog, the Beaver was throttling back to touch down on the water. Bruce was at the end of the jetty—in less than a minute Momo had turned the plane around and thrown a mooring line out to him.

The back door opened.

Momo greeted all three of them with "Bloody good timing."

"For what?" said Wilderness.

"Take a seat."

"On what?"

Momo passed out a box, then another and another. Then he sat in the doorway of the plane, clutching a clear bottle and three small shot glasses and a plastic cup.

"I'm not the fuckin' queen, mate. You can all sit down."

Then he splashed something as transparent as Wilderness's cover into the glasses and handed them out. Pastorius got the plastic cup.

"Bottoms up."

Bruce spoke first. "This is good stuff. Not sure we've ever landed better."

"Vodka?" said Wilderness.

"That'd be one name for it, but it's got dozens. Kilju . . . pontikku . . . ponantza . . . tuliliemi . . ."

"Moonshine?"

"Yep."

Wilderness realised he was sitting on a case of the stuff. He peered past Momo into the cabin, half-expecting to see a piano and Fred Astaire poised to fly down to Rio, but it was packed with boxes. More than he could count.

"You seem to have cornered the market."

"Neatly put, mate. Niilo?"

Bruce had knocked his drink back and was on a second glass. Niilo was sipping slowly at his, as though finding it or the plastic distasteful. He stared into it, swirled it pointlessly.

"Yes. Of course. How quickly we get to the point. Yes, I think we may have cornered the market."

"Well, you did say they had other fish to fry. Not sure where the 'we' comes in, though. Are you part of this . . . racket, Niilo?"

"Racket?" Momo said. "You cheeky fucker!"

Pastorius held up his hand—a cop stopping traffic.

"Of course it's a racket. You wonder at my role? I'm the protection. The guarantee. Nobody bothers Momo or Bruce while I'm around. As far as Supo are concerned, they're still patrolling the border for us. Their flights across the restricted zone are sanctioned. They can reach places you'd have difficulty getting to by road. Hence, we have been able to attain a virtual monopoly. But I can only do so much. My cover might be as obvious as yours, but so far most believe it. I pull too many strings, lean on too many policemen, and it won't be. Do you follow?"

"I think so. I'm waiting for one of you to tell me why you're telling me."

"I've local cops looking the other way. Out on what passes for the highway . . . not possible . . . other airfields . . . airfields down south . . . they're looking out for us . . . or people like us. But, of course, the market is down south. Nobody buys moonshine in Lapland, because they're all making their own. With stuff this good, and it isn't always quite this good, there's a ready market in Helsinki. It's just that we can't reach it."

"A . . . *black* market?"

Such a familiar phrase, he found he was all but savouring it.

"A black market . . . yes. One we cannot reach. But you can."

A voice in Wilderness's head said, "slowly."

He tacked away.

"What is it, grain?"

"Barley mostly," said Momo. "Touch of spud. There's some real rubbish about . . . just sugar and yeast . . . you might drink it if you were desperate. Drink too much and you might end up blind. But the blokes who make this are a class act."

Wilderness allowed Momo to top him up. Sipped slowly. It burnt, but not too much, and it had some flavour, hints of herb, to play around with on the tongue. Perhaps the distillers were a class act. All the same, it was nothing he'd ever drink out of choice, it was a notch or two above rotgut—but this wasn't choice. It was diplomacy.

"OK. What is it you three think I can do for you?"

The Aussies looked at Niilo.

Niilo said, "Our police will not stop a car with diplomatic plates. To search it would be . . . an . . . incident."

That word again.

"You have plenty of room in the Mog. We fill it up with vodka. You drive back to Helsinki. Don't go directly to the embassy. Leave the Mog in a public car park. Keys on top of the front wheel, driver side. Find a bar. Have a drink. Come back an hour later. The van will be empty, the keys back on the wheel . . . and an envelope full of markka. You need never meet the men at the other end."

"That simple?"

"Probably not . . . you know . . . plans . . . mice . . . men. But by and large it should work."

"And the split?"

"Equal shares. A four-way split."

Wilderness held out his glass once more, bought himself a moment of time.

"What's the markup on this? A hundred percent? Two hundred?"

Pastorius smiled, Bruce and Momo guffawed.

"Fuckin' hell mate. We weren't born yesterday. Nah. Make that a thousand."

Wilderness broached the matter that was bothering him the most.

"What makes you lot think I'm bent?"

And then they all fell about laughing.

§42

That night Wilderness screened *Carry on Cabby*. It brought the house down. Momo was merely one of dozens busting their sides at humour about as sophisticated as a whoopee cushion. He chalked one up to Farr—the battle for hearts and minds wasn't going to be won with kitchen sink drama, but with the updated version of music hall and panto. On the other hand, if that was true then most Soviet cinema didn't stand a cat in hell's chance. It was all as deadly serious as a tract by Karl Marx. He'd go back to Farr and put in a request for *Les Vacances de M. Hulot* and pass the buck for resisting communism to the French.

He slept in one of Joeerämaa's small hotels, something like a spruce shack, a spruce shack with attached sauna—he'd never stayed in a youth hostel but he imagined they must be much like this. Basic. Barely comfortable. Forgettable.

In the morning, he drove down to Persereiikkä. The back of the Mog crammed with moonshine, Pastorius dozing fitfully in the passenger seat. A deep pothole shook him awake.

Pastorius yawned and muttered the word "boredom."

"Eh?"

"I was thinking of that line from Hamlet."

"Which one? Every line in Hamlet is a line from Hamlet."

"'Thus conscience doth make cowards of us all.' It's boredom makes villains of us all. If I really had something interesting, something worthwhile to do . . . I'd probably be an honest man."

"German has an excellent word for it. *Schieber*. We were always *Schiebers* back in the days of the Berlin blockade and the airlift. A versatile word . . . smuggler, black marketeer, gangster, drug dealer . . . covered a multitude of sins."

"And you wear it as a badge of honour?"

"No," Wilderness replied. "I wouldn't go quite that far."

§43

It went exactly as planned.

Two days and two cinematic fiascos later Wilderness parked the Mog in Helsinki. Called the number Pastorius had given him. Gave the password "Greta Garbo." Hung up. Killed an hour in a bar.

When he collected the truck, the keys and a fat envelope of Finnish currency were on the near-side front tyre.

He drove the truck back to the chancery's underground car park, logged in with no one and went home.

He'd been in the flat about an hour and a half, rinsed off the days on the road in the shower and was just contemplating the prospect of Estonian Burgundy and wishing there were another choice when there was a knock at the door.

Janis Bell stood on the landing with a bottle of red wine in her hand. She glanced at the corkscrew in Wilderness's hand and said, "Seems we have the same idea."

"You were passing?"

"No, I live on the top floor. Most people in Paradise Apartments work for the embassy."

"What kept you?"

"I didn't want you to think I'm easy."

"And I didn't want you to think I was available."

"It's OK. I've read your file. I know you're married. And to whom. The son-in-law also rises."

"Not funny, not funny at all."

He handed her the corkscrew.

"If you can't be funny at least be useful."

While she uncorked the bottle, he found glasses and tucked the envelope of cash into the cutlery drawer.

She held up the burgundy.

"Can you honestly drink this muck?"

"No. I drink it dishonestly. Why? What have you brought?"

"Moldavian claret. A Purcari 1952."

"Good stuff?"

"Good enough for the Tsar in its day. Call it one of the perks of the deeply ambivalent relationship this country has with its big next-door neighbour."

She slipped off her shoes. Curled her legs under herself on the sofa. Wilderness hoped she'd told him the truth, that this was not a seduction, as he could feel his resistance melting.

"The blokes on the gate say you got back at four."

"Sounds about right."

"You didn't report to the boss?"

"As I would have had to pass your desk, you know damn well I didn't."

"She's . . . concerned."

"Would that be the same as pissed off?"

"Perhaps either term is an understatement. You've made two trips north and reported back on neither."

"There's nothing to spy on. Not a damn thing. Lapland seems to have early closing day every day. A perpetual Wednesday. There's nothing to report. Just the buzz of tourism. It'll peak in a day or two then tail off for the autumn and peak again around Christmas. All so predictable as not to be worth comment."

"And when there is?"

"When there is, I'll consider what to tell her."

"She is Head of Station. She could just have you packed off back to Blighty."

"You don't know how happy that would make me. 'Who do I have to fuck to get off this movie?'"

"Or she could just make your life hell."

"I doubt that. But . . . why are you telling me this?"

"I suppose I think you deserve a warning."

"Deserve?"

"You've earned it."

"How?"

"By being the first person posted out since I got here who isn't a total bore."

Oh yes, he really hoped this was not a seduction. As she took the plastic slide from her hair and let it tumble to her shoulders he all but prayed it wasn't.

"OK. What are you warning me about?"

"The coded letters you had Charlie send to London. She knows about them. I'd tell you Charlie can't be trusted, but the truth is he's doing what we trust him to do. His job."

"He hasn't cracked the code?"

"No. You've hurt his professional pride there. Whoever came up with it was one clever bastard."

"My Number Two—Eddie Clark. I don't have that kind of mind."

"But if he does crack it?"

"He won't. But Mrs. Burton can always tell him to stop transmitting for me."

"Then you'd just find another way."

"Yep."

"Hmm . . . well, she hasn't told him to stop. She's hoping Charlie will crack it and then she'll have you by the balls."

At that moment Wilderness hoped sincerely that no woman was about to approach his balls.

"What are you up to, Joe?"

"As you said not a moment ago, just doing my job."

She shook her head, the black mop swaying from side to side . . . the grass skirt on a hula dancer . . . the fifth or sixth of the seven veils.

"No . . . no . . . noooo. You're not a cultural attaché, you're a spy, and if there's nothing to spy on . . . what are you?"

One aspect of his new-found relationship with Niilo and the Aussies still nagged at him. When he'd asked, "What makes you lot think I'm bent?" they'd roared with laughter, but none had actually answered.

He knew exactly what Janis was going to say next. She scarcely needed to utter it.

But when she did he felt the touch of the feather as it knocked him down.

"You're a *Schieber*, aren't you?"

"How do you know that word?"

"First class honours in Modern Languages, Cambridge 1962. Just think, we went to the same university."

"I suppose so, but it's a strained comparison. I was never an undergraduate. I have no degree, no diploma. No affiliation to any college."

"I read French and German at Newnham. I've taught myself Russian since and I'm dabbling in some of the languages between here and there . . . you know, the *Mitteleuropa* alphabet soups . . . Polish . . . Czech."

"And yet here you are, typing letters for Mrs. Burton."

"Strictly pro tem. I have diplomatic status. I'm a Third Secretary in Her Majesty's Diplomatic Service, not a shorthand typist. Not my fault if 'secretary' is a bit too bloody literal at the moment."

"Aha."

"Aha, bollocks! I intend to run MI6. One day."

"When you grow up."

"Of course, when I grow up. And you, Joe Holderness, what will you do when you grow up?"

"Define my being grown up. When will I know I've got there?"

"That's easy, Joe. When you stop nicking things."

§44

Wilderness had not stocked the narrow galley that passed for a kitchen. Eating out emphatically meant "out" of his flat. Anything was better.

Advice to agents serving abroad always included the patronising "do not establish a pattern to your movements"—which Wilderness habitually ignored.

His "pattern" was to take breakfast most days in a café just a hundred yards from his flat—the Egg & Sausage diner, *Muna Ja Makkara*, or as the sign read simply, *M&M*. If the KGB wanted to assassinate him, they'd know where to find him, and perhaps they'd all have a cup of coffee before the guns came out.

The guns did not come out—a "gun" came in, in the person of Tom Rockford.

Wilderness had met Rockford half a dozen times. He'd been the CIA's man in Vienna and in Lisbon. He'd been in Madrid that time the Spanish had locked up Wilderness and then banned him from ever visiting Spain again.

He slipped into the booth opposite Wilderness.

"Joe."

"Rocky."

Wilderness didn't know Rockford was attached to the Helsinki embassy, but then he hadn't asked. The CIA were everywhere. Sooner or later they'd make themselves known.

"Welcome to Finland."

"You took your time. I've been here nearly a month."

"Didn't want to show my hand too soon."

"Don't make me laugh while I'm eating, Rocky. Could be messy."

"I hear you've been up to Lapland."

"Yep. It's no secret."

In Finland, Wilderness had concluded, nothing was a secret.

"I just wondered if there's anything you'd care to share."

"There's nothing to share."

"Aw. C'mon."

"No, honestly, I mean I've learnt nothing. There's fuck all happening up there."

Rockford decided it was time to order a coffee, and while he flagged down a waitress neither of them said any more.

Once the girl had scribbled on her notepad and moved away, Rockford lowered his voice.

"We're . . . kinda thin on the ground these days."

"I had noticed."

"I mean . . . that asshole George Fosse . . . blundered all over the place in '62 . . . took liberties the Finns wouldn't put up with . . . got himself kicked out and a few dozen good guys along with him."

"Don't worry. You'll be back. And I can't believe there's anything about Lapland you don't already know. I heard you mapped every bog and ditch."

Another awkward silence as the waitress plonked a milky coffee in front of Rockford.

"All it amounts to," Wilderness continued, "is that the Finns put an end to spy tourism."

"That's cute. You just make that up?"

"Find me a better term for what you lot were up to."

"It leaves a gap."

"No it doesn't. You're missing nothing but bird migration. And I don't think the arctic terns and the snow geese work for Brezhnev."

"Fosse was an idiot. Didn't think to pay off the Supo."

"Perhaps some people can't be bought," said Wilderness, suppressing any thought of Niilo Pastorius.

"You know we had a reciprocal on intel with the Finns," Rockford said.

"No. But I'm not surprised either."

"They cancelled on us last year."

"Really? The words shit, creek and paddle come to mind. Has it occurred to Langley that perhaps the Finns don't trust you?"

"Joe . . . for fuck's sake . . . we're their ally . . ."

"If I were Finland—the Spam and mustard filling in a Soviet-American sandwich—I wouldn't trust anybody. Nothing personal, Rocky, but if I were unearthing anything vital up in Lapland I wouldn't tell you. The Finns think the Russians are the threat, but it's you lot, isn't it? Tell me you haven't got a scenario to nuke the shit out of this country if you have to deny it to the Russians. Tell me every bridge, every port and railway junction doesn't have a target number assigned to it. Tell me you're not still adding targets. Tell me you won't leave Lapland as scorched as the Nazis did. Tell me all that and I'll call you a liar. You dig your bunkers at home and you prepare to nuke the rest of us. Rocky, I've even heard you lot have a term for your nuclear policy—'So What? Optimism.' Marginally better than 'Mutually Assured Destruction.' I suppose 'Couldn't Give a Flying Fuck' was already taken?"

Rockford was one of those big men whose emotions were oft as not made manifest in their cheeks. He was the kind of man to turn red in the face about three-tenths of a second before he lost it.

"Jesus H. Christ, Joe—whose side are you on? Whose fuckin' side! And if the Finns are so damn goody-two-shoes why are they buying MiGs?!"

"Say it louder, Rocky. I'm not sure everyone in the restaurant heard you."

Rockford got up, all bustle and rage.

"Special relationship, my ass. Fuck you, Joe."

It had been worth provoking him. If "fuck you" was the limit of his verbal armoury then Wilderness felt reassured. If Rocky had known about Pastorius, he'd have used it.

§45

For two days Wilderness drove the poet Prudence Latymer to readings. She was devoutly Christian—not an f-word passed her lips—and seemed dedicated to simple rhyming couplets celebrating dance, spring, renewal, the natural world and the smaller breeds of English and Scottish dog. It was as though T. S. Eliot had never lived.

By the third day Wilderness was considering shooting her.

Instead he rang Janis Bell and said, "I'm off up north. She's all yours."

"You're not supposed to do this. The boss'll be really angry."

"Fine. You do it."

"What do I tell Burton?"

"How about . . . I felt the call of the wild?"

"Fuck you, Joe."

§46

A pattern established that was neither fulfilling nor intolerable. He would arrive in Persereiikkä after stopping in two or three rural backwaters—he had learnt almost at once the trick of sleeping through a film whilst appearing to be awake, and now found the opening score of *The Titfield Thunderbolt* soothingly somnolent. His only worry was that he might show the same film twice to the same village and not realise it.

After a night in Persereiikkä he would press on to Joeerämaa the next morning, load up with moonshine, show Momo another *Carry On* film and follow a different route, via different villages and with any luck different films, back to Helsinki.

The first time he handed over the envelope, Pastorius said, "You haven't opened it?"

"Why would I?"

And Pastorius had riffled through the money with the dexterity of a casino dealer and divvied up four equal shares. Wilderness did not bother to count his, merely weighed it on the palm of the hand. After two more runs he reckoned he'd got the equivalent of three months' pay tucked away at the back of the cutlery drawer. After six he might have felt rich, if he'd bothered to count it.

He also had, and this puzzled and surprised him, a hint of that forgotten feeling of belonging that only came with "partners in crime." The *Schiebers* revisited. None of them was Eddie, the ultimately reliable man, but Pastorius was honest in his dishonesty, a crook you could trust to play fair, and while Momo and Bruce were ne'er-do-well piss artists . . . neither of them was a Frank Spoleto.

But on the Sunday night following a late August black market trip, he arrived home to a note under the door:

```
You must tell Burton something. She's in London
for ten days as of yesterday. And you can bet
your bottom dollar she's complaining like hell
about you. Joe—please give me something I can
put on file and show to her the minute she
gets back. I know nothing's happening up there,
but couldn't you dress that up as a positive?
All quiet on the northern front? Or some such
nonsense?
    Janis
```

Wilderness liked to think he could take good advice when he saw it. To have the Brocken Witch kick up a shit storm just when he was starting to make serious money would be counterproductive. He typed up a no-names account of Pastorius's ferreting expeditions and presented it as evidence of no Russian activity. He threw in handy phrases such as "on the one hand" and "all things considered" and wondered about "under the circumstances" . . . but he couldn't think what circumstances there might be.

On Monday morning he got into chancery ahead of Janis Bell, put his puffed-up piece of nonsense on her desk and whilst hoping to make a run for it before she arrived, could not help pausing to read the schedule for "the week in culture" that she had left next to the IBM—two more poets and an expert on Norman architecture.

He scribbled "called by the wild" across the schedule and set off north again. He had, after all, a new treat for the culturally deprived Finns—a three-year-old BBC recording of the wedding of Princess Alexandra to the Hon. Angus Ogilvy in Westminster Abbey. Who could resist? Once Finland had seen that, the Cold War was all over bar the shouting.

§47

The tourist agency was closed up. Pastorius was not expecting him. He'd shown no films on the way and managed the journey in one long, exhausting twelve-hour stint. Three breaks along the way for coffee or he would have fallen asleep at the wheel.

Instead he skipped dinner, fell asleep in bed at the White Nights and told himself it was not so much running away as tactical withdrawal.

In the morning he went down to breakfast. Asked if there were any messages.

There was one:

Ratbag! Yrs Bell.

"And," said the bloke at the desk, "a man was asking for you about half an hour ago."

"For me? Who?"

"Well, for the Englishman, and you are the only one here. He didn't leave a name. A German gentleman, I think."

Wilderness was inhaling the aroma of his first coffee when he felt the man looming. Not the plump looming of an Eddie but a tall skinny looming, although when Wilderness looked up at him, the first thing he thought was that time had filled him out rather well. Flesh on his bones and perhaps the nervous twitch had vanished from his cheeks.

"*Kein Wort auf Russisch.*"

(Not one word in Russian.)

"Are there any Germans called Kostya?"

"Joe. Please."

"For fuck's sake, Kostya. Just sit down."

Oh, but the twitch was still there. All too apparent as he looked around to see who was listening. If *Carry On* ever made a *Carry On Spying*, that look, so damned hammy, would be perfect.

"You're looking well. Shall we stick with German?"

"Yes. And thank you, I am indeed well."

"And your mother? Did she invest the money she stole from me with her peanut butter scam? Buy her own private salt mine?"

"You are joking?"

"Of course I'm joking. She made general. Everyone in Six knows that. Everyone at Langley knows that. Quite an achievement. Volga Vasilievna Zolotukhina, captain of netball and head girl of the KGB, eh?"

"Not quite. Not while Krasnaya still lives."

"But she must be seventy by now."

"Sixty-eight. There is talk she might retire at seventy. Then my mother is, what you said . . . *head girl.*"

Wilderness didn't think he'd ever seen Kostya out of uniform before. A business suit in a dark shade of nothing—a briefcase set down beside him in the booth. All a disguise for what?

"And you . . . Am I about to handle your defection?"

"And still you joke. No. I am very loyal. I too have been promoted. I am a captain."

"And I'm just a fucking sergeant. Would you bloody believe it?"

Kostya looked around the room again. It wasn't even a quarter full. The twitch had spread to his lower left eyelid.

Wilderness beckoned to the waiter, ordered breakfast for two. Who knew how long it would take Kostya to get to the point? They might as well eat.

"We're in a neutral country Kostya. Eat your neutral eggs and your neutral toast. Drink your neutral coffee. I don't know how you got here, but if you've just nipped across for a decent meal, tuck in."

Over poached eggs Wilderness managed to wheedle out of him that he was based just across the border at Rayakoski and had driven over, via the narrow isthmus of Norway, swapping the plates on his car and his Russian passport for a German one between countries. As far as the Finns were concerned, he was a German. A commercial traveller.

"In . . . in . . . Вот дерьмо . . . oh shit . . ."

"If our dodgy trade has any rules, fairly high on the list has to be 'get your cover down pat.'"

"Machine . . . machine parts. That's it. I am traveller in machine parts."

"Good one. Nicely vague. That should cover you for anything from a pencil sharpener to a tractor engine."

On his second coffee Kostya seemed to relax a little. His look around the room took no more than five seconds, then he said, blurting it out all too rapidly, "I hear you have cornered the market in vodka."

"Really Kostya—*how* do you know this?"

"The flyers. The pilots. Your pilots. We took down one. We could have taken down all three. We preferred instead to keep track of them. It was possible they were more use to us alive than dead."

"And how do you keep track?"

Kostya shrugged.

"We have people on the ground. People here."

"A network?"

"No. Nothing so structured. The odd person willing to sell us gossip. Nothing more than that."

"Not the local Communist Party?"

"What local Communist Party? The Finns are like everyone else. They just want to be Americans. *Bonanza*, Kellogg's Corn Flakes, Dick van Dyke and peanut butter."

"Don't you dare mention peanut butter to me."

"Of course. Sorry. No, it's strictly a cash deal. No ideology whatsoever. Capitalism at its most basic. 'You sell us the rope with which we will hang you.'"

"Lenin?"

"Correct."

"And this . . . person . . . told you I was running vodka?"

"No. I was told it was an Englishman. That's all. I didn't get a name. It never occurred to me it might be an MI6 operation. I paid extra for a photograph. Not even a good photograph, but enough for me to know it was you. I learnt your *nom-de-guerre-froide* less than half an hour ago, Mr. Young."

"And you are?"

Kostya slid a passport across the table.

"Pohl," Wilderness read. "Gertan Pohl. From Munich?"

"One place was as good as another. Just so long as it's in the Bundesrepublik not the DDR. I have plates on the car to match."

"It's a good fake. Almost Erno standard."

Kostya blinked first.

"You fucker! It is an Erno fake, isn't it? I don't even remember introducing you."

"You didn't. Nell did."

Nell had taken a shine to Kostya. At least two years younger than he was, she'd treated him like a little brother and all but combed his hair and scrubbed his cheeks with a spit-hanky.

Wilderness pushed the passport back.

"Let's stick to our new names, shall we, Herr Pohl?"

"You think I want it known I'm Russian? I'd get lynched."

"I'm sure you would. I heard it said not that long ago that Finns can smell a Russian. But, backtrack a minute. This isn't an MI6 operation. And I don't think you ever thought it was. It's private enterprise . . . why would your lot be interested in it?"

"Private enterprise? Just like Berlin?"

"Just like Berlin."

Kostya seemed to lose his voice. For a minute he said nothing, would not meet Wilderness's gaze. And when he spoke it was scarcely more than a whisper.

"I am here to buy."

A dozen thoughts collided in Wilderness's mind. That Kostya was in Lapland to buy moonshine vodka was but one. And all the others told him not to believe it.

"You want me to sell vodka to Russia? Ездить в Тулу со своим самоваром?"

"Yes. That is it. Are we . . . are we back in business?"

"We might be," Wilderness replied.

§48

They took a mid-morning stroll through Persereiikkä, down to the river once more. It always seemed to Wilderness that the town smelled of sawdust. It was odd that he never heard the sound of a chainsaw.

It wasn't a pretty town—it was a town in permanent transition. Rising from its own ashes again and again. Twenty years on it could not lose the smell of burning, that ever-present hint of charcoal left over from when the Germans razed the entire town.

He could see a reaction in Kostya. He could smell burning too.

"Your first visit?"

"Yes. I arrived in darkness last night."

"And?"

"I tell myself we did not do this. The Nazis destroyed Persereiikkä."

"Don't pat yourself on the back. There's an awful lot more you have to answer for."

"Could we not discuss the sins of the Soviet Union? If we do I might have to lecture you on the Murmansk Expedition of 1919. All those frozen Tommies stranded at the end of the world. Great Britain's futile attempt to nip Communism in the bud?"

"Fine by me. Let's get down to business. Vodka."

"We have a national shortage."

"What?"

"We are short of everything. I don't think that's any secret. Your Moscow watchers in London are a waste of money if they don't know that. The cost of defence, the cost of the space programme—President Kennedy knew exactly what he was doing when he promised a man on the moon . . . a challenge we could not refuse, but a race we could not win. Add two successive low-yield harvests and Brezhnev's Russia is as poor as it was under the Tsars."

They stopped. Kostya, with fewer nerves than he usually displayed, looked Wilderness in the eye.

"You don't believe me, do you?"

"I'm sceptical."

"Joe . . . two months ago I approved an order for the reuse of every piece of paper on the base. Do you know what for? For lavatory paper. The Soviet Union has run out of bog roll. That soft stuff you used to sell to us in Berlin is now as highly prized as fresh fruit or Scotch whisky. We wipe our arses on documents marked Classified, Secret and sometimes even Top Secret. And the damn stuff won't flush. So once a week a surly corporal lights a bonfire of Soviet secrets and Russian shit."

Wilderness hoped he wasn't reacting visibly to this.

"And vodka? Surely there are illicit stills on your side of the border."

"There were, but we're a controlled country—"

"You mean a police state."

"We have rules. We enforce rules. Eighteen months ago the militia raided over a hundred illegal distilleries in Karelia and Murmansk Oblasts and put them out of business. All perfectly legal."

"Legal but stupid."

"Legal but very stupid. Can you imagine how difficult it is to control the average Russian soldier if he can't get a drink? We simmer at the point of mutiny day after day. I'd rather break the rules and have slightly tipsy and obedient men."

"How much would you want?"

"Not a lot. Half a dozen cases a week."

"And you'd take them back with you?"

"No. I'm taking no risk with my own people. But . . . I have to pass through Finnish and Norwegian customs. One random search and I'm blown. The flyers also have an amphibian, do they not? It's a short flight for them. Completely below radar. Only a matter of minutes. We'd open up a leak in the fence. Somewhere on the far side of the lake. North of Nellim. I've picked out a suitable place. You'll be less than five kilometres from the border and maybe twenty from Rayakoski. And it's a place impossible to reach by road. Your men cannot be followed, and nor can we. Two of my men will meet them. The day of each flight I will come over ahead of it as Gertan Pohl with cash payment. Up front."

"In what currency?"

"In Berlin you would deal only in dollars. So . . . dollars."

None of this added up. Flying the vodka across the lake did, Kostya continuing to drive across didn't. Keeping up the Gertan Pohl disguise didn't make any sense. Perhaps he didn't trust a couple of Russian grunts with the money, perhaps he didn't trust the Aussies. Paying in dollars? It wasn't that he'd agreed too readily—Wilderness hadn't even asked.

"These pilots aren't working for me. They're my partners. I will have to discuss this with them. I can't give orders. You understand?"

"Yes."

"They're based up at Joeerämaa—but you know that. I'll go up there later this morning. They often finish any flying by noon and once the cap comes off the beer they're home for the rest of the day. I'll come back to you with an answer in the morning. Meet me at breakfast as you did today."

"Another night in Persereiikkä?"

"You have a problem with that?"

"Not really. I should not be in Finland too long, but the only person with a right to ask about my absence from the base is the Political Commissar."

"Which just happens to be you?"

"Of course."

Kostya smiled. Perhaps for the first time. A hint of the boy he'd been when they first met.

And he hadn't even asked the price.

§49

At the lakeside, they were in deck chairs again. Judging by the half dozen empties tossed onto the grass, just short of their ever-growing pile, they'd been home at least half an hour.

"What load of shite have you brought us this time, Joe? I've a yen to see that *Alfie* thing with Michael Caine."

"No films. This is strictly a business trip. Where's Niilo?"

"Taking a piss in the woods."

But Niilo had come up right behind them. An open beer in each hand.

"Nothing will disguise the sound of your Mog, Joe. I heard you coming several minutes ago."

Wilderness took the proffered bottle.

"Forgive me if I'm cynical," said Pastorius. "But unexpected visits are almost never good news."

"You may well be right. A while back you told me there were no KGB on your patch."

Pastorius said nothing.

"Yet . . . I had breakfast with a KGB agent this morning at the White Nights."

Pastorius wasn't visibly rattled.

"Someone new to Persereiikkä?"

"Yes. So he said. But not new to me. I met him in Berlin back in '48."

"And he got here . . . how?"

"Drove in from Norway on a fake West German passport. A fake good enough to fool anyone."

"Well . . . that seems plausible. What does he want?"

"Vodka. He wants us to sell him vodka."

The gurgling noise puzzled Wilderness for a moment. Then he recognised it for what it was. Two Australians laughing so much they had choked on their beer.

"Vodka to the fuckin' Russians? Gold nuggets to fuckin' Kalgoorlie, mate!"

"It appears," said Wilderness with a straight face, "that there's a national shortage of vodka in the Soviet Union."

Momo laughed and rocked with such force the deck chair collapsed under him.

Bruce tried to pick him up. Wilderness was certain he'd seen this act on the halls before the war—how to disentangle a drunk from a deck chair. It was the sort of thing the Crazy Gang might do . . . or Mr. Pastry.

"Seriously, mate . . . seriously . . ."

Pastorius spoke. "Yes, Joe. Seriously, what would you have us do?"

Wilderness pulled up a wooden beer crate and sat down.

"When I'm sure I've got your attention."

"Yeah. Sorry, Joe . . . it's just so bloody absurd."

"I agree. But we're going to do it anyway."

"Really?" said Pastorius.

"We need to string him out until I find out why he's really here."

Bruce said, "You're kidding, right? Just tell him to fuck off."

"Not kidding at all. He's here to buy vodka as a cover for something else. So in the meantime we sell him vodka."

"Are we back in the spook game then?"

"Sort of. But all you have to do is fly the Beaver to the other side of the lake, perhaps once a week."

"And what? Meet Russkis?"

"I think that's inevitable."

"Don't like Russkis, mate."

"This time they won't be shooting at you. You drop down this side of the border."

"Still don't like it."

Pastorius said, "Joe, may I have a word with you in private?"

"Don't mind us," Momo said. "The less I know about spook stuff, the more I like it."

They walked along the lakeshore, neither speaking until Pastorius was sure of privacy. Wilderness heard the clink of another empty bottle landing on the pile, then nothing but the lapping of water.

"Joe, I have to report this."

"No, you don't. Play the *Schieber* a while longer. If you tell Helsinki . . . well for one thing there's already an American agent sniffing around. He's too lazy to come up here on a whim. He gets wind of KGB activity . . . the CIA will be all over this, just like they were in '62 when your government had to kick them out en masse. And then there'll be no more vodka profits for anyone."

"String him out, you said. How?"

"He's in Persereiikkä now. I left him cooling his heels. I won't go back until the morning. Get on to one of your men and put a watch on him. Where he goes. Who he sees. He's at the White Nights under the name of Gertan Pohl."

"I don't have the manpower to follow him. In fact, the man in manpower is me."

"Niilo, find someone. Bribe someone."

"Alright. I'll make a few phone calls. But I promise nothing."

"Thank you. Now, can we talk these two into going along with us or are we stuck at the 'spook' thing?"

"Gavin's death hit them hard. Don't think that they're too rough-and-ready not to care. They cared greatly. That they don't know what really happened to him burns."

"I know."

"You do?"

"They shot him down. The Russians had been onto your ferreting for a while. They could have shot down Momo and Bruce as well, but chose to let them escape and keep tabs on them."

"And . . . and that's how they found us?"

"Yes."

"Do they know about me?"

"Your name hasn't come up yet. But they knew an Englishman was involved. I imagine that rang a few alarm bells—and somehow they managed to photograph me. That's what brought Kostya Zolotukhin across."

"And he told you about Gavin?"

"Yes."

"Don't tell Bruce or Momo. They'll kill him if they get the chance."

"I wasn't going to. The risk is obvious."

"Will they meet him if they take on this run across the lake?"

"Probably not. Kostya plans to pay us in advance in person. He'll drive in from Norway and pay us in cash. No reason they have to meet him."

"Cash? Markka?"

"Dollars."

Pastorius pulled a face. Wilderness knew why and spoke for both of them.

"It doesn't ring true, does it? American dollars? Sounds like a seduction. Visiting in person when he could run all this from Russia, and if not from Russia then from some spot only metres from his hole in the fence? He may well want the vodka, but it's a handy cover for what he's really after."

"I agree. Now, we should go back to the Aussies, have a beer, get them on board, change the subject, show a film in Joeerämaa . . . create the illusion of a normality we are about to fuck up so royally."

$50

Wilderness let Momo pick the film. Momo chose *Doctor in the House*. Twenty-five Joeerämaaans laughed themselves silly at a hospital romp in which English actors ten and twenty years too old for the roles played medical students—beer, bottom jokes, nurses and stethoscopes. In the war of words, the battle for the soul of Finland, Marx-Engels-Leninism took yet another pasting. One more point to Mr. Farr.

Early the next morning Momo and Bruce, although somewhat hungover, shuffled out to their Bedouin camp by the lake and grunted their continued assent.

"Just don't get us shot, right?"

Walking back to the Mog, Pastorius said, "I managed to put a tail on your man. He ate alone at the hotel. Took a stroll around town. That takes all of ten minutes. Looked at his watch a lot, as though willing time to pass more quickly. Picked a couple of English language magazines off the rack in the lobby and went to bed early. He spoke to no one except waitresses and the concierge. Made no phone calls."

Less than two hours later Wilderness was back in Persereiikkä. The dot of nine. An impatient Kostya, sitting in the booth they'd occupied yesterday.

"What kept you? I've been sitting here half an hour. I'm beginning to think Siberia is more fun than Finland."

"And you might be right," Wilderness replied. "I'm here because the British are punishing me. Why are you here?"

"You mean in Rayakoski?"

Wilderness said nothing. He meant whatever Kostya took it to mean.

"I'm not being punished. There's no stick. Just a carrot."

"And what's the carrot?"

"Promotion to major with my next posting. All I have to do is stick it out at Rayakoski till next winter."

"I don't suppose you remember Frank asking you if everyone in the KGB is a major?"

"I try not to remember Frank at all."

"Well, good luck with that. Eddie's been trying for twenty years."

Then the all-too-furtive glance around the room. Wilderness supposed Kostya might make major. But it was a miracle he'd ever made captain.

"Joe? Do we have deal?"

"I think we do."

"And the price?"

At last. First things saved till last.

Wilderness gilded the lily. Named a price he hoped was too high. It was.

"That's . . . that's . . . what's the word . . . steep."

"It's what it goes for in Helsinki."

"But this isn't Helsinki. It's ten miles across the lake. Easier for you by far."

"I could offer a discount. But there'd be a quid pro quo."

"I'm listening."

"When you take delivery of the vodka, I want your men to load something else onto the plane."

"We've nothing you could possibly want."

"Bring me the sacks of bog paper."

Kostya looked dumbstruck. He said nothing for the best part of a minute.

"You know. I was about to order breakfast. I don't think I'll bother. Joe, what in God's name do you want with bog paper?"

"You said it yourself, yesterday. Before it encountered Soviet arseholes, it was Classified or Secret or Top Secret."

"But it's covered in—"

"I know."

"And it's secret."

"But it's covered in—"

"Stop, stop, stop!"

"It's because it's covered in shit that you can give it to me. Unless my people can find a way of cleaning it up without losing the print, it's worthless, therefore it can't be secret anymore, can it?"

"That's very specious reasoning, Joe."

"Specious? It's pure sophistry. But let it salve your conscience. You'd be giving me something worthless."

"Might your people clean it up?"

"I've no idea. I don't care. I just want the pleasure of mailing them sacks of Russian shit in the diplomatic bag."

Another pause for thought. The waitress approached with her notepad. Kostya just shook his head, and with it seemed to shake off all doubt about the deal.

"How much of a discount?"

"Ten percent."

"Twenty."

"Fifteen."

"Done."

"You are your mother's son after all."

What, Wilderness wondered, brought the blush to his cheeks? The mention of Volga Vasilievna Zolotukhina or the mistaken assumption that he'd just negotiated well with the enemy and scored a few points?

§51

Wilderness left Persereiikkä with a Russian-made map of Lapland in his hand, a creek just north of Nellim ringed in blue biro, and a dozen questions in his head. Some of them he'd put to Eddie as soon as he could.

Chaplin looked at the encrypted message.

"Another wedding? So soon?"

"No. A funeral. My great-grandmother died. One hundred and fifteen."

"Unbelievable."

"Yes. Isn't it?"

"I'll have to tell Mrs. Burton."

"Has she told you not to send?"

"Not yet, but she will."

Wilderness to Eddie:

—**What do the Watchers say Mother is short of?**
  And don't give me a lecture just a list.

The replies:

—Such as?

—No prompts just tell me what they think.

—Zinc's OK. Copper's down. Nickel's all but
wiped out. Steel's booming.

Second biggest uranium reserves on Earth.
Mountains of coal. Petrol pouring in from
Roumania. Will that do?

—Crops?

Two lousy harvests in a row, but you could have
found that out from the Daily Express. Is this
leading anywhere? I've got work to do y'know.

—What have you heard about a crackdown on
illegal stills?

—Oh, they've been moaning about that for a
while. It takes a bushel of grain to make a
gallon of vodka.

—What the fuck is a bushel?

—About 60 lbs. It takes 10-12 pounds of grain
to make a bottle of vodka. Mother can't spare
the grain. Been importing grain for years. One
bottle of vodka gets one bastard drunk for a
day.

12 lbs of grain makes enough bread to last a
family for a week. Simple maths really.

—So they really are short of vodka?

—And spuds.

—And paper?

—That too. There's a story going round the
office that the poor buggers stationed
in East Germany are so short of bog roll
they're wiping their backsides on classified
documents.

—You have to wonder, don't you? Who makes these
things up?

§52

It was still summer, but soon enough September would begin to look autumnal and presage a winter of almost unimaginable cold.

To be sitting by a sun-dappled lake on the edge of the arctic circle, sipping a Belgian beer, watching sand martins and swallows take insects on the wing, made life in London seem exactly where it was—a thousand miles away.

"You know," said Pastorius, "your friend Kostya might have fucked it up for us all."

"How so?"

"You have been bored."

"Are we back to Hamlet again?"

"Whereas I have been happy."

"Busy doing nothing?"

"Which, as we know, is a crime."

"You didn't have to listen to Prudence Latymer . . . and while you oblige me by sitting through the worst that British cinema has to offer . . . you don't have to."

"Kostya . . . has made us spies again. I was happy as a sleeper. I might even say I was happy as a travel agent. But you, you want the bit between your teeth, don't you?"

"I was content enough trucking the vodka around."

"But now you seem to have a real spy. And if you have a real spy . . . so do I."

Kostya had shown up the night before at the hotel in Persereiikkä and paid in full for the seventy-two bottles of 105 proof vodka currently winging their way across the lake, with all the potential for drunk, puking and blindness.

Wilderness had watched the Beaver take off, as improbable as an albatross or a giant bumble bee. Wings too small, feet too big. As speed and lift broke the meniscus of the water it was as though something organic had snapped and the plane popped skyward.

Now it was returning, just visible in the east, all but touching the treetops. He doubted they'd flown much higher at any point on the trip.

"Of course—"

Pastorius paused as the Beaver dropped sharply, as though it would just bounce off the water.

"Of course what?"

"Of course we still don't know he's a spy. And if he's not a spy then he's just a crook—in short, he's one of us."

"Oh, he's a spy alright. We just haven't proved it yet."

"And were he to be a spy . . . what is there to spy on? The trees and the lakes are all too apparent . . . the mines are underground . . . there's no industry to speak of and absolutely no military bases. The Russians and the Americans have photographed every square metre and the Swedes have mined the highways. In short, everyone knows everything. We are the naked country. Stripped bare as your Lady Godiva in our spurious neutrality."

The Beaver dipped to the left, the near wing seemingly inches above the water—a graceful 180-degree turn—the engine died and as the propeller fluttered down to zero Momo set the plane neatly at the end of the jetty.

A thing of beauty, Wilderness thought. Some part of him wished he'd learned to fly, that would have given an extra touch of credibility to being in the RAF—but he hadn't even finished basic training before MI6 had nabbed him.

The door opened. Bruce stood on the jetty, stretched, yawned, yelled.

"You bastards. You pair of complete and utter fucking bastards!"

Momo threw a large plastic sack out of the plane, to land at Bruce's feet.

"Stuff, you said. We'd be carrying 'stuff' back. This isn't stuff, it's shit! Leastways it smells like shit. My plane stinks like a Borroloola dunny on a summer's day. You bastards!"

"What's he talking about?" Pastorius asked.

"Niilo, if I told you, you wouldn't believe me."

"And there's six of them! You fuckers!"

Over beer and more beer, Momo said, "All those Russian phrases you had me learn were no fuckin' use. All the Ivans do is grunt."

All? There'd been four—Здравствуйте (hello)—Джо послал нас (Joe sent us)—Положите их сюда (put them here)—Спасибо (thank you).

"OK. Next time I'll come with you."

"For real?"

"Why not? I've spent my life since I was eighteen studying Russia and Russians and this side of the lake is the closest I've ever been. Who knows? I might even put a toe over the border."

"If you like I could fly that bit further, kick you out and let you walk back. Shit bags, Joe. You've got me hefting shit bags around for a living. The next time England takes on the Krauts you can whistle *Land of Hope and Glory* and fly your own fucking Spitfires."

§53

Wilderness found his way to "Dispatch," one floor below ground level at chancery.

It was a little like being backstage in a theatre—more like a packing shed than an office. England was not on display—no gilt, no paintings on loan from the National Gallery, no mirrors, and just one royal photograph above the desk and that both old (George V & Queen Mary) and dusty.

A bloke in a brown warehouse coat looked at the sacks. Then he looked at Wilderness.

"Six at once?"

"Yes, please. Next diplomatic bag."

The man bent down and sniffed.

"Bit whiffy, aren't they?"

Oh, the gentle English art of understatement.

Then he bent lower, inhaled too much and began waving his hand madly as though trying to disperse a fart.

"S'truth!"

Wilderness knew he was dying to ask what was in the sacks, but the rules didn't allow for that. And if he mentioned a Borroloola dunny the man would be none the wiser.

"SIS, you say? What department?"

Forensics or Decryption? Wilderness wondered. He settled on Forensics. If they could clean it up to the point where text was visible then the paper could go to Decryption.

There might, he thought, be something in this, there might not. Either way there was a pleasing surge of satisfaction in being able to mail six sacks of shit to MI6.

Time to celebrate.

On the way home he bought two bottles of Moldavian claret.

§54

A couple of hours later Janis Bell appeared on his doorstep, burdened with five boxed reels of film.

"What, no wine?"

"Take them off me. They weigh a ton."

"What is it?"

"What you asked for. *Alfie.*"

Wilderness took the reels off her and dumped them on an armchair. Janis kicked off her shoes and parked herself on the sofa. He nipped into the kitchen, thinking to open the Moldavian claret, when she called after him.

"You haven't shown any films lately. Farr says he hasn't seen hide nor hair of you."

That gave him pause for thought. Suspicion always did. Her tone verged on making the sentences into questions.

He waited until a shriller, more enquiring "Joe?" echoed out of the sitting room. Instead of wine he picked up a bottle of the Lapland vodka and two shot glasses. Set all three down on the coffee table.

"And what conclusion do you draw from that, in your capacity as the future head of service?"

"That you've found something else to do. Either you're working a fiddle, as you seem to have done everywhere you've ever been posted, or you've found something genuine."

"Run that adjective by me again."

"Genuine . . . legitimate . . . of interest to the Service."

"And if I tell you?"

"Oh, I'm not Mrs. Burton's girl. I'm not your girl either. I'm my own. Whatever you tell me you tell me, and it stays with me."

"What if I say it's a matter of national security?"

"I'd say you were full of it."

"OK. Curl up, have a drink and I'll tell you. Vodka OK?"

He gave her a neat shot of moonshine, without warning, that left her gasping, "Water! Joe, for fuck's sake, water!"

"So glad to have got your attention."

She knocked back half a pint of tap water in a single gulp.

"You sod," she said at last. "You sod. So that's it? Eh? Reindeers and moonshine not polka dots and moonbeams? You sod."

"You'll understand if I say the second glass is just a prop. You couldn't pay me to drink any more of that, at least not neat—and, by the bye, it's considered the good stuff."

"Who in God's name does drink it?"

"Much of Helsinki, it would seem—suitably thinned with tonic water, and given a measure of taste with a twist of lemon or a splash of Martini, I'd guess. Unthinned, taken neat . . . most of the Russians out at their base in Rayakoski."

"Oh God . . . you're selling vodka to the Russians? Have you gone completely potty?"

"No. Think of it as bait."

"Bait?"

"I've hooked a KGB captain."

"You're kidding?"

"Absolutely not."

"What? He just strolled over and asked to buy a bottle?"

"More or less."

"Can you be certain he's real?"

"Yep. Knew him in Berlin during the airlift. And it's bottles plural. Seventy-two so far. Kostya will be running some sort of racket on the other side. Selling on at a profit. It's what he did in Berlin."

"So two peas in a pod, eh?"

"I'll try to take that as a compliment. The difference is . . . in those days a racket was just a racket. Now it looks more like a mask for something else. We played at spies . . . the smuggling, the black market were what was real. Now . . ."

"Now you think he's spying for real?"

"I know he is."

"On what?"

"I don't know. Which is where you come in."

"I do?"

"If you want to run MI6 you have to start somewhere."

"OK . . . you really do have my attention now."

"Find out what in Lapland, anything north of Rovaniemi, is worth his attention on a regular basis. Go through what we have on industry, armaments . . . anything. Including things the Finns might not think we know about. Pastorius is quite convinced there are no Russian agents on his patch, so I need to know more about his patch."

"You know your man . . . but Pastorius knows his territory. If he says there's nothing worth spying on . . ."

"I suppose that sentence had to end in three dots."

"How long have I got?"

"Well . . . I'd like to be out of here by Christmas."

§55

It took forty-eight hours for the shit to hit the fan.

He was in what passed for his office, a room as perfunctory as his apartment. One desk, one chair—no in/out trays, as though neither person nor paper would ever pass his way—and a phone that never rang.

Burton just stood in the doorway and yelled.

"In my office now!"

He followed, far from meekly. Janis Bell managed to find herself in need of a file as they passed through her office and put a six-foot metal door between herself and any scrutiny.

Then they were in Burton's office. The door slammed behind Wilderness, and Mrs. Burton assumed her position behind the desk, pigeon-puffed with rage.

"How dare you?"

Wilderness had heard that phrase all his life. From schoolteachers, officers . . . people who felt the dignity on which they stood had been violated by oiks like him. He still didn't know what it meant.

"I've no idea what you're talking about," he lied.

"Really? So you know nothing about six sacks of—I can hardly bring myself to utter the word . . . why . . . I'm getting . . . I'm getting complaints from Dispatch here, from Forensics in London. Six sacks of paper . . . covered in—"

"I'll make it easy for you. The word is shit."

"And you mailed six sacks of it to London! In the diplomatic bag!"

"Mrs. Burton. Before you bollock me any further, why don't you wait and see what Decryption have to say. It isn't ordinary paper, it's classified Soviet paper . . . which just happens to be covered in—"

"Do not say it again!"

She sat down in her chair with a thump—if a thump could sound petulant, it was a petulant thump. She pushed the London memos towards him.

"Read for yourself."

"No thanks. Nothing they say, until Decryption get back to me, matters a damn. Let's just wait."

"How did you come by classified Soviet documents?"

"I'm a field agent, it's a field matter, you know that."

"I'm the Head of Station!"

"Which is why you have to be free to disown any field agent, if you have to. Right now, the less you know the better."

"So you're keeping me in the dark?"

"What you don't know can't hurt you. It's in everybody's interests."

If Wilderness had been Head of Station, his next sentence would have consisted of the words "off" and "fuck."

"Get out!" she said. "Get out! Get out! Get out!"

Such are the limitations of a vocabulary lacking constructive obscenity.

§56

He packed for the north. He took Janis Bell's hint and let her book him and his projector into a couple of villages on the Gulf of Bothnia.

Where Farr had managed to find *Les Vacances de M. Hulot* with Finnish subtitles was a mystery little short of a miracle. It received the best reception yet, and Wilderness began to wonder if Jacques Tati hadn't hit upon the universal language.

He'd time getting to Lapland for Kostya's next visit. And if Momo didn't care for *M. Hulot*, there was always *Alfie*.

§57

Wilderness realised he could set his clock by Kostya. If not always punctual, then predictable. He was at the White Nights when Wilderness walked in.

They had dinner together. The tourists milled around. Most of them seemed to prefer being outside with a good chance of seeing the northern lights, but there weren't half as many as there'd been in June. Lapland was about to enter the temporal equivalent of no man's land.

Kostya had stopped looking around. He might even have relaxed.

They talked about their childhoods—Wilderness took the attitude that the KGB were rubbish if their file on him hadn't mapped out his ragged years in Stepney and Whitechapel—and talked freely . . . of death and poverty and theft.

All the same, he was struck by the contrast. Throughout the starvation years, the purge years of the 1930s, Kostya had led the privileged life of the child of a high-ranking party member—no holes in his trousers, no shortage of shoes and, above all, no father to beat the living shit out of him on a whim. First in Leningrad and then in Moscow, as the great purge, the Yezhovshchina, left the Party looking gap-toothed and moth-eaten and the survivors moved inward and upward. His mother's career prospered under the patronage of Krasnaya, and as long as Krasnaya was safe so were Kostya and his mother.

"If we had a god, Krasnaya would be my godmother."

Wilderness did have a godmother. He just couldn't remember who it was. Some aunt out in the wilds of Essex? One of those pinafored, flour-dusted, hairnet and safety pin, needle and thread old gypsies out beyond Epping? Certainly no one as glamorous—was that the word?—as Krasnaya. He could still see that poster in his mind's eye. One of the London galleries had included it in an exhibition of Soviet art about ten years ago. Along with all the miners, factory workers and tireless peasant harvesters—pick-axes, hammers and sickles—there was the warrior goddess with baby and Fedorov machine gun. The unflinching gaze of Krasnaya, her eyes locked onto infinity and the promise of an attainable, socialist future. And the boy in the crook of her left arm—no more than three or four, his eyes equally unflinchingly looking out at the observer.

If a Frenchman had painted the poster Krasnaya would have had one breast, or possibly both, exposed. But this was Mother Russia.

When they'd finished their meal, Kostya put a folded newspaper on the table—yesterday's *Paris Herald Tribune.*

"Enough for ninety-six. Can you manage ninety-six?"

"I think so. Sales going well, are they?"

Kostya said nothing to this, but, thought Wilderness, if he's trying to kid me they're all given away in Rayakoski in the interest of boosting morale among the Ivans, silence will not work. He'd bet on half the bottles finding their way to Leningrad or Moscow, to the tables of the privileged, the "class" to which Kostya belonged.

"I think we can," he said. "We'll land at noon. On the dot."

After Kostya went up to bed, Wilderness hung around outside till midnight to see if he came out again. He didn't, but by midnight Wilderness was fed up waiting and went to bed anyway, none the wiser as to what Kostya was up to. It occurred to him to come straight out and ask him. But there was something of the hermit crab about Kostya. One alarming note, one wrong word and he'd be back in his shell.

§58

Wilderness borrowed a pair of overalls, which might have been white ten or twenty years ago, and flew with Bruce to the far side of the lake.

He'd seen Hamburg and Berlin from the gun turrets of Lancasters, flown with pilots only too willing to scratch the chimney tops to show him the ruins and show off their skills—but he'd never flown as low as this. Bruce skimmed the water like a flat stone thrown as they flew down the inlet, pulled up to the treetops where it narrowed, and dropped the Beaver down to the water again as though eighty-foot pines were no more than sheep hurdles.

He looked at his watch as they splashed down. It had taken just seventeen minutes.

Out of the trees crawled a battered Russian World War II half-track—a ZiS 42. Wilderness had seen plenty of those in Berlin—a half-destroyed half-track had sat in Unter den Linden for the best part of two years until someone thought to have it dragged away.

It crunched to a halt at the end of a makeshift jetty, everything beneath it crushed out of existence. Two of Kostya's men got out, a corporal and a private.

For a second the corporal looked at Wilderness as though he might ask a question, query his presence, thought better of it and just barked at the Ivan to unload the vodka.

It was all over in five minutes—no more than a dozen words uttered by either side, Wilderness's grasp of their language all but superfluous, and as the half-track backed away Wilderness stood by eight shit bags, looking towards Mother Russia and wondering.

"Chatty lot, aren't they?" Bruce said. "I know what you're thinking and the answer's no."

"Really?"

"You're thinking we could take a stroll in the woods, have a peek at Russia, maybe stick a foot over the line . . . see if it feels any different . . . like testing the bathwater with yer big toe. Forget it, Joe. All it takes is one idiot with a Kalashnikov."

Wilderness knew Bruce was right, and the world was full of lone idiots armed with a Kalashnikov or an M16. But this was Russia—the be-all and end-all of his job for twenty years. An interest rather than an obsession, but compelling nonetheless. And this might well be as close as he'd ever get. He imagined it was how astronomers felt, gazing at the moon and knowing they'd never get there.

§59

They'd been back the best part of an hour, more beer, more complaints, but more of the great pacifier—money—when Pastorius drove up.

"I kept an eye on your Russian as long as I could. He checked out, drove north. I didn't follow. I don't think he spoke to a soul, and the man on the desk says he neither made nor received any phone calls. You were the last person he spoke to and I fear you're barking up the wrong tree."

"You're telling me you believe him?"

"I'm saying no such thing, but since we have no evidence that he is spying then all we have to go on is your knowledge of him. Quite simply, based on past experience, would you trust him?"

Wilderness thought about this. It was a straightforward question without a straightforward answer. To say simply "He's Russian" seemed inadequate if acceptable enough.

"I . . . we . . . me and Frank Spoleto . . . got scammed by his mother during the airlift back in '48. Frank took it personally, but then he always does. It was a few hundred dollars, no more. Kostya had nothing to do with it. She set him up as surely as she set us up. If I'd not been there Frank would have thumped three hundred dollars' worth out of Kostya's hide. I paid Frank off, but he wouldn't do business with Kostya again. I did, occasionally. Nothing went wrong. But it was only a matter of months before the whole racket went tits up. Frank and I were pulled out of Berlin. Until now I'd no idea what had become of Kostya. He didn't show up in any Berlin or Moscow reports that crossed my desk. His mother did, but then she was the rising star of the KGB.

"If I'd heard that Kostya had quit the KGB and become a schoolmaster or a wages clerk, a poet or a composer, I'd be less surprised at that than at him making officer and political commissar. He was, he still is far too nervous. In a sense he's too nice . . . I've never been able to imagine him hitting anyone, let alone shooting anyone. Kostya was born to be anonymous. But he's like Christopher Robin or Lon Chaney Jr.—no one was ever going to let him be anonymous. He is forever his mother's son. I like Kostya. I might even trust him. I'd never say that of his mother."

"Fortunately we are dealing with the son."

"A small mercy."

"Unless of course his mother is back in Moscow pulling the strings."

"This, whatever it is, is far too small to interest her."

"But, as you said, 'She set him up as surely as she set us up.'"

"I honestly do not think that's what's happening."

"So what now?"

"Now? We show another bloody film and I crawl back into Helsinki by way of every one-horse town in Finland that's put itself on the embassy's list."

"For which we will be eternally grateful."

"Shut up, Niilo."

§60

Alfie was a hit. The sad but funny tale of a man utterly devoid of self-knowledge, a 1950s wide boy adrift in the London of the 1960s, uncomprehending as the city and its values change around him, armoured and immunised by a well-honed, conscience-denying philosophy that two hours later leaves him back at square one.

It left Wilderness wondering what might have become of him if Burne-Jones and MI6 had not "rescued" him. He was in the RAF, although he'd never wear a blue blazer with RAF wings on the breast pocket as Alfie did. And he'd been a London wide boy, a thief rather than a conman, but a skilled thief. He might have gone on making a living robbing the rich to feed . . . himself. And, God knows, MI6 had made enough use of his skills at safecracking and burglary.

Wilderness felt sorry for Alfie.

There but for the grace of Burne-Jones.

Momo and Bruce loved *Alfie*.

His last sight that night was of them pissed as farts, lobbing empty beer bottles into the lake and tunelessly singing over and over again,

"Wossitallabout
                 wossitallabout
                                 wossitallabout
                                                 Alfeeeeeeeee?"

§61

Wilderness saw no reason to go into the office. Given a choice between a grim apartment and a grim office, he chose the apartment. Difference? A kettle and packet of Co-Op tea, considerately packed into his suitcase by his wife.

But the telephone rang.

"Did you mail off more you-know-what in the diplomatic bag yesterday?" asked Janis Bell.

"Yep."

"You'd better come in. She's asking for you."

"I can read lists of touring Morris dancers and lecturers on the English water colourists at home if you just drop them off."

"Actually, the next tour is 'the English Folk Movement of the early Twentieth Century,' Vaughan Williams, Delius, and Cecil Sharp."

"Hours of harmless fun."

"All the same you have to come in—or she'll make my life hell."

§62

Janis Bell showed him into Burton's office with a look of contrived neutrality. It was almost as though they'd never met. Not a nod, not a wink, thank God. But if Janis was his coconspirator it was because she had chosen the role herself.

"It pains me to tell you this," Burton began. "But it looks as though you were right."

She shoved a teleprinter decode across the desk to him.

```
Parcel from agent most valuable.
Request more from same source.
Top priority.
```

But there was not a hint as to what in six shit bags had proved valuable.

"Read it? Good. Now, get out."

In the outer office, Janis Bell handed him the *Week in Culture*.

He shoved it unread into his pocket and made his way down to the cypher room.

"Don't tell me," Chaplin said. "Your grandmother just died."

"No, it was the family dog."

"Fido?"

"Rover. I'll just jot down a quickie for you, Charlie. Won't take a minute."

Wilderness to Eddie:
```
—What was on the bog paper?
```

The Replies:
```
—About seven-eighths of a detailed plan for the
 New Year Red Army exercises in Murmansk and
 Soviet Karelia. With clear indication that it
 is just another exercise not you-know-what.
```

Wilderness agreed with the anonymous assessor. It was "valuable." Every year in the DDR, the joint forces of the Warsaw Pact staged military exercises all around Berlin. And NATO never knew whether it was exercise, dress rehearsal or prelude to invasion.

```
—Anything else?
—They're still working on it. That and the
 package that arrived this morning. They're
 both pleased and annoyed. Pleased to have the
 intel, annoyed at how they get it. Your name
 would be mud here if it weren't shit. But I
 suppose you're earning your keep.
```

§63

Wilderness drove Professor Joan Cooper LRAM to small towns in the west and found that he had quite a taste for Delius, who had previously played only to his deaf ear. Professor Cooper was good company, but he knew in his bones it would be a mistake to get to like this aspect of the job—to fall for your own cover.

Ten days . . . or maybe two weeks later—he was losing track of time, as each day and each town began to blend into the other, and the cover swallowed him alive—he was back in Paradise Apartments.

When he opened the door to Janis Bell, she was clutching neither wine nor films, but a sheaf of paper.

She knelt on the floor, on the patternless rug in eight shades of brown, and spread out her pages.

"Shall I begin at the end?" she said.

"Why not."

"That chap from the Supo who told you you were in the town where nothing ever happened was right. There's nothing going on north of Rovaniemi that the Russians won't know about. It's all too . . . easy. My conclusion is . . ."

Her hand slapped down firmly on a bundle of paper.

"The only thing worth spying on in Lapland is *you*."

This had occurred to Wilderness.

"I'm the reason Kostya is out in the open, but I don't think I'm the reason he's there. I've heard your summing up . . . give me the arithmetic."

"I did what you asked. I looked for anything that might be worth their attention. I ruled out forestry and agriculture right away. Industry? They mine significant amounts of copper and nickel. Again . . . how could that be a secret worth spying on? It isn't. But . . . statistics . . . Finland produces more refined nickel than any other country on Earth . . . far more than is mined . . . so it's an importer of nickel . . . and hence probably the world's biggest smelter of nickel."

"Where? All over the country?"

"Nope . . . just a couple of sites . . . one in Harjavalta . . . that's in—"

"Satakunta . . . about five hundred kilometres from Lapland."

"Ah, you know it?"

"I was there last week. They loved Elgar."

"OK. Searching for sarcasm but can't detect any. Shall I continue?"

"Please do."

"I asked myself, again, what might be worth it? What might be secret? This is what I came up with . . . just after the treaty with the Russians Finland developed a rapid smelting process . . . patented in 1949 . . . extended to cover improvements in 1963. It's that process that's made Finland top dog in refined nickel. And I think this might be it."

She sat back, heels tucked under her backside, looking just a touch smug.

"Let's have a drink," Wilderness said.

When she'd got a glass of Moldavian claret in her hand he said, "A couple of smelting plants, you said?"

She set the glass down and scrabbled among the pages.

"Yes. The other's at . . . er . . . I seem to be missing something."

"No matter."

"I'll remember. It'll come to me."

"It doesn't matter. And there's a reason it doesn't matter. You said the process was patented."

"Yep. Twice."

"Then anyone who wants to know how rapid smelting works doesn't need to spy. They can go to the patent office and ask to see the application. It isn't secret, just protected."

"Yes. Protected—under international law so they can't just steal it!"
Wilderness said nothing. Just looked at her and waited.

"Oh God. I've been a complete bloody fool, haven't I? Does Russia
give a flying fuck about international law?"

"Let's come at this sideways. You have your finger on the right page
but not the right picture."

"Sorry, Joe. I'm not following you here."

"My man back in London, Eddie, gave me a hit list of current Russian shortages . . . vodka, bog paper, nickel and copper were all on the
list . . . and I find myself wondering. Paper, vodka . . . nickel. How do
these all connect?"

"Rock, paper, scissors would make more sense. Oh God, please get
me another drink."

"Of course—and I'll ask Eddie in the morning."

$64

Wilderness to Eddie:
```
—Why are copper and nickel down?
```

The replies:
```
—Earthquake collapsed half a dozen copper mines
  somewhere near the Mongolian border last
  autumn. Altai? Anyway, it was big. Richter
  7.6. This January an explosion at Pechango
  near Murmansk took out one of their biggest
  nickel mines. Cause unknown. It used to be
  part of Finland. On older maps it's still
  Petsamo. If you want my two pennorth it's a
  blip. They'll fix it.
—Can you look into production? Annual stats et
  al?
—As if I'd nothing better to do.
```

§65

The next few runs became little short of domestic—almost conjugal. Having exhausted their life stories, Joe and Kostya took to playing chess after dinner in the bar at the White Nights. Three times out of four Kostya won. Wilderness reassured himself that it was Russia's national game, tempting the delusion that he might win at something more English such as darts or soccer and knowing full well he wouldn't. He could kick arse at three card monte, but you only played that with a mark and whatever Kostya was he wasn't a mark.

As Kostya's hand hovered over a bishop, Wilderness got fed up waiting and asked, "What are you up to?"

"I'm about to put you in check. Mate in three, I think."

"No—I mean here, here in Lapland."

"Joe, we've had this out time and again—"

"No we haven't."

"Yes we have. You just haven't said anything. It's all been going on inside your head."

Wilderness let it drop. Let his king topple. Leaned back and gazed around the bar. The same old faces. The same half a dozen men in business suits he'd been seeing all summer. He thought too little of it. It was all too familiar. Part of the new-found domesticity of espionage. Once upon a time he might have enjoyed that—Berlin had been somewhat like that, sitting in *Paradies Verlassen* with the enemy in plain sight, with the enemy buying him cocktails, trading gossip, flirting with him. But that was BTFWWU—Before The Fucking Wall Went Up. A break point in history on a par with the ending of the last Ice Age.

Niilo withdrew the watch on Kostya with a single word, "Pointless."

Wilderness had a suspicion, that he wished was a theory, that he wished might be evidence. He did not tell this to Niilo—that too would have been pointless. But it was, all the same, all he had.

§66

West Berlin: November

They sat in the mayoral Mercedes-Benz at the corner of Hessische Straße, about a hundred and fifty yards east of the Invalidenstraße Crossing—East Berlin to the British Sector of West Berlin: Germans Only.

Nell had flown in from Bonn specially for the meeting—any chance to be at home again, to sleep in her own bed, eat in her favourite café, walk on what she saw as "her own streets."

It had been a waste of time. A risk and a waste of time. A risk in that a clandestine meeting in the Adlon Hotel with the Soviet ambassador to the DDR would go down like a lead balloon in Bonn—when or if they found out. A waste of time in that Piotr Andreyevich Abrassimov had appeared to have only two replies to anything Brandt said: "No" and "We shall see." Perhaps that was the secret to all diplomacy—never commit, never reveal, never agree, never disagree. Nell had spent over an hour in the same room as the ambassador, and while it was obvious that he liked Brandt as a man—there had been not a hint of personal animosity—what the ambassador thought about the policy suggestions Brandt had ventured was a mystery. She wondered if the mayor was any clearer about it than she was herself.

He wasn't asleep, he just had his eyes closed. Rubbing at his forehead as though easing pain within.

"*Keine Rose ohne Dornen.* No rose without thorns," Nell said.

"What?"

"He rolled out that phrase as though it were poetry. What does it mean?"

"I've no idea."

"Is the rose meant to represent a unified Germany at some future date? And the thorns are what . . . every obstacle he'll ever throw at us?"

"Nell, honestly, I didn't give it a second thought. He was just showing off his knowledge of German idiom."

The car jerked forward as the queue speeded up.

The East Berlin border guards were checking papers. Less than precise, more than random.

Nell wondered if they were doing this—late on a Sunday evening as hundreds of West Germans allowed east to visit "those left behind" made their way home—just to slow down the mayor. But there were no markings on the car, no flag—just an ordinary top-of-the-range Mercedes in a pleasing shade of black. At this distance there was no way they could know who was sitting in the back seat.

When at last the car rolled under the floodlights into the concrete corridor, and a border guard shone his torch on the documents the chauffeur held out to him, the inspection was cursory—he didn't even glance at Nell and Brandt.

§67

When the chauffeur asked "where to?" Nell was surprised Brandt said "office" not "home." It was Sunday, a dark, miserable, drizzly Sunday evening. Berlin did dark and miserable in spades—she would not change it for the world. But surely even Brandt would want to be home with his wife and kids . . . with Rut and Lars and Mathias? At the very least there'd be a new episode of *Bonanza* to watch.

From her office she heard a thump. Something falling. Someone falling?

She found Brandt sprawled on the floor, out cold.

She should have spotted the signs. The fingers pressed to the temple, the uncharacteristic snappiness about Abrassimov's rose conundrum.

She found a pulse in his neck, heard the rasp of his struggle to breathe and grabbed the phone.

"Doctor to the mayor's office now!"

"Fräulein Burkhardt. It's Sunday, there's no one here. Only cleaners."

"Find someone. Brandt is ill!"

A few moments later an elderly cleaning lady shuffled in. Put her bucket and mop by the door and leant down over Brandt.

Nell had him on his back, a cushion under his head, his tie loosened. He lay exactly where he'd lain the day she'd found him listening to Schubert.

The cleaner slapped Brandt sharply on both cheeks.

Nell was about to yell out, when the cleaner said, "He's only fainted. Trust me. I seen lots of it during the war. People dead from the blast. Not a bleedin' mark on 'em. People blown apart. And people who just drop down dead on account they was tired o' living. Most of 'em . . . most of 'em had just fainted with the shock of it all. C'mon Mr. Willy . . . Wakey wakey!"

Brandt's eyes opened. His breathing slackened off.

"I . . . I was choking . . . I thought I was choking."

"'Appen you was, but you'll be right as a rain after a nice cup of tea."
She turned to Nell.

"Won't he, dearie?"

And Nell realised what her role was in the crisis.

§68

Stretched out on the office couch, Brandt balanced a cup and saucer on his sternum and seemed more inclined to inhale tea than drink it.

"I meant to tell you . . ."

Nell said nothing. Wondered how long he'd pause.

"Bonn," he said at last.

"Yes. That place in the west. Think of all the interesting cities on the Rhine and then pick the one that isn't. Bound to be Bonn."

"Have you finished?"

"Never. But I am listening."

"The new coalition of the Bundesrepublik . . ."

In the pause Nell heard bad news begin to whisper. He'd said nothing in the last few days about this latest development, the end of Ehrhard's government. All the same she knew he wanted a government post—Minister of Research. A title she found hard to credit with meaning.

Was he now going to tell her he'd got it? Or perhaps, he hadn't and they'd be returning full-time to Berlin?

"I'm not going to be the minister of research."

Nell said nothing. The whisper was still there. Berlin? Bonn?

"They—that is, the party—are rather insistent I become foreign minister."

"They? The party?"

"Yes."

"And the new chancellor?"

"I thought you'd have something to say about that."

"Do we work with Nazis?"

"Kiesinger was a *Mitläufer*. A fellow-traveller. Never . . . committed to the party."

"A Nazi all the same."

"I can't remember who said this—indeed I wish I had—Kiesinger is a man 'always on the lookout for a four-leaf clover.'"

"An opportunist."

"If you want to put it as cruelly as you can—yes. Now, Nell, you won't work with a Nazi—goes without saying. But can you work with an opportunist?"

Nell said nothing.

The cleaning lady came back to check on her patient.

"Sit up straight, Mr. Willy, an' drink yer tea."

And Nell wished she could speak to Brandt as plainly as that.

§69

Persereiikkä

The first heavy snow fell in early November. Snow that would not be washed away by rainfall or melted by the sporadic sunshine. The thermometer had plummeted.

Out at the lake Momo was dismantling their camp.

"What do you do now?"

"Do?"

"Where do you . . . live?"

"Oh, we built a cabin in the woods about half a mile back. Three walls of pine stuffed with whatever we could pack in the gaps. Straw mostly. You got any books in English you're through with, bring 'em up next time. We can always use books in winter. I read that *War and Peace* a couple of years back. We kind of hibernate, y'know, like a couple of old bears. 'Cept we do emerge before spring from time to time . . . wine, women, song . . . work. Did you know lady bears don't even wake up to give birth?"

Having nothing to say to this, Wilderness ignored it.

"Work? So you carry on flying?"

"Some. We fly some. Tomorrow we'll fit skis to the Bobcat. They're on a pantograph . . . y'know, like the top of a tram. There's up for wheels and down for skis. All depends on the terrain. But you can bet your last razoo that we'll be landing on snow from now on. But . . . you bring me nicely to a point. How many more Russian trips were you expecting?"

"I hadn't thought. Enough to keep my Russian on the hook till I find out what he's up to."

"Well I'll tell you now, just looking at the sky . . . forget it. You're in *Napapiiri*."

As Momo looked up, Wilderness did too. The eastern sky was curiously pink. He'd never seen that before. Some phenomenon of light, cold and latitude, all melding into pink. Pink was a colour almost anyone would associate with warmth . . . his twin babies, the cat's nose, the wife's knickers . . . but it didn't look that way.

"*Napapiiri*?"

"Means you're inside the arctic circle. So don't be fooled by a good summer. Once the lake freezes . . . you can forget it. There's nowhere on the far side flat or smooth enough for wheels or skis and I won't land skis on ice . . . too fuckin' dangerous. You can go into skid and who knows where the fuck that might end. Wrapped around a fir tree with your bollocks up in the branches with the pine nuts. The lake'll freeze solid any day now. And I do mean solid. Right now the ice is like glass. Thin and brittle. Solid—you can stomp on it with pit boots and not see a crack—for all I know you could shoot holes in it and not see it shift. Before it freezes solid we'll haul the Beaver out of the water, and once we do then the Russian run's over."

"Of course," Wilderness said. "I wouldn't want to put you at risk."

For a moment Wilderness thought Bruce might laugh, but then it was immediately obvious he was holding laughter in to make another point.

"Joe—you are a risk, everything you do is a risk. Don't get me wrong, you're a nice guy—not like those ponces I served with in the RAF—but I hate this spook business and I won't be sorry to see the back of it. The Helsinki run? Happy to carry on if you are—as long as we can put the bobcat down somewhere, we can get the vodka and you can peddle it down south. Come spring—if you're still here I'd rather not resume flogging vodka to the Russians. So, if you want to nick this bloke . . . you're gonna have to spin him a yarn and spin it pretty damn quick."

"Not sure I can do that. My people want me in the east—more villages, more films. My arrangement with Kostya is for December. An appointment I mean to keep."

"Then, like I said, you're going to have to spin him a yarn."

"I've been doing that for weeks. I'm just hoping he shows up regardless of the weather. He's not a flyer . . . he may well not work it out."

"If you can nick him . . . what do you want to do? Arrest him?"

"I don't have that authority. I could shoot him."

"So, you're licensed to kill? Like 007?"

"No. That double-0 stuff is just bollocks. I mean, if I could get him somewhere as remote as this I could just shoot him and no one would ever find the body."

"Bears might."

"Do bears eat dead people."

"Course they fuckin' do. They eat dead anything."

"Then I refer you to my previous answer."

"Joe, there are times you rip me up. For a cockney spiv you can't half turn on the toff. 'I refer you to my previous answer'—you wanker."

$70

Mid-December

The east looked pretty much like the north, more lakes, more villages, more polished pine rooms, more saunas. Wilderness took his "British Night Out" to Mikkeli (four times) to Imatra (three times) and to a couple of dozen villages along the Karelian border with Russia, up as far as Lake Pielinen. On several occasions he calculated he was less than a hundred miles from Leningrad. Winter brought one blessing—the exquisite poets, the chroniclers of English folk music and the historians of Celtic archaeology didn't want anything to do with a sub-zero Finland or a Finland under snow. Wilderness travelled in white silence.

Momo proved to be the bellwether of Finnish taste. The avant-garde received a glacial gratitude and the *Carry On* films left them wanting more.

It became almost a delight—but not quite—to get back to Helsinki and news from home.

Eddie to Wilderness:
—I've got a barrow-load of statistics for you. Boring as hell but you did ask.

Wilderness could not remember why he'd asked. He glanced through, flipping pages far too quickly. It had taken him over an hour to decode and he was already getting impatient.

—Most nickel comes out of former colonies. Belgian Congo, Northern Rhodesia, now just called Congo and Zambia. China's on the rise, but still lags a long way behind the Congo. USA hardly charts, UK not even on the map. Russian production fair to middling.

Get on with it, Eddie!

   —But here's something you didn't ask about.
   Cobalt. Number 27 on the periodic table. Most
   cobalt is derived from nickel ore. It's not
   rare. 32nd most common element on Earth. But
   there's rarity and rarity. Most nickel ore
   comes out of central Africa. Most refined
   cobalt comes from Finland, simply because
   they import and refine so much nickel on top
   of what they mine themselves. I can't find
   any figures for Finnish cobalt for the last
   two years. Or for that matter for Russian
   cobalt. But I've gone over all the stats
   for cobalt from the Congo since 1948. The
   Congo got its independence from Belgium in
   1960. Ever since then it's been in a state of
   intermittent civil war, Katanga, Lumumba and
   so on . . .

Get on with it, Eddie!

   —. . . and that's disrupted production and
   accounting. Figures for 1959 are pretty
   consistent with figures for the previous ten
   years. No figures for 1960. 1961 appears
   to record a surge in production that I
   find unbelievable. Production drops every
   year since, so it looks as though the war
   is taking its toll. It doesn't make sense.
   I would have expected a pattern showing
   production trailing off right from the
   outbreak of hostilities in 1960—the one
   year for which I don't have figures. So I
   went over them all again. You know what?
   Sometime between the 1959 stats and the 1961
   stats some dozy apeth put the decimal point

in the wrong place. There was no surge and
production has trailed off steadily for over
five years. I reckon that there is only 10%
of Congolese cobalt in "circulation" than
what is currently estimated from the stats.
For all that it's a common element, the world
is short of cobalt right now. As I said,
there's rarity and rarity. Shares in cobalt
stocks may be undervalued by 40-50%. If I
were that sort of bloke, and I'm not, I'd be
buying cobalt stock as fast as I could.

§71

"I'm sort of following you here, Joe . . . but what does it mean? What does it all add up to?"

Janis Bell tucked her legs up. Wilderness had long ago concluded she was part cat.

"Let me begin with a tangent."

"If you must."

"Do you remember the *Tsar Bomba* the Russians set off over Novaya Zemlya in '61?"

"Do I? I went on a demo in protest in my last year at Cambridge!"

"Cambridge? OK. Here . . . they were somewhat closer to it. The bomb broke windows even in Sweden. It was five hundred megatons, and utterly impractical . . . can't fit it onto a missile, few planes are big enough to carry it and even then you're sending the crew on a suicide mission. It may just be the most pointless big bang in history. Five years later the Russians haven't attempted anything else on that scale and no one is copying them."

With a cheek he admired rather than resented, Janis Bell took herself off to the kitchen and returned with wine and glasses.

"I get the feeling it's going to be a long night."

"So . . . if big bombs have proved their uselessness, what is a country to do?"

"I dunno . . . join CND?"

"Think about it, Janis."

She knocked back a big gulp of red, did her best to assume the expression of someone drinking and thinking. Then another.

"Mini," she said at last.

"Eh?"

"You make the Morris Mini of bombs. Put the engine on sideways or summat like that. It's a metaphor, you will understand."

"I will?"

"Make something smaller and better."

"By George, I think she's got it."

"So . . . how do you make a smaller atom bomb as effective as a big one."

"Sorry, Professor 'Iggins. I shot my bolt with the Mini."

"You make the outer casing out of cobalt-59."

"In what way does that differ from cobalt?"

"It is cobalt. Cobalt-59 is the atomic mass of cobalt's most stable isotope."

"I hear a 'but' coming."

"But cobalt-59 is turned into cobalt-60 by the thermonuclear explosion that sets off a chain reaction and beta decay. Cobalt-60 is not a stable isotope. It's a law of nature, in a manner of speaking, that matter is always in search of stability. Imagine a sinking ship jettisoning cargo until it's buoyant again. Unstable isotopes throw out stuff until the atom is stable. The stuff-thrown-out, for want of a better term, is what makes for radioactivity. It stops when the atom is stable again—the eventual stable atomic isotope from cobalt-60 is nickel-60. Meanwhile cobalt-60 is highly radioactive. It has a half-life of 5.27 years."

Janis Bell shook her head like a wet dog on the threshold.

"Hmmm . . . Sort of leaves me breathless. Dumb admitted here. What does that mean?"

"It means that its radioactivity diminishes by half every 5.27 years. Anywhere the fall-out from a cobalt bomb lands will be radioactive and uninhabitable."

"For . . . 5.27 years."

"No . . . halving the radiation every 5.27 years still leaves you with a toxic level a hundred odd years later. It can't be outlasted. You can't live in a fallout shelter for three generations."

"So our American cousins digging big holes in the ground are wasting their time?"

"Yep."

"And how many of these . . . er . . ."

"They're known as dirty bombs."

"How apt. How many dirty bombs would it take to wipe out life on Earth?"

"Not many . . . trade winds would do the work the bomb couldn't do for itself."

They'd reached a natural break. Wilderness poured himself a drink and listened to the wheels of cognition engage in Janis's mind.

"OK. Dumb again. So I shall ask the silly question. What's all this got to do with your pal Kostya?"

Wilderness was still wondering whether to answer. He had an answer. He'd been kicking an answer around for two days now and still was not convinced of it. It made sense. It did not make sense. It added up. It did not add up.

"He's not spying, he's buying."

§72

"Russia has suffered disasters in nickel mining. As a result it is not producing cobalt. China is, but relations with China are not what they were. China will not sell to Russia. For Russia to buy on the open market, from the Congo or Zambia, risks alerting the British and hence the Americans. The simple solution is to buy next door, which just happens to be the world's largest producer of refined cobalt."

"Surely it has other uses than just making bombs more deadly?"

"Yes, it has. X-ray technology uses cobalt. Cobalamine, which is cobalt-derived, is also known as vitamin B12—"

"—OK. OK. Even I'm not naïve enough to think Russia is running a covert vitamin programme. But."

"But what?"

"But you still have no connection to Kostya or to Lapland."

"Did you find out where the Finns' other nickel refineries are?"

"Bugger. Not yet."

"You forgot?"

"Yes. I forgot. Sentence me to typing Ma Burton's letters for the next thirty years!"

§73

Wilderness set out his theory in a long, coded letter to Eddie.

The replies:

—I said I didn't have figures for Russian cobalt production. You might deduce that as they're stuffed for nickel they may well be stuffed for cobalt. But equally you might not. And just because Russia isn't producing cobalt right now it doesn't mean they haven't got stockpiles of the stuff. Are you sure about this?

—No.

—Okey dokey. So what, in your uncertainty, do you mean to do about our old pal?

—Confront him.

—I get the feeling you've been putting that off?

—I asked once and he just dodged the bullet.

—That's a metaphor, right?

—It was last time. It won't be this time.

—Oh fuckin' Ada.

§74

He arrived in Persereiikkä early. Not yet five and only vaguely dark as a full moon turned snow and frost into winter's wonderland. He had a couple of hours before Kostya would show up.

Pastorius arrived minutes later, sat opposite him in a booth in the bar at the White Nights. Plonked down a martini for each of them.

"Cheers."

"Are we celebrating something?"

"Of course. Did you think olives grow on trees? Yes. End of term. We break up 'for the hols' as you English say. Let's drink to that."

"What are you on about?"

"Look outside, Joe. Frost everywhere. The lake's frozen over. It froze six weeks ago, not long after your last visit."

"Have I really been gone that long? I've shown mouldy old British films in so many one-horse Karelian villages since then I've lost track of time."

"Well—the Beaver's out of the water. No more Russia runs."

He seemed inordinately pleased at the prospect. Held out his glass to clink. Wilderness didn't match him. His drink sat untouched between them.

"I'm still expecting Kostya."

"I'm afraid he won't be getting any more moonshine this winter."

"I told him I'd be here today. He thinks we have one more run left."

"Well . . . you'll have to disappoint him—if he comes. And I suppose he might. If he hasn't driven out to the far side of the lake, it's just possible he may not know it's frozen . . . he's Russian after all—what do they know about snow and ice? Or does he not realise the Aussies won't fly once it's frozen?"

"He's a city kid. And he does sort of define naïve. He always has."

"But you don't. You knew the lake would be frozen."

"Of course."

"Then why did you arrange to meet him today?"

Wilderness said nothing.

Pastorius stared out of the window

"Look at it. Would you take a plane up in this?"

At the second bidding he did look. Snowflakes the size of half crowns floating weightlessly in midair. In the west a plume of white vapour was winding its way into the moonlit sky, a floating stairway to the stars. He'd never noticed it before.

"Niilo, what's that?"

"What's what? Oh, you mean the smoke or steam or whatever. That's Hirviämpäri. About ten miles away."

"Hirviämpäri what? I've seen no heavy industry this far north."

"A nickel smelting plant. It's been shut down for the last eighteen months."

"Why have you never mentioned this?"

"You've never asked . . . and there has been . . . no, there still is . . . an element of secrecy."

"About what?"

Niilo seemed to shrug, stared down into his martini for a few moments.

"I know we are as nothing to you, to the Americans and possibly less to the Russians, but we are a nation, however small, however young—after all we are not yet fifty—and we have our secrets just as you do. Not, perhaps, the secrets of world annihilation but secrets nonetheless."

"Are you going to tell me?"

"Are you going to beat it out of me?"

"Of course not."

"An accident. Nothing sinister. An accident."

"I'm listening."

"A leak into the river. One hundred thousand kilos of nickel. It rendered the river toxic. Raised the nickel levels in the water to five hundred times what is held to be normal and then swept out into the Gulf of Bothnia. You couldn't drink the water, you couldn't wash in it and every life form that lived in it died. Do you understand now why we kept this secret?"

"Yes, and I'll keep your secret."

"The clean-up took more than a year. All this summer, right up until the end of last month the Hirviämpäri plant has been subject to modifications and checks and rechecks to ensure it never happens again.

The men in suits we see in the bar here, time after time—remember you said they didn't look like tourists? They're not. They're engineers, executives and government officials—all here to get Hirviämpäri up and running again. It reopened ten days ago. We are once again producing nickel—"

Not spying, buying.

"And cobalt?"

Not spying, buying.

"I'm not so hot on chemistry, but yes I believe that is a by-product."

Not spying, buying.

Wilderness excused himself. Put a phone call through to chancery and caught Janis Bell just as she was leaving for home.

"This won't take long. Does the name Hirviämpäri ring any—"

"Bells? Irony upon irony. Yes. That's the name I couldn't remember."

"OK. That's all. I know everything I need to—"

"Joe, she's on the prowl!"

"What?"

"Burton's bitten my head off a dozen times today. She knows something. Dunno what, but she knows. Maybe she's worked out you've gone north not east? Whatever you do next . . . and I've no idea how that sentence should end."

Wilderness had. He knew exactly how it was going to end.

§75

"Niilo, can you get up to Joeerämaa first thing in the morning?"

"Of course."

"Tell Momo and Bruce to make themselves scarce. You too. I'll be there about noon."

"Should I be asking you why?'

"No."

"And now?"

"Now, I play one last game of chess."

§76

Another copy of the *Paris Herald Tribune* slid across the table to him.

"A hundred and twenty? Or is that too many?"

Wilderness stuck out his fists, a pawn concealed in each.

"No, that's fine. Tap."

Kostya took white.

They played for over an hour and a half. Wilderness dug in. Losing struck him as far too symbolic. He sought new reserves of tenacity.

"Well played," Kostya said as his king fell to a bishop-knight pincer.

They met again at breakfast.

Wilderness glanced at the men in suits, the executives, the engineers, the government officials, once more outnumbered by the tourists as Christmas loomed.

Kostya looked at no one and nothing. They might have been invisible.

"Leave your car and come with me."

"Where to?"

"Up to the lake, to Joeerämaa."

"Why?"

"Something you should see."

"Something or someone? Joe, it would not be wise for me to meet your Supo man."

"That's OK. He doesn't want to meet you either."

Out on the snow, the Mog warming up, minutes before they set off, the receptionist came out and handed Wilderness a note:

Urgent. Call me. JB.

Bad timing.

Jenny Burton the Brocken Witch could go to hell.

$77

The morning was crepuscular. Nothing was light or dark enough. A dawn that refused to break and preferred to remain cracked.

Wilderness could see, had seen for weeks now, why the Finns got stuck on, and also probably stuck in, Lapland. It was strangely beautiful—he resisted words like "ethereal"—and even with the chugging of the Mog's engine strangely quiet. He doubted he could ever adapt to it—he was a city boy through and through, London . . . Berlin—but he could see why Momo and Bruce had.

Kostya looked slightly bored. The other city kid—Leningrad, Moscow. He said next to nothing, asked far too few questions, as though his curiosity for the landscape and for Wilderness himself had been muted. When they hadn't played chess they'd usually talked books—but even that seemed exhausted.

About an hour out Kostya said, "Joe, did you ever really think I might be defecting?"

"Probably not."

"You know, the only reason I make these trips in person is to get out once in a while. I thought I would enjoy being in a foreign country. I haven't been out of the Soviet Union for more than twenty-four hours since Berlin. If I'd had more time I might even have visited Helsinki. I would never defect. I'm loyal to my country, Joe. Whatever deals we have done—in Berlin or here—I remain loyal. Finland might be dull . . . and Murmansk is duller. But I'd never defect. Think of the embarrassment it would cause my mother. If I weren't loyal to Mother Russia I'd still be loyal to my mother."

At the lake, engine off, he heard the crunch of his boots on the snow. It was said you could tell how cold it was by the tone registered in the crunch. But one look at the lake told him. It was frozen solid.

"Is this where you take off?"

"It was."

He'd no idea where Bruce and Momo had their cabin, but hoped it was far enough away.

The Beaver was under the corrugated tin roof about thirty feet from the water—the plane Wilderness couldn't identify sat on the shore where it had always been, and there was no sign of the Bobcat.

"Is no one here?"

"Looks that way?"

"The men you said I should meet? The pilots?"

"Gone. The lake looks solid. I don't think you'll be getting a shipment today.

At this point Wilderness had been sure Kostya would smell a rat. Instead he put a foot on the ice and then another. Stamped as though proving its solidity to himself.

Wilderness had his last payment in a brown envelope, closed by a rubber band.

"You'd better have your money back, Kostya. No deal, no dollars."

Kostya stopped stamping on the ice and looked up. He was about six feet from the shore now. Wilderness threw high and badly. Kostya spun rapidly in an attempt to catch the package, slipped and slid another ten feet on his backside.

Kostya laughed to himself, bent to pick up the money, and when he turned Wilderness had his Smith & Wesson aimed at his chest.

"Joe?"

"Have you read *War and Peace*, Kostya?"

"Have you read *Oliver Twist*?"

"Touché. The chapter when Dolokhov leads his squadron out onto the frozen lake. The ice breaks. They drown. He survives. Tolstoy never explains how he survives, but it's obvious. Despite his wounds he reaches the other side of the lake. Abandons everyone else to their fate. Bit of a bastard, really."

"Joe, what is wrong?"

Wilderness put a bullet into the ice about a yard to Kostya's left. The ice cracked and the shot echoed for several seconds.

"Tell me the truth."

"The truth about what?"

Another bullet a yard to the right.

"Vodka my arse. Tell me why you're really here."

"That is why I'm here."

Three more bullets, rapidly, all around him. The echoes rebounding and rebounding.

Now Kostya clapped his hands to his ears. Now the ice beneath him began to move.

"I've wondered all along why you had to make these trips in person. It wasn't about money or not trusting your own men. And it sure as fuck wasn't the jolly day trip you mentioned on the way here. It was all so you could meet those grey-suited buggers at the White Nights. I was naïve. I had you watched to see where you went when you left the hotel, but you didn't need to leave the bleedin' hotel did you? All your contacts, from government and industry, were already there."

"Joe—for God's sake. I've no idea what you're talking about. Government officials? I can't meet government officials. I can't even meet your Supo man. The risk is too great. A KGB man caught in Finalnd, disguised as a German? They'd lock me up and throw away the key. If I could deal with the Finns why on earth would I be asking you to be the middle man in the vodka game?"

One more bullet.

Water began to lap around Kostya's boots.

Wilderness took a speedloader from his pocket, flipped the chamber and slipped in another six bullets.

"You were sent here to set up a deal. You're buying cobalt, because Russia is making a dirty bomb."

Kostya looked incredulous.

"Joe—if we wanted Finnish cobalt why would we not just send a trade mission to Helsinki and buy it openly?"

"Because the Americans threatened to nuke Finland when you silly buggers sold it MiGs—openly. So it all goes covert. Instead of a trade mission, they send you. The undercover man. But then you realised I was here and you had to do something to throw me off the scent."

"No, Joe. No."

One bullet, the ice broke and began to sink under Kostya's weight, water rolling over his boots, up to his ankles.

"Why are you here?"

"Joe, I'm sinking."

"Why are you here?"

"Joe, for pity's sake."

The ice tipped sideways. One leg vanished into the water.

"Why are you here?"

"Joe . . . Joe . . . Joe."

"Why are you here?"

Wilderness took aim at Kostya's head.

Kostya floundered, his gloved hands finding no grip on the ice.

He sucked in air, tried to shout and his voice all but failed him. Chilled to a croak.

"Because . . . because . . . Joe, I'm just a fucking *Schieber!*"

§78

Back at the White Nights, Wilderness found he'd missed another phone call.

You're fired. Report back now! Burton.

Only then did he realise who'd sent him the first message.

§79

"I got the into-my-office-door-closed treatment. Charlie had cracked your code. That was a surprise. I had Charlie down for a complete prat. I stood there like a fifteen-year-old schoolgirl caught skiving off hockey. She didn't ask me what I knew, she told me what I knew—the vodka, Kostya, the cobalt refinery . . . the lot . . . a catalogue of your sins—and mine. I was your collaborator . . . or was it conspirator? Either way I had betrayed her trust—not that she ever trusted me with a damn thing. I tried to warn you, but you never called."

"A slight confusion over initials."

"Oh fuck. Never thought of that. Anyway, she went ballistic. I don't know where she is now. When you didn't show up with your tail between your legs she just vanished. I'd guess she's in London."

"So would I."

"Joe, am I in trouble?"

"I think we both might be in trouble."

"Ah well, so much for my brilliant career."

Now the shoes came off, kicked into the middle of the room, and her head went back and her hands locked into her hair in a silent scream.

"I don't suppose you kept a bottle of best Lapland rotgut, did you? I think it's just come into its own."

When she fell into a woozy sleep, Wilderness put a blanket over her and emptied the cutlery drawer into a briefcase. He'd counted neither markka nor dollars but it hefted up as a small fortune.

He put a thousand dollars into one of the shoes she'd kicked off before hitting the bottle, and then he went to bed.

When he awoke Janis Bell had gone.

§80

It was a snowy Heathrow. The kind of landing weather to make the faint of heart grip the armrests white-knuckled. He could see nothing out of the window as the engines turned snow into dense white mist. As the plane slid along the tarmac it felt like being inside a glass snow globe, just waiting to be dropped from dead fingers.

A Special Branch copper intercepted him ahead of the queue for Passport Control.

"Mr. Holderness?"

It was Ernie Leadbetter. Wilderness didn't think they'd exchanged more than a dozen words, but he'd known him by sight for ten years or more. Leadbetter had always struck Wilderness as a copper who might have a bit of imagination—the kind of copper who knew enough not to dress like a copper—a deep blue Aquascutum overcoat wrapped around his boxer's frame, a black cashmere scarf and, rather than a grubby, greasy trilby, no hat at all. What was it about the Branch and hats? A hat passing as an identity?

"'Scuse the formality, sir, but identity—a quick look at your passport?"

Wilderness had it open at the photo page. Leadbetter nodded, waved at the bloke up front and steered Wilderness past the line and out into the Arrivals hall.

"I've a car waiting, sir. It's rush hour but they'll all be heading out of London, not in. We should be there in forty minutes or so."

He held open the back door of a Foreign Office Rover 95.

Wilderness wondered, and then he asked.

"Ernie, I'm not under arrest, am I?"

"Lord no—the Colonel just wants you there in time for dinner."

"So we're going . . . ?"

"To Campden Hill Square, sir."

Leadbetter closed the door, walked round to the other side, sat next to Wilderness and set the car in motion just by uttering the driver's name.

"Ernie," Wilderness said as the car took the ramp down to the London Road. "What rank are you now?"

"Chief Inspector, sir. Have been for two years now."

"Then drop the 'sir'. I'm just a sergeant and I haven't been promoted since 1948."

They said nothing for a while. Leadbetter was not the kind of man to want to bring Wilderness up to date on how his favourite soccer team had done over the past six months.

As they hit the Chiswick flyover, Wilderness said, "Ernie, what's the buzz back at the office?"

"You mean about yourself?"

"Of course."

"Let me put it this way . . . some of us are hoping for a bottle of duty-free vodka."

Well—if that was all they knew . . .

§81

Burne-Jones opened the front door in person. Less for him than for the wife who bustled out, swathed in fur and headscarf, before Wilderness had even rung the bell.

"Joe! Joe . . . Joe."

Each softer than the one before. Then the double kiss.

"Alec's such a rotter, nabbing you before you've even seen Judy. Must dash. Theatre, y'know."

Wilderness stood, gathering a fine layer of snow about his shoulders. Burne-Jones glared after his wife.

"Bloody woman. What she forgot to tell you was that I'm not monop-olising you at all. She and Judy are taking your children to a panto."

"Aren't they a bit young for that?"

"It's more for Madge than for them. She feels about panto much as she does about farce, and Lonnie Donegan as Wishee-Washee proved irresistible. If he sings *My Old Man's a Dustman* she'll be in seventh heaven. Now, don't just stand there. Come inside. It's going to be a bollock-freezer tonight."

Wilderness hung up his coat. Sniffed the air.

"Madge left us dinner?"

Wilderness had eaten hundreds of Madge's rather perfunctory pot-luck dinners.

"Of course. Quid pro quo. There's a nice little bourguignon on the hob. She's become quite the cook. Ever since she discovered *Len Deigh-ton's Cookstrip* she's been unstoppable. Calls it *cuisine à la spook* . . . her shorthand for it is spy-fry."

§82

". . . And then Burton told me I was fired. I took a couple of days getting back to Helsinki. For once it was convenient to show films."

"You ignored her?"

"I dragged my feet. Needed thinking time. And I find I can think very well if I'm sitting through a stock-in-trade British comedy I've already seen twenty times. Alec Guinness has such a soothing voice. When I got back to Helsinki, Burton wasn't there. She'd left a letter ordering me back to London. Following orders has never been my forte, but I wasn't going to argue with that. And I find myself wondering what I could have done to get myself sent back three months ago. I merely sent an encode to Eddie asking if you were in the picture. He said you were. I assume Burton was here, raising hell."

"More or less. Certainly wasn't out to make friends and influence people."

"So I cleared my flat . . . cleared my desk . . . although there was nothing on it . . . and . . ."

"And here you are."

"And here I am. Back in Blighty. Has the risk diminished?"

"You mean Thwaite? No, absolutely not. But they're on their Christmas recess already, so we don't need to worry about old Reg until the New Year. No . . . we need to worry about what you unearthed. You will recall I said not to go poking around?"

"Hardly matters now, does it?"

"It does and it doesn't. You haven't actually exposed the fact that the Finns are selling cobalt, that's a given, didn't need exposing—it's the business they're in. But you have rightly deduced the nefarious end product of one particular export of cobalt."

"The dirty bomb."

"Quite. Excellent work on your part, although I detect Eddie's hand in this too, but it raises a problem. You see, we already knew Finland was selling bomb-grade cobalt."

"Then what the fuck was I doing in Lapland and why wasn't that fact in my brief?"

"Slow down, Joe. Don't get mad. We already knew because the Finns aren't selling cobalt to the Russians. You utterly misjudged your old chum Kostya. It seems as though he really was just buying vodka off you."

"I don't get this. I don't get any of it. The Finns are selling bomb-grade cobalt. You don't deny that. If they're not selling it to the Russians then to whom are they selling it?"

"To us."

Wilderness heard his knife and fork hit the china. Had they fallen from his hands or had he slammed them down?

"We're making a dirty bomb?"

"'Fraid so. Out in Oz. Place called Maralinga in South Australia."

"And we need Finnish cobalt to do this? We've been ripping the heart out of Africa for a hundred years—it's what the fucking empire was for—surely we have all the copper, nickel and—fukkit—cobalt . . . we need."

"So one would think. But I'm told it's a question of purity. Too many impurities and the chain reaction fizzles out like a wet banger on Guy Fawkes Night. Not so much the quality of the ore as the quality of the refining. In that area the Finns lead the world. Quite possibly the only one in which they do.

"We've tried before, on a much smaller scale. But some bright spark thought we might give it one more go. Something to put us at the top table in the nuclear club. It's proved a divisive issue, to say the least. And the reason you weren't told about the Finnish connection was that you didn't have clearance. I didn't have clearance. When I read your encodes to Eddie I had to go upstairs and ask what it was all about. That's when . . . well I think words failed C. He asked where you were, but you were out of touch in Lapland by then. In the meantime Burton's man at the embassy had cracked the code you and Ed invented and she hit the roof. And it was blown. Too many people knew. Burton hasn't done herself any favours, insisting on her right to know as Head of Station. Ridiculous. Even the ambassador didn't know. I'm afraid Mrs. Burton's days in the service are numbered."

"Then promote the woman in her outer office. Janis Bell is twice as smart as Jenny Burton."

"I'll bear that in mind. And while we're discussing personnel. There remains the problem of you."

"I thought that might be the case."

"There are people who'd like to shoot you and people who want to give you a medal."

"So nothing's changed, then?"

"Bear with me, Joe. For a while—more a moment, actually—we thought we might have to take young Kostya out. All depended on how much you'd alerted him to what was really going on."

Wilderness would have hated that—for all his flaws, naïvetés really—Kostya was a likeable man—almost a friend, if field agents had friends. When he'd pulled him from the water, Kostya had sobbed like a boy. And when they'd followed the tyre tracks and found the Australians' cabin it had taken hours and hours to get him warm again. Bruce asking him, "What kind of a bastard are you, Joe?" Momo boiling kettle after kettle of water. And Kostya staring at him over the top of his mug of cocoa, with those big blue eyes, more in utter incomprehension at the betrayal of trust than in hatred.

"But you haven't taken him out and you won't."

[Pause.]

"No. No, we won't. Don't let this go to your head, Joe—but you did us all a favour. It was a dodgy, disgusting project. Absolutely divided the general staff and the top brass at the MoD. The idea that it might have been compromised was the last straw. The project's been axed. Much to the delight of the Australians who never wanted it there in the first place. One wishes they had said so sooner. I can't pretend you've returned home a hero . . . but . . ."

"But the world's a safer place because of me."

"Oh dear, I see it's gone to your head already."

§83

Judy collected him from Campden Hill. The winter hardtop on her two-seater MG glistening with snow under the lamplight.

She stood on the doorstep and hugged him. Blew her father a kiss from the palm of her hand.

"Chop chop, Joe. Can't hang about. Ma's on girl-duty. I said I'd relieve her before eleven."

She chattered amiably, affectionately. He did not listen.

By Regent's Park, Wilderness asked her to pull over and threw up at the side of the road.

"Anything the matter? Or is it just booze?"

He was staring into his own vomit. Staring at the clay-coloured slush he was standing in.

"Joe?"

"No. Not booze. Something else. I don't know what."

But he did.

"Will you make it home?"

"Yes. Just give me a minute."

Now he stared at the sky, slightly surprised not to see the sky over Joeerämaa or Persereiikkä, the London city sky perceived through a distorting haze of sodium lamps, but then everything had been a distortion—everything. He'd been living in a hall of mirrors.

§84

He lay on his back, staring at the silver stars Judy had painstakingly stuck to the Tuscan-blue bedroom ceiling—a ceiling that Wilderness could not help but think of as cobalt blue. Even the toothpaste was cobalt blue. He'd showered in seconds, but he'd scrubbed his teeth vigorously for minutes to lose the taste of vomit.

"Tell me," she said simply.

He said nothing.

She wriggled sideways and gently headbutted his shoulder like a demanding cat.

"Tell me."

"Alec's being very nice about it. I might just have received the gentlest bollocking of my life. But it remains. I fucked up. I didn't have enough facts so I invented something that made sense of the facts I did have."

"Y'know, when I was at Cambridge the lit critters had a word for that."

"What?"

"Fab . . . hang on . . . fab something . . . fabulation."

"Lies is simpler. Only one syllable."

"You lied to yourself, you mean?"

"Thus boredom doth make liars of us all."

"OK. Now you really have lost me."

"Liars, thieves and spies."

"Ah . . . back on the rails. I'm with you now, but let's drop it. Spilt milk, spilt vodka. Who really cares?"

"I came close to killing a man."

"An innocent man?"

"No . . . he was never that."

"And if I understand a lifetime with my father and the best part of fifteen years with you, the agent in the field, like it or lump it, is copper, judge, jury and occasional executioner. Lonely place, the field."

"Innocence doesn't matter. You lose your innocence the minute you strap on the holster. I almost killed . . . almost . . . a friend."

"Was that 'I almost killed a friend' or 'I almost killed someone who was almost a friend'? Almost in the latter instance meaning 'not quite.'"

Wilderness said nothing

"OK. Let's drop it. You're home now. This isn't the field, it's a queen-sized bed and I am your wife-sized wife."

She was silent for a few minutes but he knew from her breathing that she had not fallen asleep.

Then he felt her fingernails walking sharply up his spine and she began to sing softly.

"My old man's a spookman . . . he wears a spookman's hat . . ."

§85

In the morning Judy left five minutes after the nanny arrived. Wilderness took the opportunity to hide the stash he had brought out of Finland. He still hadn't counted it and didn't now—it was whatever it was, less the thousand dollars he had given to Janis Bell.

As a scarcely reformed thief he was well aware how difficult it is to hide anything from the probing, devious mind of a cat burglar. As hiding places went, mattress, chimney and cistern were little better than planting a flag reading "here's the swag." The discerning man needed to go a step further to keep his ill-gotten gains from the next ill-getter.

Years ago, before he was married, he'd set a safe into the wall behind the lavatory cistern. Your average burglar would lift the lid on the cistern—he'd be unlikely to go in for the plumbing required to turn off the water and unmount the cistern to find the nine-inch metal door it concealed.

His Finland stash joined the remnants from other rackets, some now quite distant. He really should take those white five-pound notes into a bank—they'd not been legal tender for five years now. They'd been the foundation of what he thought of as his running-away-from-home fund. It was just that he'd never found running away from home to be necessary.

Bolting the porcelain cistern back into place he wondered why he'd never told Judy about it. He and Judy had much in common and many differences. The one that sprang to mind, monkey wrench in hand, was that she believed a husband and wife should have no secrets—and he didn't.

Vienna

§

Vienna, The Imperial Hotel: September 1955

Standard procedure that felt nothing of the sort. By the book, but what the book didn't say was what you did now.

Standard procedure. One bullet to the heart, one to the head. Not six feet from his target.

In the confines of a small, tiled hotel bathroom his Browning 7.65 sounded like artillery, a cannon to the ear.

Surely someone must have heard, was Wilderness's first thought.

And his second was that the Russian's eyes were still open.

Half his brains splattered across the wall and still his eyes were open.

VI

Armagnac and Easter Eggs

§86

They got through Christmas without incident. He always thought they would. Judy could structure Christmas in such a way as to avoid overexposure to her family—she had three sisters, Wilderness had no one . . . no one that he knew of, no siblings, no cousins, no parents . . . to the extent that Burne-Jones had dubbed him "the Perfect Spy," the man without ties and constraints—until the day Wilderness had married his daughter . . . and late in the marriage had made him a grandfather for the fifth and sixth times.

The twins were still of an age when Christmas presents were of less interest than the paper that wrapped them. Wilderness put this to the test and wrapped them each an empty box. Molly opened the box, peered in, held it upside down to see if anything fell out, then returned gleefully to the wrapping paper. Joan shook it once and, not hearing anything rattle, put the box aside without opening it and proceeded to iron out the creases in the paper without the advantage of an iron.

"You're a bastard," said his wife.

"So people keep telling me."

So the Australians had told him, too. What other word would fit? He could still see the look on Kostya's face as life and warmth crept back into it. Kostya had not called him a bastard. And it occurred to Wilderness that there probably wasn't a word in Kostya's vocabulary to convey what he thought of Wilderness at that moment.

He hadn't told Judy what he'd done out on the ice. He'd also never told her about the one man he had killed, in a hotel room in Vienna ten years ago. If he did, then she might see the point in his unspoken rejection of her "let's have no secrets"—he had no wish to prove that point by revealing secrets she didn't know he had kept only to have her say "I wish you'd never told me that." Most of the time she asked him questions he could answer. Most of the time she knew when it wasn't worth asking the question. Most of the time he could sit on the loo without thinking of the box of secrets behind it. And he'd told her very little of his last Berlin venture. She'd figured that one out for herself.

One of Judy's ways to structure Christmas was to decline all her mother's invitations to spend it back in Campden Hill Square. That visit she and Wilderness could usually hold off till the day after Boxing Day, when a representative handful of presents and babies would be scooped up and dumped in the back of a cab.

"Why does it feel as though we've done this dozens of times? It's their third Christmas. We've done this precisely twice."

"Dunno," Wilderness replied. "How often have you imagined it?"

"A lot. I suppose. And I suppose there'll come a point when I'll miss the time when we could spend three days completely alone without phone or post, and burping babies will not seem like the bliss it is now."

"Bliss?"

"If bliss can be said to be pleasure beyond your imagination's a priori notion of what pleasure is, yes. Not that bringing them up single-handed doesn't have its ups and downs. You were gone an age."

Wilderness knew where this was leading, and looked out of the cab window rather than catch Judy's eye.

"Has Pa told you how long you'll be at home?"

"No. But he will."

§87

The moment came sooner than he had anticipated.

Madge had served up curried leftovers. Goose this, spud that, something green, something stuffed. The remains of a Fortnum's Christmas pudding that might once have been a moon of Jupiter.

Then she plonked down a decanter of Armagnac, looking relieved when every head shook in response to her "Coffee, anyone?"

Burne-Jones got to his feet, reached for the decanter and said, "Joe, let's adjourn to my study for a while, shall we?"

"You've got it all wrong, Pa." Judy said. "Ma and I are supposed to withdraw while the gentlemen reorganise the League of Nations or compare todgers or whatever."

"I shall ignore that."

"And why do you call it a study? Do you actually study in there?"

Madge chipped in, "I once caught your father with his shoes and socks off, staring at his feet. So I assume he studies feet. Does that answer your question?"

"Partly. When he presents his paper on 'Feet' to the Linnaean Society I might be convinced. Particularly if it undermines the theory of evolution."

With the study door closed, Burne-Jones said, "What's got into her?"

Wilderness said, "She's anticipating what you're going to say."

"I see. That obvious, is it?"

"You said yourself, Thwaite will be after my guts in the New Year. So she's expecting another foreign posting."

Burne-Jones prodded the fire to life with a poker—the half-hearted glow of the smokeless briquettes that were all London's smog laws would allow. He plonked himself down in one fireside chair and waved Wilderness into the other one. Wilderness didn't care what Alec studied or whether he studied at all. He could simply sit, just be, in a room like this and roll the clock back eighty years—a padded cell for the sophisticated man, deep chairs, heavy velvet curtains, shelf upon shelf of books, a harmonium no one ever played.

Burne-Jones poured out two hefty Armagnacs.

Wilderness wondered if he was going to take his slippers and socks off, but he didn't. He sipped once at his Armagnac, sighed with pleasure and said, "She's right of course. Pity of it is that you really should be at home with your daughters, enjoying them while they're enjoyable. When they're older . . . well there are times I think Judy could suck the fun out of Sunday Night at the London Palladium. However, be that as it may . . . you can't stay in England just yet. But it won't be a posting. Not as such. Tell me, Joe. How good's your Czech?"

"Patchy. I tend to get by in German. Not the most popular language in Czechoslovakia, but I don't get punched in the jaw for speaking it."

"I want you back there before whatever it is that's going to blow blows. But we can spare a few weeks for you to scrub up."

"OK . . . but Cambridge University is still in England or did it move while I was away?"

"Of course you can't go to Cambridge. No, no . . . it's Dublin. We've done a deal with the Russian and Slavonic faculty at Trinity. Matter o' fact we set up it up after Hungary in '56, when Cambridge simply couldn't cope with the number of new recruits we were sending them. You start the week after next. If Thwaite asks, you're still abroad. No need for him to know where or why. And he'd be an idiot to ask either and risk being reminded that the service he scrutinises has the word *secret* in front of it. You'll be nicely off radar and you can come and go without showing a passport. That's one reason I had Ernie pick you up at the airport. No one saw your passport, so no one who doesn't need to know knows you're here."

"The invisible man."

"Quite."

§88

He travelled under his own name and enrolled under his own name. When he checked in with Eddie and Alice Pettifer before setting off for Euston and Holyhead for the crossing to Dún Laoghaire, Alice gave him his cover folder, the address of the lodging they'd found for him, a street map of Dublin and a bankers' letter to enable him to draw expenses and salary in punts from the National Bank of Ireland in O'Connell Street.

"And," she said, as he stuffed papers unread into his briefcase. "Leave the gun."

"What gun?"

She spun the briefcase round to face her and pulled out his Smith & Wesson before he could even reach out a hand to stop her.

"Exactly," she said. "What gun?"

"Alice . . ."

"No Joe. No soft soap. I'm following orders and so should you. You don't need a gun."

"I rather think I do."

"You're a student. Students don't carry guns. They carry biros. And . . . just think of the trouble guns have got you into."

"Think of the trouble they've got me out of."

"Burne-Jones's orders, Joe. You're not allowed so much as a pea shooter."

Wilderness looked to Eddie. Eddie strived for expressionless blank and said, "Coffee, anyone?"

§89

The MS *Inishmaan* ploughed through rough seas.

Wilderness slept.

Wilderness dreamed.

Dreamed dreams that might have haunted Macbeth or Richard III.

Not that anyone told him to "despair and die," but the dead wanted words with him all the same.

Yuri Myshkin dead in his armchair at the Adlon Hotel in Berlin, dead but speaking, "Another fine mess, eh Joe?"

His father walking out into the North Sea stark naked, repeatedly as though in a time loop, "Make a better job of the life thing than I did, son. Life thing. Life thing. Life life life."

And his grandfather, who had fallen from a rooftop in Hampstead, glass cascading all around him, with not a cry nor a word. Yet in dreams Wilderness heard the old man calling his name over and over again, "Joe, Joe, Joe." In a slow diminuendo mimicking the fall.

And the living. Kostya sinking into the frozen lake, "I'm just a fucking *Schieber*! *Schieber*! *Schieber*!"

Oddly, the one man he had killed in the twenty years since Burne-Jones had rescued him from the glasshouse, the KGB agent he'd shot dead in Vienna back in '55, failed to put in an appearance in his dreams. For once the man had no echo. No accusation. Wilderness was quite certain—well almost certain—he felt no guilt about the killing. "Him or me" seemed perfectly adequate. His intermittent recurrence was hardly proof of conscience, merely of memory.

But waking, Wilderness wondered . . . about himself. About the KGB agent whose name he had never known. And he wondered about the others. Was a conscience really needed? There was nothing he could have done to save Yuri or his grandfather, there was nothing he *would* have done to save his father . . . and Kostya? Well, he had saved Kostya. After he'd nearly killed him.

§90

A cab took him through hypnotic, prismatic drizzle from the port to the address Alice had given him: Duke Street, just south of the Liffey, halfway between St. Stephen's Green and Trinity College. It was a four-storey Georgian house that had seen better days—peeling paint the colour of verdigris, and a front door that looked as though it had withstood assault with a battering ram. It was also next to a pub, and as Wilderness paid off the cabbie, the name struck him as familiar: Davy Byrne's. Hadn't Leopold Bloom killed time there listening to the inane ramblings of Nosey Flynn?

He yanked on the bellpull and heard a distant ring deep inside the house.

At least two minutes passed. Bolts slid back. A key turned. A blue eye peered out.

"Would it be Mr. Holderness?"

Then the door opened wider. A small, rotund, smiling man in carpet slippers and a cardigan worn through at the elbows.

"My, but you're late. We were expecting you two hours ago."

"Bit of a rough crossing," Wilderness said.

"You must be perishing. Bring yerself in and get warm."

He closed the door, slid the bolts back into place, drew a heavy woollen curtain across. Held out a hand.

"Bob Fitzsimmons," he said. "I'll show you to yer room and then you can meet the missis."

Wilderness concluded the outside of the house was deceptive. Inside, it was clean, warm, well-maintained if archaic—a surviving fragment of the last century, dark, brown and heavy. Fitzsimmons led him to the top floor, to a big room facing onto Duke Street. Any misgivings Wilderness might have had, those inevitable comparisons to his freezing digs in Cambridge back in '46, evaporated. A vast bed, a quilt the size of Latvia, a basin, his own bath and loo, a creaking, talkative iron radiator that was almost too hot to touch. It wasn't home. It might be a home from home. Just as well, Burne-Jones was being cagy about how long he'd be in Dublin.

"What brings you to Ireland if I might be so bold?"

"Oh, I'm studying Czech at Trinity."

"And what line would you be in?"

"I'm with ICI," Wilderness replied, adhering to the cover Alice had laid down for him. "We're very keen to expand into Eastern Europe. I'm with the paint division in Basingstoke."

"Oh . . . paint. Well I never. What kind o' paint?"

"Er . . ."

"Son, you just fell at the first fence and you're sittin' on yer arse on the turf at Leopardstown. If that's yer cover, you need to put a few hours into the mugging up. ICI, you say? Would that be ICI 5 or ICI 6?"

Thank God for small mercies. The man hadn't asked where Basingstoke was. He was going to kill Alice for this.

"It's alright. I was with SOE in the last war. Your man considers me very reliable."

"Your man," Wilderness thought, was so vague it could mean anything or anyone from Alice to Burne-Jones to C to the prime minister.

"Are all your lodgers in my line of work?"

"Not all, but a fair few. Gladys and I have had the odd ICI gunman stay over the years. It's all a matter of choosing your friends and when you choose your friends you also choose your enemies. Pity of it is you can't choose your neighbours. Ask anyone from Poland. The English can be a right bunch of bastards, but I'd choose them any day over Germans or Russians."

Yes, he was definitely going to kill Alice.

"But . . . that's by the bye. Your secrets are safe with us, so come on down and meet Gladys. She'll have put the kettle on when she heard the bell ring."

§91

All Wilderness knew about paint was gloss or emulsion. Brush or roller.

Fitzsimmons had a point with paint. He'd been the first to ask. He wouldn't be the last. Wilderness had no idea what paint was even made of. Dead horses, like glue? Crude oil, like plastic?

The Fitzsimmonses kept a prewar encyclopaedia in the parlour. Twenty-six volumes, Aardvark to Zyzzyva. Wilderness duly mugged up under *P* . . . and setting off for his first day at Trinity felt he might well be able hold his own on paint . . . gypsum, clay, resin, solvent, pigment et alia . . . at least until an apposite moment arose to change the subject. Paint had one thing greatly in its favour: boring. Watching it dry . . . talking about it . . . boring. No one would ask more than a couple of questions before switching to cricket or football . . . or the existence of a deity.

He'd tucked his briefcase under his arm and was wrestling with the array of bolts on the front door when Fitzsimmons appeared.

"Young Alice called. I've a message for you."

"OK."

"No rackets, she said. Tell him no rackets. Does that mean anything?"

"Probably," Wilderness replied.

No guns, no rackets. I might as well be selling fucking paint.

§92

Czech was not the easiest language Wilderness had ever taken on, but then no language had ever struck him as too difficult. He'd yet to wrestle with Mandarin or Japanese and thankfully could not conceive of the circumstances in which Burne-Jones would require him to.

He wasn't the oldest student in the class—there were two women in their fifties, and whilst it was an unwritten rule (although he'd bet money someone had written it down somewhere) that you didn't ask why anyone else was doing what they were doing, it seemed very likely that they were "Ladies who Listened," at Caversham, the BBC's "listening post" in Berkshire. If he was learning Czech because Czechoslovakia was assuming greater importance in the great snowball fight that was postwar Europe, it was a penny to a pound Caversham and the BBC (for BBC read Foreign Office, read Government, read MI6) were upping the level of their monitoring too. Sooner or later he'd be sent into Czechoslovakia to do God-knows-what—shoot lots of people, save Fort Knox, wreck Crab Quay—and they'd be back in Berkshire, wearing headphones and listening to the Czech version of *The Archers*.

It was hard to make new friends. So he didn't try.

He hadn't been told of any other spooks on the course, so assumed there were none, and if there were what would they have to say to each other?

It was hard to make new friends. So he made none. He established a random pattern of pubs and bars—not random enough to avoid the "enemy" (whoever that was) but perhaps enough not to be perceived as a regular and get drawn into conversations that, being Irish, would inevitably be rather nosy and might even find paint interesting, and being Wilderness, would inevitably be lies from start to finish.

He'd sit in Bailey's or Davy Byrne's nursing a half of Guinness, silently cramming Czech verbs, starting with the most important:

miluji tě,
miluješ,
on nebo ona miluje . . .

And when, after cramming the principal parts of thje verb to love, he felt the need of a good glass of wine, or perhaps just a rug with no sawdust, or even a rug, he'd switch to the bar of the Shelbourne Hotel at St. Stephen's Green, order a half bottle of claret and cram again. I spy:

špehuji,
špehujete,
on nebo ona špeha

Within a month or so he was happy, or at least happy with Czech.

One night—it might have been a Wednesday, a night when pubs were less than full as wage packets waned—he sat in Davy Byrne's. With a beer. He didn't much like beer. He liked verbs. Nouns changed a bit, except in English where a noun was so stubborn as to yield only to a plural. Verbs . . . verbs . . . were motile, life-giving:

jím příliš mnoho banánů,
jíte příliš mnoho banánů,
on nebo ona jí příliš mnoho banánů

Which led with a certain inevitability to:

Ano, nemáme banány.

No bananas indeed.

Then: a figure looming over him.

Something oddly familiar about this.

"Kein Wort auf Russisch."

(Not one word in Russian.)

Odder still.

"Why, Bernard? What do the Irish think you are?"

"One of them. One so unfortunate as to lose his accent after so many years in England."

"A West Brit?"

"Exactly."

"Why not sit down. We can talk in any language we might have in common."

"German will do."

"Good. Bernard, what are you doing here?"

"Please call me Jim. It's the name you stuck me with. And I teach in the Faculty of Eastern European and Slavonic Studies. The same department you are in. I am a tutor in the Russian language."

"Of course."

"Joe, what are *you* doing here?"

"Learning Czech. But you know that."

"You're not here for me?"

"Why would I be here for you? Bernard Alleyn is in Moscow, I saw him cross the Glienicke Bridge with my own eyes. If he didn't, well . . . we'd both be in the shit, wouldn't we?"

Bernard sat. Bernard sagged. Relief all but dripped from his pores.

Wilderness stuck up an arm for the barman.

"Whiskey, large. For my friend. I think he's feeling faint."

With his hand wrapped around a glass of Old Paddy, Bernard perked up a little but still seemed unwilling to say more.

Wilderness knew almost everything there was to know about Bernard Alleyn, formerly Leonid Liubimov, now living under the name of James Wilde—a rechristening by Wilderness back in Berlin a couple of years ago. What he didn't know about was the brief life since.

Bernard looked well. He must be little short of fifty and had led a life of such duplicity, such risk, that it might well have etched itself into his face. It hadn't. His hair was greying, but in the way that elicited "distinguished" rather than "old"—if anything he was growing to bear more than a passing resemblance to Burne-Jones.

"Sorry if my being here has come as a shock. I've not come to make any trouble for you. You've no doubt made a new life for—"

"Joe, I have but the shadow of a life. Call it new or old, it is a shadow."

"But—you have a job?"

"Yes. Thanks to your friend Erno I have a job."

"References?"

"Complete and convincing fakes from universities in Bonn, Zurich and Nottingham."

"Nottingham?"

"If I'd put Cambridge somebody would know somebody. Nottingham. I've never been there and I've never met anyone that has. It might not even be a real place. Be that as it may . . . I am in Dublin. As surely as if you'd put me on the ship yourself with a ticket pinned to my lapel."

"You did ask about your wife."

"I did."

"And?"

"You are familiar with the totalitarian designation 'non-person'? I am a 'non-husband.'"

"So, she divorced you?"

"Actually no. We are 'legally separated.' And I'm not at all sure I know the difference between that and divorce."

"Me neither."

"Meanwhile my wife lives with our daughters down in Killiney, and I live in a bedsit in Mountjoy I would not grace with the word squalid."

"Not well-paid by Trinity?"

"I'm a tutor, Joe, not a lecturer. I'm paid by the hour and by results, rather than the quality of my contribution to the culture—which is close to zero by the bye."

Wilderness felt he was being blamed for Bernard's plight. For the afterlife, the half-life of the spy exposed. Not one shred of his conscience—an otherwise vital organ—felt any blame.

"And I live in one room next to this pub. A clean, well-lighted place but just one room all the same. Meanwhile my wife is at home in Hampstead with my daughters."

"Is this where you say touché?"

"No Bernard, it's where you say snap."

§93

The problem Wilderness now faced, as he saw it, was not so much avoiding Bernard or keeping him at arm's length but containing him. Of course Bernard would keep their secret—he'd kept his own for fourteen years after all—it was a matter of Wilderness keeping his in the face of Bernard's curiosity. That he'd not been a spy for eight years had perhaps diminished his spy's natural nosiness; it hadn't killed it off. Sooner or later they'd run out of small talk and large talk would leap in to fill the gap.

Wilderness tried the tactic he'd used on Kostya, avoiding idle and not-so-idle conversation by focussing his mind elsewhere.

"Do you play chess, Bernard?"

"You know where I grew up. What do you think?"

"Fine. Friday at seven? The Shelbourne bar? I'll bring the set."

On Fridays and occasional Sundays they'd meet, sometimes in Davy Byrne's, sometimes in Gladys Fitzsimmons's kitchen, mostly at the Shelbourne. They'd play chess and Wilderness would lose.

Unsurprisingly, Czech turned out to be yet another of Bernard's many languages, and whoever lost the draw for black or white chose the language they'd play in. French, German, English . . . anything but Russian.

By late February the rust and dust were out of his head and he began to win the odd game. Perhaps one in four. Losing seemed to reinvigorate Bernard, and often as not he came out of his corner chess-fighting fit.

Tonight, Good Friday, in the Shelbourne, in German, Wilderness was getting his arse kicked.

Bernard had dazzled him with moves long thought-out and quickly executed.

"I will say, Bernard, you're quite the toughest opponent I've ever had."

"Ah," the voice down to a whisper, even though the buzz in the Shelbourne would smother a cry of "murder!" in any language.

"Have you ever played a Russian before?"

"I played Yuri Myshkin. Long before he was a general. Back in the days when we might still pretend to be allies."

"Did you beat him?"

"Occasionally. But if I lost he'd always explain why I lost. He was determined I should learn from him."

"Before I was even five years old, I learnt from the best. Nastasya Filipovna Krasnaya. I could play chess almost before I could read. Something about the child's mind, I suppose."

"You knew Krasnaya?"

"You could say that."

"I met her once."

Bernard's hand hesitated over a white knight—put the move on hold. Wilderness could swear he was raising an eyebrow at this.

"May I ask when?"

"Nineteen forty-eight. You'd be worming your way into the British War Office about then."

"I shall do my utmost not to take offence at 'worming.' I imagine this was in Berlin?"

"Yes. The summer before they pulled me out. Yuri and I were running contraband into the East. Coffee mostly."

"And what did you make of her?"

"I had very little to go on. A thirty-second encounter in which I, a corporal, thought it best to stand to attention in the presence of a general. Albeit one of *your* generals, not one of mine. It was a bit like meeting a mythical creature, I suppose. Zhukov was real and I never set eyes on the man. Sokolovsky was real, and I met him more times than I can count. Krasnaya was unreal, in the way the woman in *Déjeuner sur l'herbe* would be unreal if she got dressed and stepped out of the frame to say hello. I thought she looked like an older version of the poster. *Statuesque* might be the word. The fire-engine red of her hair in the poster was just that, poster paint, but I'd always assumed she was a real redhead, and there was still a glint of gold in her hair even in '48. I suppose she'd be about fifty? You know the poster I mean, the one with the machine gun and the baby? And a slogan like 'Up the Workers.'"

"I don't think we were ever as crude as that. 'Forward with the People' seems more probable. But yes, it rings a bell. Mate, I believe."

The knight was picked up and plonked down. Lost again.

"I'm a sucker to say this, but same time on Sunday?"

"Ah no. It's Easter. I have visitation rights this coming Sunday. No—that's too formal. No one, no court has granted me the right to see my children. It's an accommodation I have reached with my wife."

"But . . . no reconciliation as yet?"

"Tell me, Joe. Do you have secrets from your wife?"

Bernard's palm went up like a traffic cop before Wilderness could draw breath.

"Of course you do. What spy could possibly tell his wife everything. You tell her what you can and hope she never asks about the rest. But at least she knows you're a spy. Kate knew nothing. As far as she was concerned, I was a former RAF pilot, of Canadian birth, doing rather well for himself and for his family in the British civil service. Everything she thought I was and everything she thought our marriage was unravelled in the course of one twenty-minute conversation in 1959. She is accommodating, but unforgiving. I take tea with her and my daughters. I do not dine with them, I do not stay overnight. It's all very restrained, very civilised and as false as the name she now lives under. As she put it so succinctly when I turned up in Ireland in '65, 'Your one big lie has forced me into a thousand little ones. My every waking moment is a lived lie.'"

"But she didn't turn you in."

"No. She didn't—or you and I would both be in prison."

Thwaite sprang too easily to mind.

"Well . . . one more fuckup and I might be."

Bernard did not ask what he meant.

"You have daughters, don't you Joe?"

"Joan and Molly. Twins. They're nearly three now."

"Mine are Beatrice and Cordelia. Teenagers. In fact, Beatrice will be going back to England in the autumn to her mother's old college, Girton. Why don't you come to Killiney with me on Sunday? Deliver the Easter eggs. I'd like you to meet my girls. It might be an incentive."

"An incentive to what?"

"To miss nothing. I didn't set eyes on my daughters for nearly seven years. The years I spent in Wormwood Scrubs. I missed most of their adolescence. They had changed from girls into young women and I missed it because I'd given my life to a cause. No cause was worth that. Yours or mine. And . . . an incentive to get out as soon as you can. Whatever mission is planned that requires you to be cramming Czech . . . make it your last. Or end up playing at being a father on alternate Sundays. I hardly saw my mother after the age of twelve. My girls saw nothing of me after the age of eight. It's no way to live."

"Is your mother still living, Bernard?"

"I believe so—but in Russia. What's Russia to me? The forbidden country."

"I gave you your chance to go back."

"And you gave me a bigger chance—*not* to go back. Let's not get into blame. Will you come?"

Wilderness decided he would meet Bernard's daughters, but silently prayed Bernard never met Judy. Ideas like his could make her impossible to live with.

§94

Time had not been kind to Kate Alleyn, née Caladine, now Howard. But then, Bernard Alleyn had not been kind to Kate Alleyn.

Wilderness remembered her picture in the papers when Bernard had been arrested in 1959. The cheaper papers, the ones Burne-Jones would "not have in the house," had made a "thing" of her—"Married to a Russian Spy! How Could She Not Know?" He supposed she was younger than Bernard, perhaps thirty-two or thirty-three at the time, a flame-haired, second-generation Irish beauty. Some wives might have sued over the headlines. She had kept her silence. And lost her beauty.

At forty-five or so, the flames were dulled and her mouth lined and puckered by chain smoking. She was civil to Bernard but spoke entirely without warmth or curiosity over tea and hot cross buns. She asked Bernard no questions. She saved those for Wilderness.

Trying to give Bernard a few minutes alone with his daughters he had, helpfully he thought, carried cups and saucers back to the kitchen—and she turned on him—a sotto voce hiss.

"What are you doing here?"

"I'm sorry?"

"You're one of them. You have to be. He's never brought anyone before."

"I'm a student at the university. I'm a friend."

"He doesn't have any friends!"

"Bernard and I play chess together a couple of times a week. I have two daughters. He wanted me to meet his."

"Bollocks. You're a fucking spy. Are you one of theirs or one of ours? Don't even bother to answer that. I don't fucking care and I'm fed up of being lied to. Just stay away from my girls. It's people like you who ruin lives."

An uneasy fifteen minutes followed before Bernard led Wilderness back to the bus stop.

Bernard was saying nothing. Perhaps it had not gone well. Perhaps it never went well. Beatrice and Cordelia had been lively and chatty—Beatrice especially when she learnt that Wilderness had studied modern languages at Cambridge. They seemed to work around the stony presence of their mother, not oblivious to it but not letting it be their cue. All the same it seemed to Wilderness that they existed stranded in the chasm between their parents, between truth and lies. Wilderness felt that he'd been shown a vision by the Ghost-of-Christmas-Yet-To-Come. The ruined life that people like Bernard could create. People like him.

§95

Something in the encounter with Kate Caladine continued to nag him.

He called his wife.

"Are you enjoying Dublin, Wilderness?"

"Sort of. But I think I need something with bigger bollocks."

"Well . . . you always have."

"Whatever comes up next has to have it."

"Isn't bollocks plural?"

"I'd moved on from bollocks to *it*—the indefinable *it*. The sort where you either have *it* or you don't."

"Oh . . . like the *It* girl?"

"Exactly."

"Well . . . whatever this *it* is . . . make sure *it*'s your last."

"Eh?"

"You're forty this year. A bit old for playing Bulldog Drummond or Richard Hannay. So make the Czech job your last."

And they had, with such ease, readily reached the point of the call. And the cards he thought he had held in his hand turned out to be in Judy's.

"That," he said. "That's . . . what Bernard says."

"Bernard? Bernard says? Bernard who?"

"Bernard Alleyn."

"You mean he's there?"

"Yep. Teaches in the department in which I study."

"Bloody hell. Does Dad know?"

"Of course not. He wouldn't want to know."

"Do you and Alleyn speak?"

"Yep. In fact we play chess a couple of times a week."

"Y'know, Wilderness mine, the world in which Dad moves has had me puzzled all my life. But the world in which you move has me utterly baffled. When is your enemy not your enemy? It's like a numbum."

"What?"

"Conundrum. My sister Eliza could never pronounce it when she was little. Same with linoleum. Linoleum was always yoeyyoeyum, and conundrum was numbum. It was the sort of thing you got on a souvenir mug or a china plate . . . 'As I was going to St. Ives I met a man with seven wives . . . seven wives with seven sacks blah blah blah . . . and all his kids and all his fucking pigs' . . . and then it asks you, 'how many were going to St Ives?' Numbum. You know? When is a door not a door? When it's ajar. When is a lamp not a lamp? And so on. When is your enemy not your enemy? When you play chess with him?"

"*How* many pigs?"

§96

Prague: Late May the Same Year, 1967

Pleasingly Warm, with Passing Clouds

The KGB were onto Ben Crosland and he knew it. He'd done the last pickup quite certain he'd been followed from the minute he left the embassy. In fact, the only way he'd got away with it was not to pick up at all. Whatever Tibor K had left for him in the gents' lavatory at the Café Dodo would stay there until K retrieved it. He turned an assignation into a stroll, walked a circuitous route back to the embassy, during which, in less than two miles, the KGB changed his tail twice. The last bloke was little, plump, pale—a passing resemblance to the Austrian actor Oskar Werner—overdressed for the weather, far too conspicuous in his belted leather jacket and flat cap; the uniform of an apparatchik.

Perhaps it was too risky for the Head of Station (Prague) to be his own courier, but they were understaffed, currently without a Second Secretary, and in Lord Brynmawr had an ambassador who seemed to have no handle on "Intelligence" whatsoever. There was no one he'd willingly trust with the job.

"I've been rumbled," he said to his wife over dinner.

"Then—" She paused. "—Then you have to stop."

"I can't. It's too important. The most I could do would be to pass it down the Service chain."

"What? You mean one of those arses who play at being your Third Secretary? I wouldn't trust either of them to go out and buy me a bloody Mars Bar."

Sarah Crosland despised most of the men Ben had ever worked with, seeing them, perhaps rightly, as public school and Oxbridge dimwits who regarded a diplomatic career as a hereditary right, happily free from the burden of work or thought. Ben was Chelmsford Grammar and Manchester University—facts which concerned him far less than they concerned his wife.

"I'll do it," she said.

"What?"

"I'll do the pickups."

Where another husband might have replied "Nonsense, darling," Ben said, "How?"

"Well . . . first things first . . . we have to throw them off the scent. You go out as usual for the next run. But we change the venue by whatever means you have of communicating with your man. Go to the Dodo, have a coffee, pretend to check out the gents. Dawdle all the way home. Give them plenty to see. Meanwhile I take Jessica out in her pram and do the pickup at a bench in the Kampa Park—one with a clear view all around so I can see whichever bastard is lurking. If you can give me a thumbnail sketch of the tails you've spotted, all the better."

"There've been three so far. As the Czech government gets weaker and more vulnerable to change the Russians may well draft in men. But."

"But what?"

"Jessica? In her pram? Sarah, she's five months old. Do you really want to risk—"

"Of course I don't want to risk anything, but do you honestly think they'll pounce on a woman with a baby? What kind of people are they?"

He knew very well what kind of people the KGB were, but refrained from saying so. Once she'd got the bit between her teeth, Sarah was all but impossible to dissuade.

It went like clockwork. Late on Wednesday afternoon Ben set off for the Café Dodo, spotted his tail straightaway and noticed no switches.

Ten minutes later Sarah wheeled the pram out of the embassy, attracting the attention of no one except the habitual, and hence ineffectual, StB appartatchik who watched the gate, and blended into the steady stream of pedestrians.

In the Dodo, down by the Legií Bridge, Ben had two coffees—more caffeine than he really needed at that time of day, but he wanted at least two men to use the gents before he went in for the pretence of a pickup. With any luck the Russians would follow one or both of the poor sods who'd pissed out of time and chance and it would be half an hour or more before they learnt the meaning of "red herring."

A quarter of a mile from the embassy in the Palác Thun, "Oskar Werner" took over and, with a diligence worthy of a British nanny in Kensington Gardens, saw him to the door.

"Went like a dream," Sarah said as she plonked a Minox film cartridge on his desk. "Your chap left his newspaper on the bench. I read bits of it for about ten minutes. Pocketed the film. Rocked the pram with my free hand, and Jessica slept through it. I saw no one I thought might be a Russian and no one approached me. If they had, I'd have woken the poor darling up and insisted she take the tit there and then. Guaranteed to put any bloke right off."

And for three weeks it worked flawlessly.

On the sixth dummy run, a familiar face followed Ben to the Dodo. It was almost tempting to wave.

Ben sat at a table in the window, nursing a coffee he would not drink, plagued as he was by insomnia, and waited for an unsuspecting phantom pisser to use the gents. One did. He'd wait for a second. He stared out of the window, the street was busy with people making their way home from work—somewhere on the other side of the passing crowd was the man he'd come to think of as "Belt-Buckle." The other two were "Oskar" and "Walrus Moustache," but it was always Belt-Buckle who stood outside the café.

And when the crowd cleared, he had gone.

§97

Jessica burbled in her sleep. Sarah leaned into the pram, wiped spittle from the baby's pouting lower lip and pulled the hood of the pram a little higher against the western sun.

She'd given it the usual ten minutes, seen not hair nor hide of anyone watching. Time to go home. She slipped the newspaper down one side of the pram, between baby and blanket, and held the black plastic film cartridge tightly in her fist—the easier to drop it down the drain if needs be.

She was about twenty feet from the park gates when a bicycle swerved in from the street and side-swiped the pram. The pram tilted, took flight, bounced, and the baby shot up into the air. Sarah screamed. Out of nowhere a man in flat cap and a leather jacket came running and caught the baby in his arms.

Now Jessica screamed and screamed and screamed.

"Oskar Werner" looked shocked.

"I am so sorry. I am so sorry. We thought it was a dummy!"

He handed Jessica back, lodged her in the crook of Sarah's left arm, righted the pram, saying over and over again, "We are so sorry. We are so sorry."

"Bastard! Motherfucking bastard!"

Sarah decked him with a swift right hook. The film cartridge firming her fist up nicely, rather like a knuckle-duster.

The cyclist bolted.

"Oskar" went out like a light and lay coldcocked upon the flagstones. Two policemen were approaching.

She slipped the film into the baby's blanket and stood firmly upon dignity and diplomatic immunity.

§98

They'd pushed Brynmawr to the limit.

He'd no idea what to say.

"I've no idea what to say," he said, and then he said it. "Mr. Novotny called me personally. Was I trying to provoke the Russians? Was I trying to start a war? Said something I didn't quite understand about poking the bear with a stick. It almost beggars belief. A Soviet cultural attaché—a specialist in nineteenth-century Czech music, I am told— knocked out in a public park by the wife of a British diplomat! And the language. What was it you called that chap?"

Part of Ben Crosland hoped his wife might feign ignorance. She didn't.

"I called him a motherfucking bastard, Ambassador."

Brynmawr turned the colour of freshly sliced beetroot. Ben doubted he'd ever heard a woman swear quite like that and was pretty certain he'd never heard the neologism "motherfucking" before. It could hardly be in common use in the House of Lords or the valleys of South Wales.

"There's only one thing we can do," Brynmawr went on. "It's come to this—you'll have to be recalled. You'll have to go home."

Ben Crosland's inner voice said "yippee."

"Both of you, I'm afraid."

And "yippee" all the louder.

§99

Dublin: June 17th

Balmy

Wilderness awoke with a hangover. He had a low tolerance of hangovers, and a low tolerance of spirits, so quite why he had agreed to trace Leopold Bloom's odyssey round the pubs of Dublin yesterday was baffling. It had been Bernard's idea. They'd take the walk instead of playing their usual Friday night game of chess, and have a whiskey in every pub Bloom had. They'd begun in Eccles Street, but nothing in his fogged morning-after memory could tell Wilderness where they'd finished.

Bernard had got him back to Duke Street, shoved him in through the Fitzsimmonses' front door and legged it. He might be an acculturated Anglo-Irishman these days, but his liver was still Russian.

Wilderness had not made it up the stairs and had woken on Gladys Fitzsimmons's sofa to a nudge from her husband.

"Young Alice phoned."

"Uhh?"

"About two hours ago. I couldn't wake you. She left a message."

Wilderness swung his feet to the floor. It swayed.

"Read it, Bob. Read it."

"Doesn't make a deal of sense. 'The dog it was that died.' That mean anything to you?"

"Yep. Needs an answer too. Give me a moment."

"I'll bring you a coffee while you think."

It needed very little thought. It was a basic code Alice had worked out a year or two ago. A six-word message meant "drop everything and get back." A four-word message meant "wind up your affairs and be back in ten days."

All that was needed was a six-word sentence to indicate he had received and understood.

Bob shoved black coffee under his nose—awful, chemical, instant coffee. A smell to make the strongest stomach heave. He'd pretend to drink it.

"Just off to roger a skunk."

"What?"

"Give that message to Alice. She'll understand. Trust me."

Three hours later he was at Dublin airport.

When Bernard called by around seven thirty only to be told that Wilderness had departed for England, he felt as though something in him had died.

$100

London, 54 Broadway

"I need you in Prague a bit sooner than I'd anticipated. We're down to the wire . . . no Second Secretary and now no First—"

"You want me in the embassy? A civil servant? I don't run agents, Alec. I am an agent."

"Have you quite finished? I had merely thought to begin at the beginning. Often the best idea. We lost the Second Secretary a while ago. He would, on occasion, do the odd job for us. Not strictly kosher. Not one of the old firm, after all. When he left, the First Secretary took over. Always unwise for a station head to enter the field, but needs must. The only virtue to it is that it keeps it within SIS. Czechoslovakia is a damn sight more important now than it was eighteen months ago—a small, faraway country about which we cannot know too much. But our man was rumbled. The other side took to dogging his every step."

"Who is the Station Head?"

"Ben Crosland. You know him?"

"Yep."

"He's on his way home. Good man. But his wife has a bit of a temper. She acted as courier for a week or two while Ben just became the decoy. She punched a KGB man in public."

"You're kidding?"

"Knocked him cold, I gather, so poor old Ben's been recalled. The Czechs insisted."

"As you said, he's a good man. Don't waste him."

"I won't. The stuff he and his wife got out of Prague these last few weeks is priceless. Almost every missive between KGB Prague and Moscow Centre."

"Everything but the date of Novotny's resignation?"

"I don't think he'll ever resign. But Ben tells me there's an . . . I think he called it an undercurrent. And I'm not inclined to ignore the idea. There's always dissidence, mostly it gets stepped on pretty damn quick. Ben reckons this 'undercurrent' will surface."

"When?"

"Damned if I know. Six months, a year? Novotny might be the dullest leader in the Warsaw Pact. That alone might ensure his survival. However, Ben's made his report and he's earned a promotion. I've suggested to Upstairs that he's posted to Washington as Head of Station."

"Philby's old job."

"Not a comparison I would have invoked. Nor a name I care to mention—but yes. Let's see who Mrs. Crosland can thump in Washington. I could give her a list if she wanted . . . J. Edgar . . . Senator Thurmond. But I digress—we have yet to find a Station Head for Prague and the FO needs to find a Second Secretary. It remains, whoever we send out, the other side will be on to them straight away. Until now we've always relied on them being strapped for cash and manpower—much as they probably do with us—but they threw everything they've got at Ben. Hence you find yourself sitting here. The only way this will work is if the decoy is at the embassy and the real agent is in deep cover."

"Might work."

"And it might not—all the same we have to try."

"How deep is deep cover?"

"How shall I put it . . . no diplomatic protection. You get caught, you're on your own."

"And this cover would be what exactly?"

"You'll appreciate that this would be a very good moment to phone A&R and send for The Dresser."

§101

A&R stood for Artists and Repertoire, a phrase Wilderness himself had pinched from Tin Pan Alley. The real purpose of the nameless department was to devise and assemble cover for field agents. The Dresser, another show biz term, was Wilderness's name for the department head, Commander Miles Grindleford RNVR, a man of firm opinion, even firmer conviction, and a man unlikely to relish a nickname of any kind. Wilderness sincerely hoped he'd never learn what his nickname was.

Grindleford rolled out his plan on the "boardroom" table in the meeting room next to Burne-Jones's office. Wilderness, Burne-Jones and Alice stood on one side, Grindleford on the other.

"First things first, am I right to assume you cannot pass as a Czech?"

"Yes. Not good enough for that."

"Would you be happier as an Austrian or a German?"

"Make me a Berliner. I've got the accent pretty well honed."

"And a Berliner working out of Vienna would be no problem?"

Wilderness just nodded. Grindleford scribbled.

"Jolly good."

Grindleford looked at Wilderness's face, scrutinising.

"And you're how tall, Mr. Holderness?"

The same tone of voice a doctor might use in asking a child's age.

"Six two."

"OK. I suppose we're stuck with that. Always possible to make a short man seem taller, but adding an inch or two to your height would be pointless. You'd be even more conspicuous."

"Hair. Does your hair grow fast?"

"Are we talking head, face or balls, Commander?"

Alice dug him in the ribs with an elbow.

"Do take this seriously, Flight Sergeant. Lives depend on it, yours included. Specifically, could you grow a moustache in a week?"

"Just about."

"Very well. Later today we'll have you made up and photographed for your West German passport. You don't wear spectacles at all?"

"No."

"Very well. A pair with plain glass would work nicely. Contact lenses, I think. Brown. Stick on 'tache, pro tem. And we'll dye your hair a shade or two darker. Mousey. Colonel Burne-Jones is confident that none of your old adversaries are currently serving in Czechoslovakia, but . . . you never know, so some disguise is called for."

Wilderness had never done any mission disguised. The novelty appealed to him.

"Now," Grindleford said, turning his attention to the spread of papers in front of him. "The McGuffin. You are Walter Hensel, you work for the Austrian company Erdbahn, the biggest manufacturer of tractors in the country, although that's not saying much. On the other hand, they do have offices in Norwich, Eindhoven, and their HQ in Vienna. And they're keen to export—"

"Are they real?"

"Oh yes. We have their cooperation at the highest level. The top man in Vienna, and the heads of their two branches in Czechoslovakia. They will all be part of this. Active cooperation will, tactically, be limited but all three chaps will be aware of your mission, and the cover could not be better. They're keen to export both parts and finished tractors to the Eastern Bloc. Last year, they opened an office in Prague and another about forty miles north near Mělník. You'll work out of Mělník. It's rural, close to the farmers you'll be selling to and it's about half an hour's drive from Mladá Boleslav. That's where Škoda are based—Erdbahn have all sorts of deals with Škoda. Their sideline, if I can call it that, is they import Škodas into Austria. Škodas are heaps of unreliable scrap metal held together with pop rivets—just my opinion, you'll understand— but the Austrian car industry has never really recovered from the war. In fact it's at its lowest point in years right now—and it's cheaper to import rubbish Škodas from Czechoslovakia than expensive, reliable Volkswagens from West Germany . . . currently Austria makes more tractors than cars . . . hence your cover story.

"In Mělník you're far less likely to be noticed by the other side, but needless to say you'll have plenty of reasons to be in Prague should circumstances demand. Better still, Czechoslovakia has only one tractor maker—'Zetor,' in Brno, about a hundred and fifty miles to the south, and on your route to and from Vienna. Erdbahn liaise with them constantly. Exchanges of ideas, new developments, that sort of thing. All sort of jolly *Ostpolitik*."

"What?"

"*Ostpolitik*. I think the meaning's pretty obvious. Willy Brandt is said to have coined it during the last federal election."

"Catchy."

"Quite. Now, let us press on. Time and tide and all that. Erdbahn . . . You'll replace the liaison chap we've asked them to withdraw. Actually I say liaison . . . salesman might be more accurate. No matter, Erdbahn have recalled him to Vienna, so the field is clear. You'll have a perfectly legit reason to be driving halfway across the country every so often. In and out of Vienna. In and out of Brno. In and out of Mladá Boleslav."

A tractor salesman?

Good fucking grief.

Wilderness had spotted the flaw in this at once and wondered if anyone else had.

"I don't know the first thing about tractors."

Grindleford pushed a glossy-covered file, an inch thick, across the table to him.

"While you grow your moustache, study this."

Wilderness looked and fought back despair.

ERDBAHN

In red capitals, and below it the company logo—a blue planet Earth suspended in space, the photograph that had left everyone awestruck sometime during the early Apollo missions—suspended in space and orbited by a sputnik . . . a sputnik in the shape of a tractor.

§102

"I'll never get used to this," Judy said, giving his new-found mousey hair another ruffle.

Wilderness had taken out the contact lenses. They stung like merry hell and would take some getting used to.

"And if you grow a moustache you might look like Dad. Not sure I could cope with that—and hanky and panky would certainly be taking a break."

"I have a week. The first couple of days will just be stubble."

"A week at home?"

"A week studying how to become a fucking tractor salesman."

"All the same, a week at home is a week at home. I'm delighted. So are hanky and panky."

"Judy. I have to study a two-hundred-page dossier."

"Oh fuck that. Just bullshit. You usually do. You're a past master of the noble art."

And with that she took the Erdbahn dossier and flipped it over her shoulder to slap down in front of the fireplace.

"And what's the name of this tractor salesman?"

"Walter Hensel."

"I've always wanted a Walter. Take me, my mousey-haired stranger. I'm yours."

"Knock it off."

"No, honestly. I don't have burglar or wicked landlord fantasies. I have rough-trade, man-on-a-tractor fantasies. A good tan, hefty biceps, bare-chested under a seriously filthy pair of dungarees. Sort of Thomas Hardy updated."

"Oh, for fuck's sake—"

"Just call me . . . Bathsheba."

Warm. Wet. Whispered into his ear.

And he knew he had lost.

§103

In the morning Wilderness and Burne-Jones met in Burne-Jones's office. No experts, no one to take notes, no one who didn't need to know. And Ben Crosland, who already knew.

"Long time no see, Ben."

"Doesn't feel that way, Joe. Your antics in Finland kept us all amused."

Burne-Jones scowled at this.

"Cut the chitchat, chaps. And get down to business."

Finland had not amused him any more than Berlin had.

"Ben's contact . . . we don't know his real name. Just as well, I suppose. Ben just refers to him as Tibor K. I don't suppose it bears any resemblance to his real name?"

Crosland shrugged.

"It does sound a little like Josef K.," Wilderness said.

"Who he?"

"The hero, if that's the word, of a couple of novels by Kafka."

"Ah," said Burne-Jones. "Never read him."

Crosland picked up the briefing.

"We began with real documents. Photocopies. Bulky. Awkward. But the diplomatic bag is capacious as you proved with the truckload of booze you got into Berlin in '65. Couple of months on, we switched to microfilm. It was almost always dead drops. Tibor and I would pass but never meet. I pinned him down to one meeting, gave him a Minox. He didn't need me to tell him how to use it. Just before I was rumbled we met again, for the last time, and I gave him the 'plum duff' kit for making microdots. He was less certain of that and the last few runs were still on cassette. It's a minor miracle the KGB didn't spot him on the last dead drop. They nabbed my wife, but they somehow missed him. Tibor is bright and he's thorough. I've no reason to think that he's not au fait with the kit by now. We simply need to work out a way to use that."

"Do we trust him? All sounds a little after the act."

"Eh?"

"He came close to being caught. Perhaps he was caught. We don't know."

"Joe, I trust him. I understand why you might not, but we don't have a choice. He is what we have. By which I mean all we have. If he'd been caught . . . well, there are, shall I say . . . other sources that would have told us."

Wilderness looked to Burne-Jones.

Burne-Jones just nodded.

Wilderness changed tack.

"Ben, honestly, you have no idea of his identity?"

"No. Nor would he let himself be photographed. Youngish bloke, probably no more than twenty-eight or thirty. Scant but terrifying memories of the war. Still a kid when the Communists took over in '48. An adolescence in an increasingly repressive state. Exactly the kind of young man you'd expect to be an opposition supporter."

"There is no opposition."

Crosland paused, looked at Wilderness as though he thought him an unrelenting cynic.

"Not as such, no. But I've been telling Alec . . . there's something in Czechoslovakia . . . well, in Prague, at least . . . that might cohere into one."

"What will make an opposition coherent?"

"Dunno. A new leader?"

"Such as?"

"Perhaps someone we've never heard of."

"We've heard of every Czech politician. That's our job."

"OK. Then perhaps someone the Czechs have never heard of."

"That's a possibility. Can't help but wonder who."

"I'm not taking any bets. Now, could we get back to Tibor?—I can guess at his sources from what he's sent us, and Alec and I agree he is Czech—I never for one moment thought he might be Russian—and we think he works in either Czech Intelligence or Counter-Intelligence. If we had a list, a Who's Who of the Czech Secret Services, we might be able to narrow it down to a dozen possibles—but we don't have such a list. Everything we get from Tibor looks to be the result of the Czechs spying on KGB Centre, Prague. The Russians may very well think they're the masters of phone-tapping and hidden bugs—but the Czechs were good pupils. The schoolboys are spying on the teachers now. After all, why wouldn't they?"

Wilderness looked at Burne-Jones, the faintest of smiles on his lips. Burne-Jones did not return it. Change the subject.

"Dead drops?" Wilderness said.

"The preferred method," Burne-Jones replied.

"I'd prefer to meet."

"Oh bugger."

"Alec . . . I'm not happy stepping into what you will not deny is a mess without knowing all the players."

"You mean meet with this chap just the once?"

"No—I mean that we meet every time there's an exchange of information."

Now Burne-Jones and Crosland looked at one another.

Crosland spoke first.

"That's an increased risk, Joe."

"If we have a long enough chain of communication, something so complex the Russians cannot follow it, then it's a diminished risk. Go on making dead drops in the caffs and loos of Prague and one day they'll be waiting for him. You said it yourself . . . a miracle they didn't bust Tibor when they busted your wife."

"The more people, the greater the risk of betrayal."

"As you said not five minutes ago, Ben, there has to be trust."

Burne-Jones cut in. "We're currently without a station head. We're trying . . . but . . . you know . . . right chap in the right place . . . but without one the chain of communication you want will be bloody difficult to set up."

"I'll take a week getting there. That's long enough."

"I'll be the judge of that."

Wilderness waited a heartbeat for the pulling of rank to slacken off, then said, "Janis Bell."

"Eh?"

"The kid from the Helsinki embassy. Where is she now?"

"Oh," said Burne-Jones. "I moved her to Bonn six months ago. In fact I did exactly what you said and promoted her. Second Secretary is her nominal cover."

"Good. Now promote her again. Station Head, Prague."

As much as he ever could, Burne-Jones looked shocked.

"She's very young, Joe. It was you called her a kid."

"'Scuse my slang. I meant 'highly capable young woman.' 'Kid' was just shorter."

Burne-Jones pondered. Crosland wisely said nothing.

"It would have to be 'Acting,' you understand."

"Whatever it takes."

"Just leave this one with me, will you?"

§104

In a dark, dirty bar behind Victoria Railway Terminus, they drank Scotch and soda beneath a cumulonimbus of cigarette smoke.

Crosland said, "Joe, what exactly did you mean 'after the act'?"

"That Tibor might have been compromised by the incident that got you recalled. Compromised and turned."

"That seems unlikely. I got compromised, not him. As far as I know the other side never got a good look at him. Sarah never set eyes on him either. As dead drops go it worked perfectly."

"Except she got nicked."

"She got nicked, Tibor didn't, and the KGB never got their hands on the film. And as for my being recalled, I can't tell you how glad I was to get out of Prague. You know, Joe, I wouldn't take this posting if I were you. It's all going to come apart at the seams. And you've no diplomatic immunity."

"Don't remind me."

"Yet . . . yet . . . you want to meet Tibor in person?"

"Yes. As soon as possible. As soon as we can set up a new chain of communication."

"Joe, please don't go in there guns blazing."

"I won't. Guns have blazed a bit too much of late."

They stood a few moments before Crosland spoke his mind.

"Then, Joe—try not to get yourself killed."

§105

Bonn, West Germany. Das Bundeshaus:
Half an Hour Later

Das Bundeshaus was a grim example of 1930s architecture. It bore more than a passing resemblance to the annex wing of an English polytechnic.

Brandt did not care.

Nell thought it suitably symbolic of living in Bonn—you were in the annex . . . the sideshow . . . the main event was happening under the big top elsewhere.

West Germany had, Brandt concluded, made a fundamental error in policy. He'd been certain of this since the visit of President Kennedy to Berlin four years earlier, when the President had publicly declared his solidarity with Berlin and Berliners whilst privately assuring him, "You're on your own, kid." A paraphrase of what JFK actually said, but neater than his statement of NATO's negative position vis-à-vis both Berlin and the Bundesrepublik. And being "on his own," Brandt had silently promised himself that he'd ditch the Hallstein Doctrine, conceived in the late 1940s—whereby the Bundesrepublik would not recognise any of the Soviet satellite states (Hungary, Bulgaria, Poland et al.) if said satellite states chose to recognise the German Democratic Republic, that is East Germany (aka the DDR: *Deutsche Demokratische Republik*). It was nonsense, it was unproductive and it was going nowhere.

As foreign minister, albeit responding to advances from Bucharest, he had managed to establish diplomatic relations with Roumania, and he'd overcome resistance in the federal government to do this. Now . . . he had his sights set closer to home, on a country with which the Bundesrepublik shared a border—Czechoslovakia, one of those oddly misshapen offcuts created when the Austro-Hungarian Empire had been dismembered like a side of pork; on the map of Europe it resembled nothing quite so much as a slice of bacon with crinkly edges. The treaty of this place, the treaty of that place . . . one or other of them had considered it a really good idea to lump the Czechs and Slovaks together into one country.

Czechoslovakia had changed very little since 1948, and the Communist Party's takeover of the country. Brandt wasn't wholly sure whether it was a coup or a putsch, but there'd been no election, so it was about as democratic as the fall of an English prime minister. Thousands had been purged from office, tens of thousands arrested, hundreds hanged—after which Czechoslovakia had seemed to settle down into a Stalinist lethargy, a torpor so profound even the Khrushchev thaw had merely wafted over the chasm.

But . . . things were changing. There was . . . what to call it . . . an "undercurrent."

"I need you in Prague a bit sooner than I'd anticipated."

Nell was not aware he'd ever needed her in Prague, either sooner or later.

"Could you be a little less cryptic."

"There's another deal in the offing. Nothing as firm as Roumania. Roumania never had to kick out all its Germans, after all, and if I were to put the idea of full recognition on the table, *both* sides would reject it. But, the Czechs have agreed to an official Cultural Mission."

"How official?"

"I'm aiming for consular status. Eventually. For now, we try it out. Cultural exchanges. We introduce our painters, writers and filmmakers—sponsor them on visits, set up some sort of arts festival, a literary prize . . . I dunno . . . 'The Attila the Hun Award for East-West Mutual Understanding'? . . . and so on—and the Czechs reciprocate, except that I rather think we'll be picking up both halves of the bill."

"Wouldn't a trade mission be more . . . more typical? You know, bicycles, adding machines . . . tractors?"

"The time is right for the Arts. There's a Czech film doing awfully well in the West. People are beginning to take notice."

Nell had taken notice. She'd seen a lot of Czech films—she'd read books by Bohumil Hrabal, and whilst she'd not yet read him she'd at least heard of this new bloke, Kondera? Kundera?—and what struck her was the difficulty of representing life in contemporary Czechoslovakia. The sheer quality of Czech cinema was undeniable, a *Nouvelle Vague* for the East, but it seemed to her to operate of necessity so obliquely to the present-day reality that it produced absurdist fantasies like *Daisies* or reflections on the Second World War—a safe subject . . . unsafe subjects would get your work banned—such as the film Brandt was surely referring to, *Closely Observed Trains*. It was tipped for an Oscar. Probably the first Czech film ever to make even this small arty dent on Hollywood. Brandt was right. The time was right.

"What do you want me to do? Help set it up?"

"No. I need you to run it. Let's start with a film festival. Get the Prague office open and then invite some of those young Czech filmmakers over here. We'll put on a film festival. Let's aim for the summer . . . say July or August."

"August '68?"

"Yes."

"In Bonn?"

"Bonn? Of course not. Berlin."

$106

London, 54 Broadway: A Couple of Days Later

Wilderness was back in the library. Still mugging up on Erdbahn. The moustache was beginning to itch horribly.

He was slowly mastering tractors and had reached the Erdbahn T64, which sounded like a type of Russian tank, except that it was available in yellow.

Forty-four horsepower with three-point linkage.

Linkage was obvious—it was surely how the tractor connected to all the other bits at the arse end . . . plough, harrow, washing machine . . . whatever. Horsepower? How powerful was a horse? Were all horses as powerful as each other? Forty-four horsepower? Didn't sound like much. Wasn't a Jag E-type two hundred–odd horses?

He was beginning to think his brain might be numb from boredom or confusion when Alice Pettifer appeared with a decode.

```
—Arrived in Prague. H.E. not happy . . . woman,
 far too young . . . blah blah blah. I have you
 to thank for this? If so, thank you, but I
 need time to get me knees under the table.
 Could you string out your journey for a couple
 of weeks? I'll arrange an embassy reception,
 something you can mingle with. Dunno quite
 what, just yet. BELL.
```

"Any reply, Joe?"

"Tell her yes. I could use the time too."

"Oh, and . . ."

"And what, Alice?"

"Burne-Jones says you should be armed for this one, so you can tool up again. But—you never really tooled down, did you, Joe?"

Wilderness said nothing. The less Alice knew about what had happened out on the ice the better. It wouldn't stop her guessing, it wouldn't stop her putting two and two together and making four, but she'd never hear it from him.

§107

West Berlin: July 6th

Wilderness insisted on travelling via Berlin. Alice did not object. It pushed his arrival a day or two beyond the fortnight Janis Bell had asked for and gave him a chance to test his passport in relative safety—if it passed muster at Heathrow, at Tegel, then he'd be sure it would at Vienna and at the Břeclav crossing into Czechoslovakia.

He preferred to avoid both the SIS station in West Berlin—badly disguised as a travel agency (the station head, Dickie Delves, was unlikely to forgive Wilderness for trashing his Triumph Sprite anytime in the next century)—and the Kempinski Hotel (which was where Delves would look for him if some silly sod back in London were to let slip that he was in Berlin). The threats Dickie had made involving Wilderness's head and a starting handle were not to be lightly forgotten.

He asked Erno Schreiber for the use of his couch for a couple of nights. Erno, the best forger Wilderness had ever come across, could check out the passport for him while he was there.

"My eyes are not what they used to be," Erno said. "But it looks real. Perhaps it is real. Who knows?"

An evening of catching up ended with the blonde from the room above making cocoa for three.

She was, Wilderness thought, oversolicitous of Erno, displaying too much care—almost to the point of fuss, and Erno, he knew, hated being fussed. Yet the old man now seemed to relish the attention. It was almost as though she had called bedtime when Erno hauled himself out of his chair and bid them both good night. And Trudie had replied, "*Schlaf gut, Schneckchen*"—the sort of thing one might say to a seven-year-old. Little snail, indeed.

Left alone, there was a clumsy silence between Wilderness and Trudie, neither really wishing to speak, each wishing the other would just bugger off.

"It's not just his eyes, you will understand," she said at last. "It's everything."

§108

Vienna: July 10th

Wilderness got five minutes with the head of Erdbahn—one Josef Voigt.

Voigt was dapper to excess in his dress—bow tie, shiny waist-coat . . . Wilderness dared not look down in case the man were wearing spats—but plain unto blunt in speech.

"I do this because I have seen Russians firsthand. I was here when they took Vienna. Need I say more? All I ask is this—whatever you do, wherever you go, do no damage to my company's good name."

Tricky one, Wilderness thought.

"And I have, as your people in London requested, arranged a company car for you."

§109

The car wasn't new. It had five thousand miles on the clock and a few dents on the body. Just as well. He wasn't supposed to be new to the business so the car should look as though it had fought its way along a few farm tracks in its time.

It was a black 1966 four-door BMW 2000 *Neue Klasse*. Boxy and unprepossessing. He'd seen better looking jeeps. "Functional" was the most positive description that could be applied to it—red leather upholstery did little to diminish this—and it was probably all he needed, a car that deliberately avoided attracting attention.

Voigt's mechanic talked him through it. Flipped open the front panel of the passenger-side footwell to show him a specially installed clip to take a handgun. Good grief, did every bugger in Austria know his secrets?

"They'd really have to be looking for it to find it," the mechanic said.

"Well," Wilderness replied, "they usually are."

This was ignored as the man went into a rambling techspeak lecture on the specs of the car, the suping up, of which he was inordinately proud and to which Wilderness was wilfully indifferent.

"Lots of modifications—"

"Don't tell me . . . An ejector seat?"

"No. Just tweaks to the engine. Gas-flowing cylinder head, twin forty Dellorto carbs, high-lift camshaft and a less-restricted exhaust. It'll be a noisy bastard . . . but with eighty hp it'll outrun any cop car."

Eighty hp? Wasn't that more than the tractors Erdbahn made? And was that eighty hp towing a plough or a harrow?

Outrun a cop car? Wilderness had not anticipated that necessity, and he thought the mechanic hadn't either. He simply had his toy so he was going to play with it.

"One word of warning," the mechanic said as Wilderness slid into the driver's seat wondering what all the knobs and buttons did.

"Didn't have time to modify the brakes . . . so mind how you go."

Ah, the standard farewell of the London beat Bobby . . . "Evenin' All" to "Mind how you go."

Wilderness found this less than reassuring. All he wanted of a car was that it should be comfortable and unobtrusive.

"Put your foot down and you'll be doing a hundred and fifty before you can blink, and it'll top out around two hundred kph."

Two hundred kph. That was . . . he totted it up . . . one hundred twenty-five mph. His wife would love this car. Turn her loose on the Kingston bypass in a suped-up BMW and she'd do a hundred twenty-five and love every second of it.

He slipped his Smith & Wesson into the clip behind the footwell. Right now he had no idea if he'd ever need to take it out again. And no wish to take it out again. He was perfectly willing to take Crosland's advice. Not only would he not go in "guns blazing," he would go in without a gun and put trust above risk.

Perhaps he wasn't a secret agent after all?

Perhaps he really was a tractor salesman?

He drove back to his hotel at a stately twenty-five miles per hour.

He was, once more, staying at the Imperial Hotel, burdened, as it was, with a memory.

Vienna

§

Vienna, The Imperial Hotel: September 1955

It was clichéd in the extreme to tell himself "I need a drink," but he did.

He closed the bathroom door—trailed the sweet, coppery smell of blood with him—flopped into an armchair, half-expecting a hammering on the door and half not.

There was no alcohol in the room. Just as well. It was only his body needing a drink, it wasn't him.

He sat a minute or more listening to the unmusic of his own pulse. Then he looked at his right hand, still clutching the Browning.

He hadn't anticipated the result. A 7.65 wasn't a powerful pistol, it wasn't known for its "stopping power" . . . but his hand must have shook . . . and what was aimed at the Russian's forehead had entered his left eye, and—meeting little resistance—had ripped through his skull and splattered his brains across the tiles. And still his eyes were open . . . well, just the one.

VII

Beer and Sausages

§110

Prague: July 12th

A Warm Summer's Friday

Wilderness had driven in from the south, from Vienna, via Břeclav. He had never been to Prague. In fact, East Berlin being the big exception, he had scarcely been behind the Iron Curtain. Burne-Jones wisely took the view that a field agent was currency to be spent carefully. Wilderness had been sent to Warsaw and to Estonia, in each case pretending to be an East German, but most of his career had been spent in the Curtain's shadow, in places whose commitment might be dubious . . . Madrid, Lisbon . . . both as suspect now as they'd been in the thirties in the eyes of SIS, and, prior to the last trip, three or four visits to Finland to pick up and evaluate Soviet defectors.

This was different. He was Walter Hensel now.

On his first day he decided he might like Prague. Erdbahn had booked him into a faded glory called the Europa Hotel on Wenceslas Square. It was a beautiful, if dirty shade of yellow—the same Art Nouveau yellow that had been the sole memorable feature of his flat in Helsinki—and like much of Prague it was ornately finished off at sky-level with . . . not frescoes, they could not be frescoes surely? . . . perhaps they were friezes? Prague had never been bombed. It wasn't Warsaw or Berlin. Its buildings had benefitted from Czechoslovakia falling to the Nazis before Britain had woken up to the threat. Saving Poland had destroyed Warsaw, who had ever tried to save Prague?

On the second day he decided he did not like Prague. Even trams and cobblestones could not make him like Prague. It hadn't been destroyed, but it had been neglected. The dirt hit him first, the pollution second and then an all-pervasive sense that everything that could peel was peeling and everything that could crumble was crumbling. After twenty years of Communism the city needed a wash 'n' brush-up. It needed a bloke to come round with a roll of wallpaper, a few pots of paint and a ladder.

On the third day he decided he needed to make more of an effort. Prague, he concluded, resembled a giant cake. An old giant Miss Havisham's wedding cake of a cake. Peeling and crumbling . . . pink and yellow . . . and way too much icing. Cake would do—until he thought of something better.

§111

On the Monday Erdbahn's Prague office opened for business, Wilderness met Helmut Kruger. The man might have been a carbon copy of Voigt, a small, pocket-sized edition, wispy red hair, a fondness for bow ties. But he was a cheerier soul, refrained from stating his anti-Communist principles and seemed in no hurry to pack Wilderness off on his way.

He showed Wilderness a printed invitation to a British Embassy reception being held for the representatives of "Foreign Trade & Culture in Czechoslovakia" . . .

His Excellency requests the pleasure and blah blah blah . . .

RSVP Janis Bell, First Secretary

So—her knees were under the table.

"We should both go," Kruger added.

Of course.

§112

Prague: July 12th

A Warm Summer's Friday

Nell had come in by train from the north, from Lichtenberger Station in East Berlin, via Dresden. She had never been to Prague. The Foreign Ministry had found her a flat in Malá Strana; Malostranské nábřeží, on the west bank of the Vltava, by the Legií Bridge—an art nouveau building with faded friezes of Greek gods and warriors complete with tin hats—a top-floor flat with dazzling views over Prague. It was a far, far better flat than she had ever had, better than the tatty attic she had shared with Joe Wilderness just after the war, better than the flat she had moved to in Charlottenburg and better than the up-to-date soulless concrete box that had been her home in Bonn until a week ago.

Growing up on the endless plains of Prussia, Nell had never known hills. Prague was wrapped in hills. They seemed to burrow into the city, and the city into them. They came right across the street to knock on doors and peer in the windows of the upper storeys. She decided she liked hills. She decided she liked Prague.

She reckoned she could walk across the bridge to work, as the Ministry had rented an office for the Cultural Mission at the far end of Národní in Jungmannovo náměstí, a square that was in fact a triangle, and an office that was in fact a shop. Prague wasn't Berlin. No distance in Prague seemed far.

The Ministry of Culture being also in Malá Strana, on her first Monday morning Nell duly presented her credentials, expecting to be given an appointment with the minister, perhaps tomorrow or the day after. The clerk took an inordinate length of time, then he handed back the two heavy, cream pages of Bundesrepublik-crested paper to her with, "Try again next week."

It felt as though she had offered him two sheets of bog roll.

"Next week? The minister cannot see me until next week?"

"Minister? If you're lucky you'll get to see the deputy minister's assistant's assistant."

And she began to wonder if Brandt had not sent her chasing wild geese. If his "undercurrent" was not so far under as to be indiscernible.

But—walking across the Legií bridge into New Town none of that seemed to matter. She was falling in love again, this time with a city.

She soon reached the office. Her assistant, Clara Wieck, had been there a week already. When Nell arrived a painter was scraping letters off the big front window. It might, she thought, mean working in a goldfish bowl, but the size of the window bothered her less than the disappearing text:

ZÁPADONEMECKÁ KULTURNÍ MISE

Clara rushed into the square, hands spread wide in a placatory gesture.

"He's fixing it, honestly. By lunchtime it'll all be fine."

"*West* German Cultural Mission? Brandt will have us shot. How long was it up there?"

"Since Thursday."

"And how many Czechs have seen this travesty?"

Clara led Nell inside and pointed to a pile of letters on her desk.

"Not one of them addressed to *West* Germany—and only one that appears urgent.

It was a printed invitation to a British Embassy reception being held for the representatives of "Foreign Trade & Culture in Czechoslovakia" . . . His Excellency requests the pleasure and blah blah blah . . .

RSVP Janis Bell, First Secretary

"OK," Nell said. "We accept, of course."

"And this."

Clara handed her a telephone message she had jotted down herself.

"Petr Jasny. Says you know him."

"Young men forget. He forgets. We were supposed to meet at the East Berlin Film Festival last year. He never showed up."

"Well . . . he seemed very keen you should attend a preview of plays he's putting on at the Blue Orange Theatre."

"What plays?"

"He didn't say. Does it matter?"

"I suppose not. We're here to spread culture. I suppose that means we're here to be spread upon as well."

"I'm sure that's not half as rude as it sounds. Shall I accept?"

§113

Mělník

Rudolf Hahn broke the Erdbahn mould. He was at least ten years younger than his bosses and did not favour bow ties. Perhaps this was the rural Erdbahn? . . . open-collared, soft-shoed . . . if he'd been English he would be wearing corduroy, Hush Puppies and one of those hideous, saggy, waxy jackets that Wilderness's mother-in-law kept solely for dog walking in the London parks.

But—he was a pragmatist.

"Most farming is collectivised. Run by committees and apparatchiks. Which is to say scarcely run at all. Czechoslovakia is one of the most inefficient countries in Europe. Their agriculture is chaos and their manufactured goods rubbish. And we, of course, operate on the cusp of the two. In the fifties we would never have been allowed near the Collectives, all decision-making would be centralised, but they want our technology . . . they simply cannot make enough tractors . . . so we can now visit both the few privately owned farms and the Collectives—the private farmers are strapped for cash, and Collectives are bound up in layers of bureaucracy that go up and up and up. All the same . . . we do sell, eventually . . . and what we sell is better by far than any Czech-manufactured equipment."

Wilderness said, "What's the difference between a Škoda and a Jehovah's Witness?"

"What?"

"It's an English joke."

"I don't know. What's the difference?"

"You can close the door on a Jehovah's Witness."

"And what's a Jehovah's Witness?"

§114

Erdbahn lodged him in the centre of Mělník. His stout-bodied land-lady introduced herself polysyllabically and all Wilderness caught was "Fudge." He doubted that could be accurate but soon found a mnemonic for the old lady.

She baked her own bread, brewed her own beer and, as the widow of the local butcher, still made her own sausages—so she was Mrs. Home-made, who served him sausages for breakfast and beer with every meal.

He liked Mělník on sight. Mostly because there was not much to it. A couple of churches, a château and a handful of bars. It lay roughly where the Elbe met the Vltava, perched on a hill above a wide plain. He had a pleasant room, nicer than he'd had in Helsinki or Dublin, but it had no river view.

In the mornings, après sausage, he liked to take a cup of coffee out to the walls of the château and look down upon the river and the far-from-endless plain stretching into the České Středohoří. It was peaceful. Watching the river flow, so still as not to seem to flow—watching the traffic lights on the canal lock turn from red to green to red. He'd never seen traffic lights on a canal before. Watching the queue of barges, stacked with massive tree trunks, backed up waiting for the lift to the next level. That was peaceful too. It was all peaceful, the distant mountains were peaceful, even the flat fields of wheat were peaceful . . . no doubt ploughed, harrowed and soon to be harvested by his future customers.

Then on the fourth or fifth morning in Mělník it came to him. The greatest mistake an agent could make had always been to forget his cover . . . to think he was Joe Holderness rather than Walter Hensel. But now it seemed the greatest mistake might be to forget he was a spy at all.

He wished he could write novels. He had a couple of great titles at his fingertips: *The Spy Who Forgot He Was A Spy* and *The Spy Who Came In From* . . . from what? What else did spies come in from besides the soddin' cold? *The Spy Who Came In From* . . . *Mowing The Lawn*? No—*The Spy Who Came In From* . . . *Selling Fucking Tractors*!

It was so peaceful.

Why did he feel like screaming?

$115

Prague

The Blue Orange Theatre was on Husova, a narrow street of Prague Old Town. For reasons best known to itself, it had chosen to have its sign in French—*L'Orange Bleu*. This heightened the Magrittean absurdity of an orange, with its chicken pox texture and crisp green leaves, depicted in viridian blue.

Beneath the sign Petr Jasny waited. He would not know Nell, but she knew him from photographs—a handsome six foot two, dark-haired with the first hints of grey appearing, and cheeks and chin permanently in five o'clock shadow. He was a playwright and screen-writer with one directing credit to his name, *Hiding in Plain Sight*, which had first shown outside Czechoslovakia at the East Berlin Film Festival in 1966.

In the twelve months since the festival, Nell had come to think better of it, and unless pressed, would not now dream of telling him that it was far too derivative of Truffaut's *Les quatre cent coups*, which is what she would have said had he kept their appointment—but, then, all these young Turks of Mittel-European film worshipped Truffaut . . . or Godard . . . or Chabrol.

"Mr. Jasny?"

"Nell!"

A double-cheeked, continental kiss to freeze her to the spot.

"Come, we are late. We don't have a curtain but if we did it would go up in thirty seconds."

They slipped into two empty seats on the end of a row, eight or nine back from the stage.

There were no programmes. She had no idea what play might be about to reveal itself.

"What is it?" she asked as the lights came up to show a middle-aged couple and a young man. The young man appeared to be playing himself at chess.

"*The Garden Party*. Václav Havel. We are committed to new work for the theatre. This is the exception. A revival. A double bill with Pinter's *The Dumb Waiter*."

She had heard of both and seen neither.

As soon as the interval began Petr was gone—backstage with the notes he had been scribbling throughout. Nell looked past the empty seat to the man who had been on the far side of Petr, but he too was scribbling.

Then they watched the Pinter, a two-hander that Petr had translated into Czech himself. It was kitchen sink, complete with a real kitchen sink, being set, as it was, in a kitchen.

She understood it more than the Havel. The Havel was repetitive, nonsensical and absurd. The Garden Party was obviously the Communist Party (or was it?) and its absurdities the absurdities of infinite layers of state bureaucracy (or were they?), a department for everything . . . a department of winding up and a department for the winding up of the department of winding up. She did not like it. The only way it would have worked was if the cast had taken it at the speed of Vaudeville, the speed of Marx Brothers patter. But they hadn't.

The Dumb Waiter was arguably more fun, but was no fun at all. Corny to think it, she thought, cornier still in Prague, but it was Kafkaesque. Dark, oppressive, inexplicable.

Only when the Pinter had finished were introductions offered.

Petr introduced the man on his left.

"Miloš Forman—if you really are putting on a film festival in Berlin next year, this is the man you need. He's probably the best film director in the country."

"Which means I'll be banned any day now," Forman said with a grin.

Petr was about to leave her on the steps. His indecision manifested in one foot up and one foot down, torn between work and woman.

"I'd love to know what you think."

No, you really wouldn't.

"I'd love to buy you a beer, but I must get back to my cast. Look . . . Forman is screening a rough cut of his new film here on Saturday. Let's meet then."

Nell felt she had been picked up, twirled around and dropped back on her feet. A fifteen-year-old at a school dance.

She walked home. Depressed by the plays. Impressed by the man.

§116

The "rough cut" was of *The Fireman's Ball*. Nell was baffled and almost bored by the film. Fortunately Miloš Forman was surrounded by people who thought otherwise and he could not have fought his way through his fans to ask an opinion of Petr or herself.

She had found the final moments touching, symbolic. An old man who has lost everything in a blaze climbs into his brass bed in the middle of a field, as snow begins to settle on the counterpane. But symbolic of what?

On the theatre steps again.

If Petr Jasny wanted an opinion, he wasn't asking—yet.

"Where do you live? May I walk you home?"

"Malostranské nábřeži."

"Really? Then I'm just round the corner from you. I have an apartment at the far end of Vítězná—the trams go right by my window."

"Let's walk . . . as you said. It's a pleasant evening."

"Well?" he asked as they crossed the bridge into Malá Strana. "Your verdict?"

She would disappoint him, she knew, but that would hardly deter her from answering honestly.

"I suppose I ought to admire the representation of the present day. Your cinema . . . Czech cinema . . . has avoided representing the present—it has done for years. You're at your best depicting the last war. But you must show day-to-day life as it is now."

"We can't do that. Everything is grey. Most Czechs could describe the colour of depression to you—that too is grey. Czechoslovakia is a hundred shades of grey—but pick the wrong shade of grey and your work is banned and you find yourself working in a scrapyard. A film accurately depicting life in 1967 would be banned. Forman was making a joke with far too hard a truth to it—he may well find himself banned. At least with films about World War II, black is ostensibly black and white is ostensibly white. Surely the same is true in Germany?"

"No. And it's for that very reason we do not make films about the war."

"Our films are part of our resistance. You need to watch for the subtleties, Nell. Nothing is overt. You've seen *Closely Observed Trains*. It drips subtlety."

"Subtleties such as printing on a girl's bare bottom with railway station rubber stamps?"

"You have to admit it was funny."

"No I don't. It wasn't."

"Did you not find *The Fireman's Ball* funny?"

"No. It's another film about dirty old men in uniforms . . . they just happen to be firemen today not station masters twenty-five years ago."

"Yet it was subversive."

"In what way?"

"Lust. Lust is subversive. Pulling that girl's knickers down is subversive. In a country where our soldiers are always courageous and our citizens models of morality, immorality is itself a rebellion. And incompetence a victory. Both films are full of weak, lazy people who barely scrape the edge of heroism. As such they are mirrors held up to life, not something plucked from a socialist realism poster. And they are jokes—and censorship so rarely gets a joke. Think how ordinary and petty those firemen are, how unlike the Stakhanovite ideal. Think of those firemen as our Keystone Cops."

He was grinning as he said it. Highly amused at his own words.

"Keystone Cops? Really?"

"Oh Nell, I may come to love your po-face."

They had reached the end of the bridge, the corner of Malostranské nábřeži and Vítězná.

Another continental double kiss, which she took less rigidly than the first.

Then he was gone, walking quickly to the end of the street. She felt sure he'd wanted more. He hadn't asked. She'd no idea what she might have said or done if he had.

He was a hugely attractive man. A bit of a dandy with his coloured shirts and his silk scarves. She was plain Nell. Frau Burkhardt's po-faced daughter. His parting quip was no doubt casual, almost thoughtless, but it was precise enough to be surgical.

Her mother had frequently referred to her as "my po-faced girl"—the child who took everything seriously, whose eyes had scrutinised and doubted everything from the second they had opened on this world to focus on it like a camera.

That had been Joe Wilderness's strength and her weakness—he had made her laugh.

Before Wilderness she had often wondered if she had a sense of humour at all. Now she wondered if she was the right person to do the job Brandt had assigned her.

The next time they spoke she told him so, but he would not hear of her quitting Prague.

"Nell, you must stay until your po-face cracks with laughter."

It was as though he'd met her mother.

§117

Čzernázemě Agricultural Collective

As a city kid Wilderness was both ignorant and blinkered. Ignorant in that rural England and certainly rural Czechoslovakia were foreign turf to him; he could tell a dandelion from a nettle; without a handy pocket crib he could not tell oats from barley. Blinkered in that, plonked down on the vast plain of central Bohemia, he might not see what there was to be seen. It came to him as fragments, or, more precisely, detritus.

He stood, backside propped against the wing of his BMW, looking at a field, putting off the moment when he had to follow the baked-dirt trail down to the farm and buttonhole the Collective's apparatchik.

It was vast . . . a square mile or more without so much as a twiglet of hedge to break it up. He was almost certain the crop was maize, not yet ripe, almost head-height, spear-like until the corn cob popped out—his bluffer's vade mecum assured him it was grown as cattle fodder. After weeds—everywhere weeds—maize might be the most prolific crop in Czechoslovakia.

He drove a snaky route avoiding potholes. Along the way he passed spuds—who could fail to spot a spud?—and hops; he knew hops, he'd been on laborious hop-picking holidays in Kent in the 1930s. But—most striking were the sporadic crops of junk and rubbish. He passed two stagnant, stinking ponds each with a rusting piece of farm machinery sitting in the middle . . . he passed a brass bed, complete with mattress, standing in a field, covered in bird shit, as though a tornado had whisked away the house that once enclosed it . . . and every few yards a pile of garbage . . . a small mountain of sinks (who in their right mind collected sinks?), a bigger mountain of broken brick and gypsum plaster, and as he swung into the farmyard a roadside crucifix tilted at forty-five degrees, its broken Christ hanging by one arm, the wooden headboard that once proclaimed INRI split in two and caked in mud. It was less like the Čzernázemě Agricultural Collective (no.1483) than the Somme after the battle. All it needed was dead tanks, and if he drove on he was sure he'd find them too.

The barn was new. Ribbed, pressed steel in plain grey. Perhaps the only evidence of socialist planning to be seen. From it emerged half a dozen grumpy-looking men. The cleanest of them, the one in leather gaiters rather than wellies, approached him, watery-blue eyes, a white walrus moustache, a nose to delight Edward Lear . . . all conveying nothing but suspicion.

"You're late."

"Ah . . . sorry about that. New to the country."

"Kraut?"

"For my sins, yes."

"Well, don't try to atone for them here. You have too many and I don't have the time. Let's see it."

"See what."

"You'll have brought a brochure."

"Of course."

Wilderness had it tucked under his arm, a glowing guide to the Erdbahn T64.

"Hmm . . . tractor, eh? I don't need tractors, I need harrows."

Oh bugger—Hahn had not briefed him on harrows.

"I can come back to that if you like."

"I don't like. And I don't like this brochure."

The old bastard rubbed it between finger and thumb.

"You haven't read it yet."

"I don't need to. It feels useless. Far too shiny."

"Too shiny for what?"

"Too shiny for wiping my arse on. Bring me paper that mops up a bit of shit and maybe we can talk about harrows."

§118

The British Embassy, Palác Thun

The embassy resembled a fortress more than a palace. Forbidding wooden gates designed to resist the battering ram that now merely opened and closed on government Humbers.

The occasion—half of Prague seemed to be queuing up—necessitated uniformed coppers, although Wilderness spotted the StB secret service dogsbody at once. He sat in a cupboard set in the stone wall opposite the gates. The oddity was that he bothered with concealment at all.

The coppers checked no documents, simply ensured that the turn-around of cars in the cul-de-sac was smooth. Inside, no one asked him for identification. He and Kruger produced their invitations and were nodded through to the reception with a smile.

It wasn't "black-tie"—just as well, Wilderness hated the black-tie events to which his father-in-law would occasionally drag him like the whining schoolboy. He'd scrubbed up, put on his best togs—Kruger had swapped his hideous paisley bow tie for one in a discreet cobalt blue.

He was impressed that Janis Bell had got all this together so soon. It was a shrewd move to bury control and agent in the biggest crowd she could muster.

He shook hands with the ambassador—he had the vaguest memory of this bloke, Lord Brynmawr . . . hadn't he been some sort of trades union leader back in the early sixties? . . . the Amalgamated Wellyboot Makers? . . . the Guild of Backseat Drivers?—and with a plump, red-faced head of chancery whose name he immediately forgot.

He hoped Janis would find him soon. There was surely a limit to the number of sausages on sticks he could eat and to how long he could make small talk in English whilst faking a Berlin accent. He sounded to his own ears like an SS guard in a 1950s POW film—"Ve haff ways of makink you eat sausage." And, as his first attempt at conversation proved, tractors were amongst the biggest chat-stoppers known to man.

Over to his left he spotted a woman in a stunning backless black dress that might have been sprayed onto her buttocks. Judy would have named the designer for him in a split second . . . Chanel? Schiaparelli? Or if it turned out to be frontless as well as backless, Rudi Gernreich.

Only one way to find out—but as he approached the woman he felt a hand settle gently upon his arm.

"Herr Hensel?" Janis Bell said. "How good of you to join us this evening. I'm Janis Bell, First Secretary to the ambassador."

Bugger. The woman in black did not turn around.

Had she done so, Wilderness would have found himself face to face with Nell Burkhardt.

"Have you seen the embassy garden? It's at its best at this time of the year."

Wilderness took the hint, muttered the right pleasantries and followed.

They went nowhere near the garden.

Janis Bell closeted them in an office on the floor above and said, "It's secure. We can talk."

"I'm listening."

"I've done what Colonel Burne-Jones asked. I've worked out a simple way for the Czechs to pass information—so long as your man really has mastered his plum duff."

She pushed a small hardback book across the desk.

Franz Kafka: Ausgewählte Kurzgeschichten (Franz Kafka: Selected Short Stories)

"Turn to the third one in."

Wilderness flipped past *Forschungen eines Hundes* and *In der Strafkolonie* to *Die Verwandlung*—Metamorphosis.

"Third paragraph, first sentence."

Gregors Blick richtete sich dann zum Fenster, und das trübe Wetter—man hörte Regentropfen auf das Fensterblech aufschlagen—machte ihn ganz melancholisch.

"Tenth word has an umlaut, so does the thirteenth. The last word doesn't. Put an umlaut over the 'o' of *melancholisch* and you have your conduit. A microdot, two if necessary. A good German speaker would spot it. Most would dismiss it as a typographic error."

Wilderness ran the tip of his index finger along the sentence.

"Would I be able to feel something? Like Braille."

"I doubt it. But I'm as new to this as you are. Nine months ago, you will recall, the most secret thing I did was type Old Ma Burton's letters. You can buy this book anywhere in the German-speaking world. Prague alone will have five thousand identical copies in its bookshops. Buy them as you need them, but not all at the same shop. Obviously. You give a copy of the book to your Czech. When there's information to receive, you just swap the doctored copy for a clean one. He is never without a Kafka and neither are you. Simple."

"Yes. It is and it'll work. Can you set up a meeting?"

"I need a few more days. I want at least six people between me and him . . . as I believe you put it to the colonel . . . a chain so long the KGB can't follow it."

"I was really hoping they'd just get bored and give up."

Janis Bell smiled, laughed.

"And when the meeting's set up," Wilderness said, "suspend the chain."

The laugh cut short, the smiled dropped.

"What?"

"Stand everyone down. Indefinitely. I'll do everything face-to-face with Tibor. From now on nothing comes through the embassy."

"Nothing?"

"Safer that way."

"So what do I do, Sgt. Holderness? Go back to typing fucking letters!"

§119

Wilderness did his best to convince her.

"Janis, you'll be the decoy. If you're looking for risk, if you're looking for danger there'll be more than enough for both of us."

"I'm not as naïve as you think. I'm not looking for risk, I'm not looking for danger. I am looking to be significant. I am looking . . . I am looking . . . to make a difference!"

"Believe me, you will."

"Fuck you, Joe."

"Not helpful, Janis."

"Me being a soddin' decoy is hardly much of a step up from typing. Did you get me here just for that? Or are we going back to showing *Carry On* films as a cover for a dodgy booze racket?"

"Cheap shot, Janis."

"At least your rackets made a profit!"

"Cheaper still."

With her last insult some of the steam seemed to go out of her. She smoothed down her dress and shook the hair out of her eyes. Looked to Wilderness to be very disappointed in him.

"I have to go. Lord Brynmawr isn't exactly the life and soul of the party. In fact, in less than a month I've concluded he's a total twat who shouldn't be allowed out on his own. And he'll get his knickers in a twist if I'm not out there schmoozing."

"Fine. Just let me know when the chain's in place."

A sigh of deep exasperation, an upward tilt of the head. In heels she and Wilderness were unflinchingly eye to eye.

"I'll get a message to Kruger at Erdbahn . . . some sort of follow-up to tonight's farce, a thank you, a suggestion to discuss things further . . . whatever . . . he'll pass it to his bloke at Mělník."

"A time and place?"

"Of course."

"Good."

"Oh, good? Happy now? Right, I'll get back to me typewriter."

§120

About a week after Janis Bell's bit-of-a-do at the embassy Rudolf Hahn handed him an envelope. Inside was a picture postcard of the Old New Synagogue in Prague.

On the back was a map reference.

"What?"

"I heard that this is how it's done. Postcards. You send each other anonymous postcards."

"It has been known, I agree, agent to agent, city to city perhaps, but we're in the same room. Rudolf, why not just show me on the map?"

Hahn looked both ways, even though there was no one else in the office, before reaching down a map from the shelf above his desk.

He stabbed at it with his finger.

It was, judging by the contours, a hill. There weren't many of those around.

"I believe it's a monument. Of some sort. Quite easy to find of course."

§121

Somewhere in the České Středohoří

Wilderness wondered if he would have chosen this hilltop for a meeting. It had advantages—you could see everything for miles around—and disadvantages—you had nowhere to hide. Anyone in a light plane or a helicopter could hardly miss you, but the Czechs seemed grounded. Czechoslovakia had more canal barges than planes. The skies did not buzz, no Cessnas, no Bobcats, no Bell Whirlybirds. Only a couple of unflapping vultures gliding.

It was a strange place. Hahn had termed it a memorial or a monument or some such, but to what Wilderness could not quite grasp. A pile of stones carefully placed in the centre of a stone circle—it all somehow seemed gladiatorial, a setting for sport or combat. No dates, no inscriptions, no roll call of the Czech dead, in a country that had dead and memorials aplenty.

Up the opposite track a maroon, dirty Škoda Octavia approached, throwing up a cloud of white dust. Tibor skidded to a halt outside the stone circle. He stood a moment half-hidden by the open door. He looked, as Crosland had said, to be in his late twenties—slightly built, about five foot nine and wearing what Wilderness thought of as the ubiquitous Czech cap.

His right hand appeared over the door, clutching a handgun.

Wilderness had expected this.

He'd left his in the footwell of the BMW.

Nobody spoke.

He slipped off his jacket, lifted his shirt, held his arms high and turned through 360 degrees.

"Happy now?"

"No. I am not happy."

"All the same, put the gun away, because you've seen all there is to see. I'm not dropping my trousers."

"You take too many risks."

"I do?"

"We have no . . . no password. We should have had a password. You have no gun. You should have a gun."

"Why? Do you want me to shoot you?"

Wilderness put his jacket back on.

"Put the gun way, Tibor."

"You know my name. What do I call you?"

"Put the damn thing away and I'll tell you."

Tibor looked at the gun as though wondering how it came to be in his right hand, then he stuck it back inside his jacket.

"I have a codename," Wilderness proffered. "Diesel."

"Really?"

"I didn't get to pick. If you like, you can call me Joe."

"*Ano ano* . . . the world is full of Joes."

"Isn't it just."

"Why are we here . . . face-to-face, Joe?"

"Dead drops and a chain of connection damn near got you caught."

"No—it didn't. The last drop Mrs. Crosland picked up was cold. I'd made it the night before. By the time the KGB pounced I was miles from Prague."

"As we are now."

"Indeed."

"If we meet face-to-face, without a chain, then you and I are the only people in the know. The embassy people go through the motions—but really they're just a decoy. Each time we meet, we agree on a time for the next meeting. If one of us fails to show, we know the other's busted."

"And then?"

"Then I drive hell-for-leather for the German border."

"And if you don't show . . . where do I run to?"

It was a good question. One Wilderness could not answer.

"And," Tibor went on. "If I have nothing to give you?"

"Then I suggest you bring a book, a ham sandwich, a bottle of beer and have a picnic."

Tibor cracked, a grin that became laughter.

"Joe—you are absurd enough, silly enough to be a Czech."

"So happens, I have a book with me."

He took the Kafka out of his jacket pocket.

"*Metamorphosis*. Third paragraph, last word. Stick your dots on *melancholisch* . . . pretend it's an umlaut."

Tibor flicked through the pages, looked at *Metamorphosis*.

"I have read the story many times. I could even say it haunts me. Some mornings I wake up and I'm surprised to find I am not a beetle. Tell me . . . do you know what the name Kafka means?"

"I thought Kafka meant Kafka."

"I suppose it does, but it sounds exactly like *kavka*. Jackdaw. The bird that collects shiny objects—gold and silver and jewels. What jewels will I bring you, Joe?"

And it occurred to Wilderness that jackdaws had no discrimination and were as likely to pick up the tinfoil cap off a milk bottle as a gold sovereign.

§122

Prague, Malá Strana

On their third "date," Nell slept with Petr.

Part way through one of his well-constructed, earnest lectures on Czech cinema, he cut himself short.

"Oh hell . . . I mean all of that or none of it . . . but right now it doesn't matter a damn."

"What does matter?"

"You do. Come home with me, Nell."

Rarely had she been so bluntly propositioned.

She was not surprised. She was not offended.

She led off, forcing him to follow her.

"On the corner, you said? Where the trams go by?"

§123

Afterwards.

"You have not been with many men, I think."

Nell was momentarily torn between outrage and curiosity at this remark.

"No. I haven't. Does it show?"

"Only when you put the light out to get undressed."

She wondered what to say and opted for truth.

"In my teens. In Berlin. Just after the war. I lived with an Englishman. He turned my life upside down. He was called Wilderness and that was what he left in his wake. Since then I have been . . . wary. I have turned out the light. An act that might be a metaphor. And I have preferred one-night stands. Does that sound awful? Does it sound promiscuous?"

"I'm male, how can I object to promiscuity? Besides it is the era of free love."

It was that summer's most overworked phrase . . . invoking girls in billowing dresses, young men with shoulder-length hair . . . it went with psychedelic rock, love-ins and flower power . . . with Haight-Ashbury not Malá Strana. And it certainly did not encompass or describe her private life in Berlin for the last twenty years—nothing was ever free. And she found his remark little short of infuriating.

"It might be the era of free love in the West. Not here. It might be in California, but . . . perhaps we are all just California dreaming."

§124

Mělník

Homework. Wilderness was doing his homework.

Erdbahn made several different types of harrow.

None more interesting than the next.

All of them of no interest at all.

Wilderness stifled a yawn and pushed on.

```
The 24 tine Spring Tine Drag Harrow, also
available to order with 36 tines. Better suited
to drier, lighter soils. Width 3.65 meters.
Suitable for both the T52 and T64 models.
```

The photos also showed that it was available in red or blue. It was like looking at the world's worst car show. Where was the scantily clad woman sprawled across the damn thing? Was there no Pirelli calendar for farm equipment?

So—be practical, he told himself—you need to be able to talk to the old bastards down on the farm—so, what does the bloody thing do? Dig, flatten, pummel? Roast, fry, simmer? Frap, flip and fricassee?

He never thought he'd think this, but right now he'd sooner be back in Lapland showing bawdy British films to drunken Finns.

If Finland had been a punishment posting, then what was Czechoslovakia . . . his own private circle in hell?

§125

Prague, Old Town: September

Prague seemed to Nell to have a theatre on every street. Petr took her to most of them in a matter of six weeks, to the Balustrade, to the Café Viola, to Laterna Magika, to the Semafor, to Činoherní Klub, to Papoušek Cécile and a dozen more—and she began to realise that for all that Czech film and theatre relished the absurd, hid in the obtuse, in the absence of free speech politics was art and art was politics.

She mentioned her brush-off at the Ministry of Culture.

"It's easy," Petr replied. "You just need to think like George Orwell. The Ministry of Culture is really the Ministry of Censorship. Extend the pattern logically and what does the Ministry of Justice become?"

"The Ministry of . . . Punishment?"

"Exactly. I think you might make a Czech after all."

Petr, along with every other writer he introduced her to, belonged to the group Writers '62—who dated themselves from the year the fifty-foot statue of Stalin, that had dominated Prague from a hillside on the north bank for seven years, had been demolished. It had been conceived in Stalin's lifetime, completed two years after his death and blown up in 1962, reportedly on Khrushchev's orders. It had been derided from the start by Prague-dwellers as "the bread queue," a reference to the artisans and workers standing in line behind Stalin.

"It was the biggest bang any of us had ever seen, and we took it as our cue. The Khrushchev thaw had arrived—long overdue and almost too late for the man himself—but we felt braver now because of it. We gathered in the Golden Tiger that night and united over beer and books."

He took her to the Golden Tiger, just a few doors away from the Blue Orange. It looked to Nell like a typical German beer hall, narrow, grubby, plain wooden tables under a vaulted ceiling—she found them depressing, but the Golden Tiger had one vital difference: writers stood and read from their works a couple of nights a week. The first time they went there it was poets hardly out of their teens she could not pretend to understand. The second time it was the well-known author of the newly filmed *Closely Observed Trains*, Bohumil Hrabal.

Hrabal read well. He seemed to have a taste for sentences as long as Henry James's and a gift for imagery that was dizzying, but he was poignant, honest, witty and funny.

Applause did not last long—hands that are clapping cannot hold a litre of beer—and as it faded Nell caught Petr looking at her.

"What?"

"You almost laughed."

"Stop it. Of course I laughed. What was that story called?"

"It's a mouthful—*Advertisement for a House I Do Not Wish to Live in Anymore.*"

"You're kidding."

"No—one day Hrabal will write a title longer than the story that follows it. He's working on a film script of it right now . . . he and Menzel have a better title, *Larks on a String*. But I think they're up against it."

"Meaning?"

"It screams out to be banned."

§126

Later, *In Between the Sheets*

"In 1956 I was teaching at the university. I was twenty-six. Young, precocious, fortunate. My brother Tomáš taught in the same department. He was eight years older than me, and a full professor. A man with a sound critical reputation. He had translated Dante into Czech. After the invasion of Hungary he published a pamphlet, privately, illegally, denouncing the Russians. It came to the attention of the state—why would it not? He lost everything—home, wife, son, life."

"Life?"

"He died in prison. I've no idea whether he was just worn out or took a bullet to the back of the head. There was no body, there is no grave. But . . . the contagion spread. He saved his wife Magda by telling the secret police he was divorcing her. All the same she withstood weeks of interrogation. He could not save me. Guilt by association. I served a year in prison. Still . . . they had a marvellous library, everything you could ever want by Marx, Engels or Lenin. I rather enjoyed Engels . . . if there's anything you need to know about the condition of the working class in Manchester in the 1840s, I'm your man."

Nell said nothing. Silently willing him to go on.

"Of course, I could not return to the university. I took to writing. First magazines—we are allowed magazines that are subscription only, a small concession—then script editing for short films at Barrandov Studios, and then a full-length film in '65. As both writer and director. *Hiding in Plain Sight* was immediately suppressed. There is, after all, no such thing as an unhappy childhood in a state that provides everything from cradle to grave, including hot and cold running happiness. The copy you saw in Berlin last year was smuggled out. Not without notice. I was charged with parasitism—that is, no obvious means of support . . . writing was not a recognised job in my case, so I got another four months, which is why I never got to Berlin. I was sent to a light engineering factory in Mladá Boleslav making parts for Škoda car doors, on a hand press—the process took four seconds, repeated ten hours a day. I've never complained of being bored since. It could have been worse. The scrapyards Forman and I joke about are real enough. I got out just after Christmas."

§127

November 1st

Wilderness had not been allowed to choose his own codename. Not that "Diesel" bothered him.

Alice Pettifer and Janis Bell had—they were, respectively, White Rabbit and Pussy-in-the-Well. Burne-Jones was, whether he liked it or not, Omelette, as it was the only dish Alice had ever known him to cook.

Pussy-in-the-Well to White Rabbit

— Much to report. First, Dubček has shown his hand. According to narks and leaks—i.e. not a word has made the papers—he went up against Novotny yesterday afternoon and challenged him to separate party and state. There's a real movement for reform, an opposition-party-within-the party taking shape around him. I can't believe Brezhnev will let this happen. If Khrushchev could crush Hungary what might Brezhnev do to Czechoslovakia?

Predictably, you stop the average Prague citizen in the street and they have no idea who Dubček is. He has emerged from Slovakia as if from nowhere. Imagine if a bloke from Basingstoke suddenly stepped up to challenge Wilson or Heath.

Coincidentally—do we believe in coincidence?—the lights went out last night. I mean that literally. Hardest hit were the student flats. No light, no work. An honesty my generation would not have admitted to. We'd have just got drunk and made babies. But this lot—about fifteen hundred or so—took to the streets. Heading for the castle. They got as far as Nerudova, only yards from the embassy, so I went down there to see for myself. They were chanting "We want Light. We want Light." Poetic as well as literal. I don't know what started it but the police laid into those kids with truncheons, tear gas, you name it. As long as I've been here—OK that's not so long really—Czechs have been telling me how much

easier things are getting. Well, this looked
like one step forward, two steps back. I've
been on student demos and, yes, the English
coppers can be pigs, but I'd not seen violence
on this scale. There's word that the injured
filled an entire ward in the Petřin hospital.
"We want light." Czechoslovakia wants light.

And I have a new bit of Czech slang for you,
make of it what you will: Radish/Ředkev.
Geddit?

White Rabbit to Pussy-in-the-Well

— Red on the outside. White on the inside?

Pussy-in-the-Well to White Rabbit

— Yep.

§128

The Night Before
October 31st

Petr all but kicked the door open, something long and loose slung
across his shoulder

"Hot water, Nell! Put a kettle on."

He hurled his package onto the sofa. A scrawny, long-haired teenage
boy with blood pouring from his forehead.

"What? Who?"

"My nephew, Jiří. My brother's son."

The flame popped under the kettle. She ran to the bathroom for a clean flannel.

"How did this happen?"

The boy's eyes flickered open.

"How do all these things happen? Coppers."

He swung his legs off the sofa, one hand still pressing the flannel to his head.

Nell took the flannel from him, wiped at the cut to see if it needed stitching. It didn't.

"You were lucky."

"Lucky I was there," said Petr.

"Do I seem ungrateful?"

"Jiří, you've never been grateful for a fucking thing in your whole life."

"Petr!"

As if she had cued him, Petr got up and left the room. She had learnt that his most frequent reaction to any confrontation was absence. She did not judge him, telling herself she had not been through what he had been through.

The kettle whistled.

"I'm going to clean the wound."

"Go ahead. I'm Jiří, by the way."

"And I am Nell."

"German?"

"Is it that obvious?"

"Just guessing. You and my uncle are . . . ?"

"Yes. We are."

"Congratulations."

"Meaning?"

"I have better luck with women than he does."

"Keep still."

"Ouch!"

"I said keep still. And try to be less arrogant. Your ego is just feeding the pain."

This seemed to work. The boy shut up and let her bathe the cut. When she'd finished she found the first-aid box and taped a thick dressing across his forehead. He was good-looking, but nothing like Petr. He was no more than five foot six, less than sixty kilos, blond and bony. Perhaps he took after his mother.

"Tea? Something hot?"

"No. Thank you. If the streets are clear I should go home."

"Where do you live?"

"Bartolomějská. Old Town. With my mother, Magda."

"Not that far then?"

"No."

"You could stay. It might be best."

"He wouldn't thank you for that."

§129

Later, *In Between the Sheets*

Petr wrapped himself around her.

"I'm sorry."

"Don't be. You probably saved his life."

"It's not that I don't like Jiří. My brother's only son. He just irritates the shit out of me. He is . . . careless . . . he takes risks . . . he never thinks. He has no idea of . . . the consequences. Czechoslovakia is a country of consequences. For every action a reaction."

§130

Prague, New Town: A Few Days Later

Nell looked up from her desk. Someone was tapping, banging, on the huge plate glass window.

There was Jiří Jasny, peering in between the N and the E of NEMEC. She opened the door.

"Shouldn't you be at the university?"

"No lectures today."

He was lying and she knew it. Petr had told her that Jiří was an inveterate skiver who drove his mother to despair.

"I was wondering," Jiří said, "if you would like to come out this evening."

"What?"

"Petr is in an edit at Barrandov. He often works all night, doesn't he?"

"Yes, but—"

"Then come to a meeting of the Žolíky."

"The what?"

"Just a bunch of students. We call ourselves Žolíky. *Spaßvögel.*"

"Ah . . . the Jokers."

"Pranksters . . . we prefer Pranksters."

"And what pranks do you get up to?"

"Oh . . . music and poetry . . . you know."

"So, it's like a meeting of Writers '62?"

"No. Not all like that. Come and see for yourself. My pal Mopslík. His dad has a warehouse just down the street from my mother's apartment. The top floor's been empty for years. He lets us have it for nothing as a . . . sort of . . . youth club."

A youth club? Nell could see no harm in that.

"We're all supposed to be in the youth league—*Svazek*—but . . . none of us give a damn about the youth league. We have better ideas. Will you come?"

"Yes. I think I will."

§131

Bartolomějská

Nell had no idea Prague had hippies. Perhaps that was not the right term, but she could think of no other to describe skinny girls with flowers in their hair and diaphanous dresses, and boys in flared jeans with paisley and velvet inserts sewn in below the knee to fluff them out to fifty centimetres. Every footstep set their jeans flapping around their ankles.

"I thought you meant it would be just boys."

"It's OK, Nell. We won't be fucking on the floorboards. Not tonight anyway."

Nell thought she should take that as a warning, but curiosity got the better of her. Jiří was a joker, perhaps that was one of his jokes? Jiří was a prankster. She hoped fucking on the floor was not one of his pranks.

There were no chairs. Everyone sat on the floorboards, getting covered in ancient dust. The light was dim, half a dozen unshaded bulbs dotted around the high ceiling. On the far wall myriad colours swirled across the brickwork as one of the boys fed projector slides with drops of tinted oil which boiled and bubbled on contact.

A record played faintly in the background . . . something about chasing rabbits.

A boy in thick spectacles got up to read, standing in the window, where a streetlamp lit him up as though in limelight.

> *"When the days are grey,*
> *The rain is purple.*
> *I sit at the feet of the stone Buddha*
> *And try to kiss the sky."*

Nell had no idea what to make of it. "Nonsense" might be a reasonable reaction.

> *"The curlew flies at sunset*
> *Into night's black mouth.*
> *I wait for starlight.*
> *And in the morning,*
> *The rainbow has frozen."*

Nell looked at Jiří for a sign of comprehension. He was pulling on a roll-up cigarette. It stank. He passed it to her.

"I do not smoke tobacco."

"S'OK. It isn't just tobacco. It's a good Red Leb."

"What?"

"Oh Nell . . . where have you been the last year? . . . Red Leb. Hashish from Lebanon."

Fed up with waiting, the girl next to her took the joint from her fingers and inhaled.

And when she breathed out, the smell of hash seemed to Nell like a Berlin mist enveloping her. Foul and all-pervasive.

A second poet got up to read, a third, a fourth and a fifth.

Nell had had enough, but then so had everyone else, it seemed.

Mopslík produced an LP in a vivid cardboard sleeve. Jiří opened two windows and placed a loudspeaker in each.

"We just got this from England."

"Got what?"

"Patience, Nell—it's time Prague heard this. Time we all heard it."

"It's half past ten. People will be trying to sleep."

"Well—we won't let them."

And the music blared out loudly, just shy of distortion—and Nell learnt that it had been twenty years ago today that Sergeant Pepper had taught his band to play.

§132

They only stopped when a neighbour stood in the street, shaking his fist and threatening to call the police. But then, she thought, that was most certainly the reaction they had wanted.

Nell left.

Jiří came running after her.

"Leave me alone, Jiří."

"Are you . . . offended?"

"That would not be the word. But I have a word for you—hooligan."

"I'm flattered."

"Don't be."

"In a world where order changes constantly whilst declaring it has stayed the same—to be a hooligan is the only sane behaviour."

It sounded to Nell like a well-rehearsed line. A position statement.

"Really? Does that mean anything? Does your group of stoned teenagers mean anything, stand for anything?"

"Does Writers '62 stand for anything? They make statements. They write manifestoes. Statement this, manifesto that . . . boring."

Ah, the cardinal sin in the eyes of the young.

"You're rather scathing. I've read some of them—"

"Manifesto shmanifesto . . . revolution by numbers."

"What's your alternative? What do you and your friends do that Writers '62 does not?"

"We rock. We make revolution for fun. We make revolution for the hell of it—and that's a quotation from Abbie Hoffmann."

"Who?"

§133

December 8th

Pussy-in-the-Well to White Rabbit
—Brezhnev is here. Utterly without notice. No
  idea what it means. It could be support for
  Novotny. Could be the chop. The real threat to
  the old order is still Dubček.
     And . . . for what it's worth there is the
  shadow of a rumour, I put it no more strongly
  than that, of an abortive military coup. I
  don't have any details.

§134

January 5, 1968

Pussy-in-the-Well to White Rabbit
—Novotny's resigned! Cue Martha and the
  Vandellas. There'll be dancing in the streets.
  Still prez, but Dubček takes over as First
  Secretary. Watch this space.

White Rabbit to Pussy-in-the-Well
—Omelette is asking "What's a Vandella? Should
  we open a file?"

$135

January 6th

Nell never seemed to know quite what determined where they spent the night. Petr was hard to part from his books and his study. She liked to wake up, especially at the weekend, with the morning sun streaming into her bedroom from across the river. One coffee at home, a second in the Café Savoy just across the square. If Petr spent all night at Barrandov, then she would always sleep at Malostranské nábřeži.

Last night Petr had fallen asleep at his desk. Nell had draped a blanket over him and gone back to the bedroom.

At eight in the morning she was ready for work—a short, productive Saturday morning with no distractions. She'd deal with all the Bonn correspondence and be back before noon. Then they'd wrap up against January and go out for lunch. The afternoon would be hers, hers and his. They might even go back to bed. An idea that, six months ago, would have struck Nell as the height of decadence.

She was making coffee for both of them.

A tapping at the door, a tapping without the heart of a knock to it.

Jiří was slumped against the door frame, bags under his young eyes, his Beatle-ish hair looking like a bird's nest.

"What's happened? You look awful. You look . . . pathetic."

"I feel pathetic. Mami threw me out last night."

He pointed to the suitcase at his feet.

"I slept on a bench in Kampa. When I woke up at seven, this was next to the bench. A message that's impossible not to get. God knows how she found me."

Nell reached down a third cup from the shelf. Jiří all but fell into the sofa.

"Why didn't you come here?"

"It was past midnight. I couldn't do that to you . . . or rather I couldn't do that to Petr and expect to get away with it."

"Why did Magda do this?"

Jiří said nothing.

"Try telling me the truth."

"We celebrated last night. Y'know . . . Novotny gone . . . the best Friday night ever . . . we did rather a lot of dope. As a rule I'd change my shirt and suck on a packet of mints—if there was time I'd even give my hair a rinse—before showing up at home. I was too stoned to think straight. And I suppose I thought she'd be in bed. She wasn't. The scene could not have been more clichéd if she'd been standing there in her nightdress clutching the rolling pin. She smelt dope on me . . . and that was it. Out. She hates illegality."

A voice from the next room.

"Can you blame her?"

Petr stood in the study doorway. Nell wondered if Jiří had just lit the blue touch paper.

"After what she went through?"

"I know what Mami went through, Petr."

"No, you don't. You know only what she's told you."

"Petr, right now I don't need a lecture. I need somewhere to stay."

Against Nell's expectations, Petr sat down next to Jiří—seemingly quite calm.

"That's a lot to ask."

Nell gave them each a cup of coffee.

Jiří sipped and sighed.

"I know. All the same I ask."

Petr gulped his coffee and held the cup out for more.

With her back to them, pouring coffee, Nell said, "There's my apartment."

She turned to see their reaction.

Petr was shaking his head, and the half-smile of latent optimism vanished from Jiří's lips.

"No. You don't know Magda, Nell. I wouldn't wish her upon you. She wants him out. Fine. I understand that. She has been through hell with the police. It's a justifiable paranoia. But if she has any bones to pick over with Jiří, she'll come looking. Better by far that she finds him here. We'll clear out the box room. A six-footer wouldn't fit in there, but he will."

"Box room? A fucking box room?" Jiří said.

"That's it, Jiří. Go on pushing your luck. And I say now, your being here carries conditions . . . you bring no trouble down on me or Nell."

The boy sensed victory and was grinning.

"You don't have to speak, Jiří. That might be too much to ask. Just nod your head if you understand me."

§136

Mid-February

On her route from her office to Petr's apartment, Nell had become accustomed to seeing graffiti. It seemed almost to be a Czech tradition. A public forum in a country that had none. Of late, since the change at the top, graffiti, or more precisely slogans, seemed to have mushroomed. The anti-government slogans were still there, aging and fading—but the new stuff seemed like sloganeering for the sake of sloganeering, a delight in that other Czech tradition—absurdity. *Credo quia absurdum.*

The long slogan, only yards from the National Theatre, sprayed rapidly and spelt badly, as though its author had had to run for it, was a quotation from absurdity's master, Václav Havel: "He who doesn't know how to wade through rye . . ."

She knew how it ended: ". . . must go to Prague for his wits."

It didn't mean anything. It didn't have to mean anything. That was Havel's point. To spray it on a wall was pointless.

But the one on the stone flags at the far end of the bridge, close to her own apartment, in English, "Six Impossible Things Before Breakfast," surely intended meaning?

And on a pair of dirty green gates directly opposite Petr's door, "Remember What the White Queen Said."

They were a cut above the usual graffiti. Someone had gone to the trouble of cutting a stencil for each word.

§137

Jiří's box room was less than six feet by six. Into this he had fitted a pitifully narrow mattress, just leaving room for a desk and a chair. When the door was opened it banged into a corner of the desk—as it did now, when Nell stuck her head around it to ask if he wanted a hot drink.

"It's freezing outside."

"I know," he replied. "I've been out in it. Not been home long at all."

Why he had been out was obvious.

The stencils for "Six Impossible Things Before Breakfast" and "Remember What the White Queen Said" were pinned to the wall above his desk, still wet, dripping red paint down the colourless wallpaper.

"What does 'Remember What the White Queen Said' mean?"

"It's Lewis Carroll. Surely it doesn't need explanation?"

"I suppose not."

Nell paused, wondering how much she could ask before he clammed up or exploded.

"Jiří, why are you doing this *now*?"

"It was too dangerous to do much before Christmas, or have you forgotten the night we met."

"No, I haven't. But . . . the old guard is gone. Or if not gone, going."

"Meet the new guard, same as the old guard."

"I don't understand. What do you mean?"

"What does one expect from an old guard?"

"I don't know. What does one expect from an old guard?"

"That they be old. What does one expect from a new guard?"

"I don't know."

"Everything."

"Everything?"

"Everything. And what do we get?"

"Whatever I say now will be wrong, so . . ."

"We get silence. Six weeks of Dubček in power and six weeks of silence. He has to say something or the change of leadership means nothing. We're drowning in Dubček's silence."

A grin spread across his face. When he thought of something, a word or phrase he might drop like a bomb into conversation, the boy was uncontainable. For all that he lied he was a poor liar. His face betrayed him.

"You must have seen those sausage stalls? They're everywhere."

"Of course."

"You know what *utopenci* are? Pickled sausages, in big jars, they sell them with gherkins. But *utopenci* translates as *Ertrunkene*—drowned men. We're all drowned men, until he speaks."

This was undeniable. Petr had said much the same thing only days ago. Brandt had sent her, tongue-in-cheek, a Disney postcard of the Pekinese dog from *Lady and the Tramp* wearing a muzzle, over which he had scrawled the initials "A.D.?"—Aleksandr Dubček.

"And what's that?"

Nell pointed at a collage on Jiří's desk—letters cut and pasted. Several discarded attempts littered the floor.

skri̯ska

"I'm designing the masthead for our newspaper."

"Whose newspaper?"

"Ours . . . us students . . . the Pranksters."

"What does it stand for?"

"*Skřitek Škatule*—Goblin Box. We are a country of demons and elves, water sprites and goblins. Czechs are very superstitious."

Another Czech tradition.

"Yes," she said. "I had noticed. And where will you get the paper?"

"Oh . . . such German practicality. I dunno . . . behind the first office door I find that isn't locked."

"You'd steal it?"

"Nell . . . please! I'd liberate it. Now, are you going to call me a hooligan again?"

"No. I'm not. You don't need to steal, Jiří. I run a foundation to foster the arts. I can give you paper."

§138

Somewhere in the České Středohoří: Late February

Wilderness had mastered the tine harrow. Also the chain harrow, which, after all, was nothing more than a bundle of chains dragged behind a tractor—and the disc harrow, available with thirty-six, seventy-two or a hundred-plus blades, which could seemingly slice ham, dice carrot and shred lettuce. God alone knew what it might do if actually towed across a field.

In the meantime he had actually managed to sell a dozen assorted harrows and four tractors and had an order for a combine harvester from the largest Collective in Bohemia, once they had been through all one hundred and forty-four levels of administration, all the way to the Fat Controller.

Much to his surprise, Erdbahn were paying him—every so often he received a Czech cheque—and it occurred to him that for the first time in his life he had a racket that was legitimate—Erdbahn commission plus MI6 salary.

He had swapped six copies of *Metamorphosis* with Tibor. He had no idea what was on the microdots. London did not tell him, and Tibor took the attitude that the less he knew the less he could reveal—Wilderness concurred, whilst lamenting silently that the process reduced him from spy to postman. At least postmen got a uniform and a bike.

The interest, as such, came in the comments Tibor threw into every meeting as almost casual asides, one gnat's hair short of gossip.

It was a bollock-freezer of a day. Tibor had brought a flask of coffee, which he shared with Wilderness as they stood on the hilltop in a biting wind.

"Do you know who I mean by General Sejna?"

"No. Who he?"

"He is a nobody. A nobody who will finally bring down President Novotny."

"Really?"

"There were rumours a while ago that he had been the instigator of a coup to unseat the reformers. This would be January, just after Novotny was made to resign as First Secretary. Sejna tried to rally the military to reinstate him—supposedly he gained the support of an entire tank division before it all collapsed around him. He's fled the country. In the last couple of days, I'm told."

This was shocking, but scarcely for the obvious reason.

"Why has Dubček said nothing about any of this?"

"Why has Dubček said nothing about anything? He has been in power nearly two months. Two months of deafening silence. But he'll have to speak now—if he doesn't he'll miss the opportunity to get rid of Novotny for good. It's not just that Sejna was on the old Central Committee. He was in business, if that's the phrase, with Novotny's son. A pair of playboys. In the midst of the most tightly controlled state in the Warsaw Pact they ran fiddles that would make the typical British spiv look like a saint. Not nylons and perfume . . . Jaguars and Porsches and Mercedes. A corruption so blatant it taints anyone who knew. And Old Novotny certainly knew. There is not a single central committee member past or present who would defend Sejna—he's fucked all their wives and the most unforgiving creature on this Earth is a cuckold. They'll see him in hell before they lift a finger—and right now I think that goes for Novotny too. It's just a matter of days."

§139

Pussy-in-the-Well to White Rabbit: March 22nd

```
—Novotny has finally gone. There is the biggest
 buzz in the city. If you want a newspaper it
 pays to get up early. They're all sold out by
 6 am. Everyone is interested. I ask myself,
 'can it last?' It's like Carnaby Street with
 politics.
```

$140

Pussy-in-the-Well to White Rabbit: April 7th

—Rumour, but one with a lot of credibility to
it. The suicide rate is rising. I seem to
hear of some old guard CP or StB man killing
himself every day. No attempt to hush it up. I
could get names if you wish, but why bother?
Yesterday's men.

Pussy-in-the-Well to White Rabbit: May 4th

—Dubček, Cernik et al. are in Moscow. I have
reports of a flight at midnight. No details.

Pussy-in-the-Well to White Rabbit: May 10th

—Half the Warsaw Pact forces seem to be
gathered on the border. Dubček has told the
country it was all pre-arranged 'manoeuvres'.
I've met no one who believes him. I think he
was taken by surprise.

   I don't know what Dubček asked for in Moscow
last week, but this appears to be Brezhnev's
reply. Scary, eh?

Pussy-in-the-Well to White Rabbit: May 18th

—A turn-up for the book. Kosygin is here—well,
you know that—but he's utterly ignoring the
Czech leadership, Acc. to our man 'Zoltan' he's
taking the waters at Karlovy Vary, twice a day.
Either he's got a touch of rheumatism or he's
come just to wave two fingers at Dubček.

Pussy-in-the-Well to White Rabbit: May 19th

—Biggest demo I've ever seen last night. Must
have been 10,000 or more. The cops did nothing

```
to stop it. Not a skull cracked. Interesting
new slogans. We're past 'Make Love Not War',
so corny after all, and into stuff so long
you couldn't spray it on a wall: "Long Live
the Soviet Union, But At Its Own Expense." Not
poetry, not catchy . . . but oh the defiance.
Six months ago the cops would have put a few
hundred in jail and as many in hospital.
```

§141

Prague: June 25th

Every so often, a so often that soon became every other day, Nell would pass a painted slogan that she knew was Jiří's work. No one else was as neat—and while many of the small army of sloganeers wrote in English, Jiří seemed unique in his fondness for, and belief in, rock 'n' roll lyrics, the subversive power of which was largely lost on Nell.

WE ARE THE PEOPLE OUR PARENTS WARNED US AGAINST

Jiří was at his desk cutting up more cardboard when she got home to Petr's apartment.

"Barrandov?" she asked simply.

"Yep. He said to tell you it'll be another all-nighter."

She paused in the doorway, wondering whether to tackle him or not.

"I saw one of yours today. You've been busy."

"No I haven't. I've only done two today. Which did you see, the John Lennon—'Strawberry Fields Forever'?"

"No. It would be the other one. It began with 'Stop'. I wondered what it meant."

"Does it have to mean anything?"

Nell felt it should.

"I can't see the point if it doesn't"

"OK, auntie—"

"Don't call me that."

"OK, Fräulein. Suggest something that does mean something."

"How about . . . Man is born free, but is everywhere in chains."

"Oh no—not Marx!"

"It's Rousseau, you idiot."

§142

Two days later a milestone in the history of dissent was published. "The Two Thousand Words" manifesto of Ludvík Vaculík. Seventy people signed, many of them writers and artists, including Jiří Menzel, Ivan Klíma, Josef Škvorecký, Milan Kundera and . . . Petr Jasny. It appeared simultaneously in four newspapers, all of which sold out.

Nell Burkhardt read it on the eve of publication, and thought it unnecessarily complicated and a far-from-easy read. She thought better of telling Petr this.

Janis Bell stuck a copy of *Literarny Listy* in the next diplomatic bag to be sent to London. Let London make of it what they would. It was an accusation, a catalogue of sins—it was not a call to arms, it was not a call to man barricades where there were no barricades, it was a call for more committees.

We do not want to cause anarchy.

But Jiří did.

Saturdays being much more "Saturday" than they had been for twenty years and more, citizens of Prague seemed to relax in a way they had all but forgotten about and could take a stroll on Václavské náměsti in much the same delightful and aimless way Italians would strut their stuff at *passeggiata*. On the following Saturday Petr and Nell walked through the heart of Prague.

Outside the Europa Hotel Jiří was selling Skři/Ška—more precisely he was giving it away. Part of Nell wondered what the boy had to say, part of her hoped Petr would not notice, but he did. Jiří thrust a copy at him with a grin. "Read all about it! Cheap at twice the price!"

Petr was still smiling as he accepted the paper. He stopped smiling as he turned to page two, and at page four he exploded.

"It's blank! You asshole, it's blank!"

Jiří pointed to the only words on the front page other than Skři/Ška. Quite literally, the small print:

```
Zero Word Manifesto
```

"You're just taking the piss!"

"I don't know about 'just' but yes, we are taking the piss. We are all of us piss-takers."

"It's only a matter of weeks since the lifting of censorship, and this is what you do? You waste paper on a prank? Blank fucking pages?"

"Which is the greater sin, to waste paper or to waste ink?"

"People die for freedoms like this!"

"Then I can count on you to defend my freedom to say nothing."

Petr hit him.

Jiří did not hit back. He moved twenty feet down the street and carried on as if nothing had happened.

Walking home, the tide of anger scarcely ebbing, Petr said, "And where the hell did he get the paper?"

Nell said nothing.

§143

White Rabbit to Pussy-in-the-Well: July 1st
—Our man in Bonn is reporting that Pravda will
 print an attack on the West German Cultural
 Mission in Prague next week. Usual thing—
 'encouraging anti-socialist forces.' This is
 run by one of Brandt's closest associates from
 his Berlin days, Nell Burkhardt. Omelette is
 asking if you've come across her.

Pussy-in-the-Well to White Rabbit: July 1st
—Oh yes.

White Rabbit to Pussy-in-the-Well: July 1st
—She is known to us. There is a connection, one
 Omelette would rather not see renewed. Diesel.

Pussy-in-the-Well to White Rabbit: July 1st
—I don't think they've met.

§144

Malá Strana: July 2nd

Kruger needed Wilderness in Prague. The request came as music to
his ears. Anywhere that wasn't Mělník or Mladá Boleslav might have
played the same tune to him.

Two nights back at the fading Europa Hotel, half a dozen mind-
numbing meetings, but evenings to himself. Warm July evenings,

evenings of pavement cafés and wonderfully pointless meanderings through the labyrinthine Prague streets. He could go to the theatre. He didn't. He could go to any one of twenty jazz clubs. He didn't. He could hear poets and novelists, unfettered by censorship, read in bars. He didn't. He drifted. Hoping to get lost. To lose himself. To lose Mělník and if at all possible to lose Walter Hensel for a while.

He found himself at dusk in Kampa Park walking slowly along the river bank.

To his left the river islands and the Old Town, to his right the narrow end of the park and a high brick wall. Every wall in Prague seemed to be covered in slogans, and after the demonstration three nights ago the graffiti count seemed to have doubled. This stretch of wall was no exception.

IT'S NO USE GOING BACK TO YESTERDAY

Neat, stark, simple. He'd no idea what it meant. Did it have to mean something? In a country that seemed to relish the absurd, the fact of a graffito—if that were the singular—probably mattered more than the words. To spray was a protest, to go to the trouble of making a stencil was a considered protest.

What was it? A Beatle lyric? The back of a Bob Dylan LP?

"*Oh Scheiße! Schon nochmal?*"

(Oh shit. Not again.)

He looked around. A small, dark woman was reading the same slogan, just a few paces behind him. All but peering over his shoulder. And she'd spoken to herself in German.

She switched to English as soon as she saw his face.

"My God!"

It was clear the woman had recognised him, and for the merest moment he had failed to recognise her.

"Nell?"

"What do you look like? What are you doing here? What do you want? Who are you supposed to be?"

"So many questions. I'm working Nell. Need I say more?"

"Spying?"

"That's what I do."

"On . . . on . . . ?"

"On the Russians. Who else?"

She shook her head, looked down at her feet, then up at him as though trying to detect the man she had known beneath the dyed mousy hair, behind the brown contact lenses.

"I cannot be seen with a spy. We are trying for diplomatic status."

"We?"

"Germany."

"I'm not spying on Germany. Are you a diplomat now?"

"I'm head of the Cultural Mission. What kind of a spy are you if you don't know that?"

"As I said, I'm not spying on Germany."

"All the same—"

"All the same . . . nothing. I am no risk to you. Nell, let's sit down and have a drink. Our first in twenty years. We've met in corridors and on staircases. Let's be comfortable this time."

"No."

And she turned to walk away in the direction of the Legií Bridge.

"Nell! What do you have to lose? I am a happily married man with two children. I cannot possibly be a threat to you."

She stopped and turned.

The look in her eyes showed not a glimmer of belief or trust, but she said, "All right. One drink. Then I go. And you are not to utter nonsense such as 'for old times' sake'—old times are old times. I would prefer them to be forgotten. I would prefer to forget them myself."

"But you can't."

"Do you want this drink or not, Joe?"

He fell into step with her, up the stone staircase to the next level, across the tramlines, across the square to the Café Savoy. She did not look at him until they reached the door.

"Happily?" she said, as though she had pondered that word and that alone for the last two minutes.

"Oh yes."

"And before we go in, what do I call you?"

"Walter."

"You don't look like a Walter."

"Does anyone?"

§145

Nell hardly touched her martini. She felt the need for control and anything that loosened her grip loosened her grip on the conversation and on Wilderness. Talking to Wilderness was like building a house of cards. One huff, one puff.

Above all she would not mention Petr. Wilderness wasn't entitled to know a thing about her life with any other man, from the day she'd walked out on him in 1948. She'd never tell him how ragged a life she had led, how work had come to substitute for almost anything and everything—until Petr.

Instead she probed him and found him surprisingly open.

"Did you want children? We never even talked about having children."

"I suppose I did. Twins came as a bit of a surprise. But I like being someone's father. I enjoy the . . . what can I call it? . . . the psychological spectacle of watching two physically identical girls manifest such different personalities."

"What are they called?"

"Molly and Joan. We went for short and simple. Judy is Judith Frances Evelyn Burne-Jones. Too much of a mouthful."

"Speaking as Christina Helène von Raeder Burkhardt I could relish a little simplicity myself."

"Nell."

He held up his glass to clink on her name.

She did not.

"Erno?" she said, tacking away from the surprising, sudden intimacy of her nickname and his ham-fisted gesture. "When did you last see Erno?"

"On my way out here nine months ago."

"Did you meet Trudie?"

"Oh yes."

"And?"

"Possessive. Pushy. She might just overdo the loving care and hasten Erno into his grave."

"Oh God, you're such a . . . such a man."

"He hates fuss."

"But he needs care."

"When did you last see him?"

"Six weeks ago. Joe, he is not well. You must make the effort and get to Berlin."

"I'll try."

Wilderness knocked back the last of his martini.

"One for the road?"

Then he noticed that she had only sipped at hers.

"Well. I'm having one."

He went to the bar, not looking back at her. But she could read him easily at this moment. He was wondering if she'd still be there when he turned around.

She was.

She tacked away from the personal once more.

"What do you make of the Czechs?"

"Not a lot. I deal with farmers. There are three types—anachronistic peasants, who distrust everyone and always have done, and care for nothing but muck and money—apparatchiks at the Collectives who seem incapable of thinking for themselves and consult the rule book at every turn—and a hybrid of the two, the apparatchik who has never stopped being a peasant. All of them are usually out to rook you. They're all on the fiddle. If they're not trying to con the state, they're trying to con me. And you?"

This would be as close as she would ever come to mentioning or describing Petr—and a body blow to Wilderness's cynicism.

"The Czechs are remarkable. I deal with actors and film directors and playwrights. They are delightful, original, charming, funny optimists. They might be the funniest people in Europe were it not for you English."

And then Nell paused. Wondering about the demands of truth. She owed Wilderness nothing. To whom did she owe truth? To herself? To Czechoslovakia?

"That's on the outside," she said. "On the inside they're just waiting for the hammer to fall."

§146

Outside the café. A darkness just penetrated by ancient streetlamps. The residual, heady warmth of a summer evening. A time and a place that might be loaded with potential for romance were it any other man and woman.

"Would you like to meet again?"

"What? Over dinner? A romantic tryst with sausages and dumplings?"

"Nell, it's a simple enough question."

"And a simple enough answer. No, Joe, I would not."

"For old times' sake?"

"The very phrase I asked you not to use. Shall I tell you why? Shall I? For a long time all I had was old times. I nurtured them, I treasured them and then I got over them. Why would I add to them now only to deplete them?"

"I see," said Wilderness not seeing.

"Besides, each time we would meet the risk would go up. If I were to be seen consorting with a British spy Brandt's *Ostpolitik* would be set back ten years. No one in the East would ever trust him again."

"Consorting?"

"That's it, Joe. Seize on the least important word in the sentence."

§147

"I met my old lover on the street last night."

"What?"

"The Englishman I told you about."

"He's here? What's he doing here?"

Nell had no wish to lie to Petr. What Wilderness had told her was undoubtedly a lie, or if not a lie a fiction—but she repeated what he had told her.

"He's selling tractors."

"British tractors?"

"He didn't say. It hardly matters, does it?"

"Was it pleasant?"

"Disturbing. Joe Wilderness could enrage a saint and make the Pope spit."

Petr rolled onto his side, one arm on the pillow, one arm around her, pulling her closer.

"But he did not disturb me half as much as I disturbed myself."

A pause, a minute of silence interrupted only by the rattle of a tram passing the window.

"Tell me."

"I asked what he made of Czechoslovakia, what he thought of Czechs. His reply was callous, but probably accurate. He deals with farmers, after all. I countered by telling him just a little about you . . . and Forman . . . and Hrabal . . . and Writers '62. I mentioned no names, just that you were creative and outgoing and . . . optimistic."

"That's OK. I know how to take a compliment."

"Then—and I don't know why I said this and I wish I hadn't—I said that beneath that optimism you were all waiting for the hammer to fall. I don't know that I know that. It just came to me. Intuition, I suppose. More likely repression. Not sure how well the phrase translates."

"Oh, its meaning is obvious. And you are right. I cannot speak for Forman or Hrabal, but, yes, I *am* waiting for the hammer to fall."

She rolled onto her side, chest to chest, face to face, her finger to his lips willing him to say no more.

But he did.

"Of course, I may not wait for the hammer to fall."

VIII

Jam Roly-Poly

§148

Mimram, Hertfordshire, England:
Late August, 1968—Probably the 24th or 25th

Sunshine with Occasional Clouds
Temperature: 72° F
No Prospect of Rain

It had been a good year for spuds. Troy and the Fat Man had beaten blight with a hefty dose of copper sulphate. Troy always liked the look of potato plants when healthy green leaves glistened with speckles of the purple mixture—iridescent might be the word, although if one were to believe the newspapers, "psychedelic'" was the vogue term for such things. He wasn't wholly certain what "psychedelic" meant.

They'd put off lunch to take the muck cart to the muck heap at the farm a mile or so down the road. On the Fat Man's advice Troy had bought a 1946 Ferguson TE20 tractor, known to anyone in farming as the "Little Grey Fergie"—a delightfully crude beast by modern standards with a mere two-litre engine, but it would run on paraffin, haul anything that needed hauling and, in all probability, run for ever and ever.

He was not allowed to drive it.

"I seen the way you drives yer Bentley, cock. You best leave tractors to them as knows."

"And I suppose that means you?"

"Yus. You have no idea what you don't know about what I know about tractors."

Troy could not find anything approaching sense in that sentence, and so had never attempted to usurp the Fat Man from his rightful place on the metal seat. They looked most uncomfortable anyway—like something a giant might use to strain a giant's spaghetti in the kitchen at the top of the beanstalk. Half an hour on that seat and you'd have rings on your backside the size of florins.

So today he followed a wagonload of manure from Home Farm back to Mimram, in no way finding it unpleasant or symbolic to be stuck behind the muck cart.

A few yards from Troy's gateway the tractor stopped. Troy looked around the cart. A uniformed copper was speaking to the Fat Man. Not a copper he knew. Ever since old Trubshawe had retired three years ago village bobbies had come and gone with the regularity of one-hit teen idols.

"You can't bring that in here!"

The Fat Man turned off the engine.

"Eh?"

"I said you can't bring that in here."

"Tell you what, cock. Why don't you ask his nibs?"

A thumb over the shoulder gesturing at Troy.

"Are you responsible for this?"

"Guilty as charged," said Troy.

"Eh?"

"Yes. I own the load of manure and I also own the house behind you and I'm also getting fed up with this rigmarole."

Ever since his brother had become Home Secretary in 1964, Troy had had to get used to his weekend visits and the occasional presence of a guardian in the shape of a policeman—or two. The least they could do, he thought, was remember who he was.

A second copper appeared. Plain clothes. A Special Branch officer. One Troy had known in his days at the Yard, Chief Inspector Ernie Leadbetter.

"Sorry about this, Mr. Troy. It's just that today's a bit different."

"Different enough for me to be denied access to my own property, Ernie?"

"Of course not, but if you'd allow me, I will just call your brother from the squad car."

"Be my guest."

Thirty seconds later, Ernie was back.

"He's coming down."

"Shouldn't I be going up?"

"Said he wants a quick word first."

"When I shoot him, just look the other way, would you?"

"Be my guest."

It was several minutes before Rod appeared, panting as though he'd run all the way down the drive.

"Sorry. Honestly, I just forgot."

"Forgot what?"

"You."

"Who is it this time. Ringo Starr? Taylor and Burton? The Pope?"

"No, just Harold."

"Harold who?"

"Wilson."

"Harold fucking Wilson?"

"Manners, Freddie. The prime *fucking* minister."

"It's Saturday afternoon. He should be in his constituency handing out leaflets and platitudes. What does he want?"

"You."

"Me?"

"You."

"And yet you *forgot* about me."

"Just come inside and get cleaned up. We'll explain everything."

"I haven't had lunch yet."

"Freddie, you're just prevaricating."

"I haven't had lunch—*he* hasn't had lunch!"

Troy pointed at the Fat Man, still perched on the tractor.

"And they can hear his stomach grumbling in Poland!"

$149

Troy declined to clean up. Skipping lunch, not making Wilson wait till he'd eaten, was all the concession Rod was going to get. If the Prime Minister of the United Kingdom of Great Britain and Northern Ireland wanted Troy's attention he'd have to take him as he was in his grubby boiler suit, smelling somewhat of cow shit.

He took his wellies off.

Wilson and Rod were in Troy's study, without so much as a by-your-leave. Troy knew why Rod had done this. It was an icebreaker. Anyone who visited Mimram was curious less about the Troy brothers than about their father, Alex (deceased 1943), a near-contemporary of Churchill, and a quondam ally and sparring partner—they'd go months without speaking. The study had been Alex's before it was Troy's, and showing the enquiring pol in there bought time, answered questions by giving them a slice of history—the detritus of life in Russia and Austria, every object—the room was cluttered—every object an anecdote.

Wilson was smoking a postprandial cigar, thereby confirming what Troy had always thought, that the pipe was as much a prop as the plastic mac he habitually wore, if slightly less repulsive.

"Harold. What brings you all this way?"

Rod hissed in his ear, "Prime Minister!"

Troy hissed back, "Fuck off."

Wilson had to be slightly deaf not to have heard them, but sat back down after the handshake, unperturbed.

"You'll have heard the news?"

"Yes. New Beatles LP delayed until the autumn. Tragic."

Troy felt Rod's shoe tap sharply against his stockinged foot.

"No . . . no. I meant about Lord Brynmawr."

Troy's first and only thought was "Who the hell is Lord Brynmawr?" Helpfully, Rod read his expression right down to the punctuation.

"You knew him as Hywel Thomas. He was our planning minister."

The name rang a bell—little tubby bloke from South Wales. Union man—miners or steel workers or something.

"Oh. When was he kicked upstairs?"

"Not a phrase we use, Freddie."

Wilson affected a chuckle.

"Not kicked, Freddie. Jumped. I needed an ambassador in Prague. Hywel fitted the bill. And he jumped at the chance. Never happy in Planning. Foreign Affairs was much more his sort of thing. But I could never move him to the Foreign Office with George still around."

George was George Brown. Wilson's deputy and until his sudden resignation, in a huffy fit about six months ago, he had been Foreign Secretary. He was a free-speaking piss-artist, a pain in the arse to

Wilson, and, for that reason if for no other, Troy and Rod quite liked him.

Troy said, "Why are you talking of Hywel Thomas in the past tense?"

Wilson said, "You haven't told him?"

"I missed Freddie at breakfast and he's only just got in for—"

"—for the lunch I haven't had yet," Troy muttered.

"Hywel died last night, Freddie. Heart attack, I believe. Harold received a phone call early this morning. Dreadful news."

"Sorry to hear that," Troy said. "But what has this got to do with me?"

"Hywel died at the worst possible moment," Wilson said.

Troy did not need this explaining. Just before midnight on the twentieth Russian tanks had rolled into Czechoslovakia and clipped short the Prague Spring.

"We need to a get a new man in place as soon as possible. By next week, in fact."

"Well good luck with that. I can't think of anyone I might recommend, so—"

A toe-shattering tap on the foot from Rod's size-twelve beetle-crushers.

"You're being an ass. Harold is offering *you* the job."

Troy—almost speechless, but not quite.

"What?"

"I need a man right away," Wilson said. "Above all, given that the Russians will not be withdrawing any day soon, I need a good Russian speaker. Someone who can talk to them face-to-face without an interpreter."

Troy could only conclude that whatever file MI5 and Special Branch had on him had not been read by Wilson. He'd not seen it himself, but he'd readily conclude that every scrape he'd got into and got out of was recorded, and the fact that he had been cleared every time, exonerated every time, would not do a damn thing to diminish the suspicion that he was not entirely kosher, not entirely pukka and not entirely "one of us."

"You're mad. Both of you. Mad as hatters."

A little more of the Wilson fake chuckle.

But Rod wasn't laughing.

"Do excuse us a moment, Harold."

Rod bundled Troy, approximately half his size, out into the corridor.

"Stop acting like a spoilt brat!"

"I'm not. I'm being honest."

"Freddie, get back in there, be polite and hear the man out. He's our prime minister for God's sake."

"You never liked him! We used to call him Mittiavelli. You've always taken the piss out of him—remember? 'How can you tell when Wilson's lying? His lips move.' I've heard you crack that one a dozen times."

"I was probably pissed. But I'm sober right now and he's not lying."

"Rod, he's a conman in a Gannex mac."

"Not the point. I serve under him, and I'm happy to do so."

"Happy?"

"OK. Not happy, but willing. Freddie, just hear him out and tell him you'll think about it."

Back in the study Wilson briefly outlined to Troy the duties of an ambassador. Troy didn't ask any questions.

"And of course, the real advantage to us, the government, is that you're free now—you retired last year, didn't you?"

Troy had retired five years ago but said nothing.

"And you know the Russian mind."

His heart sank. This was the anglicised version of the nonsense he had heard so often as child whenever two or three Russians were gathered together in the same room—the Russian Soul, that agonising, self-tormenting, invisible, elusive and possibly nonexistent organ. Berdyaev had written the lot—*The Soul of Russia*, *The Fate of Russia* and *The Russian Idea*. It would not surprise Troy to learn that there were ten or twenty books called *The Russian Mind*. He hadn't read any of them. The Russian Mind/Soul/Idea/Fate were just more reasons to get drunk and maudlin and sing songs about women with black eyes.

Troy gave Rod what he'd asked for.

"I'll think about it," he said.

"Good, good," Wilson replied. "Think about your title while you're about it."

§150

When Wilson had gone, Troy said, "What did he mean by 'think about your title'?"

"Hywel took Lord Brynmawr. It's where he was born in the Welsh valleys."

"I know. But what did Mittiavelli mean?"

"Ah . . . I see. Hywel was a lord. If we were to send you out as plain Mr. Troy, the Russians, not understanding titles any more than the Americans do, would see it as a sort of downgrading. Hence they'd assume Czechoslovakia meant less to us and that would make any negotiations we might undertake, any demands we might have, less effective. 'Oh, they've only sent a bloke not a lord, so he doesn't matter much.'"

Oh shit.

"You're not kidding, are you?"

"'Fraid not."

Oh fuck.

"Isn't one title in the family enough?"

"Ah . . . it wouldn't be hereditary, just a life peerage. You wouldn't be able to pass it on to all those sons you don't actually have."

"Wanker."

"What?"

"You're a wanker, Rod. A complete and utter wanker."

§151

Down in the kitchen the Fat Man was tucking into bangers and mash.

"I saved you some. It'll be a bit crisp. It's in the bottom oven."

Troy salvaged a not-quite-burnt offering.

The Fat Man said, "It'll come up a treat with a dollop of HP sauce."

"I'm sure it will. Tell me, do you think they put the sauce bottle on the table at lunch in the House of Lords?"

"Dunno. Why you askin'?"

"Believe it or not. Mock me if you must. But Rod and Wilson have just offered me a peerage."

The Fat Man sucked air through his teeth like a plumber looking at a rusted stopcock.

"Peer like a lord? Lord like a toff?"

"Yep."

"Well . . . you come to the right man, old cock. I been around lords and toffs all my working life."

"I know. You told me."

"Thing is. There's toffs and there's toffs."

"You don't say."

"There's yer bruv for one. He's a decent enough bloke. Bit of a plonker from time to time and he can talk the backside off a donkey when he's a mind. But, all things considered—"

"Six of one, half a dozen of the other."

"That's it . . . a bit of give-and-take . . . he's alright. Wouldn't want him on my side in an up-the-garden-wall contest, but he's alright. A bloke as you can trust. Same goes for the guv'nor. Uses words a damn sight more ju . . . ju—"

"Judiciously."

"That's the feller . . . more thingy than Rod, but you'd trust him with yer wallet and yer life."

"Is this leading anywhere?"

"Course it is. Now most toffs . . . as in there's toffs and there's toffs . . . you shake hands with them and feel to see if yer watch chain's still there. How do you think they got to be toffs in the first place?"

"I say again, is this leading anywhere?"

"Yeah. Why would *you* want to be a toff?"

"This is where I came in."

"You don't wanna be a toff."

"Of course I don't. No . . . hang on, why don't I want to be a toff?"

"Cos you got it made, that's why. You got everything a man could ask for. You got yer rozzer's pension. Nice little town house, crackin' place in the country, yer own orchard, yer own spud patch and yer own pig. Why would anyone want to have to go up to London, dress up in ermine, wear a crown, make speeches, worse . . . listen to speeches, when they could be at 'ome, in their orchard with their pig. To say nothing about being at 'ome, in their orchard with their deliciously fat pig . . . and their deliciously buxom missis."

Oh shit.

Troy had given no thought to what the missis would say any more than he'd wondered what the pig might say.

He walloped the bottom of the bottle and a pleasing slick of brown sauce coated his bangers and mash.

He really didn't fancy raising this topic with his wife. There was no knowing which way she might jump. Best to string out lunch until teatime.

"Did you, by any chance, find the time to knock up a pudding?"

"O' course. Get that lot down yer and there's jam roly-poly to follow. You don't get grub like this in the House o' Lords, I bet."

§152

They got through dinner without the subject coming up. Troy had told Rod he'd thump him if he mentioned it.

And when he asked the Fat Man to bide his time, he received the reply, "Knobs to that. I ain't getting between you and yer bruv in a keep-shtum contest. I'll have me dinner in front of the telly. You lot just fight amongst yourselves. Besides, it's Billy Cotton tonight—Wakey! Wakey!"

For a brief moment Troy thought he might enjoy an evening of tuneless big band nostalgia, as the BBC wound itself effortlessly back to the 1950s and wiped five years of satire, sex scandals, Mods and Rockers, Mersey Beat and Swinging London off the clock—but then his brain kicked in. The problem was not Rod, the problem was his wife.

He did not choose the right moment.

Thinking she was safely tucked up in bed, and the half-open, half-closed bathroom door a minor Maginot between them, he raised the matter at his night's ablutions.

"Can you hear me?"

"Not gone deaf since dinner time!"

"Harold Wilson came over this afternoon."

"Bet that pleased Rod."

"Well . . . actually. It was me."

"Me what?"

"He came to see me."

"Huh. What on earth does the slimy bugger want with a retired copper? Does he want you to be Black Rod? Pink Rod? Although I can see that might have obscene overtones. Or just governor-general of Tristan da Cuhna?"

It amazed Troy how close she had come to the target whilst doing no more than take the piss.

"Not exactly."

"How *in*exactly then?"

"He offered me a peerage. I said—"

The flat of her hand between his shoulder blades caused him to spit toothpaste all over the mirror.

"Tell me you said yes!"

He swung around, coughed and spattered her with what was left of the toothpaste.

"Tell me you said yes!!!"

"No."

"No—you won't tell me?

"No. I mean I said no."

She punched him in the solar plexus. Not hard enough to double him up but enough to make damn sure her displeasure registered.

"You ass. You complete and utter fucking ass!"

He sat down on the loo with a bit of a thump.

"I don't want to be Lord Whatever of Wherever."

"Did you even think about me?"

"Of course not."

She stomped off back to the bedroom. He followed, wiping minty-green toothpaste off his face and chest. And with it his ring of confidence.

"I bet you bloody didn't. Well . . . I want to be Lady Troy."

"We already have a Lady Troy. We had dinner with her not two hours ago."

"Cid won't mind another. Besides she's been Lady Troy since I don't know when."

"Nineteen forty-three."

"So she'd still be top dog . . . I'd be . . . the soubrette. Fawned on by couturiers and waiters . . ."

She swept around the room holding her night dress like a regal train.

"More caviar, Lady Troy, more champagne, Lady Troy . . . more vinegar with your mushy peas, Lady Troy."

"Tell me you're kidding."

"I'm not. In fact I'd love it. I began life as Anna Victoria Sara Coward. Spinster of this parish et cetera. Gave that mouthful up to become Mrs. Angus Pakenham—someone absolutely destined to become a widow."

Troy could not, would not argue with that. Angus was always a disaster waiting to happen.

"And then, three years ago you finally popped the question."

"Actually it was two, and you proposed to me."

"All I did, Freddie, was take the words out your mouth, as t'were."

"So you don't like being Mrs. Troy?"

"It's been bliss. A happiness I didn't think I was ever going to get and I'm damn sure I don't deserve. But then I think to meself, if I don't deserve happiness who the fuck does? Certainly not you. You don't deserve me. After a lifetime of indecision and infidelity I rather think you deserve your own circle in hell next that chap who ate his own children."

"Count Ugolino."

"Yes. Him. But . . . to be serious for a moment. Freddie, one of the reasons you and I took so long to get to where we are, disregarding for the moment the wife and the mistress—or two, or three—is that I always thought you'd end up with a bullet in you."

"Well—there has been the odd one."

"I mean, a fatal one. One that hit you when Kolankiewicz was not around. Without Kolankiewicz, without me, you'd be several times dead."

§153

Rod was up before him. If "up" included not-yet-dressed-still-in-dressing-gown-odd-socks-on-hair-not-combed. Troy found him on the south verandah, sipping a large mug of black coffee, his minister's red box and a scattering of papers on the table beside him. Rod had spent every Sunday morning this way for the best part of four years. He never seemed to tire of it, as though thirteen years in Opposition had left him with untapped reserves of energy. Troy had long thought the military/civil service slang for paperwork—"bumf," as in "bum fodder"—to be spot on, yet to Rod it was meat and drink . . . and coffee.

Troy picked up a paper, glanced idly at it, only to feel Rod slap him on the back of the offending hand.

"Secrets, Freddie! Anything that comes out of the red box is a government secret."

"Until one of you chooses to leak it to the *Daily Mirror* or the *Guardian*."

He flopped down into the empty chair.

"Besides, I've a right to know."

"Really?"

"I'm a citizen."

"Oh . . . bollocks."

"I'm a ratepayer."

"More bollocks."

"I'm a voter. I even vote for you."

"The least you could do."

"And I would appear to be Her Majesty's new ambassador to Prague."

Rod spilled his coffee, most down his dressing gown, some spotting a government paper on rising drug use among the under-twenty-ones.

"You changed your mind?"

"Let's just say I got my arm and several other more vital organs twisted overnight."

"Ah. Anna wants it, eh?"

"In spades. Don't ask me why."

"I must buy her flowers."

"Don't even think of it."

"Then we have to move quickly. You'd better come up to town with me in the morning. There'll be no time for any formalities—"

"You mean I don't get to meet the queen? No ermine, no coronet?"

"Not just yet you don't. We need to get you on a plane to Prague by Wednesday or Thursday. I can't tell you how tricky things are going to be in Czechoslovakia. You'll have to be briefed. Intelligence and all that."

"You mean spook stuff?"

"Of course. They'll want you in the picture. We'll get a bloke from the FO or Six to talk to you in the afternoon. They'll give you the latest status report and tell you what we have in the field."

"Field?"

"We have people in Czechoslovakia. We're not sure how safe they are, but this is the wrong time to pull them out and most certainly the wrong time to send anyone else in. Think of it as a war zone—no names, no pack drill and so on."

"No wives?"

"Eh?"

"Anna wants it. I told you. She has every intention of coming out to Prague."

"Oh bloody hell. Not a good idea. Gwyneth Brynmawr will be on her way back within forty-eight hours. It's no place for a woman."

"Really? I thought they tore up their petticoats to make bandages and reloaded the Winchesters."

"Do take this seriously, Freddie. I say again—no place for a woman."

"Fine. You be the one to tell her that."

§154

Anna was musing. Togs off. Nightie on. Musing.

"Is Troy the right title? Shouldn't we have something with a place name in it? You know, like 'Oxford and Asquith' or 'Baldwin of Bewdley'?

Or 'the MacGregor of MacGregor' . . . but, for all the years I was married to a Scotsman I never knew what that meant."

The prospect of impending ennoblement had brought out the snob in Anna. He knew how to kill that.

"Well . . . I had thought about using my mother's maiden name."

"And what was that?"

"Chekhov-Tsvetayeva."

"Next."

Try again.

"But if you're really keen on a geographical connection, I believe the title of Lord Scunthorpe is vacant."

Troy thought the name of a grim, northern steel town somewhere in Lincolnshire or Yorkshire, or anywhere north of the Trent, might be the last word, but all she said was, "I've never been to Scunthorpe. Somehow the urge passed me by."

"Nor have I. How about something completely different? In keeping with the innovations of the new classless age Wilson keeps banging on about."

"Freddie, you no more believe that load of old bollocks than Rod does."

"How about Lord and Lady Gloucester-Old-Spot? After the pig. Very chic, very now. Very down-to-earth."

"You'll be telling me next that it's 'funky,' whatever 'funky' means. However . . . fuck off."

"Fine. Lady Troy it is then. Speaking of which, Her Majesty's Government—"

"You mean Rod."

"—would prefer it if Lady Troy were not to accompany her husband to Prague."

"I refer the honourable member to my previous answer. Fuck off. There's no way I'll agree to be left out of this."

"Good. Start packing in the morning."

"What was that line of Sir Richard Burton's . . . when he was ambassador to God-knows-where? You know, the one everyone quotes."

"Pay, pack and follow."

"Ah . . . then you pay, I'll pack and no one follows."

$155

After lunch on the Monday, Rod introduced Troy to the minister of state at the Foreign Office with particular responsibility for Intelligence (Central Europe)—one Eliot Spicer, a rising star of the Labour Party and a junior minister after less than five years an MP.

They met in Rod's office, the protocol being that Rod was by far the senior and did not go to junior minister's offices but summoned junior ministers to his. And protocol seemed to matter more than Intelligence. Nothing Spicer said to him sounded in any way like an Intelligence briefing.

"Of course, we have agents in the field."

"I know. Rod told me."

"And it's terribly important that we know what the Russians are up to. But I think it wiser if their immediate control in Prague briefs you."

Troy thought this a bit of ducking and diving, although more likely to be sheer ignorance. Spicer had come in carrying one of the ubiquitous civil service buff folders, and seemed obliged to consult it from time to time, as though he didn't really know his subject.

"Who would that be?"

A flip of the folder for a fact that should have been on the tip of his tongue.

"Er . . . First Secretary . . . half a mo'. Chap's name should be in here somewhere."

Half a dozen sheets of paper slipped to the floor. Spicer gathered them up, turned a couple this way and that.

"I . . . er seem . . ."

"To have lost it?"

"Er . . ."

"But whoever this chap is, he's MI6?"

"Er . . ."

"I'll take that as a yes."

"Quite . . . he's responsible for all liaison with field agents, and more importantly he handles the ambassador's liaison with the government in Bonn."

"Why is that?"

Rod stuck his two pennorth in.

"West Germany doesn't officially recognise the government of Czechoslovakia. Our man in Prague—that's you, Freddie—acts on their behalf."

"Shouldn't be a problem," Spicer added. "If there are problems they'll be very much Czech problems. And, of course, your biggest problem is going to be refugees."

Of course, it would be. "Of course" was a phrase to render the obvious more obvious if that were at all possible.

"Of course . . . all this has caught us on the hop, to say the least. They're already banging on the embassy door, as it were. But we can't take the average Czech refugee. Simply don't have the facility, but if a *prominente*, a *politico*, comes hammering . . . well, then we have to act. We have to consider political asylum . . . and the er . . . validity of the application."

This startled Troy.

"Are you saying there are circumstances in which we would hand a known dissident back to the Russians?"

"I rather think I am. Can't house them all, can we? We'd have to put up tents on the embassy lawn."

Spicer smiled complacently at his own tasteless joke. Troy made a mental note to buy tents.

"There's only so much we can do," Spicer continued, "Often as not it will be a matter of finding the right way of saying no."

"So . . . I'm just there to fill a void, am I? A powerless puppet dressed in red, white and blue?"

A deep intake of breath on Spicer's part. A look of increasing exasperation.

"I can't tell you how important it is that we fly the flag."

"Why?" said Troy.

This flustered Spicer.

"Well. Isn't it obvious? Democrats . . . our side, as it were . . . ousted by the Warsaw Pact . . . Russians with snow on their boots, that sort of thing. We must demonstrate our position, our support . . . publicly."

"Publicly?"

"Of course."

"Because in private you're getting ready to dump them."

"Freddie!"

Troy ignored his brother.

"Don't tell me," he said to Spicer. "It's a small, faraway country of which we know nothing."

"I say, that's a bit bloody steep. You're comparing the PM to Chamberlain."

Politics is a world of rapid change, but Rod performed the quickest volte-face Troy had ever seen with, "He's right though, isn't he? Harold will fly the flag and then leave the Czechs in Soviet hell."

Spicer said nothing. Did he sigh? Troy could not be certain. At last he said, "Rod, far be it from me to question your loyalty, but cabinet is a collective—"

Troy cut him short.

"Mr. Spicer. If you want me to do this, then shut up now and stop spoon-feeding me the party line like yesterday's cold rice pudding. Or you know where you can shove your peerage and your ambassador's job."

Troy knew he should quit now, and go back to his farm, his fat pig, his fat man and his buxom wife. But he didn't.

"We will, as you put it, fly the flag. Tell me. What is the amabassador's car in Prague?"

Spicer looked puzzled, flicked through his folder for a few seconds.

"I believe it's a Humber Imperial. Most of our embassies have Humbers now. Rolls-Royces were beginning to look a bit too old-school, wrong image . . . the empire and all that. Despite the name, the Imperial's the right image for the New Britain. After all, we could hardly put an ambassador in a mini, trendy though they are."

Troy winced inwardly at both "New Britain" and "trendy."

"When I was in Berlin in '48, General Robertson was in charge of the British sector. He had a vintage Rolls, with a little flagpole on the bonnet, flying a little union jack. Have it shipped to Prague, would you? Just now it's the *right* image."

§156

Troy was still with Rod when Spicer's PPS phoned to say that the Rolls was still in West Berlin and had been mothballed since the wall went up in 1961, but in the absence of any instruction to the contrary had been garaged, and serviced on a regular basis. And yes, it would be waiting for him in Prague.

"Wanted to see how far you could push him, is that it?" said Rod.

"Something like that. Ignorant little prick. Y'know, I don't know how you stick these people."

"I compromise. Something you don't know how to do."

"Do you want me to compromise in Prague?"

"You'll be a diplomat. Diplomacy is all compromise. You'll have to learn how to do it. And I have every confidence you will."

"But whenever Wilson wants to speak to the Russian command in Czechoslovakia, I shall be called upon to speak the Wilson line to whichever Russian is running the country . . . knowing we'll give in to pretty well anything. That's not a compromise. That's a capitulation."

"You can do some good here, Freddie. Try to see it that way."

§157

Fly the flag.

Much as Troy agreed with Dr. Johnson on the definition of a patriot, he was going to fly the flag and three days later managed to do so twice within a matter of hours.

A few telephone calls on the Tuesday and he had secured the use of a Lockheed Jetstar, painted red, white and blue, with a large union jack adorning the tail fin.

"God almighty Freddie! The treasury will have a fit!"

"Have this one on me, Rod."

"A private jet? What are you thinking of?"

"Actually I was thinking of Goldfinger and Pussy Galore. And perhaps I was also thinking of Anna, whom you have corrupted completely by making me take this fucking job. How am I gonna keep her down on the farm? Et cetera . . . so she might as well have her ladyship, her private jet and her Rolls-Royce. If she ever floats down to Earth I'll be sure to let you know."

When the plane touched down at Ruzyne on the Thursday, a second union jack was waiting for him, not, as his memory told him, flying from the bonnet but from a tiny flagpole on the roof of a 1935 Rolls-Royce Phantom II. A uniformed chauffeur was at the wheel, and a tall, dark-haired young woman in a Biba-but-businesslike twin set was standing by the open rear door. Both plane and car had been directed to a far corner of the airport—cordoned off from the main buildings by half a dozen jeeps. At the perimeter as many tanks sat idly by, aiming, he hoped, at nothing, and beyond them a couple of huge Antonov troop transports.

"Ambassador, I'm Janis Bell—SIS station head."

A northern accent. Not unlike Wilson's own. Not the received pro-nunciation he'd been expecting.

She shook his hand like a bloke.

"Nice touch," she said, looking up at the plane.

"Alas," said Troy gazing round at the *arabia deserta* of the airport. "No one appears to be looking."

"Oh, but they are. They most certainly are. I think you've made your point."

Watchers one cannot see? thought Troy. Well, he'd just have to get used to that.

Troy introduced Anna, who, as she settled into the back seat, whispered, "She's quite a looker. Do remember to keep it in your pants, Troy."

Troy ignored this.

Janis Bell asked for their passports and took the seat next to the chauffeur.

"You can talk freely, Ambassador. We know the car isn't bugged. Can't be wholly certain about any room in the embassy, though."

He'd have to get used to that too, although quite how eluded him for the time being.

It took only seconds and the merest scrutiny for the men at the barrier to let them through.

"If that seemed too easy," Janis Bell said, reading Troy's mind and turning in her seat, "it's just that they'll not want to rock the boat quite so soon. There'll be a period of good will if only to mask what they're really up to. Ordinarily a new ambassador would present his credentials to the president, but, almost needless to say, you won't be doing that just yet. President Svoboda has had his hands full this last week—he flew to Moscow on Friday to try and get Dubček released. I've even heard that Dubček was led away in handcuffs, but he was returned to Prague on Tuesday. I'd hardly term it 'released.' He's just a prisoner here rather than in Moscow."

"Meanwhile," Troy said, "the Pope showed him the instruments of torture."

"Exactly," said Janis.

"What?" said Anna.

"Galileo . . . recanting."

"Oh."

"Not," Janis added, "that anyone has recanted anything yet. And from what I gather there was torture of a kind. The usual Russian thing . . . sleep deprivation . . . no washing . . . they looked dreadful, all of them. As though they lived in their suits rather than just wore them."

§158

As they reached central Prague, the streets were lined with tanks, parked as neatly as commuter cars, nose to tail, thirty or forty in a line. Some looked closed, lids down, locked up like the garden shed, and those that weren't were surrounded by protesting Czechs.

Troy wound down the window as the car slowed to a crawl.

He couldn't understand a word of Czech, but the meaning was clear.

"*Vraťte se do Ruska!*"

Go back to Russia!

And the reply even clearer.

"Пошёл на хуй!"

Fuck off!

One or two heads turned at the sight of a Rolls-Royce, but more, far more, were focussed on the tanks and the half dozen unfortunate Russian Ivans set to guard them.

Janis Bell said, "As I'm sure you can see, the heat's gone out if it. The Russians have had a week to work out where they are."

"What?"

"Oh, some of them had no idea what country they'd invaded. Whole battalions who thought they were in East Germany or Austria."

The car stopped, a crowd of protestors surging across the street.

Troy tapped on the glass to attract the driver's attention.

"I think I'll walk from here."

Janis Bell turned in her seat.

"What? Sorry . . . I mean why? Do you really think that's a good idea?"

The car turned into a side street and stopped.

Anna said, "I wouldn't bother, Miss Bell. He's stubborn as a mule."

"You might get lost."

"No, I won't," said Troy. "And it's the last chance I'll get to see for myself. By lunchtime tomorrow your people or their people or both will be watching. So if you don't mind I'll take this opportunity to walk about as an anonymous citizen."

He got out of the car. The chauffeur was already at the boot.

For some reason there were bullet holes in it.

Troy did not ask.

The chauffeur opened the boot, pulled the outer lid down and took out a flat leather cap and a beaten-up leather jacket.

"I keep these in case I want to go into a bar and not look like an Englishman, a chauffeur or an embassy official. You might find them handy, sir. I don't know what it is about Czechs and leather caps . . . but they all seem to have them. And Miss Bell's right, you might get lost. So here's a street map for you. The embassy's on the other side of the river. Take any bridge facing roughly west and you'll get there eventually."

Troy slipped on the jacket, pulled the cap down on his forehead.

"Perfect, sir. You look just like a Czech."

And Troy thought, "Thank God I don't look like a Russian."

"Thank you, Mr. er . . ."

"Just Broadbent, sir. Tony Broadbent. No 'Mr.' necessary."

§159

Troy had lived through war. Never through invasion. He'd seen London bombed by the Luftwaffe, and on two occasions had been far too close for comfort. In the Blitz, he'd been in an East End synagogue that had received a direct hit. It had taken an age to dig him out and when he emerged it looked to him as though there was nothing left of London. In the Little Blitz of '44 he'd been on the Underground when a bomb fell through the air shaft. He'd no idea why he had survived. It was against all logic. He should have suffocated. Everyone else had.

Prague did not look like London. It did not look demolished—it had been pecked at by modern warfare . . . a shop front caved in here, a flattened tram there—what could flatten a tram? It was almost inconceivable, but that's what tanks did, and the tanks were everywhere. Some of the buildings reminded him of the Brandenburg Gate, pitted with bullet holes like a bad case of architectural acne.

Dubček had asked the people not to resist, and the Czech army had stayed on it bases with not a shot fired. But resistance was not the same as protest. And he'd issued no injunction against that. An obvious protest was slogans, most as simple as "Go back to Russia"—as though every kid in Prague owned a can of spray paint. The most obvious was people. Troy felt Miss Bell was right, the heat must have gone out of it after a week, and certainly the retaliation was low—he didn't hear a single shot fired, and Russian troops looked to him worn down by insult and piss-taking—but there still seemed to be ten people in the streets for every tank.

A beer hall disgorged half a dozen men in their forties. Emboldened by booze, they turned their backs on a tank, dropped their pants and wiggled their arses. The Russians on the tank looked away, more bored than offended.

There were thousands of flowers in the street. Every bunch marking a death. And every so often he'd see a teenager silently holding a flag, a calm memorial to yet another victim.

He drifted west in the direction of the river—along Vinohradská, where the Prague radio station had been the centre of last week's most violent conflict. Twenty-two dead. Prague had defended itself—on either side of the street the Czechs had dug trenches, but trenches do not stop tanks.

He found himself in the Old Town Square, which was home to the most famous structure in the country. His father had visited Prague around 1908, and years later the old man had described to him the wonder that was the Old Town Astronomical Clock.

Four mechanical figures emerged when the clock chimed the hour. Troy looked at his watch. By chance he'd timed it right—three minutes to the hour.

The mechanism jerked into life. One figure was Death. He'd no idea what the other three represented, but few people had ever seen them as they were this August day. Some brave soul had shinned up the outside of the Town Hall. One figure wore a blindfold, the second had gaffer tape over its ears and the last over its mouth. See no . . . hear no . . . speak no . . .

If only all governments could be toppled by satire. In England it took a sex scandal to bring down a government.

$160

He reached the other side of the river, just north of Kampa Park, pretty certain he was heading in the right direction for the embassy.

There was hardly an inch of wall without a slogan.

He was reading one that was fresh, dripping with wet paint—it sounded vaguely familiar.

THE LIFE YOU WANT TO GRASP MIGHT BE THE YOU THAT WANTS TO GRASP IT

He was sure he'd read that somewhere. He just couldn't remember where.

Between him and the slogan was a short, dark woman in a beautiful summer dress of swirling reds and greens. She was muttering to herself in German, swearing softly. Then she turned, realised she was not alone, apologised and walked on.

Troy and Nell never having met, neither recognised the other.

§161

Palác Thun

He found the embassy, hiding in a cul-de-sac in the shadow of the presidential castle, looking deceptively small, and deceptively more like a prison than a palace. It dawned on him as he walked along Thunovská that when he'd got out of the car Janis Bell still had his newly minted diplomatic passport—so new the ink was scarcely dry. He did not relish the idea of explaining this to a Russian.

But when he turned the corner, there was no battalion of Soviet troops, just two Prague coppers, whiling the day away in conversation with Miss Bell. Her Czech seemed to him surprisingly rapid and free from hesitation—not that he understood a word of it.

"Oh, you found us. Good. You went off without your—"

"I know. Are these chaps here to arrest me?"

"No. They're not actually unfriendly. Just coppers doing what they're told."

"Ah. I wasn't that kind of copper."

"So I've heard."

"All the same, we'd better get inside. The head of chancery, that is, Mr. Crawford, is a bit miffed that I was the reception . . . it should have been him . . . protocol and all that."

"He hasn't got the entire staff lined up waiting, has he?"

"No—but if I'd given him notice he would have. Please follow me and watch where you put your feet."

Janis Bell's last sentence baffled Troy but its meaning became clear soon enough. The route to the ambassador's office was like a building site. Rooms that been elegant enough to justify the word *Palác* were being divided up and buried in plasterboard by a small army of workmen—cables and drills and hammers strewn across the floor. In one corner of what had once been the main dining room three men were demolishing a spiral staircase so beautiful Troy wished he could buy the bits and have it reassembled in Mimram.

"I know what you're thinking, desecration, but believe me it's necessary. We're trying to get as many of our people as possible into offices with no exterior walls. Since the Russians arrived we've had people drilling through the outer wall. We think they were trying to plant microphones or some such. Didn't work. And I haven't registered a complaint. They're hardly likely to listen after all. But—we rearrange."

Troy's office was two floors up, at garden level, partly shaded by a gnarled old chestnut tree. He liked it at once. Until all this was over, it might well be a good substitute for his study at Mimram.

Janis Bell said, "Of course, Mr. Crawford is chafing at the bit. It would be as well to get him up here now."

Troy waved this away with his hand.

"I'm sure he has a point, and I'm sure we bruised his pride, but the protocols aren't what they were. No doubt he has a small army of civil servants in chancery—"

"Actually it's not much more than a dozen. Mr. Crawford has four assistants, second and third secretaries. I don't count. Needless to say. And of course we employ a fair number Czechs, who are not technically civil servants."

"Miss Bell, I'm not a civil service appointment. I couldn't give a toss about garden parties and receptions, first nights at the National Ballet, his pecking order or his protocol. I'm here for one reason and one reason only. To deal with the Russians. That's why Wilson and my brother appointed me. Wilson doesn't much trust MI6—he sees conspiracies everywhere; after all, George Brown wants his job, Five and Six want to topple the government . . . he probably pokes under the bed every night with a broom handle—so he sent me, a retired copper. And I have been known to stand up to our Secret Services . . . when needs be."

"I'll get me coat."

Troy laughed out loud. Janis Bell just grinned.

"I'm sure we can work together, Miss Bell."

"I'm sure we can, Ambassador."

"Troy. Behind these doors, I'm just Troy."

"So long as Mr. Crawford never hears me call you that."

"Tell me a little about yourself. As MI6's woman on the spot."

"Well . . . I'm twenty-eight. I joined the Service while I was at Cambridge. I got the tap on the shoulder. Must admit I was quite surprised. I wasn't known for my conservative ideas. But, no, Britain was changing. And a new Britain needed people like me. Apparently."

"Female?"

"And working class, and a northerner, with a first in modern languages, not classics. Someone who'd actually read a book written since Cicero put down his pen. It was MI6's early venture into kitchen sink drama. I fitted a scenario for them, as if I'd stepped straight out of a Shelagh Delaney play or a Stan Barstow novel. I was the 'right image' for the 'New Britain'—a phrase that makes me want to spit. I was three years in London. In '65 I was posted to the Helsinki embassy as an assistant to Jenny Burton, the Head of Station— which meant I typed her soddin' letters. In '66 I thought I'd ruined my career, but it turned out it was Mrs. Burton who'd ruined hers. She got posted to Pitcairn Island or somewhere not much bigger. I was sent to Bonn with the cover of Second Secretary—quite a promotion in terms of embassy status, but I was a small cog in a very large machine—and then here last summer. I'm Head of Station, my cover is First Secretary—in both cases prefaced by the word 'acting,' which, believe me, is reflected in my salary. There hasn't been a permanent Head of Station since that summer when Ben Crosland was suddenly recalled. They've had more than a year to confirm my appointment . . . haven't done it."

"Do I have that authority?"

"Nope. As you said not five minutes ago, you're neither a civil servant nor a spook. Only Six can make me permanent head, only the Civil Service can confirm me in the pretence of First Secretary."

"Give me some time. I am an expert at blackmailing the Home Secretary. I've had fifty years of practice. Why was Crosland recalled?"

"You mean they didn't tell you. Good bloody grief."

"Assume they told me next to nothing."

"Well . . . Crosland was acting as a decoy, by which I mean he was ostensibly running a contact personally . . . his wife made the dead drops. After a few weeks the Russians worked out that she was the real agent, not her husband—they made their move and she knocked a KGB bloke out cold in the Kampa Park."

Troy pondered this.

"It'll pay you to keep an eye on my wife too. She's quite capable of that. Tell me, are you running the contact now?"

"Yes, that's my job. But we have better systems in place now. Next to nothing, you say? So you've no idea of operations?"

Troy shook his head.

"OK. I've two men in deep cover dealing with Czech contacts. In Brno there's 'Zoltan'—but he's gone quiet since the invasion, and I rather think we'll have to pull him out, and there's 'Diesel' in Mělník. He has his head down, but he's active. I know from London that he still makes regular reports. Never met 'Zoltan,' and while I avoid direct contact with 'Diesel'—at his insistence, I might add—I have worked with him before. By the bye, we never refer to them, even in the most confidential corners, by anything other than their codenames. I've just realised I said 'we'—there is no 'we.' Mr. Crawford doesn't actually know Zoltan and Diesel are here."

"It's that secret?"

"Open this and you'll be the only other person in this building who knows Diesel's real name."

She pushed a thin red folder across the desk. Red—meaning "Top Secret Never To Be Removed From Office."

There was only one page to the dossier, and the name of the agent—an uneven line in smudgy type:

```
Joe Holderness.
```

Janis Bell read Troy's expression.

"You know him?"

"Oh yes."

"I suppose you think he's trouble."

"Of course, but no more than I am myself."

"Contact has been minimal. He's chosen to go it alone. I'll admit that annoyed the hell out of me when we first got here, but he was right. The StB constantly monitor . . ."

"StB?"

"My God, you really did get the short briefing. StB: *Státní bezpečnost.* The secret police. Plain clothes, a kind of poor man's Gestapo . . . they harass our Czech staff and most of our UK nationals. Drivers, cleaners, doormen . . . we have a remarkable turnover of local staff as they resign or just vanish rather than be blackmailed.

"They watch us from a sort of hole in the wall right opposite the front door of the embassy. It can't be much bigger than a broom cupboard, but some poor bugger in the StB sits in there all day and photographs everyone who comes and goes. I wave to him now and again. No idea if he waves back. And, almost needless to say, since the invasion there've been uniformed Czech coppers right outside. For our own protection, as it were. I suppose we should be grateful they're not Russians.

"I'm privileged, as was Ben Crosland. I get the personal attention of the Russians. They trail me everywhere. After all, it was a KGB man Ben's wife thumped, not an StB agent. It's almost as though the Russians didn't trust the StB. But that was a year ago . . . the 'almost' is wholly redundant. They really don't trust the StB now. Hence the KGB follow me around Prague, like a dog at a fair, as my Mum would say. But I think 'Diesel' was counting on that. They've never dared stop me after the Sarah Crosland incident. I'd like to think they think I'm better at it . . . that I make contacts and dead drops that they miss. Truth is, I do bugger all but lead them on a bit of a dance. But while they think I'm picking up information they're less inclined to look for anyone else. And they get lazy. Some days they'll all but follow me into the ladies' loo . . . other days I won't see hide nor hair of 'em."

"Should I expect to be followed?"

"Probably not. As ambassador you'll be too prominent to be doing anything suspect, and your public appearances will be known to them in advance . . . so . . ."

Janis Bell shrugged off the end of her sentence.

"The locals. Do you know of any they've turned?"

"We've sacked half a dozen in the time I've been here, two in the last month, but no one is attracting my suspicion at the moment."

"And bugs?"

"Oh . . . forgive what I said at the airport. It was a poor joke on my part. No, we sweep for electronic devices every day. There's nothing at the moment. On the other hand, if you visit any of their buildings assume every word you say is being recorded. And as it's summer, assume anything you say in the garden can be picked up by a directional microphone from the palace gardens just up the hill. They overlook every inch of the embassy garden. And, please . . . don't go on walkabout alone. Make today's your last."

"Of course," Troy lied. "Now, is it time I met Mr. Crawford and smoothed down his feathers?"

§162

That night Aleksandr Dubček broadcast to the nation. Troy turned on the large, prewar radio in his office—in the age of the transistor, the British Embassy still ran on valves—and Janis Bell translated as Dubček improvised. Even to Troy's uncomprehending ears Dubček sounded as though he was ad-libbing and exhausted:

```
We beg you, dear fellow citizens, to help us
prevent any provocations by some elements who
are interested in worsening the situation.

To ignore the real situation could only lead in
some places to adventures and anarchy.
```

"I'm not sure about 'adventures' . . . can't think of a better word, but he might not mean that. Oh, hang on . . . he's having a go at the new radio stations . . . 'spreading mistrust and doubt.'"

When Dubček had finished, Janis turned off the radio and said, "Basically he's saying what he's said all along—do nothing. It's significant how many times he used the words 'extraordinary' and 'normal.' I tried to count and got a bit lost."

Troy said, "*Some* elements?"

"That would cover just about everyone in Czechoslovakia."

"Tell me. Have you ever seen the Charlie Chaplin film *Modern Times*?"

"Yes, it was on at FilmSoc when I was a student. Don't remember much about it."

"There's a scene in which Chaplin is crossing the road. A lorry stacked with timber passes by and its red warning flag falls off. Chaplin picks it up just as a workers' demonstration comes around the corner and he unwittingly finds himself carrying the Socialist flag at the head of a hundred marchers. Isn't that Dubček?"

"Isn't that a very harsh reading of the situation?

§163

Somewhere in the České Středohoří: September

When Wilderness arrived at the stone circle on the hilltop, Tibor was sitting on a rock the height of a footstool that he'd rolled in from somewhere. He'd rolled in two, and between the two were a sandwich tin and two bottles of Budvar.

"A picnic?" Wilderness asked.

Tibor shrugged.

"It was your idea. When there's nothing to give, nothing to report, you said I should bring beer, sandwiches and a good book."

Wilderness sat opposite him. Accepted the gift of a sandwich. Peeled back the top slice. Sausage. Again.

"Nothing?" he said. "After all that's happened in the last two weeks?"

"It may well be because of what's happened that there's nothing. The Russians have wrapped us in their iron fist. I don't have the access this week that I had last week. May not last, of course. Meanwhile all I have is gossip, and you can get that in any bar in Prague."

"I haven't been to Prague in weeks. And the only gossip in Mělník concerns pigs, turnips and the baker's flighty wife."

"Oh well . . . in that case I may have a salacious snippet for you. Čierna nad Tisou. You know to what I refer?"

Of course he did. At the end of July, Brezhnev had met the Czechoslovak leaders at a railway junction on the Ukraine border—Čierna nad Tisou. It might well go down in history—the third most famous railway station in the world, after Crewe and Astapovo. The Russians rolled across the border in fifteen green sleeping cars and each evening they rolled back into a siding on the Soviet side, while Dubček remained on the Slovak side. As if to demonstrate that ne'er the twain shall meet, even the track gauges were different. In the day they met for discussion in a railwayman's club. It had yielded platitudes. Dubček had returned saying nothing of meaning and playing his cards closer to his chest than ever.

Tibor flipped the caps on the beer and offered one to Wilderness.

"They tried to . . . shall I say . . . persuade Dubček."

"Of course."

"Or shall I say . . . seduce him?"

"Eh?"

"They sent hookers to his sleeping car."

"I'm not sure I believe you."

"It's just what I hear. Make of it what you will. But it's the point when I think the Russians washed their hands of him. If you can't get a man's mind with Marxist logic, that's one thing. If you can't get a man by his cock with a couple of whores, then he's beyond redemption. After that any pretence they would not invade was a smoke screen. Brezhnev had already made his mind up."

They sipped beer.

"And here we are," Wilderness said.

"Yep."

"Unemployed. Out of work."

Tibor almost choked on his beer.

"Don't make me laugh, Joe. It's a waste of good beer."

"We're redundant. Think about it. We are spies with nothing left to spy on. *It* has happened."

"*It* is a cock-up. And when *it* has run *its* course to nowhere, the Czechs will blame the Slovaks, the Slovaks will blame the Czechs and sooner or later they'll both blame the Jews."

"Meanwhile, what do we do? Run a book club and meet to rehash Kafka? I've read every word he's written in the last year."

"I did, as you suggested, come with sandwiches, beer *and* a good book."

Tibor stuck his hand in his jacket pocket, pulled out a tatty German paperback.

Faust by Goethe.

"I'm only halfway through . . . but . . . fascinating."

"I read it years ago," said Wilderness, taking the book from him. "I doubt I was even twenty. There are lessons for us all in these pages."

He flipped through to find the line he was looking for.

"*Doch der den Augenblick ergreift, Das ist der rechte Mann.*"

(He who grasps the moment, he is the proper man.)

"Carpe diem?" Tibor said.

"Oh, far too late for that," Wilderness replied.

$164

Pussy-in-the-Well to White Rabbit: September 25th
 — `Joke. When will the Russians leave?`

White Rabbit to Pussy-in-the-Well: September 25th
 — `OK. Tell me.`

Pussy-in-the-Well to White Rabbit: September 25th
 — `When they find out who sent them the`
   `invitation!`

White Rabbit to Pussy-in-the-Well: September 25th
- Ha bloody ha.

§165

Prague Old Town: October

Someone had been telling the truth about Jiří J.

§166

Jiří was short of money. Again. Partly because of the cost of paint. He had more than two dozen stencils made up and could spray a ten-word slogan in well under a minute. It was great fun, dodging the coppers, ducking and diving, in and out of the alleys, finding an untouched wall and desecrating it. His latest was:

I AM THE WALRUS

Meaningless, but in a system that arrogated to itself such irrationalities as "the inevitability of history," meaninglessness was the final protest. The revolutionary power of nonsense. Dada pure and simple. History is on our side! History will absolve me! . . . dada dada dada dada dada dada.

Since the invasion the number of slogans on the walls had multiplied tenfold. Every Prankster had a spray can. He still thought he was the best and had never stooped to the obvious—"Go Home!" or "Freedom!"—and he avoided obscenity. Vepřové Václav didn't, but then he was much more visual and took time and risks to create cartoons, usually of Brezhnev engaged in sex with animals. And František had taken the biggest risk, pulled off the biggest stunt of all the Pranksters—he'd climbed up the façade of the Old Town Hall and gaffer-taped the mechanical figures.

Jiří felt speed was essential. All the same you couldn't stencil "Do You Know Which Way the Wind Blows" in just a few seconds. Eight words that had almost got him caught. He'd had to drop the can and the stencils—and he'd made the mistake of telling Nell, who had all but begged him to stop.

His mother might be good for a few crowns. Since he had moved in with his uncle, she had seemed better disposed towards him. She complained less about the length of his hair, asked fewer nosy questions, and while she had never offered money, there was always a cup of tea and a slice of bread and bratwurst set in front of him.

As he walked to her flat in Bartolomějská it occurred to him that if the police were clever they'd stop chasing him through the streets—any kid in plimsolls could outrun a copper in boots—and instead keep an eye on who bought spray paint in hardware shops. Then it occurred to him that they probably did. He pushed the thought to one side and let himself into his mother's apartment.

"You little sod!"

"Is that any way to greet your only son?"

"What have you been up to?"

"Nothing, Mami."

"Then why have I had the coppers banging on my door before breakfast? Not just ordinary coppers. StB—and they had a Russian with them!"

Oh shit.

"They've never bothered with me before."

"Jiří, for God's sake. They never bothered with you because you were a kid. You're eighteen now. That's when they start their secret files. Some apparatchik probably typed your name on a folder the day you turned eighteen. And ever since, you've been filling it for them. You and your stupid stunts."

"You didn't tell them anything?"

"Of course I didn't. I told them I hadn't seen you in months. But I don't want you here. I went through all this with your father. Months of accusation and interrogation. And at the end of it all I was a widow. I won't go through that again. If I am to lose a son, I'd far rather it was because he just buggered off than fell into the grip of the beast. So, Jiří, find a way out of Prague, find a way out of Czechoslovakia—and just bugger off."

"I have no money."

Magda vanished into her bedroom for a minute. Returned with her handbag. Tipped it out onto the kitchen table. A moment's ferreting around and she plucked out half a dozen bank notes and thrust them at him.

"There. That's all I've got. Take it and go."

"Mami—"

"Mami nothing. Don't try and soft-soap me. Just go. And remember this. Your father died for a principle, not for some silly teenage prank."

§167

Jiří weighed up the risk of going to Petr's flat. It all depended on whether the cops had worked out where he really lived, by which he meant someone might have finked on him, and whether or not their sense of drama would be ruined if they banged on a door in the middle of the day rather than at daybreak. You should never underestimate the cop love of showing off.

He turned up his collar, pulled his woolly hat down to his eyebrows and took the risk.

Nell was in the kitchen. He could hear Petr clacking away on the typewriter in his study.

"We're eating in. Care to join us?"

Before Jiří could answer, Petr's voice boomed from the study.

"He can buy his own bloody food. This is not a soup kitchen!"

"He's joking," Nell said.

"If only," said Jiří. "Nell. I have a problem."

"Money? You're always broke."

"Well . . . of course . . . but there's more . . . the secret police are on to me."

Petr had ears like a jackass. He would hear a gnat fart as a tram went by. Now he stood in the doorway.

"What?"

"They came to Mami's apartment this morning."

"And you came here?"

"I've nowhere else to go."

"You stupid little fucker."

"Petr! Please," Nell said. "Let the boy speak."

"He's said it all. The cops are after him, so he leads them here?"

"Were you followed, Jiří?" she said.

"No. And I don't mean to put either of you at risk. I just . . . well I have no money."

Petr grabbed Jiří from behind, his right hand locked into the scruff of his neck, twisting his shirt collar. With his left he opened the door wide and had thrust the boy halfway into the stairwell before Nell body-slammed him with her shoulder and forced him to let go.

Nell banged the door shut.

"For God's sake, Petr. He's your own flesh and blood."

"Flesh dies, and blood bleeds. My flesh and blood died in prison ten years ago. This . . . this is a parasite!"

"Which is what the Party used to call you!"

This stopped Petr. Whatever he had to say next went unsaid. Instead he spoke more calmly.

"If he stays here, if he is found here . . ."

"I understand. He can stay at my apartment."

"No, he can't. It's diplomatic territory. You're the consul. That won't stop the StB searching your apartment, but it will spread the fallout if he's found there. A diplomatic incident. Think of Brandt's reaction. Even the Americans aren't taking in refugees, for just that reason."

Nell turned to Jiří.

He was rubbing gently at the bruising on the back of his neck. His expression unchanged, unmoved by all this. So used to Petr's rage that it bounced off him. He hadn't resisted, and he wasn't cowering.

"Then . . . then you must go to the British. Go to the embassy. They represent my country, they have a legal obligation to me. I will give you a letter. You must ask for Janis Bell. Remember the name: Janis Bell."

"Nell," said Petr. "The American Embassy is surrounded by police. What makes you think it will be any different at the British?"

"I was there yesterday. No Russians. No StB. There were just two regular police. Jiří will have to take his chances with them. May I use your typewriter?"

§168

Palác Thun

Jiří got to the British Embassy in the last light of day. The spook in the broom cupboard opposite the main entrance was having a less-than-crafty fag, smoke billowing out from the observation hole.

Right in front of the embassy's intimidating wooden gates two uniformed policemen were holding back a crowd of twenty or so. They were all kids of his age, all boys, and he knew all of them by sight and three or four were friends from way back, from kindergarten . . . Tommo, František, Mopslík . . . Vepřové Václav.

Mopslík said, "The cops are trying to round us all up. They came to my mother's flat."

"They came to my mother's too."

"Looks like they're out to get all the Pranksters."

"Maybe we're not as harmless as we thought?"

"Right now, Jiří, that's fuck all consolation."

"Will the English let us in?"

"Not if this pair have a say. They've kept their guns holstered, but if any of us take so much as a step towards them the night sticks come out. Perhaps we should try the Americans."

"Forget it—more cops and KGB than the Kremlin."

The side door to the embassy suddenly opened. A small, dark woman, dressed for the evening in a classic little black dress, came down the slope, clutching a silver tray as though she might be about to serve tea and cucumber sandwiches to the cops.

Both cops turned and looked down at the tray in expectation. It was bare.

Before they could look up the woman bashed them both about the head with the tray and went on bashing until one of them fell to his knees and the other stepped back to flip the stud on his holster. He stepped back into Vepřové Václav, bounced off one hundred and fifteen kilos of flesh and fell flat on his face.

The main gate to the embassy courtyard opened as if on cue, wide enough to allow a car *out*, wide enough to allow twenty kids *in*.

They froze.

"What the fuck is going on?"

"Move, you morons!"

"What?"

"Imshe, mush—inside!"

They ran for gate, the madwoman not far behind them, urging them on with cries of "Head 'em up, move 'em out, Rawhide!"

Then the gates closed behind them.

The sound of iron on oak, so reassuring.

A collective breath drawn, a collective sigh exhaled.

A warm tide seemed to Jiří to be spreading outwards from his heart across his ribs, down through his belly. Chaos and mystery washed away by this new-found sense of safety.

§169

Janis Bell said, "Do you think that was wise?"

And Anna replied, "Yep, gotta keep them dogies movin'."

"Where are we going to put them all?"

"We've bags of room. This place is huge."

"No, we haven't. Honestly. And if there's just one Russian agent among that lot—"

"OK, OK. I see your point. Don't want the little buggers roving around the embassy, poking into stuff. Hmmm . . . hmmm . . . got any tents?"

"Well . . . sort of . . . we have two or three small marquees we use on the back lawn for receptions in the summer. You know, just big enough to keep the rain off the cucumber sandwiches."

"Super. Have them put up on the lawn, send someone into town in the morning to buy sleeping bags—they all look like hippies, they probably enjoy roughing it—and speaking of sandwiches, rustle up a pile and see the little buggers get fed—and . . ."

She handed Janis Bell the silver tray.

"See if the odd job bloke can straighten this out, will you? It would appear it once belonged to Mad King Ludwig of Bavaria. Be a shame to leave it looking quite so dented."

§170

The Morning After

"Have you gone completely mad?"

"Sorry Rod, not sure I follow you."

"Some woman in your embassy clobbered a Russian soldier with a tin tray and let a dozen refugees in. I had the Cabinet Secretary on the phone before breakfast! I got summoned to No. 10!"

"That's not true."

"All of it? Some of it?"

"First—it wasn't 'some woman'; it was Anna."

"Oh bloody hell."

"The tray was silver, not tin. And they were Czech coppers, not Russian soldiers. The Russians didn't arrive till this morning. But now the place is crawling with them, so no more refugees."

"How many do you have?"

"More than a dozen."

"How many?"

"Twenty-seven."

"Oh bloody hell. Oh bloody hell. What do you intend to do with them?"

Zzzzzzfzzzzzzz.

The crackle on the line from London gave Troy just the excuse he needed.

"Sorry, bro . . . the line's playing up."

And Her Majesty's Ambassador to Czechoslovakia put the phone down on Her Majesty's Principal Secretary of State for Home Affairs.

It bought Troy time, and he needed time. He was in awe of his wife's courage and bloody-mindedness, but unlike her he had to work out what to do with twenty-seven refugees, none of whom was much past childhood.

Rod had asked what he intended. He would certainly ask again.

§171

Later the Same Day
Around Six in the Evening

Nell arrived back at Vítězná to find Petr throwing clothes into a suitcase.

"You're packing?"

"I'm leaving."

"Leaving me?"

"God, no. Leaving Czechoslovakia."

"But I'm in Czechoslovakia."

"You don't have to be. Go home, grab what you need and we can be in Vienna by midnight."

"Petr. I have a job to do. More of a job than it was ever supposed to be. I have a duty to Germany, a duty to Brandt and like it or not a duty to Czechoslovakia."

"Nell. Please come with me. I beg you, please come with me."

"No."

"No?"

"First you tell me why."

"Jiří. He has made us all vulnerable. You as well as me."

"He's just a boy."

"He is a dangerous boy."

"Dangerous? He paints graffiti, Petr. That's all he does."

"And people go to prison for less. I spent a year in prison simply because I was someone's brother. I spent four months in a factory turning scrap metal into hinges because my occupation was deemed parasitic. I'm not going back to either of those simply for being his uncle. Why do you think his mother threw him out?"

"She threw him out because she caught him smoking pot!"

"And because he was a liability to her. I took him in on condition he brought no trouble down on us. Now the police are looking for him."

"They looked at Magda's, not here."

"They will look for him here. Perhaps tonight, certainly tomorrow."

"You should be proud of Jiří."

"I'm fed up with his childish antics. And I'll find room for pride when I'm free."

"So, what do you propose to do?"

Petr took a sheet of headed paper from the tabletop and handed it to her—Ministry of the Interior.

"What is it? You'll have to tell me. It's too . . . too official. Too many ticks and too many boxes."

"It's an exit permit. I was supposed to attend the Cannes Film Festival in May. They abandoned the festival after the troubles in Paris, so I didn't go."

"I remember. That was over five months ago. What use is it now? Anything issued before the Russians arrived is surely worthless?"

"They forgot to date it. All I have to do is type in the date."

Nell held the sheet of paper out to him.

"Then do it. I won't be coming with you. Go on, take it."

Nell had never thought of herself as leaving Wilderness. She had walked away from him, left him in his bed at the American Hospital in Tempelhof, but she had not *left* him. He had left her. He had told her lies of leaving for months on end. Every lie a mendacious mile.

She heard the rapid click of typewriter keys in the next room, took her coat and let Petr leave her just seconds before he reappeared. He called down the stairwell to her.

She did not look back.

He had left her.

§172

Palác Thun: The Same Evening

The madwoman was handing out sleeping bags. It had been a warm October night—cold just the same. They had clustered around Vepřové Václav, who seemed to exude heat. He also farted a lot, but . . . beggars . . . choosers.

It dawned on Jiří that this must be the Janis Bell Nell had mentioned.

"Excuse me, Janis Bell," he said, assuming she spoke no Czech. "I have a letter for you."

The madwoman looked at the embossed envelope:

NĚMECKÁ KULTURNÍ MISE

"No. Not me. But I'll see she gets it. And you are?"

"Jiří Jasny."

"Well, I'm not Miss Bell. I'm the ambassadress."

This was baffling. She might just as well have spoken to him in Polish. Too many *s* letters, and too many syllables.

"My husband is the grumpy-looking bloke you can see staring at us from his office window, just behind the chestnut tree. He is the ambassador. Hence I am am-bass-a-dress."

She nodded too much. Talking to an idiot.

"Mrs. Basdress?"

"OK. That'll have to do. I'll deliver your letter."

§173

Janis Bell slid a paper knife into the envelope, saying as she did so, "It's from Nell Burkhardt."

"Who she?" Anna asked.

"She runs the West German Cultural Mission. Not long before the tanks rolled in, Brandt and Dubček agreed to consular status for her, although as with either of my titles it's prefaced by the word 'acting.' Dubček had appealed for the normalisation of relations with West Germany. Upgrading Nell was about as far as it got. She's been very *active* in her time here. Signed up almost anyone who was anyone for a festival in Berlin, which unfortunately was scheduled for the week of the invasion."

"And the boy? Is he anyone?"

"Yes and no. Nell says they're after him as one of the 'sloganeers.' They've been the most marvellous thorn in the side of the Communists—even before the invasion. I rather admire them—just a bunch of kids with spray cans, but more effective than any manifesto. He is also the nephew of the film director Petr Jasny. Jasny is a discreet dissident. He might sign a petition, he wouldn't throw a Molotov cocktail. Can't blame him for that, with two prison terms behind him. But the boy's father was Tomás Jasny. MI6 are pretty certain he was executed in the fifties. So . . . the boy comes with baggage."

"And what is Miss Burkhardt asking?"

"That we grant him entry . . . well you did that off your own bat last night, didn't you?"

"Asylum?"

"Doesn't mention that."

"Do we have that . . . er . . . power?"

"Troy does. He could give them all, all twenty-soddin'-seven of them asylum. Doesn't mean he'd get them out of Czechoslovakia or even out of the embassy. They might be here for years. And there'd be ripples in Westminster. Brezhnev has made it clear that this is an 'internal' matter and he doesn't want or expect to see asylum granted. For the first week you were here the border crossings were loose . . . not open, just loose . . . and I think this was in the hope that the real dissidents would just bugger off. I doubt any of them did. And now they're tight . . . y'know, camel's arse and all that."

"Ripples in Westminster?"

"Oh yes."

"Then don't say that to Troy or he'll do it just to annoy his brother."

§174

Prague, Jungmannovo námesti:
The Morning After

Janis Bell sent a courier out with a letter for Nell.

Clara Wieck opened all the mail at the Cultural Mission.

"Good Lord!"

"What?"

"That boy . . . the nephew . . ."

She held out the letter to Nell. Nell had been waiting for something like this.

```
Nell—Jiří is fine. He got into the embassy. And
so did twenty-six other kids. They're all safe
for now, but in the long term I've no idea what
to do with them. Let us keep in touch about this.
                                      Janis Bell
```

"I should go there."

"Don't," said Clara.

"I'm sorry?"

"That would be really rather stupid. You're the consul. If this goes wrong . . . well, far better to let the StB pick on me. I'm a nobody. Not so much a diplomatic incident, more an irritant. Besides, I don't live with a known dissident."

Nell had not told Clara that Petr had left. She might never tell her.

"You may be right."

"I know damn well I am."

"I have a plan to get Jiří out of Czechoslovakia, it's just that it will take time."

"OK. Put what you want him to know in a letter. I'll walk over after lunch and try my best to look casual."

§175

Neither Nell nor Clara yet had diplomatic passports. Clara wasn't sure which would attract more suspicion. She showed her ordinary green German passport to the policeman in the cul-de-sac that led to the British Embassy. He looked at the photograph, looked at her, handed it back and turned to the Russians with a muttered "Just another bloody *Skopová hlava*" (muttonhead).

Inside, she asked for Janis Bell, whom she had met before, and a woman she'd never met before appeared and introduced herself as Anna.

"Ah, I know him," Anna said, reading Jiří's name on the envelope. "The skinny one, the runt of the litter."

"I'm sorry. I don't understand."

"That's alright. I'll see he gets it."

§176

"It just says to stay put," said Jiří.

"As if you had a choice," Anna replied.

"I can't stay here!"

"The trouble with your generation is you have no patience."

"And I bet that's what your parents said to you."

Indeed it was, but Anna would never admit that to this lippy little kid, who looked like someone who'd failed the audition for the Rolling Stones.

"I'm doing my best. So make the best of it."

Anna had sent out for more blankets and had bought half a dozen Primus stoves to let them make hot drinks for themselves.

A thank-you would have been nice.

Up the hill, in the castle gardens, a platoon of Russian soldiers looked down upon the embassy garden, day and night. Their every move was under scrutiny. It was so tempting to shrug off being Lady Troy for ten seconds and hold up two fingers.

§177

A week passed before Clara Wieck delivered another letter.

When he'd read it Jiří said, "Mrs. Basdress, do you have a camera?"

"Show me."

The letter asked for two passport-sized photographs.

Anna went in search of Janis Bell and asked the same question.

Janis made two replies.

"Yes, I have a Brownie 127 . . . somewhere."

And . . .

"Anna, what are you up to?"

§178

Wilmersdorf, Berlin: November 15th

Strange as it was to be back in her old apartment, Nell found no mental space for nostalgia.

She dropped off the roll of film with an overnight developer.

She ate at the first restaurant she passed, one that prompted no memories. She was not even sure it had been there the last time she had spent a night in Berlin.

Then she went to bed early and censored her dreams.

In the morning she collected the prints and walked to Grünetümmlerstraße.

As ever, the door to Erno's flat was an inch or so ajar, and a wave of heat hit her as soon as she pushed at it.

Erno was at the table. Half past ten in the morning but he appeared to be having lunch—and scowling.

"Erno?"

The scowl became a smile. He half-rose from his seat, but she gently pressed him back down with a hand on his shoulder.

"No, no. Please finish your . . ."

"It's nettle soup. Trudie insists it is good for me. I would as soon tip it down the sink."

"Nettle soup? Where does she get nettles in November?"

"I daren't ask. I might find out she's a witch who can make flowers bloom at Christmas. But the truth is, Nell, I have had a touch of pneumonia, which on top of all the ills that old age brings . . . perhaps Trudie is not a witch but she may well be an angel."

He was, she thought, as pale as a sheet. He'd lost weight too, and when he looked at her he was screwing up his eyes.

It gave her pause.

She sat opposite him. Slipped off her coat and unwound her headscarf. She'd no real idea of Erno's age. He was a veteran of the First

World War, but that could mean anything between seventy and ninety. He had always been a crepuscular creature. She could not remember when she'd last seen him outdoors. He liked to be indoors in warmth, with the curtains drawn and the light in pools of his own choosing. It had helped to render him inscrutably ageless in her eyes. Now . . . now he seemed to resemble a mole.

"Erno, there is something I need."

"Ask, child. I have never yet denied you anything."

"A passport."

"Hmm."

His head shook gently from side to side. Not a "no," more a consideration. He spooned up another mouthful of soup.

"What nationality?"

"Bundesrepublik."

"And who is the supplicant?"

Nell opened her handbag, placed the photographs of Jiří on the table.

A gust of cold air.

Suddenly she was aware of another person in the room.

Trudie stood in the doorway.

"Nell, may I have a word. In private."

Erno answered.

"No, you may not. Whatever you have to say, Trudie, say it here and say it now."

"As you wish. Nell, Erno is not well. You ask too much."

"I can see that, Trudie. But—I am desperate. There is no other word for it. I must get Jiří out of Czechoslovakia. He is virtually a prisoner in the British Embassy—"

"Nell—I say again. Erno has been very ill—"

Erno threw down his napkin, let his spoon rattle on the crockery.

"Ladies, please. It has been fifty years since women fought over me and, flattering as it is, I can live without it. What Nell asks is simple. Forging West German passports is the nearest thing I have to a production line. I could make them in my sleep. Forgive me, Trudie, but I shall take a little time off from our health regime and do as Nell asks. And if you insist that I am too old for this kind of thing and that this should be my last, I would not gainsay you. This will be my last. Now, if you would excuse me."

He shuffled off to the bedroom. The door closed quietly behind him, not a trace of anger remained.

Trudie said, "Show me."

Nell picked up one of the photographs.

"Oh God, he's just a boy."

"Yes," said Nell. "He is."

§179

Somewhere in the České Středohoří: November 29th

Wilderness kept his appointment with Tibor. He left his car halfway down the slope and walked the rest of the way.

Part of him relished meetings with Tibor. They might be the only time in any month he didn't feel like a tractor salesman.

As he reached the stone circle, Tibor stood with his back to him, staring out at the landscape.

But this wasn't Tibor. This bloke was too tall and too skinny.

Wilderness wondered how much noise he'd made. Had this bloke heard his car or his footsteps on the stone trail? And he regretted that his gun was still in the footwell of his car where he'd put it that day in Vienna. A year and more in Czechoslovakia and he hadn't felt the need of a gun.

The skinny bloke turned around.

Wilderness asked the obvious question.

"Where's Tibor?"

"Мне жаль."

(I'm sorry.)

"Kostya, for fuck's sake speak English."

"He's dead, Joe."

"How?"

Kostya hadn't killed him. Wilderness could not imagine Kostya killing anyone.

"His interrogators . . . they were . . . clumsy."

"So he got beaten to death in those torture chambers you buggers have under the embassy on Pod Kaštany."

"That seems likely. I only arrested him. I wasn't one of . . . I have only been in this country a month . . . this is my first case."

"I don't care—stop making excuses. Why isn't this hillside crawling with KGB? Tibor gave you the place . . . but you could not have known he was meeting me . . . he never knew me by anything but a code name. Why are you here alone?"

"Call me Joe, you told him. *Call me Joe.* A six-foot London Joe who talked to him of Kafka and Goethe? Of course I knew it was you."

Wilderness looked around, expecting nothing, seeing no one.

"You really came alone?"

"Yes."

"Then you're not here to bust me?"

"I'm here to tell you you have twenty-four hours to leave Czechoslovakia."

"Generous."

"I'm in charge of this case, Joe . . . Sooner than later, I have to report to men far more important than I am. And I may not be able to save you. I'm just a major. Right now, I'm the only person who knows about you. That cannot last. If you are alone, go now. If you had a team . . . well, they got lucky Tibor died before our men could get any more out of him, so tell them to leave at once. You . . . you have twenty-four hours."

Wilderness spun slowly around, not doubting Kostya was alone, but still wondering about he knew-not-what. He came face-to-face with him.

"Make it forty-eight hours."

"What?"

"There are loose ends."

"No Joe, no!"

"Forty-eight . . . that's all I ask."

"Joe, why must you always drag us to the point where one of us might get shot?"

"It's the game we're in."

"And so . . . you would make me into your executioner."

"Give me those extra two days. I promise you, there'll be no fuck-ups."

"OK. But I speak only for myself."

"I understand."

"Forty-eight hours, Joe. After that it's out of my hands."

For a moment Wilderness thought Kostya was about to shake his hand, or make some equally sentimental gesture, but he turned and headed for the northern slope out of the stone circle.

"Kostya."

He stopped.

"Where can I contact you?"

"What? Why on earth would you need to contact me?"

If all this went pear-shaped, Wilderness could envision the kind of contact involving a gun to the head.

"Perhaps I just want to say goodbye."

"Again? All we have are goodbyes. Twenty years of goodbyes."

"Indulge me."

Kostya weighed this up. It took him several seconds to answer, his eyes fixed on some point way out in the hills.

Then he looked straight at Wilderness. Eye to eye.

"Alright. Don't come near the embassy. That would be so stupid. But I'm billeted in Malá Strana, and most evenings I have dinner at the Café Savoy."

"I think you've chosen the one Prague restaurant I actually know how to find."

"До свидания, Joe."

$180

Clara delivered one last letter to the embassy.

Janis Bell no longer bothered to open them. There had been more than a dozen in the last month. She passed them straight to Anna and did not enquire what happened next.

Anna read the letter, and stood while Jiří read it:

It will be tonight. Find a way out of the embassy. I will be
waiting in Klárov at nine. Be on time. I will not risk the curfew.
I will also not risk arrest and will leave promptly at 9.01. Look
for a Blue VW Beetle with German plates. Dress for a long,
cold journey.

Nell

"Find a way out? Hasn't she seen those Russians at the door?"

"Probably not. But I'm sure we can find a way."

Jiří pointed up to the next level, to the terrace carved out of the hillside in front of the presidential palace, only forty feet above the embassy garden. It had crossed his mind many times that the wall was climbable, covered in thick old vines of ivy, but the Russians manned it day and night. In the day he saw the sunlight reflecting off the lenses of their cameras and at night he could see the ends of their cigarettes.

"Just look up there, Mrs. Basdress. How many Russian soldiers do you think are watching us?"

"Dunno. Don't care. And if I thought it would distract them I'd walk around the garden naked. But it wouldn't work and it'll be tit-freezing cold tonight, so we need another way. Just leave it with me—and above all, Jiří, and I say this knowing something of your nature, don't do anything stupid."

§181

Wilderness said goodbye to Mrs. Homemade, who was insistent he take a string of sausages with him—pork and pork-flavour.

Then he phoned Hahn and Kruger and used a prearranged code, some nonsense about a sales conference they all had to attend in Vienna. It took Hahn a nudge or two before the penny dropped. Kruger got it at once, but Wilderness knew he was silently cursing that this would cost him the life he'd made for himself in Prague.

To check into the Europa seemed like tempting fate, so he parked his BMW in Klárov and walked to the British Embassy.

A group of Russian soldiers looked at him almost devoid of expression, but it was a regular Prague copper who checked his German passport. It occurred to Wilderness that the man might ask what business he could have with the British at eight o'clock in the evening, but he didn't.

It was the British who were suspicious. The woman on the other end of the intercom told him they were closed, as though an embassy were no more than a provincial greengrocers on a Wednesday afternoon.

Wilderness said, "I'm here to see Janis Bell. Just say one word, 'Diesel.'"

Janis could not have been far away. Less than a minute later the door opened. And then it slammed behind him.

"Good grief, Joe, you like risk, don't you?"

"The risk is out there, not in here."

"I mean . . . coming here . . ."

"I'm busted, Janis. The Russians know everything. Busted and knackered. I need a bed for the night."

"Let me see what I can do."

She led him up to the top floor of the palace, to a room so low anyone taller than Wilderness would have to stoop. All the same, it was well furnished, clean and warm.

"This is the Foreign Secretary's room. We're not expecting him. In fact, he's never been here. Tomorrow we should tell the ambassador what's happening. I'd tell him now but he's having dinner with Dubček."

"I won't be here long. I've no intention of becoming a refugee. I'll get out of the country as soon . . . as soon as I've finished."

Janis Bell stood in the window, high above the embassy garden.

"Refugee? Just look out there. It's like Chipperfield's Circus."

Wilderness found himself looking at the tops of a scattering of tents. "How many?"

"Twenty-seven. Not one of them over the age of twenty-one."

"What can you do with them?"

"Dunno, but I imagine that's why Troy and Dubček are meeting. Now, tired, you say. Hungry too?"

"Haven't eaten since breakfast."

"I'll have something sent up."

When she'd gone, Wilderness kicked off his shoes and lay on the bed. The exhaustion wasn't physical. It might even be relief that this was all over—almost all over.

Janis hadn't asked what he meant by "finished."

Finished was Nell. He did not want to leave Prague without seeing Nell. He'd asked Kostya for time. A day to find her . . . and a day to escape.

§182

The eastern terrace of the embassy was not watched to the same extent as the garden. Anna concluded that after dark someone dressed in black could probably go over the wall without being seen.

She'd reconnoitred the route late that afternoon. Twelve feet or so below the wall was the sloping roof a building that stood in a courtyard just off Sněmovní. The door to the courtyard was not locked. A drainpipe ran from the lower end of the roof to ground level, and what teenage boy could not climb a drainpipe? Once in Sněmovní it was a five-hundred-yard dash to Klárov, the broad square where the trams stopped before they snaked their way up the next hill, and where Nell Burkhardt had said she would park.

At ten minutes to nine, feeling faintly ridiculous in a black balaclava, she held Jiří by one hand, leaned out as far as she dared and dropped him onto the roof below.

She heard the tiles crack beneath his weight.

He looked up.

"Goodbye, Mrs. Basdress," he said in a stagey whisper.

"Jiří . . . bugger off and bon voyage."

§183

Nell parked her Beetle in front of a dirty black BMW that looked as though it had spent its life in ploughed fields.

It was three minutes to nine.

Punctuality was not one of Jiří's finer points. Stupidity was.

But on the dot of nine the passenger door was yanked open, and Jiří slid into the seat.

"Did anyone see you?"

"No one that matters. I didn't run. I walked at a normal pace. I didn't look suspicious."

She handed him his passport.

"Learn who you are supposed to be."

"Horst Burkhardt, born 21.9.52, Wiesbaden."

"You're my nephew. You understand?"

"Yes, but . . . I'm eighteen, not sixteen."

"For God's sake, Jiří, think! Who are the border patrols more likely to be interested in? A sixteen-year-old schoolboy or an eighteen-year-old student. It drops you neatly below the line of interest."

"OK. OK."

Nell started the car. Felt her bumper thump the BMW behind her, but drove on.

"Nell. Where are we going?"

"Berlin."

§184

The Following Morning

Working with Lord Troy reminded Janis Bell of working with Joe Holderness. They were both . . . more than a bit dodgy . . . although, in mitigation, Lord Troy was not as dodgy as Lady Troy.

It was late in the morning when his dodgy Lordship sent for her.

"I don't suppose you have any way of contacting Joe Holderness."

"Actually I was waiting for a chance to tell you about Joe. He's here."

"Here where? In the embassy?"

"Upstairs. I put him in the room we keep for the Foreign Secretary."

"And the reason he's here?"

"He tells me his cover is blown. He got here last night while you were with Dubček. Didn't want to risk a hotel. The Russians have given him forty-eight hours to leave . . . he's already used up about twenty of them. If it were me, I'd have just driven to the border and got the hell out of Czechoslovakia. I honestly don't know why he hasn't."

"I think I can guess why. More accurately, I think I can guess who. Would you ask him to join us? There's been a development I think he'll want to know about."

§185

Janis Bell caught Wilderness just as he was preparing to leave. Overcoat on, wondering if the bulge of the gun in its shoulder holster might be a bit too obvious. He'd dug the gun out of its hidey-hole when he parked the car last night. He could not now imagine taking it off until he left the country. He thought too about ditching the farce that was "Walter

Hensel"—he wasn't Walter anymore . . . a tractor salesman with a Smith & Wesson?—but thought better of it.

"Joe?"

"Things I have to do. Someone I need to find."

"Troy's asking for you."

"This is urgent, Janis. And that's an understatement."

"Troy said you'd want to know."

"Know what?"

"How the fuck should I know? Just come with me, Joe."

She all but shoved Wilderness through the door to Troy's office, but as she closed the door, Troy said, "Would you mind staying, Janis? It'll save me having to say this twice."

There was an awkward pause as Troy seemed to clock Wilderness's "Walter Hensel" appearance. Troy looked down at his notes then back at Wilderness. Janis Bell hovered, part of it and not part of it, sensing trouble, wanting to be there and not be there.

"Sorry we have to meet like this after such a long time, Joe."

"Yep. It's been a year or two."

"But the devil drives. Ten minutes ago I received a telephone call from the German foreign minister, Willy Brandt. As you may imagine the German Foreign Office has spies and narks all over the place. Early this morning Brandt received reports that a West German citizen, resident in Prague, was arrested late last night at the border, attempting to smuggle out a wanted dissident. A student. He doesn't know the name of the boy, but the woman has been named as Nell Burkhardt."

"Is he sure?"

"Sure enough to make it a diplomatic matter. I act for the Bundesrepublik in this country. If it is Fräulein Burkhardt . . . the responsibility is mine. Of course it may be a case of mistaken identity or simply a mistake per se."

Janis Bell knew she wasn't hopping from one foot to the other like a nervous schoolgirl—it just felt that way.

"No!" she blurted out

"No what?"

"No, it's not a mistake."

Both men turned to her.

Troy said, "Spit it out, Janis."

"We lost a refugee in the night. At teatime yesterday there were twenty-seven, and only twenty-six at breakfast. Jiří Jasny went over the wall. He'll be the dissident they've got."

"Which one is he?"

"The little one. The cheeky one. The one your wife's pally with."

Wilderness said, "And Nell? How does she fit in?"

"Ever since Jiří got here he's been receiving letters from Nell at the Cultural Mission. Never in person. Her deputy, Clara, calls a couple of times a week. The last letter was yesterday afternoon. Clara gave it to me. I gave it to your wife. Your wife will have given it to Jiří."

"And then Anna helped him over the wall while I was with Dubček?"

"I didn't say that."

"You didn't need to."

Wilderness said, "Where is Nell? Did Brandt know?"

"No—he just said the KGB had her. Joe, I will move heaven and earth to get Nell back."

"No," Wilderness said. "That's my job."

§186

Troy and Anna met for lunch in the ambassador's private dining room. He told the staff to leave everything—they would serve themselves.

"I suppose you don't want them to hear the bollocking you're about to deliver?" Anna said. "Go ahead. I did it. I helped little Jiří wotsisname over the wall. I've no regrets."

This was not the time to tell her that Jiří would probably spend the next two years in prison.

"And I have no regrets. It's my congratulations I didn't want the staff to hear."

"Good Lord. When I think of all the times I've urged restraint on you over the last twenty-five years, I didn't think you'd miss a chance to get back at me."

"Perhaps you're turning into me. Y'know . . . Charlie and Oona Chaplin?"

"Or Nikita and Mrs. Khrushchev? Not fucking likely."

"I wanted to ask you," Troy said as he ladled out an indeterminate soup, worthy of any British factory canteen, to his wife, "do you have any plan for getting the others out?"

"Isn't that what you and Dubček were discussing last night?"

"In part, yes."

"Oh God—this soup's disgusting. What is it, Ye Olde Czechy Sock recipe?"

Troy ignored this.

"Dubček hasn't got much time left. He is a nominal leader at best. It won't be long before he's packed off back to Slovakia to supervise pig insemination or some such."

"Well, you're the expert on that. How long, roughly?"

"He'll be gone by the new year."

"Bugger—so we, or as I now realise, *I*, have got just a few weeks to strike a deal over these kids, is that it?"

"No. That isn't what I'm saying. Dubček cannot put a foot out of line and would never do anything . . . underhand."

"Not with you here, husband mine."

"Dubček will be replaced by some hard-line bastard of whom the Russians approve. Someone who would never put a foot out of line."

"*Plus ça change.*"

"But . . . someone who might be open to bribes."

"You're going to buy these kids their freedom?

"Well, the thought had occurred to me."

"If you got it, spend it?"

"Something like that."

"Ah . . . I begin to remember why I married you. Just a flicker."

"One I shall cherish. But . . . more precisely. I'll need photographs of each of them. Can you arrange that?"

"Yep."

"And when you've done that, I shall issue visas for the United Kingdom, and then when the time is right, I'll find out who to bribe for twenty-six safe passages to the border. May take a while, but . . ."

"I hate 'but.' It might just be my least favourite word in the English language."

"But we have another, more immediate problem."

"I'm listening."

"Joe Holderness is out there now, in the city. He's a loose cannon."

"Hmmm . . . do you know how often I heard you described as a loose cannon back when you were a copper?"

Troy said nothing.

§187

Vítězná, Malá Strana

Wilderness hated killing time, but to go to the Soviet Embassy on Pod Kaštany would have gained him nothing. It was a boulevard of vast villas, with nowhere to hide, and the Russians would have spotted him in minutes. During the war the Germans had occupied the building. They'd built the torture chambers . . . the Russians continued to use them all the same.

He could lurk in the shadows at the far side of the Legií Bridge, looking and feeling like Harry Lime, and watch the entrance to Café Savoy until he caught sight of Kostya. Instead he asked for a table, ordered a beer, sat down to wait.

For some reason he thought of all the times he had sat in the bar at the White Nights in Persereiikkä waiting for Kostya—he'd set out the chess set and play an imaginary game, plan attack and defence, and as often as not Kostya would slice through his plans in half a dozen moves.

When Kostya came in he didn't see Wilderness at once. The maître d' pointed him out, and thirty seconds of whispering followed before Kostya approached him.

"I don't believe you're doing this. I don't believe you're still here."

"Sit down, Kostya."

As Kostya sat, a waiter stuck half a litre of beer in front of him. He ignored it, kept his eyes on Wilderness.

Wilderness said, "The last time I sat at this table I wasn't facing a Russian. I was facing a German."

"And your point is?"

"Who do you think that was?"

Kostya pushed back his sleeve and looked at his Red Army–issue Pobeda watch.

"Less than sixteen hours of your forty-eight left and you want to play guessing games?"

"It was Nell."

"Ah, yes. I had heard she was here. Some sort of cultural liaison, I think."

"Where is she, Kostya?"

"What?"

"You have Nell. The KGB have Nell. Where is she?

"I don't know anything about this."

"I could very easily have a gun aimed at your groin right now Kostya."

"But you haven't."

"But I will if I don't get answers. Nell was arrested at the border with the DDR late last night. You, the KGB, have her. Fuck your sixteen hours . . . you've got till midnight to set her free or I will find you and I will blow your fucking brains out."

The shock on Kostya's face looked far more real than Wilderness's threat, and Wilderness had known for years what an unconvincing liar he was.

"Joe . . . Joe . . . I know nothing about this."

And Wilderness believed him.

"Drink your beer, Kostya. You've gone paler than a ghost."

They each took a gulp of beer, an armistice written in Budvar.

"If . . . if . . . if Nell were being held at Pod Kaštany, I'd know. Dammit, that's my job."

"Can you find out where she is?"

"Probably."

"No Kostya, you mean definitely."

"Joe, please!"

"Tomorrow morning."

"That's . . . that's—"

"Yes, Kostya."

"But . . . but not here. Not where we can be—"

"Seen? OK. Meet me on the hilltop at one o' clock."

§188

Somewhere in the České Středohoří

Wilderness parked at the bottom of the limestone trail. After walking less than a hundred yards he could see Kostya on the skyline, back to him.

At the sound of shoes on stones Kostya turned. He was dressed for the winter weather, a scarf around his neck, hands sunk deep in the pockets of his mackintosh.

It spelled gun.

Much as Wilderness's hidden hand spelled gun.

Wilderness drew level.

"Let's both take our hands out very slowly, Kostya. Try not to shoot yourself in the foot."

They drew—the slow-motion shoot-out of a spaghetti western.

They each stood with a handgun loosely on the thigh.

Kostya looked to have a German SIG . . . some wartime souvenir . . . the same model Wilderness had first learnt to shoot with. He'd never trust his life to such a gun. He had his Smith & Wesson .44, a body-slammer.

"So tell me."

"I did not do this thing, Joe."

"Maybe not, but you have her. Tell your people to let her go. See us safely to the Austrian border and—"

"Joe, she's in Berlin! The Czechs didn't arrest Nell at the border. They called the Stasi and had her and the boy picked up just short of Dresden. The KGB have her in the East Berlin compound now."

It crossed Wilderness's mind to shoot him now and have done. But if he spent his rage on Kostya, Nell would pay the price of that rage.

"Then get her back."

"Joe. I can't . . . this is . . . you would say . . . out of my league. I'm a small fish in a small pond. I'm powerless."

"But your mother isn't. This isn't an East German thing or a Czech thing, we both know that. It's a Russian thing. So call your mother."

For the first time Kostya took his eyes off Joe's, looked away, muttered something Wilderness took to be the Russian for "Jesus wept" at the mention of his mother.

"This isn't a few dozen jars of peanut butter, Joe."

"I know. It's Nell. Do you think I'd consider blowing your brains out for anyone else?"

The sound of a car approaching. The guns were levelled in an instant, Kostya's hand shaking like an autumn leaf. He'd be lucky to hit Wilderness even at this close range. Wilderness held a steady bead on Kostya's head.

Then Kostya looked away again, down the hill.

"What on earth is that?"

Wilderness turned, lowered his gun.

"That," he said, "is a 1935 Rolls-Royce Phantom II."

"What's it doing here? Did you know you were being followed?"

"Why me? Why not you?"

"We don't have vintage Rolls-Royces in the Soviet Union. Joe, Joe . . . tell me you have not set me up."

Wilderness holstered his gun.

"Of course I haven't. Put the fucking gun away. You're not going to shoot the British ambassador."

As though cued by his title, Troy got out of the Rolls and crossed the few yards of stone and dust between them.

Wilderness said, "Have you considered being less conspicuous, Troy?"

Troy said, "Why? The Russians know everything. They didn't even bother to follow me. They knew where I was going."

"Troy, this had better be good."

"As good as I can make it."

Troy turned to Kostya.

"Major Zolotukhin, I presume? I'm Frederick Troy. Her Britannic Majesty's ambassador to the Socialist Republic of Czechoslovakia. I have spoken with President Svoboda in Prague and with Herr Brandt in Bonn. I have placed calls to Comrade Gromyko in Moscow that he seems most unwilling to take. And to Ambassador Chervonenko with hardly more joy. He dismissed me in eight words. Nevertheless—I am authorised to negotiate on behalf of the Bundesrepublik for the release of Nell Burkhardt. And in the absence of any other Russian willing to talk to me I am here to negotiate with you."

"Что?"

"You'd like me to say that pompous load of twaddle again?"

"Twaddle? What is twaddle? No . . . no . . . it's just . . ."

"Brandt wants her back. Name your price."

Wilderness spoke. "You're serious?"

"Would I be stuck on this hillside with you two if I weren't?"

"Then take your hand out of your pocket and off your gun. Nobody here wants to shoot anybody."

Troy took his left hand from his overcoat pocket, showed them the Baby Browning he'd been clutching, then slipped it back into his shoulder holster, and they stood, each about ten feet from the other, patient gunmen on an impatient errand.

"A handbag gun," said Wilderness. "I don't believe it. Both of you with fucking handbag guns."

Then he said, "Kostya, you can trust this bloke, he's kosher."

"Kosher?"

"Кошерный," Troy translated. "Major, please take our offer to Moscow. Please, take it to your mother. That is all I got from Chervonenko, eight words—'Tell him to take it to his mother.' You can liaise with me in person at the British Embassy. No one will be surprised at a visit from a KGB officer in the midst of the present crisis. In fact, it might be harder to receive Joe than you. He's supposed to be a secret secret agent, after all."

Wilderness shook his head.

"No. I'm utterly blown. As you said, they know everything. I have only hours left playing Bulldog Drummond."

Troy looked to Kostya.

"He's right," Kostya said. "He has little or no cover left. The sooner he leaves Czechoslovakia, the better."

"Then you need to move quickly, Major. Come back to me with your terms. We want Nell Burkhardt back—unharmed."

"It will be difficult. It might even be impossible."

"I'll be waiting. If you can, phone me—if you don't want to be overheard, polish the brass buttons on your uniform and pay me a formal visit. I understand . . . the difficult you do right now, the impossible takes a while."

Kostya looked at Wilderness, said, "What does he mean? He talks in riddles."

"He's being a smart arse. Troy family weakness. Use ten words where two would do. He was quoting a popular song. Cole Porter? Jerome Kern? I dunno. But he really is the British ambassador and he's just handed you a blank cheque. Find out Moscow's price, and short of complete NATO nuclear disarmament you'll probably get it."

Kostya was staring at nothing again, then he was staring at the ground, then he was staring at Troy, then he was staring at Wilderness.

For a second or so Wilderness could see a frozen lake in Lapland.

"Joe, Joe . . . I am out of my depth. This could get us all killed."

"We were out of our depth in Berlin, we were out of our depth in Finland, yet here we are. Alive and kicking. The thing is . . . the thing has got to be . . . not to shoot each other."

"The thing is to free Nell. I want to see Nell walk free as much as you do."

"Of course you do, Kostya. We have to know who to trust. And we have trusted one another for a very long time. Now, if you two ladies stick your popguns back in your handbags, we might find a bar."

§189

They let Kostya buy. A mostly empty bar in Mělník.

Troy said, "He seems like a boy."

"He's the same age as me. He's just worn better."

"Berlin? I heard Berlin."

"That was round about the time of the airlift. We really were just boys in Berlin. *Schiebers*, black marketeers, smugglers . . . we thought nationalities and frontiers didn't matter. Naïve and cunning at the same time. That combination got me shot. In fact, it was Kostya's boss who shot me—Yuri Myshkin. All a bit of a cock-up. Yuri claimed he wasn't aiming at me."

"You believed him?"

"Yes. I had the chance to get even a couple of years ago. I didn't take it. Nature took its course instead. You probably read about his funeral . . . but by then Yuri was a full-blown KGB general and had gone back to using his real name, Bogusnik. He was a rogue. Weren't we all? Kostya's mother was a rogue—these days she's also a KGB general. But Yuri took care of Kostya even if his mother didn't. Kostya got out of Berlin without a scratch. I didn't see him again until Finland in '66."

"Ah . . . yes . . . I heard about your Finland posting."

"Of course you did . . . we're a secret service . . . which means every bugger knows our secrets."

"It's far simpler than that. Your wife has coffee with my brother's wife . . . they—"

"Natter?"

"I'm sure they do. So . . . you and Kostya ran another racket in Finland? Let me guess—vodka?"

"We don't call them rackets, Troy. We call them ventures."

"No, Joe. That was a racket. This is a venture."

"A venture I'd rather London knew nothing about."

For a few moments Troy said nothing, then, "That's a lot to ask. I am, after all, London's 'man-in-Prague.'"

"I know. But, if London knows . . . well they'll just fuck it up, won't they?"

"Of course they will. So . . . yes . . . OK . . . they'll hear nothing about it . . . until it's too late."

"Now if you could get that through to Janis Bell—"

Kostya was coming back. His hands still shaking, drops of Uzbekistan's Finest "Scotch" were splashed all over the tin tray.

He downed half his glass in one gulp.

Wilderness and Troy both stared at him, neither touching a glass.

Kostya said, "What is the matter?"

Troy said nothing.

Wilderness said, "There's nothing to be scared of."

"Are you crazy? You've met my mother. There's everything to be scared of."

"She'll do it."

"I wish I shared your confidence."

"She's a businesswoman—"

"She's a general."

"She's a *Schieber*."

"Meaning?"

"There's a deal to be done. We simply have to make it attractive enough for her to give us what we want. Nell is being held by the KGB in Berlin. Your mother can get access to the compound—she barks, they jump—your mother can strike a bargain with us."

"Are you offering money?"

"Kostya, I don't have any—"

Troy cut him off, "I do. If General Zolotukhina is looking for a bribe, then I shall bribe her. I doubt she would want so much as to break the bank."

"You are a rich man?"

"Yes."

"A capitalist millionaire?"

"And the rest."

"He's telling the truth, Kostya," Wilderness said. "The man is seriously rich. Take the money for granted. Just strike the deal."

The other half of Kostya's imitation Scotch went down without touching the sides. Troy quietly slid his glass towards him.

"Спасибо."

§190

After Kostya had gone, Wilderness said, "He might still fuck it up."

"It felt like giving Pinocchio a blood transfusion, but I think your pep talk helped."

"But? I can hear another 'but' waiting in the wings."

"If push comes to shove . . . could you shoot our little wooden boy?"

"I've no idea. I just wish they'd sent someone else."

Out in the car park Wilderness looked at the boot on the Rolls-Royce. Ran his finger over the bullet holes.

"I can hardly believe this. You had it shipped from Berlin?"

"It hasn't been used since the wall went up."

"And in twenty years they haven't got around to fixing the bullet holes. There are times my life seems like a circle."

"Meaning?"

"Berlin '48. The one that didn't hit your Roller hit me. Wanna see the scar?"

§191

Palác Thun

It was late the following afternoon.

The switchboard operator called Troy.

"Ambassador, I have a Russian on the line. Bad line and very bad English. Won't give a name."

"Put him on."

"I think it's a woman."

Already?

"You are the Lord Frederick Troy Umbatsator?"

Guttural. A voice deeper than his own spoke to him of a lifetime of cheap cigarettes.

"Yes."

"I am Volga Vasilievna Zolotukhina."

"How nice of you to call, General. How may you help me?"

"Ha . . . ha . . . ha. So funny. How say? You English . . . you kill me."

"General, I'm happy to speak Russian if it speeds things up."

So they switched to Russian.

"I got your message. I'm in Berlin. That's the 'how' of this."

"And Fräulein Burkhardt is well?"

"She is unharmed."

"And the boy?"

"This is not about the boy. The boy is not part of any deal."

"So, are you calling me with a price?"

"Да, конечно."

"How much do you want?"

"Wrong question."

"What do you want?"

"Wrong again."

"General, I'm running out of interrogatives."

"Try . . . не сколько а кого?"

Кого . . . *Who* might I want?

§192

Troy yelled for Janis Bell.

He'd never done that before.

She ran in.

She'd never done that before.

"Where's Joe Holderness? Is still in Prague?"

"He's downstairs right now."

"Get him up here."

§193

"Zolotukhina doesn't want money."
   "What does she want?"
   "Bernard Alleyn."

§194

Wilderness opted for the shortest route to Berlin—out via the Zinnwald-Georgenfeld Crossing, into the DDR, on through Dresden to East Berlin, then into West Berlin at Invalidenstraße. He'd have to stay as Walter Hensel. He felt that as keenly as if someone had stubbed out a fag end on him.

He'd left it late. Waiting on news, any news from Russia. He'd left as soon as Troy had given him the news, but by then it was dusk and as he approached the border it was darkness. He was tired. The last thing he had imagined had happened. The last thing he had wanted was happening.

About five miles south of Teplice he felt a wave of exhaustion roll over him and, as he snapped to, realised he had let the car drift into the opposite lane.

Oh for a cup of coffee. He thought he might kill for a couple of dexies.

By the magic of thought, less than a mile on, nestling on the edge of the forest that surrounded Velemín, a shack appeared. A shack with an illuminated sign boasting beer, sausages and . . . coffee.

He pulled over into a car park, empty but for one beaten-up, steely-grey Trabant.

A man was painting a slogan on the wooden fence at the back of the car park.

"Отвяжись, Иван!"
(Fuck off, Ivan!)

The man turned. It was a boy, no more than eighteen or nineteen, and once he had perceived no threat in Wilderness he carried on spraying, no doubt heading for one of the predictable taunts that had been flung at the Red Army since August . . .

> Иди домой . . . Наташу нужно ебать
> (Go home now . . . Natasha needs a shag)
> Кто ебет твою жену, пока ты ебешь нас?
> (Who's fucking your wife while you're fucking us?)

Wilderness went for coffee. Stirred in two sugars. Hated the taste but needed the energy.

He sat long enough to feel the caffeine bite, and when he emerged from the shack he saw four Russian soldiers and a half-track with a rear-mounted machine gun.

The soldiers had the boy on the ground and were kicking the shit out of him. The boy was groaning, but when he stopped, they stopped and for a few seconds the only sound was the idle purr of the half-track's engine. Then they started laughing, laughing like drunks at a post-rugby piss-up.

They looked at Wilderness as he approached, and the laughter began to subside. No one interfered as Wilderness knelt down and put his left hand to the boy's carotid artery.

He was dead.

"Он умер," Wilderness said, turning to look at them, his left hand still resting on the boy's neck, his right gripping the butt of the Smith & Wesson tucked into his shoulder holster.

This started them laughing again.

Wilderness stood up. Fanned the hammer with the edge of his left hand. Took out the first three with shots to the forehead, but hit the fourth in the throat. The man lay on his back in a spreading crimson tide, both hands under his chin.

Wilderness looked down. The man stared back.

Wilderness shot him through the forehead.

Then he heard the grinding of gears and saw the half-track begin to reverse.

He'd not noticed that the driver was still behind the wheel. So dark, he could see no one in the cab. He had only one shot left, but one was all it took to kill him—fired at a face he never saw. The half-track continued on its unmanned trajectory and demolished half the fence before it came to a halt.

Wilderness looked back at the shack. No door had opened, no face pressed to the window. They could hardly fail to hear, but not to see was wisdom.

He got back into the BMW and changed course.

If this was reported the first thing the opposition would do was look for him at the crossing a few miles down the road, so he headed southwest for the Waidhaus Crossing, which would lead him straight into West Germany.

The road was empty, and he had a car that could touch two hundred kph.

Troy's question had troubled him, but he knew the answer to the question now. He could shoot their little wooden boy. If he had to.

§195

He checked into a hotel on the outskirts of Nuremburg. And slept.

Vienna

§

Vienna, The Imperial Hotel: September 1955

Brain set like mortar.

No one had told him this.

It was possible that he had just surpassed his instructor—the inimitable Major Weatherill—in that the major might well have shot nothing more animate than a cardboard target. He was, after all, paid to teach men like Wilderness how to kill, not to kill in person.

He had sat too long.

It was almost dawn.

He'd have to take a lavatory brush to the wall.

§

Wilderness dumped the body in the bath. The Russian was a little bloke, no more than five feet five, and less than ten stones.

He ran the cold tap until the man was completely submerged.

He reached in and closed the remaining eye, but the movement of water caused by removing his hand sent out a ripple that opened the eye again. It wasn't looking at Wilderness, though. It wasn't looking at anything. It was no more than the glassy eye of a goldfish in a bowl.

Wilderness looked at the wall.

Picked up the bog brush.

Brain set like mortar.

He knew what he was going to do. He was going to leave the man in the bath and leg it. Leave it to whoever found him to sort it out.

So—said one part of his mind to another—why scrub the brains off the wall?

All the same, he did.

Tipped the grey, crispy mess into the loo and flushed until it went.

§

Wilderness went through the pockets of the Russian's jacket. Took his wallet and his passport.

He put on the shoulder holster and the Browning for no other reason than that it seemed the simplest way to carry them. Then he went through his own small suitcase and stuffed his jacket pockets with anything that identified him—as well as his toothbrush, razor and a spare shirt.

He looked at himself in the bedroom mirror. The jacket bulged. Nothing to be done about that. He hung a Do Not Disturb sign on the doorknob and went down to the lobby. With any luck the sign would buy him about forty-eight hours.

As he walked past the concierge, he felt like Harpo Marx in *Room Service*. Dodging out without paying the bill, and wearing everything he owned.

IX

Black Coffee

§196

Nuremberg

He'd had the dream again. But it was the last time. He sat on the edge of the bed and shook his head, and in that shaking freed himself. The dead Russian never visited him again.

§197

For over a year now the first thing he'd done on waking had been to put in Walter Hensel's contact lenses. This morning he dropped them onto the bathroom floor and ground them to dust with the heel of his shoe. Then he smashed Walter's glasses, flung the shoe at the wall and stepped into the shower and stood under the jets until the water ran cold.

There was nothing he could do about Walter's mousey hair. It would grow out or he'd dye it back to his natural off-blond. But the moustache vanished in four swift strokes of the razor.

He stared at his own face in the mirror.

He did not know himself.

He wasn't Walter Hensel anymore.

He wasn't Joe Wilderness either.

He'd have to wait for Wilderness to turn up.

Bad penny, as his grandfather used to say.

§198

He put the Smith & Wesson back into its hiding place and took out the plastic bag, bound up with rubber bands, that contained the other versions of himself. He opted for a British passport, one with all the right stamps. He'd have to make an effort to remember the name.

It was a dogleg to get to the western end of the Berlin Corridor at Marienborn, adding another two hours driving time, but it was the only way. Once he was into East Germany, autopilot would take over, he'd done that route so many times. He'd be in Berlin by five o' clock.

§199

He couldn't stay at the Kempinski. He might bump into someone from Berlin Station. He might even bump into the deeply unforgiving Dickie Delves. And Delves would rat him out to Burne-Jones at the drop of a hat. The situation called for anonymity—a cheap, 2-star hotel in Wilmersdorf, one he'd never stayed in before, one walking distance from Grünetümmlerstraße.

There was no irrefutable reason to be in Berlin. He knew how this had happened. He wanted to ask, he wanted confirmation and he wanted to kill recrimination before recrimination killed.

He knocked on the door around 6:00 p.m.

The German girl answered . . . Trudie? Traudl? Standing in the doorway, her body a blockade.

"Erno is very sick. You must not come in."

"I won't keep him long. Is he awake?"

She didn't answer. Tried to stare him down.

Wilderness pushed past her.

"You're not the first visitor today," she yelled at his back.

Wilderness turned around.

"Stop playing games with me. Who came? When?"

"It was a Russian. Asking for Erno. I told him what I tell you. He had no manners either."

"Oh for fuck's sake."

Wilderness opened the bedroom door quietly.

Erno lay with his eyes closed, but the rhythm of his breathing was not sleep's rhythm, and a reading lamp cast its arc on a small green book that looked as though it had only just slipped from his fingers.

His eyes opened.

"What kept you? I have been expecting you every hour since that damned Russian showed up."

"I was in Prague—had to take the long way round, through Bavaria. What did the Russian want?"

"To gloat. He termed it a courtesy call, but he came to gloat. Left me this."

Erno picked up the book, and Wilderness realised it wasn't a thin volume of Goethe or Schiller but a West German passport. He looked at it, turning the pages.

"Pretty good."

"Not good enough. It's what got Nell arrested."

The photograph was of a teenage boy, the name was Horst Burkhardt, date of birth given as 21.9.52, Wiesbaden.

"I bungled it, Joe."

"Erno. It looks pretty damn good to me. Maybe they got a tip-off."

"You're just being kind."

Wilderness was "just being kind." He knew what they both knew. Of course the passport had got Nell busted. She'd been spotted at the border, and the Czech patrol had alerted the East German police, who had let her and the boy, whoever he was, get as far as Dresden. Thereby the Czechs managed to pass the problem, the culprits and the paperwork onto someone else. Typical cop laziness.

"Count the numbers on the cover."

"Six."

"There should be seven. It's my eyes. Joe, I simply cannot see the small things anymore. The things that matter."

"I came to tell you not to blame yourself and not to worry. I have it all in hand. When was Nell here?"

"She came twice. Once with the photograph of the boy, and then ten days later to collect the passport. Joe, who is this boy?"

"I've no idea."

"Could he be so important? So important that she takes a risk like this?"

"I don't know that either. But I'll get her back. We'll get her back . . . me, Eddie and Frank."

"Ah . . . the *Schiebers*. I could almost be nostalgic for our days as *Schiebers*, were it not for Frank. But dying men are beggars and beggars can't be choosers. If Eddie comes to Berlin, bring him to see me, and if that means bringing Frank . . . so be it. I shall say goodbye to you all."

$200

"Do you need anything?" Wilderness asked Trudie.

"Money would help," she replied.

Wilderness gave her two hundred US dollars and told her what she didn't want to hear.

"I'll be back."

$201

Southwark, London

It was not a feeling he cared for in the least. To be abroad in the town he called home—he'd known no other—and to be homeless.

His plane had landed at Heathrow at three. By five thirty he was in Borough High Street in search of Swift Eddie. Eddie was not home. He might not be home for an hour or maybe two—but Wilderness could not go home to Hampstead. Nor could he go to the office.

He sat an hour in a greasy spoon, drank three cups of tea the colour of fencing creosote, and waited. He had a view of Eddie's front door. Another half hour and he saw Eddie walk straight past his own door and head on down the street.

Of course, the chippie.

He'd let him order first. Let him get his choppers round a few mouthfuls of cod and chips. Always more amenable when eating.

Another ten minutes and Wilderness went to the chippie, found Eddie head down in trencherman mode and pulled out the chair opposite.

"What . . . *chomp* . . . do you . . . *chomp* . . . want?"

"Nice of you to ask, Eddie. Fish cake, mushy peas and a small chips."

"I mean . . . *chomp chomp* . . . what are you doing here? Aren't you supposed to be in Prague?"

"I have . . . *we* have a problem."

"We?"

Wilderness explained in short, simple sentences, just shy of telling him what the trade-off was to be.

"I really don't want Burne-Jones finding out about this."

"Well, you wouldn't be sitting here if you did, would you?"

"Or Alice. If she knows, he knows."

"Or Judy? Have you thought what you're going to tell her?"

"I'm not going to tell her anything until we have Nell back."

"Makes sense, I suppose. All the same, 'We'?"

"The Russians will trade Nell."

"What, like we did with that twat Masefield and ole wotsisname . . . Bernard Alleyn? Look how that worked out."

"It's Bernard Alleyn they'll trade for."

The knife and fork clattered down.

"I think you just killed my appetite. Y'know, I was happy at the Yard."

"Maybe, but you had no future there."

"I say! I was happy at the Yard, and then you come along after . . . fuckin' ada . . . fifteen fuckin' years and the next thing I know I'm back in bloody Berlin with Frank bloody Spoleto. Joe, have you never heard of the quiet life? I do me crossword over breakfast, I have a pint in a pub at lunchtime, I come home at six to a nice beef bourguignon or a plate of fish and chips, then I wipe the floor with the toffee-nosed kids on University Challenge and go to bed with a good book. Right now I'm on Iris Murdoch."

"Have you finished?"

"I don't need a 'We.'"

"I need you to come to Dublin with me."

"What's in Dublin?"

"Bernard Alleyn."

"Oh bloody Nora. How long have you known?"

"Since January."

"And he's agreed to the trade."

"Not yet. That's why I need you to come with me."

"I have a job, Joe. I work for Burne-Jones, remember. I can't just swan off."

"No. But you can get sick."

Eddie cogitated. Looked longingly at his cooling cod but made no move to resume eating.

"Frank. Promise me there'll be no Frank this time."

"Can't do that, Ed."

"Why not? He's back in New York. He won't want to come to Berlin."

"I need the bridge. We do this in the British sector, we're fucked. It has to be the American, it has to be Glienicke. And to get Glienicke, I need Frank."

"How long?"

"Four days, maybe five."

"And when it's over you'll come clean with Burne-Jones?"

"Ed, I'll let him tear off my epaulettes and break my sword over his knee."

If I live through this, that is.

$202

"I suppose you want to kip at my place?" Eddie said.

"Yes. I can't go home. And I'll need to use the phone."

"If you must."

Around half past ten Wilderness put in a call to New York. With any luck he'd catch Frank on his first bourbon of the day.

"You got some nerve."

"Well, you were never one to bear a grudge."

The last time they had met, Wilderness had all but knocked him cold. And Frank could bear a grudge for eternity and a day.

"Right. That's me. Job. Hit me with a plague of boils, why don't you."

"It's more serious than that, Frank."

"I don't care. Hear me? I don't fucking care!"

"It's Nell."

"So?"

"The opposition have her."

"Oh Jeezus H. Christ. How did that happen? I thought she was tucked away safely in Bonn working for the Krauts."

"They posted her to Prague. Then the British posted me to Prague—"

"And you let this happen?"

"No Frank, I didn't let it happen—it happened."

"So . . . you make a mess and call on your old buddy to clean it up. Joe, I should just let you sink in the shit. You hear me, kid? I should just let you fuckin' sink."

"But you won't."

Silence.

Steaming time.

Wilderness knew that when Frank finally spoke he would be positive.

"Nell. Right. What do you have in mind?"

"They'll trade."

"What? Like last time?"

"Exactly like last time. I mean *exactly*."

"You're kidding! You mean they still want—"

"Not out loud, Frank."

"Sure, sure . . . but fukkit . . . you'd think they'd have given up by now."

"Yeah, well . . . they haven't."

"Do you know where he is?"

"Yes."

"And you figure you can talk him into it?"

"I don't know, but I'm going to try. Just . . . get me the bridge, Frank."

"What's wrong with the British crossing?"

"Would I be calling you if that were feasible? Think about it."

"OK. Sure, sure."

"It has to be the bridge. And if the guns come out, I'd be happier on the bridge than out on a road. Less . . . exposed."

"You're planning a shoot-out at the Glienicke Corral—again?"

"Not planning, just allowing for."

"Jesus H. Christ. Joe. You could get us all killed."

"You won't be on the bridge, Frank. It'll be like last time. You get to keep your feet in West Berlin."

"One shot. All it takes is one shot and your career in MI6 is over."

"It's not a career. It's a job. But yes . . . it's over. Shot or no shot, it's over."

"Did it ever occur to you that it might be the end of my career too?"

"Not if you play your hand right."

"Did it ever occur to you to ask why I'm going along with this cocka-mamey scheme?"

"Many times in the last two minutes. I think you might just give a damn about Nell."

"Oh sure . . . suddenly I'm Mr. Softee. OK. Maybe I do care about Nell. But . . . Goddammit . . . I'm fifty-six years old."

Wilderness had never had a real idea of Frank's age. When they met, twenty and more years ago, Wilderness had been a teenager, so had Kostya, and Eddie not much older. Frank was a different generation.

"I'm fifty-six years old. And I'd like to retire. But you can't tell the Company to go to hell. They tell you to go to hell. Win or lose they're going to hate this. They'll pension me off and hope my involvement stays under wraps. Meanwhile . . . meanwhile I have the ad agency. It's not just a front, it's a real Madison Avenue advertising agency. Cigs, whiskey and automobiles. Steve Sharma, the senior partner you met in '63, died last year. They need a figurehead. Someone who'll swank in three or four times a year, chomp on a Cuban, hand out the bonuses and bonhomie and quietly pick up his obscenely large share dividend. I'd be happy to be that man. Very happy."

"Of course, but let's remember this is about Nell."

"Sure. We rescue Nell. We move heaven and earth and Berlin to rescue Nell. We'll be the Lone Ranger and Tonto. Just don't get me shot before I light the Cuban and pick up my dividend. Capisce?"

"Oh yes, *capisco.*"

"One shot, Joe. One shot and we are fucked!"

"And on that note . . ."

"What?"

"Are you still in touch with the Kopps?"

There was a malign silence. Frank Spoleto was never stuck for words. If he was thinking what to say they might well be in trouble. Wilderness could almost see him looking over his shoulder, switching the phone from one ear to the other.

"They . . . er . . . still have an account with us, yes."

Which meant Frank still had an account with them.

§203

One day in 1948 Frank had caught two kids raiding his "warehouse" at Tempelhof. How they got in was not important. The base was about as tight as a sieve.

It would have been typical of Frank to have banged their heads together and put the fear of Frank up them. He didn't, and, as he explained to Wilderness the next time the *Schiebers* met at *Paradies Verlassen*, it would have been a waste of time.

"These kids just don't scare."

"I can imagine."

"I mean . . . they're fifteen . . . at twelve they were in the Hitler youth, defending Berlin against the Red Army. One of them, don't ask me which, they're as alike as two peas . . . one of them actually got a medal pinned on him by Hitler. I mean personally . . . the day before the fucker shot himself."

"So what did you do?'"

"I put 'em on the payroll. All those ragbag gangs of kids we run into from time to time, trying to steal from us . . . well, these two will see 'em off. Think of the gangs as wolves and foxes. We just hired two sheepdogs that could rip the guts out of a tiger."

Wilderness and Eddie OK'd this. Misgivings only began to set in when Wilderness met them. His own childhood had been one of parental vacancy and neglect, but it had not left him as stripped of emotion as Rikki and Marti Koppenrad. These boys were hardened. Full metal jacket, full metal trousers.

It came as a shock but no surprise when they killed their first.

Hans-Jürgen Richter.

Frank was furious.

They'd collared the boys in the back room of the club.

"For fuck's sake! The guy worked for us!"

Wilderness interrupted.

"Frank, is that us . . . as in you, me and Eddie or us as in American Intelligence."

"He worked for Uncle Sam. You idiots just took out an American agent!"

Rikki spoke. Softly but uncowed.

"He was a Nazi."

"So? Berlin is full of fuckin' Nazis. We can't round up all of them, we can't prosecute every last one of the fuckers . . . so some of them end up working for us."

Rikki was absolute in his simplicity.

"We kill Nazis."

"For fuck's sake, why?"

"They destroyed our country. More than Monty's tanks, more than your Flying Fortresses. We kill Nazis."

"I do not fucking believe this!"

Wilderness never knew what bargain, what compromise, Frank had reached with the Kopps, as Eddie dubbed them.

Every so often, almost till the day Frank and Wilderness had left Berlin, a former Nazi would be found dead in the street. The Kopps had their trademark—whatever the organ they'd aimed at, head or heart, they'd put a bullet through each hand . . . a bizarre parody of the crucifixion's nails.

Throughout the 1950s and well into the '60s Wilderness had heard stories of Kopp kills. The boys, grown to men, had become expensive contract killers, although it was said they would still kill any Nazi for free.

$204

"Set up a meeting," Wilderness said.

"The Kopps? The fuckin' Kopps! That's your plan?"

"That's my plan B."

"Jeezus, Joe. The more I hear, the less I like this. I say 'one shot could get us all killed' and you say 'hire the Kopps'!"

"Try to see them as our safety net."

"I have a problem seeing a couple of whack-jobs as anything but a couple of whack-jobs."

"Then I'm surprised you still handle their account. But they must have been very useful to your *Company* over the years."

Wilderness, in his own mind, had put a capital C and italics on Company—and Frank had clearly heard.

"You can drop the sarcasm. Didn't I already say I'll do it? This is for Nell—that's the only reason, right?"

"Yes. Be in Berlin the day after tomorrow. A *Schieber* meeting."

"OK. I get it."

$205

It said something about the conflict Eddie felt between his very vocal complaints and his oft-silent loyalty that they were on a plane over the Irish Sea before he said, "Why do you need me in Dublin?"

"I can talk Bernard into this. He may not take much convincing, but if he's left alone . . . it's his nature to look at things from half a dozen different angles, like a threepenny bit, and that's the precursor to worry. So we won't leave him alone. I need to be in Berlin. I don't want Bernard in Berlin until the last minute. If the Russians get preemptive and try a snatch we'll have nothing to trade. It's not as if they'd have any difficulty finding him in Berlin. So you sit with him—in Dublin."

"I'd be his minder?"

"Yes. Keep him occupied. He likes a game of chess. You like a game of chess. That ought to work. He's hard to beat, by the bye."

Eddie just said, "A threepenny bit has twelve sides."

§206

Dublin

Wilderness checked them both into the Shelbourne.

Then he called Bernard Alleyn.

"Pawn to Queen's Bishop 2."

"Ah . . . you're back. Another language or a refresher course?"

"Neither. I'm here to see you."

"OK. Hmmmm . . . How about lunch tomorrow?"

"I'd prefer tonight."

"Tonight? Alright. It'll be after nine. You're in Duke Street?"

"No, I'm at the Shelbourne. Room 202."

Nothing in Bernard's words conveyed a hint of suspicion. Innocence or training? The guileless guile of a man who'd lived a double life for twelve years and surely suspected everyone and everything.

When they'd rung off, Wilderness said to Eddie, "When he gets here give it thirty seconds of polite and chummy, then lose yourself for an hour."

"Glad to, but I've never been to Dublin before."

"This is Ireland Ed—Dublin—there's a pub every twenty yards. Or have you changed the habit of a lifetime?"

§207

"I want you to come back to Berlin with me. To the Glienicke Bridge."

Bernard nodded. Much the same as he did when he watched Joe make a poor judgement in chess. If he felt shock or surprise it lurked well below the surface.

"I see," he said, and Wilderness was quite certain he didn't.

"I wouldn't ask if there were any other way. A West German was arrested just outside Dresden a few days ago—smuggling a wanted Czech dissident into the West. I've talked to the Russians, who've taken this out of the hands of the East Germans, and struck a deal or the makings of a deal. They'll trade the German for you. And . . . I didn't offer. They asked."

"For me? They asked for me. Not just any old has-been spy?"

"For you. They asked for Bernard Alleyn, but they meant Leonid L'vovich Liubimov."

"I see," Bernard said again.

"I wouldn't ask—"

"Yes, yes . . . I know, you just told me that. This must be very important."

"It's . . . vital."

"Literally so? Vital as in a matter concerning life and hence concerning death?"

"Yes."

"My death?"

"That's not my intention. For one thing, I'll be in the line of fire too."

"Well . . . If I must die on the Glienicke Bridge with a Russian bullet in me . . . I could not choose better company. But why would either of us choose to die? For what would we be risking death? For Germany? East or West? For a matter of state? Another shuffle on the Cold War's chessboard. Knight takes pawn, bishop takes knight. Does any of it matter more than that? Are affairs of state so important to either of us anymore? East Germans arrest a West German. Charges of spying or subversion will be bandied around. Someone goes to prison. Someone gets ransomed. If not for me then for someone else. Does it, any of it, have any impact on us? We're in Ireland, Joe. It's not John Bull's other island anymore. It is, mercifully, a country of no significance on the world stage whatsoever. As far as the Cold War extends, we might as well be in Laputa or Brobdingnag. And yet you think we should risk everything for the life of one man?"

"It's a woman. I'm doing this for a woman."

"She must be a very important woman."

"The most important woman in my life . . . after my wife, that is."

"Ah," a touch of incredulity. "Surely not your mother?"

"No. My mother died hunched over a gin and lime in an East End boozer almost thirty years ago. She left me to fend for myself. I wouldn't lift a finger if it were her in this mess."

"But she died."

"And in dying, left me."

A flicker of something surfacing in Bernard.

"My mother left me. My mother left me and she did not die. It would have been easier for me to understand if she had died."

"You never talk about your mother. Do you really want to talk about your mother?"

"Of course not. We should talk about the woman we are to rescue. You haven't yet said who she is, and I can only assume you want to know I'm on board before you do tell me."

"It's Nell. Nell Burkhardt."

"Oh my God."

Bernard had required not a moment to remember. Nell had sprung his memory open like a jack-in-the-box.

"Of course," he said. "We must. I understand. Really, I understand."

"You'd trade yourself for Nell?"

"My life is a series of ragged ends, ten years in tatters. Who knows? Going back might gather up the threads. I have almost nothing to lose. Kate despises me, my girls will soon be at universities in England—the one place I dare not visit. Who knows why Russia wants me back? A quick trip to a gulag, a long day with Ivan Denisovich—or the Order of Lenin. If you think we can save Nell . . ."

"Thank you, Bernard. I can't do this without you. But I've no intention of handing you over."

"Then . . . what? What is the trade? What happens at Glienicke?"

"What happens is that the other side gets a look at you and knows it's you. Just enough for them to think we'll trade."

Wilderness flipped open his briefcase. Laid a Walther PPK-L 7.65 on the bedspread.

"If it gets tricky we may have to shoot our way out. In fact, I'm damn certain we'll have to. Just try not to shoot me or Nell. Every other bugger is fair game."

Bernard picked up the gun.

"You do know how to use one?" Wilderness said.

Bernard felt the weight in his hand.

"Hmm . . . Lighter than they used to be."

Flicked out the magazine.

Looked at it.

Pushed it back in.

"I'm a trained agent, Joe. Just like you. But I haven't fired a gun in . . . oh hell . . . twenty-three years. Do the hand and the eye forget?"

"No idea. I've never given mine the chance to forget. But, times move on. If we get close enough I can kill an apparatchik with a Barclaycard."

"Whatever that is."

Bernard took aim at a vase of dried flowers perched upon the mantelpiece. Wilderness was reassured to note that his hand was rock-steady.

"Now," Bernard said. "Tell me you have a plan B."

$208

Hampstead, London

There was, it turned out, a worse feeling than being homeless in your hometown. It was sitting in a caff only yards from your own front door, waiting for your wife to go out to a coffee morning or some such, so you could sneak into your own home like a burglar.

He sat in *Il Barrino* on the corner of Perrin's Lane, where he'd a good view of anyone coming out of Perrin's Walk. He'd been there about twenty minutes when, right on time, Judy appeared with the twins in their double pushchair—Molly chattering away, Joan looking at everything as though directing her first film.

They turned left up Heath Street and left again into Church Row.

11:00 a.m. Coffee with Lucinda Troy, sister-in-law of the Troy in Prague. Judy would be there an hour at least.

The cistern on the upstairs loo came off the wall easily enough. Inside the little safe was his entire stash from the Finnish rackets, a few hundred in white fivers, about five hundred dollars acquired in various dodgy deals he'd rather his wife never knew about, another clutch of passports from half a dozen countries in half a dozen names but all bearing his photograph, and the Baby Browning with which he'd killed the KGB agent in Vienna. He left the gun. He left the sterling—his once-upon-a-time, running-away-from-home fund. He'd never run away from home. Until now.

He was in and out of the house in less than twenty minutes—all bathroom fittings back in place. He'd swept up the dust, mopped up the small splashes of water with his handkerchief—Irish linen, a real honker of a hanky, a red J embroidered in one corner, a Christmas gift from his mother-in-law. He dropped it in a bin in Heath Street. And then—and then . . . temptation struck and nailed him to a chair in the corner caff. Rationality and irrationality went *mano a mano* inside his head. He wanted to see Judy come home. He wanted to see his girls come home.

Three-quarters of an hour later they did. On the opposite side of the street, moving slowly as the girls peered in every shop window from patisserie to estate agent.

Joan was still looking around. Her eyes turned to the caff, and to him. Then her hand came up, pointing at him. She said something—her vocabulary was huge but her pronunciation could still be babyish. She might have said "Daddy," she might not.

All the same, Judy tucked her into the pushchair, folded her arms back into the blanket, and Wilderness was pretty certain her lips had said, "It's rude to point."

Then they rounded the corner into Perrin's Walk and vanished from his sight.

§209

Wilmersdorf, Berlin

"Who is this bitch?"

Frank was on the doorstep at Grünetümmlerstraße.

"Name's Trudie. She has my old room on the top floor."

"She wouldn't let me in to see Erno. When you said *Schiebers*, I figured you meant to meet here."

"I did. But—she's appointed herself Erno's guardian. Let me talk to her."

As they climbed the stairs, Frank said to Wilderness's back, "I mean, is Erno really that ill?"

Wilderness stopped, turned.

"He's dying, Frank. Let's not piss this woman off any more than we have to."

The door was open. Trudie stood sentinel.

"You too?"

"Trust me," Wilderness replied. "Erno does want to see us. We are old times to Erno. The last of old times."

"I do not doubt you, but now is bad times."

"I understand. I'll come back later. We'll both come back later."

"And this is the wrong place for a meeting of your 'Council of Criminals.'"

"What?"

"Not now, Frank. Just pipe down."

"Fuck this. I have a suite at the Kempinski. We don't need to duck and fuck like this. Council of Criminals, my ass!"

"I can't go near the Kempinski. Nor can Ed, and Bernard sure as hell can't. It's always crawling with English spooks. All it takes is for just one of them to recognise one of us—"

"OK. OK. I get the picture."

"The room I had at the Hotel Prignitz . . . we'd need to have Ed's beer belly surgically removed to get him in there. I'll get a better hotel for Eddie and Bernard somewhere we can all—"

"I said. I get it."

"May I make a suggestion?"

They both looked at Trudie.

"For the last two weeks I have slept in this room. On the sofa. You wish to see Erno. I understand. I want peace for Erno. *You* will understand. Why don't you take my room on the floor above? Little has changed since you lived there, Joe Holderness. Light the fire and do what you must."

$210

The twins looked around the room. Wilderness had lit the fire. It was still scarcely better than freezing.

Rikki spoke.

Wilderness was not sure he'd ever heard Marti speak.

"I never thought I'd set foot in this room again."

"You're looking good Rikki. You both are."

With their Crombie blue overcoats, their cashmere red scarves, their handmade shoes and their pigskin gloves.

"We prosper, Joe. Frank says you have a proposition for us."

"I do. The Glienicke Bridge, Friday. I need back up."

"You want someone killed?"

"Only if it all goes wrong."

"And you think it might?"

"Yes. We're exchanging prisoners. On the bridge, on the line. If it goes wrong, you'll know. You can ignore any raised voices. I can handle shouting. But if there's so much as a single shot, take out everyone on the other side except the woman."

Rikki looked silently at his brother. If there was an exchange of meaning between the two, Wilderness could not see it.

"Who will be on the other side? East Germans?"

"Russians."

"A moment if you would."

The twins went into a huddle by the door. Wilderness could hear just Rikki's whisper. If Marti was replying it was in nods and ticks.

Then they came back to face Frank and Wilderness.

"We . . . kill Germans."

"I know."

"If you want us to kill Russians the risk goes up and so does the price. It doubles."

"From what to what?"

"A German would cost you a thousand pounds each—so four thousand sterling."

Wilderness pointed to the black bag on the table.

"There's about four grand in dollars, and the equivalent of about another three thousand dollars in Finnish markka. I don't have any sterling and I have no way to get any. It's a take-it-or-leave-it."

"We take it."

Rikki was literal. He had taken the bag and handed it to his brother before he'd reached the end of his very short sentence.

"Friday night? What time?"

"Midnight."

"We'll be ready. And, Frank—Langley still hasn't paid us for von Pfeffel."

"Guys, guys . . . not in front of the children."

And Wilderness wanted to slap him.

When the twins had left, Frank said, "Three grand in Finnish moolah? You been running rackets I don't know about?"

And Wilderness wanted to slap him.

§211

Wilderness booked a hotel for Eddie and Bernard, out of sight. Out of the over-populated, over-policed city centre—a Bismarck-era villa in Dahlem, once the home of a Berlin baron of industry or trade. Something the Nazis had confiscated from its owners, that the Americans had confiscated in turn and sold to the highest bidder.

He could have stayed there too. Waited for Eddie to arrive.

He didn't.

Trudie had given him choice.

And temptation.

Lying on a rug, on the floor of his old room, under the eaves at Grünetümmlerstraße, listening/not listening to Berlin settle, it seemed to Wilderness that time was unwinding, that he was caught in its loosening spring, its cosmic clockwork, heading inexorably back to 1948 . . . 1947 . . . that trickster memory was playing with his ears. He could hear airfreighters dropping down to Tegel and Gatow, all those Lancasters and Yorks, all those Douglas C-54s, keeping Berlin alive as Stalin's grip tightened around it. Bread and beef and coal. Then he could hear Nell trying to make coffee as quietly as possible to avoid waking him—an effort that always failed. And then he could hear the heavy tread of Yuri Myshkin's boots upon the stairs—for a small man he seemed incapable of the light touch.

He dragged the eiderdown off the bed. A pillow for his head. He couldn't sleep in that bed. God knows, the mattress might have been changed half a dozen times in twenty years—it was the axe with four new handles and two new blades, but still the same axe. It was the same bed. He couldn't sleep in that bed. Not without Nell.

§212

In the morning he went down to Erno's. Trudie was raking hot ash out of the stove, red and pungent.

The coffee pot sat on top of the stove. Three china cups on the floor next to her.

"I heard you get up," she said simply.

Then, "He's asking for you."

She poured. The smell of coffee conjured up thoughts and memories for Wilderness that were probably beyond her imagination. Two years spent as *Schiebers*, smuggling coffee. It seemed to him he had reeked of coffee, that his clothes had reeked of coffee, that his flat had reeked of coffee—as Nell had so often pointed out. Time's spring unwound again for a moment.

"Take Erno's cup in with you. He's been awake for hours. Always with first light. It's why he sleeps so much in the day."

Erno was just about sitting up. Glasses on the end of his nose, reading yesterday's *Tagesspiegel*.

"Did I hear Frank yesterday?"

"Yes. Sorry about that. It seems he'd like to see you."

"And I him. If this is endgame, I'd like a sense of an ending."

"Meaning?"

"A fond farewell, even to those of whom I was not particularly fond?"

"Well . . . I'll bring him when this is over. Ed will be here in a couple of days. And Bernard Alleyn too."

Erno plucked the glasses off his nose.

"It seems we have been here before."

"We have . . . I'm trying not think about Marx's tragedy and farce line."

"It is most odd to think of you all here again. All the *Schiebers* in one room. You have a life in London. A wife. Children. A life without men like Frank. I thought you had turned your life around, Joe."

"So did I."

"But have you?"

"You tell me."

"No. Let me ask you a question. Do you expect to pull this off?"

"I don't know. But, as you said, it's endgame."

"And when it ends?"

"I don't know that either."

§213

Glienicke, Berlin: Friday, December 13th

"Are we set?"

"Yep. My guys are briefed. They know to keep out of the way and to keep their mouths shut. As far as they're concerned this is strictly a Company matter."

Frank had arrived first and had parked under the trees where it was darkest. He stuck his head through the window of Wilderness's rented Mercedes, twenty yards back from the American side of the bridge.

"What's your name today, Frank?"

"Fuck. I forgot already. I dunno. Molloy or Murphy, something like that. Just call me 'Colonel.' It's safer."

The great advantage of the Glienicke Bridge, which in better days had linked Berlin to Potsdam, was that it was not a designated crossing point, it was hardly ever used—no regular human traffic—so the road leading down to it had become little better than a cul-de-sac. It had a simplicity that border crossings in central Berlin could hardly afford. No floodlights, no barbed wire, no concrete chicanes, just well-mannered guards from the USA and the DDR. They probably swapped cigarettes and moaned about boredom to each other.

Wilderness saw the lights of a car coming up behind them.

"That's Eddie," he said. "Don't bug him."

"Yeah, yeah—as if . . ."

Wilderness and Frank met Eddie and Bernard between the two cars.

Bernard was very formal, shook hands with both of them. He'd be polite to his own executioner, Wilderness thought.

Eddie looked worried, but he always did. It was a cold December night, under a sliver of moon. He'd far rather be in bed. In any situation like this his mind would be saying, "Can I go now?" while his lips said nothing.

Wilderness said, "Are we waiting on the Kopp brothers?"

"Nope. We got here half an hour ago. They've been scoping out the opposition with night sights."

"And?"

"Hard to tell. Let's just say the Russians haven't mobilised a division. Six, maybe seven guys."

"So, where are the Kopps?"

Frank pointed to his car under the trees.

"They're over there by my car."

"I can't see anyone."

Then one twin or the other moved. He was completely black—a tight-fitting black track suit, black gloves, a black balaclava, burnt cork all over what little of his face showed—and a Russian-made, gas-operated Dragunov sniper rifle in matte black. The only reflective surface was the lens on the night sight.

"If you can't see me, neither can they," Rikki said.

Wilderness looked at his watch. He couldn't even see the hands. Rikki looked over, his eyes accustomed to the dark.

"Six minutes to twelve. Don't go just yet. I have something for you."

He opened the boot of Frank's car and took out a bulletproof vest.

"I could only get one," he said. "Put it on."

Wilderness hefted the vest.

"I'm not the target," he said. "Bernard, take off your overcoat."

"Joe, really?"

"Just do it."

The Kopps fitted the jacket around him—death's tailors.

Wilderness said, "Bernard. You have your gun?"

"Yes. In my pocket."

"Safety on?"

"Oh yes."

"Then flick it off and rack a bullet into the chamber. And don't get between these blokes and their targets."

"I'm sorry?"

"Give them a sight line. When we're facing people try not to stand directly opposite."

"Do we know *what* we're facing?"

"Frank reckons six or seven at the most."

"Ah."

"Ah what?"

"If they're all on the bridge at the same time . . ."

"Then yes, it will be a shoot-out."

At two minutes to midnight a US Army corporal raised the barrier—a touch of the ludicrous as he saluted—and they set foot on the bridge. Somewhere behind Wilderness the Kopps had chosen their positions, but he did not look back.

They'd taken twenty paces and Bernard asked softly, "Have you ever killed anyone, Joe?"

"Yep."

"I haven't."

"Bernard, you picked a fine time to tell me."

A couple of feet beyond the centre line, the official border, over the Havel, Kostya stood with his hands in his greatcoat pockets. He looked about as comfortable as Eddie. A small woman wrapped up against the cold stood six feet to his left. There was no one else.

"Nell. Show me your face."

Nell unwrapped her headscarf.

She did not smile, she did not speak.

Kostya said, "We must wait."

"Wait for what?"

Wilderness could see movement at the East German end of the bridge, figures vague as ghosts. The Russians might have their own snipers, and he'd never know.

"We wait. That is all. Not for long."

"You have Nell. I have Major Liubimov . . ."

"Please, Joe. This will not take long."

He could outshoot Kostya blindfolded.

He could shoot Kostya now and the three of them could run for it.

He didn't want to shoot Kostya.

He did not want to run for it.

He wanted to walk away quietly with every piece of the puzzle back in place.

From the far end of the bridge, a stately, possibly fat figure lumbered towards them, the hips swinging slowly, the feet wide apart, plonking down with bodily weight, the head swathed in fur and scarves.

As it grew near Wilderness could see a silver box clutched between gloved hands—about big enough to hold a large chess set. Then proximity told and he perceived the outline for what it was—female. And with proximity, uniform—a full-blown KGB general.

She clutched the box with one hand, and with the other pulled off her hat; a mass of greying ringlets cascaded down and Wilderness found himself looking once again into those brown and beautiful sad eyes. General Zolotukhina . . . Volga Vassilievna.

She dropped her hat and touched Nell lightly on the arm.

"Go now," she said.

Nell looked baffled, did not move.

Wilderness called on her by name.

"Nell?"

Nell looked back at him—eyes wide.

Wilderness said, "Nell, just walk past me, keep on walking and don't look back."

Nell crossed the line on the far side of Bernard Alleyn.

Wilderness was tempted to look back in her direction, but did not want to find her looking back at him. He listened to the click of her heels on the asphalt, every step sound-diminishing, every step nearer her freedom.

Bernard waited. Did not move. Hands in his pockets. One of them, Wilderness hoped, wrapped around the butt of his gun, safety off.

Wilderness could not hear Nell anymore.

Silence. Wind upon water.

Then Volga looked straight at Bernard.

"Comrade Liubimov. I am the bearer of sad news. Your mother, Krasnaya, is dead—Nastasya Fillipovna died in April. Died like so many, in the first breath of spring. She was a loyal servant of the Union of Soviet Socialist Republics, and was cremated with all military honours. And she was my dearest friend. Shoulder to shoulder we stood in October 1917. Side by side we took Berlin in 1945. I have here her ashes. I am sorry to drag you away from the life you have made, but I felt I should deliver them in person, and as I could not come to you, you needs must come to me. My deepest condolences, comrade. Krasnaya was a hero. May she rest in peace . . . in Ireland."

She held out the silver box.

Bernard took it, the perplexed look in his eyes yielding to tears.

Such is irony that for the first time, Wilderness could discern in this tearful adult the little boy sitting on his mother's left arm, looking out at the world from half a million posters—Krasnaya and son—defiant.

Then Volga turned to Wilderness.

"You see, Joe. You need to know who to trust."

She smiled. Held out her hand for him to shake.

One shot rang out.

§214

Frank kicked the gun out of Rikki's hands.

"Everybody down!"

"It was an accident," Rikki said softly.

"Shuttup! Everybody down, I say!"

Silence.

More silence.

The volley of fire Frank was expecting didn't seem to be happening. A minute passed.

He rose to a crouch, looked behind him. Eddie was a large blob upon the tarmac, struggling against nature and corpulence to lie flat. Nell had not moved. She was still standing, staring out across the bridge like Queen Christina on the prow. The wind shifted and the bridge was suddenly wrapped in river mist. Frank stood up. If he couldn't see the Russians, they couldn't see him.

"What the fuck just happened?"

"It was an accident," Rikki said again. "I slipped."

"Who were you aiming at?"

"I wasn't aiming at all."

"Did you hit anyone?"

"I don't know."

Nell started out across the bridge, paused to kick off her shoes and ran. Frank lunged for her, tripped, reached for her ankle and missed.

"Nell, for fuck's sake!"

But she was gone, folded into mist.

§215

Nell slammed into someone.

Arms embraced her.

She put her head against his chest.

"Joe, Joe, Joe."

A moment's stillness, then, "It's me. Bernard."

She drew back just as the wind changed again, and his face became visible.

"Where's Joe?"

"Joe's been shot."

"Is he . . . ?"

"I don't know. The bullet hit him in the back."

Nell thrust off the restraint of Bernard's arms and tried to move past him.

"Nell!"

"I must."

"The Russians have him."

"What . . . is he dead?"

"Nell, the Russians have him. Dead or alive, the Russians have him."

"No. Oh no. Oh no."

Her strength drained away. She leant her head against Bernard's chest, sank slowly to her knees and wailed like Hecuba. The wind turned again, the river mist wrapped itself around them once more, and they vanished from sight.

End

Stuff

Finland
The first part of this book was always going to be set in Finland, but it might not have taken the course it did had I not read *The Most Dangerous Game*, by Gavin Lyall (Hodder & Stoughton, 1964). But for that I don't think I'd have included pilots. That I named one of them "Gavin" may be taken as homage.

Russian Shortages
These are recurrent in the history of Russia, be it Imperial Russia or the Soviet Union. The Soviet Union has imported grain ever since the last famine of 1947–48. However, I know of no mid-sixties crop failure after the disastrous harvest of 1963, which led to increased imports of grain from the West and to bread rationing—nor was there any shortage of cobalt that I've heard of. I made both up. In fact, 1965 was a bumper year for both wheat and barley. Unless I'm mangling the statistics . . . (always been crap at maths—living proof that you cannot educate kids with your fists, but . . . the English are like that, so fukkem). What I didn't make up was the shortage of bog paper and the attempts by MI6 to obtain it and clean off the . . . That happened in East Berlin.

Cobalt
As far as I know, the UK is the only country ever to have tested a dirty bomb, in 1957 in South Australia. It wasn't large, but the area around Maralinga is still polluted. The idea that the UK were ready to try again in 1966 is entirely fictional.

Most of what I say about cobalt, nickel et al. is true . . . at some point. I've moved dates around for purposes of plotting. Russia did suffer earthquakes, Finland did pollute a river with nickel (more than once)—but in neither case in the year I give.

Years ago (1978, I think) I was in the 100 Club in Oxford St. (London) sharing table with a recently retired "city gent." "Retired?" I said. "You're no older than me." He then told me how he had cleaned up £250,000 on cobalt as he had spotted that a decimal point was in the wrong place, bought shares, and waited for someone else to spot the same mistake. This duly happened, and I think his quarter of a million to be about £6,000,000 at today's prices.

Alfie

I am well aware that the song sung by Bruce and Momo in chapter 60 wasn't in the original version of the film. *Alfie* was released early in 1966 without the eponymous song. Alfie himself had been around for several years by then . . . as a radio play on the BBC and as a stage play at the Mermaid. I suspect Bill Naughton had been working and reworking Alfie since the 1950s. Its final form was as a novel, and I think I read that before I saw the film. It's often held up critically as the epitome of the sixties values. Hmm? That's complete bollocks. It's very much a 1950s work and even in the film Alfie is portrayed as a fifties man (RAF badge on his blazer?—about as cool as Alan Partridge) somewhat lost in the sixties. Alfie doesn't know that, but then, what does Alfie know? What's it all about, Alfie? A question directed at the wrong man.

West German Cultural Mission in Prague

What Czechoslovakia agreed to was a trade mission, and eventual consular status. But I had no use for a trade mission.

SIS HQ

I'm well aware that SIS had moved to Century House by the time this book opens—indeed it had for much of the action of my previous Wilderness novel. I left it at Broadway/St Anne's Gate for no other reason than that Century House, their London home in the mid-1960s and for some thirty years after, was an ugly monstrosity—the sort of architecture that brings to mind the Prince of Wales's "carbuncle" comment—and I have no wish to attempt to describe it. I wanted "C" to be in an office like the one "M" and Moneypenny have in the Bond films . . . with lots of dark wood and green baize on the doors and one of those curly hat rack things you can frisbee your hat at and . . . (er . . . that's enough. Stop kvetching. ed.)

Embassies

The wife, pram, baby thing actually happened in Moscow, not Prague. The tents full of refugees also happened elsewhere and elsewhen (I think I might just have made up a word) in that it was at the West German Embassy in Prague in 1989, when around two thousand East Germans sought refuge there.

My memories of the British Embassy might be flawed. I first visited Prague during the Velvet Revolution of 1989 to meet Václav Havel. The British Embassy welcomed me and the film crew. We sat in the embassy garden—cup of tea, bit of a chat with the ambassador, can't remember if there were biscuits—not imagining I'd need to write about it thirty years later. Fool that I was, I took no notes.

In 2018 the embassy couldn't even be arsed to reply to my letters—ringing the doorbell got me a curt "What do you want?" rather than a courteous "How may I help you?"—and after the second attempt I gave up. "Fuck off" would have been straight to the point, with the added benefit of brevity. This will now lead to a two-page rant of unparalleled umbrage on "whaddafukk do I pay my taxes for?" . . . (er . . . no it won't. ed.) . . . OK, OK . . . let's leave the usual disclaimer: "No Ambassadors Were Harmed in the Making of this ~~Film~~ . . . er . . . Book." 'Nuff said.

Bohumil Hrabal

Advertisement for a House I do not Wish to Live in Anymore is the title of a collection rather than an individual story. Reading the collection, watching the film *Larks on a String*, it might seem that "based upon" is not really precise. Unless I'm mistaken, the book was not translated into English until 2015, almost twenty years after Hrabal's death and almost fifty years after the film was made. The film was banned in Czechoslovakia until 1990.

Malá Strana

I am grateful to long-serving travel writer John Bell, of Islington and so many other places, for lots of tips about Prague, in particular for steering me towards the "other" bank into Malá Strana.

William Goldman

A couple of lines in the final chapter are paraphrases of lines Goldman wrote for *Butch Cassidy and The Sundance Kid*. Goldman died while I was writing this—so did Nicholas Roeg and Bernardo Bertolucci; 2018 was a bad year for film. Goldman was the first writer ever to make me want to *read* a screenplay as well as watch the film . . . Truffaut and Pinter soon followed, but it began with Goldman.

Jiří's Slogans

They're mostly fakes, but fakes I would hope capture the spirit of the age, or they're paraphrases of slogans that were in use in 1968—some of which I saw sprayed on walls at that time. Alas, so many of them were song quotations, Dylan, Lennon, Jefferson Airplane and so on . . . just a tad costly to repeat here . . . anyone reading the line "Remember What the White Queen Said" will surely think of the original? And I would refer anyone seeking the most cryptic of sixties slogans to the back cover of Dylan's *John Wesley Harding*—and the last four words of the opening paragraph. "Key to what?" I have been asking for fifty-two years.

The only line I'd hold up as being 100 percent authentically sixties is "We are the people our parents warned us against." That much is real.

Volga

Volga Riccucci died while I was writing this book. I'd already pinched her name and her appearance at the suggestion of her daughter, Alessia Dragoni—an idea that helped my plot come together. Volga may well have been the last Tuscan Communist I will ever meet, a member of the Partito Comunista Italiano (PCI), and whilst I doubt they meet today, the plaque on the outside of their local HQ might be regarded as a memorial to the Riccucci family, and hence to Volga.

Here endeth the **Stuff**

Acknowledgments

Gordon Chaplin
Ann Alexander
Sam Brown
Sarah Teale
David Mackie
Clare Drysdale
Peter Blackstock
Clare Alexander
Cosima Dannoritzer
Alessia Dragoni
Ion Trewin
Giuliana Braconi
Christine Hellemans
Nick Lockett
Pile Wonder
Bruce Kennedy
Patrizia Braconi
Keith Caladine
Sue Bold
Ugo Mariotti
Allison Malecha
Gianluca Monaci
Erica Nuñez
Tim Hailstone
Sarah Burkinshaw

Morgan Entrekin
Amy Hundley
Joaquim Fernandez
Emily Burns
Alicia Burns
Caroline Trefler
Brian Patten
Justina Batchelor
Alan Latchley
Barbara Eite
Lesley Thorne
Nazareno Monaci
Deb Seager
Karen Duffy
Angela & Tim Tyack
Sue Freathy
Anna-Riikka Santapukki
Nev Fountain
Zoë Sharp
Kevin O'Reilly
Maggie Topkis
Valentina Memmi
Anastasia Zolotukhina
&
Volga Riccucci

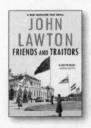

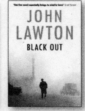

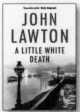
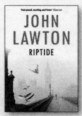